Work h

so

His To

The Housekeeper

Three favourite authors bring you
three fabulous stories!

HIS TO COMMAND DUET

September 2013

October 2013

His To Command
The Housekeeper

Sharon Kendrick
Emma Darcy
Christina Hollis

MILLS & BOON

Mills & Boon, an imprint of Harlequin (UK) Limited, Eton House, 18-24 Paradise Road, Richmond, Surrey TW9 1SR

HIS TO COMMAND: THE HOUSEKEEPER
© Harlequin Enterprises II B.V./S.à.r.l 2013

The Prince's Chambermaid © Sharon Kendrick 2009
The Billionaire's Housekeeper Mistress © Emma Darcy 2010
The Tuscan Tycoon's Pregnant Housekeeper © Christina Hollis 2009

ISBN: 978 0 263 90287 7

010-1013

Harlequin (UK) policy is to use papers that are natural, renewable and recyclable products and made from wood grown in sustainable forests. The logging and manufacturing processes conform to the legal environmental regulations of the country of origin.

Printed and bound in Spain
by Blackprint CPI, Barcelona

THE PRINCE'S CHAMBERMAID

Sharon Kendrick

Sharon Kendrick started storytelling at the age of eleven and has never really stopped. She likes to write fast-paced, feel-good romances, with heroes who are so sexy they'll make your toes curl! Born in west London, she now lives in the beautiful city of Winchester—where she can see the cathedral from her window (but only if she stands on tiptoe). She has two children, Celia and Patrick, and her passions include music, books, cooking and eating—and drifting off into wonderful daydreams while she works out new plots!

To Judy Hutson, Catriona Smith and Narell Thomas, who were there at this story's inception and who inspired me—as did the green fields of West Sussex and the wild splendour of Cornwall.

And to Rachel Thomas
for her invaluable research on head-hunting.

CHAPTER ONE

FOR a moment she thought she must have misheard him. Either that, or she was going crazy. And maybe she was. For hadn't her foolish dreams of love just been dealt a death-blow in time-honoured fashion? From her position behind the reception desk where she was covering for the receptionist's lunch-break, Cathy stared up at her boss in disbelief and tried not to think about the crumpled-up letter which was lying in the bottom of her handbag. Or the battering to her self-esteem which had left her feeling lonely, and wounded.

'Sorry.' She cleared her throat, wondering if he was having some kind of joke at her expense. 'For a minute then, I thought you said—'

'A prince? Yes, I did.' Rupert's smirk was supercilious, his upper-crust English accent even more pronounced than usual, as he paused to allow the significance of his statement to sink in. 'A royal prince is going to be gracing our hotel with his presence—what do you think of that, Cathy?'

'A *prince*?' Cathy echoed in disbelief.

Rupert's smirk became even more pronounced.

'Prince Xaviero of Zaffirinthos. I don't suppose you've heard of him?'

Cathy bit back the defensive response which sprang to her lips. Just because she was a chambermaid who'd never really qualified for anything didn't mean that she was a complete write-off, did it? The implication being that such a woman would barely recognise the name of a member of the English royal family—let alone a rather more obscure foreign version. But Rupert was right, damn him. Despite doing her best to keep up with world events via newspapers and books, it seemed that Zaffirinthos had somehow slipped off her radar. 'N-no,' she answered uncertainly. 'No, I haven't.'

'Then let me enlighten you. He's next in line to an island kingdom, a world-class polo player—and a lover of beautiful women,' said Rupert, puffing out his chest. 'In fact, the most glittering VIP we've ever had.'

Cathy stared at him, screwing up her eyes in confusion because something didn't make sense. They both knew that important guests were few and far between—despite the fact that there was a world-famous polo club nearby as well as some pretty impressive stud farms. But there were also other, more upmarket hotels and she couldn't imagine why on earth a *prince* would choose to stay somewhere like this. Yes, the building was listed and yes, originally it had been a very elegant private home before it had been turned into a hotel. But Rupert's general mismanagement and dwindling guest numbers had left house and grounds in a pretty run-down condition, which didn't tend to attract VIPs.

'But why?' she questioned. 'I mean, why's he coming *here*?'

Rupert's smile disappeared as quickly as a ray of

April sunshine. '*Why* is none of your business,' he snapped back, but then seemed to relent—glancing round to check that the coast was clear and paying lip-service to discretion, but clearly busting to tell someone. 'Well, keep it to yourself—but he's moving over here from his home in New York and he's about to complete the purchase of the Greenhill Polo Club.'

Cathy's eyes opened wider. She thought of the acres of valuable real estate which housed the prestigious club, which brought international celebrities flocking there every weekend during the polo season. 'A place like that would cost an absolute *fortune* to buy,' she said slowly.

'For once, you're right, Cathy—but that won't be a problem, not in this case. You see, this man is not just any old prince—with genuine blue blood coursing around in his veins—he also happens to be outrageously wealthy.' Rupert's eyes narrowed calculatingly. 'Which is why there are going to have to be some changes made before he and his entourage arrive.'

Cathy had been working for Rupert long enough to know just when to sense trouble. 'Changes?' she said, hoping that she was hiding the instinctive alarm which sprang up inside her. 'What kind of changes?'

'Well, for a start—we're going to have to spruce up the public rooms to accommodate a man of his calibre. They'll all need a lick of paint—especially the downstairs washrooms. I've organised for a firm of decorators to come in and start work first thing tomorrow morning.'

Cathy stared at him. 'That quickly?'

'Yes, that quickly. Someone will be in later to measure up—and you'll need to show him around,' said Rupert testily. 'The Prince will be arriving next week and there's a lot to be done between now and then if it's to meet royal expectations. Apparently, he only sleeps on Egyptian cotton sheets—so I'm going to have to send to London for those. Oh, and one other thing.'

His eyes roved over her in a manner she had always found offensive, but Cathy had learnt to ignore the suggestive way her boss looked at her, just as she had learnt to ignore his other annoying traits. Because no job in the world was perfect. Nothing was. Everyone knew that. 'What?' she questioned apprehensively.

'You'll need to do something about your appearance. All of the staff need some sort of overhaul, but you need it more than most, Cathy.'

It was a criticism he had levelled at her more than once. But Cathy never really had the inclination to use anything other than a little honest-to-goodness soap and water and to drag a brush through her pale and disobedient hair. Her chambermaiding duties meant she had to be up much too early to make a fuss and, besides, the great-aunt who had brought her up had been a no-nonsense woman who had scoffed at make-up—and had taught her great-niece to do the same.

Cathy hated the way Rupert sometimes made her feel. As if she were only half a woman. Why did he do that? *Because he gets a kick out of it, that's why. And because he's never got over the fact that you once rejected him.* But insecurity could sometimes get the better of you and she found herself asking, 'What's wrong with my appearance?'

'How long have you got?' Rupert smoothed back the lock of hair which flopped over his forehead. 'The point is that the Prince is a connoisseur of beautiful things and beautiful women in particular. And while I'm not hoping for a miracle, I'd like you to make a bit more effort while he's here. Some make-up wouldn't go amiss, for a start. And you'll be getting a brand-new uniform.'

Most women might have liked the thought of a new uniform but something in Rupert's eyes made Cathy feel instinctively wary. Infuriatingly, she could feel herself starting to blush—a slow heat travelling all the way down her neck and beyond, to the infuriatingly heavy weight of breasts which had always been too lush for her tiny frame. 'But—'

'No *buts*,' said Rupert. 'I'm the boss, Cathy. And what I say goes.'

Well, she certainly couldn't argue with that. Cathy bit her lip as she watched Rupert sweep out of the reception area in that over-dramatic manner of his.

In a way, she had been in the job too long—and sometimes she wondered if she would ever have the courage to leave. Yet familiarity was a powerful tie, especially to the emotionally insecure, and she had never known anything else but this place.

She had been brought to this village as an orphan—delivered into the care of her great-aunt—a formidable spinster who had had little idea how to cope with a grieving child. Cathy had missed her parents badly—she'd fretted and cried at nights. And her great-aunt, though well-intentioned, had been unusually strict with her, extolling the virtues of clean living, early nights and plenty of book learning.

But Cathy had proved to be something of a disappointment. Not a particularly academic child, she had achieved little in the way of qualifications except for a commendation for cooking and a special mention of the contribution she'd made to the school garden.

When her great-aunt had become ill, Cathy had been

happy to nurse the old lady—wanting in some small way to repay the woman's kindness to her. And after her death Cathy had experienced that same terrible tearing sense of being alone as when her parents had died.

The job as chambermaid at Rupert's hotel had never been meant to be anything other than a temporary post while she decided what she really wanted to do with her life. It had provided an undemanding refuge from the cruel knocks of life. But the days had drifted into months, then years—until she had met Peter, a trainee clergyman. Friendship had turned into dating and a slow-burning romance. Peter had provided sanctuary, and gentleness— and when he had asked her to marry him, Cathy had said yes, seeing a simple and happy future spread out before her, with a straightforward man who loved her.

Or so he'd said. He had taken a job up north and the plan had been that she would join him at the end of the year. And then yesterday, the letter had arrived. The one which had destroyed all her hopes and dreams and made a mockery of all she stood for. The one which said: I'm sorry, Cathy—but I've met somebody else and she's going to have a baby...

She was so lost in her troubled thoughts that at first she didn't notice that anybody had walked into Reception. Not until a faint movement alerted her to the presence of someone moving towards the desk. A man. Cathy sat up straight, automatically pinning a profes- sional smile of welcome to her lips.

And froze.

It was one of those rare moments which chanced along once in a lifetime if you were lucky. The sensa- tion of being sucked in by a gaze so mesmerising that you felt as if you were being devoured by it.

Dazed, she stared up into the most startling pair of eyes she had ever seen. Eyes as golden as a late-afternoon sun—all richness and lustre—but under-pinned by a cold and metallic gleam.

Unseen beneath the reception desk, Cathy's fingers bunched themselves into two little fists. She was unable to stop herself from staring at the rest of his face—at arrogant, haughty features which looked as if they had been carved from some rare and gleaming piece of metal. At lips which were curved and full—the corners mocking and sensual. But they were hard, obdurate lips, too, she realised as an instinctive shiver iced her skin.

His hair was dark and ruffled, and his olive skin was faintly flushed, glowing with health and vitality as if he'd been engaged in some kind of violent exercise. Tall and broad-shouldered, his physique was powerful yet lean—a fact which was emphasised by the T-shirt he wore, which clung lovingly to every hard sinew. The muscular torso tapered down into narrow hips and the longest legs she had ever seen. Legs which were encased in mud-spattered denim so faded and old that it seemed to caress his flesh like a second skin. Cathy swallowed. Her heart was racing and her throat had constricted, as if someone were pressing their fingers against it.

'I'm…I'm afraid you can't come in here looking like that, sir,' she said, forcing the words out.

Xaviero studied her—though without quite the same awestruck intensity with which she had been studying *him*. He had noticed the way her pupils had darkened and the way her lips had parted with unconscious longing. But he was used to having that effect on women—even when he'd just come from a long, hard session of riding, as now. Her stuttering response was not unusual either—though it usually happened when he was on official duty, when people were so caught up with the occasion and the protocol which surrounded him that they couldn't think straight.

The most important thing was that she hadn't recognised him—of that he was certain. After a lifetime of being subjected to idolatry and fawning he was an expert in anonymity and in people pretending *not* to recognise him.

His eyes flicked over her in brief assessment, registering that she was tiny and fair. And that she possessed the most magnificent pair of breasts he had seen in a long while—their thrusting pertness noticeable despite the unflattering white overall she wore. Too big, surely—for such a petite frame? His eyes narrowed in expert appraisal. And yet completely natural, by the look of them.

'Looking like *what*?' he questioned softly.

Cathy's mouth dried. Even his voice was drop-dead gorgeous. Rich, like dark sweet molasses and with a strange and captivating lilt to it. An accent she'd never heard before and one she couldn't place at all. But who cared when somehow he managed to turn each syllable into a poem?

Oh, for heaven's sake, she thought. *Pull yourself together. Just because you've been dumped by your fiancé, there's no need to behave like some old spinster— eyeing up the kind of man who wouldn't look twice at you.*

And yet she could do nothing to prevent the powerful thundering of her heart. 'Looking like…like…' Like what? He looked like danger, that was what. With the faintly disreputable look of a womaniser who had probably left his motorbike outside—and she knew

Rupert's opinion about *bikers* staying in the hotel. *So get rid of him. Direct him to the B&B down in the village. And do it quickly, before you make even more of a fool of yourself.*

'I'm afraid that all our guests must be properly attired in smart-casual clothing,' she said quickly, echoing one of Rupert's stuffy directives and embarrassingly aware of the mocking twist of the man's lips. 'It's…it's one of the rules.'

Xaviero almost laughed aloud at the pompous restriction—but why knock something which had the power to amuse him? 'One of the rules?' he repeated mockingly. 'A very old-fashioned rule, I must say.'

Cathy risked moving her hands from beneath the desk and she held her palms up in a silent gesture of helplessness. She totally agreed with him—but what could she do? Rupert was still mired in the past. He wanted formality and ostentatious symbols of wealth—he certainly didn't want people walking into his hotel wearing mud-spattered clothing. Yet Cathy thought of the dwindling guest numbers and thought that her boss could do with all the help he could get.

'I'm very sorry,' she repeated softly. 'But there's nothing I can do. Our policy is very strict.'

'Is it now?' he murmured as he stared down into a pair of wide aquamarine eyes. 'And you don't make any…*exceptions*?'

How could he make such a simple query sound as if…as if…? Her mouth drying like sand, Cathy shook her head, trying to quell the haywire nature of her thoughts, thinking that most people would be happy to make an exception for *him*. 'I'm afraid we don't. Not…not even for guests.'

As she shrugged her shoulders apologetically the movement drew his attention to the sway of her magnificent breasts and, unexpectedly, Xaviero felt the sharp stirring of lust at his groin. For there was no sweeter temptation than a woman who responded to him as a man, rather than as a prince.

Placing one lazy denimed elbow on the counter which separated them, he leaned forward and gave a conspiratorial smile. 'And what would you do,' he queried softly, 'if I told you that I was not here as a guest?'

Cathy's heart gave a lurch. Up close, he seemed to exude an air of raw masculinity which had short-circuited her brain and was making her breath come in short, shallow bursts. What *was* the matter with her? Struggling out of the befuddled haze of her thoughts, she realised that his answer hadn't really surprised her. After all, he didn't really *look* like a guest, did he? 'You're...you're not?'

'No.' He paused while he thought about who he would like to be. Whose skin he would like to step inside for a brief moment of complete freedom. It was a game he had always liked to play when he was younger—when he had gone away to mainland Europe to college—and it had always driven his security people mad.

For Xaviero—or, rather, Prince Xaviero Vincente Caius di Cesere of Zaffirinthos, to give him his full title—liked to remain incognito wherever and whenever possible. Anonymity was his rarest and most precious possession. He liked to play at a life that could never be his for more than a few minutes at a time. A world in which he was judged as other men were—by appearance and demeanour, and by what he said. Where chemistry counted more than privilege.

Didn't matter that outside in a bullet-proofed car sat two bodyguards with guns bulging at their breast pockets—or that a further two were lurking somewhere in the grounds. For as long as this woman remained ignorant of his true identity, he could pretend he was just like any other man. 'No, I'm not a guest,' he added truthfully.

Suddenly it all made sense and Cathy wondered how she could have been so dense. 'Of course! *You're* the painter and decorator,' she said slowly, her lips parting in a wide smile. 'And you've come to measure up the washrooms.'

Xaviero's eyes narrowed at her outrageous assumption—but he could hardly berate her for insubordination when she had no idea who he was! He had been about to deny her laughable assertion, but now she was rising to her feet and instead he found himself utterly captivated by her lush little body—and by the sheer sunny quality of her smile. When had anyone last smiled at him that sweetly? Or treated him as just a man, instead of a privileged member of one of Europe's richest royal houses?

En route from the polo club to the airfield which housed his private plane, he had called in here on a whim. The sweat from a hot, hard ride still drying on his skin, he had been curious as to how the place looked before it was made ready for his official visit. But now he wondered whether the hand of fate might have stepped in. Had he been guided here by some unseen and benevolent hand, to have sexual hunger awoken in him once more by a lowly woman who was completely unaware of his true identity?

'That's right,' he said slowly, doing his best to hide another sudden stir of lust. 'I've come to measure up the washrooms.'

'Right. Well, in that case—Rupert has instructed me to show you around.'

Xaviero smiled. So he wouldn't even have to deal with the crashing snob of an Englishman who set his nerves on edge. This was getting better by the minute. 'Perfect.'

Cathy could feel the skitter of her heart as his eyes drifted over her. She remembered the discarded letter which lay in her handbag and yet hot on that memory came the realisation that no man had ever made her feel like this before. Not even Peter—the man she had thought she'd loved enough to want to marry!

Was this what love *really* felt like? The thought flew into her mind unbidden, before she firmly sent it packing. *Oh, for heaven's sake, Cathy—have you finally lost sight of your senses? You've only just met him. You don't know him. He's a stranger who's clearly aware of just how devastatingly attractive he is. And if he's going to be working on-site there's no way you can keep dissolving in a puddle at his feet every time he flicks you that curiously arrogant glance of his.*

She gave him an efficient smile. 'So if you'd like to follow me.'

Xaviero tried to imagine how a painter and decorator might respond in such a situation. Especially one who was mesmerised by a woman's petite beauty. Wouldn't he flirt a little? Especially in view of the way she had been staring at him—like a starving cat who had just been confronted with a plate of food. Was she as hungry for sex as he was? 'I can't think of anything I'd rather do,' he murmured.

His provocative words were tantalising—but they were daunting, too. Cathy came out from behind the reception desk and then half-wished she had remained behind its protective barrier. Because standing so close to him, she felt so…*exposed*…so intensely aware of his towering height and his hard-packed muscular body. Her knowledge of men was laughably small—but even she realised that this man exuded a sensual kind of aura which spelt danger. So what did you do when you encountered danger? she asked herself. You put some physical distance between you, that was what.

'Let's go,' she said quickly.

'Mmm. Let's.' Like a snake lured by a charmer, he watched the seductive sway of her body as she led the way. She really was a tiny little thing—like a pocket Venus—with those curiously old-fashioned curves which made her bottom look so eminently cuppable. He knew from ex-girlfriends who haunted the international fashion shows that clothes looked best on lanky bean-poles without any bust or hips—but he realised instantly that this was the kind of woman who would look best with no clothes at all…

Cathy was trying to walk normally—though how could she do that when she could feel his gaze on her back, burning into her like golden flames shot from a blowtorch? She made the decision to leave the wash-rooms until last—because how embarrassing would it be to have to stand pointing out the peeling paintwork behind one of the cisterns? Instead, she stopped in front of a set of double doors and, pushing them open, stepped into a large, high-ceilinged room.

'Here we are,' she said brightly. 'This is our formal drawing room—where guests sometimes bring their coffee after dinner. It…well, it hasn't been used very much lately.'

Xaviero looked around at the general air of neglect. 'So I see,' he said wryly.

The furniture was much too faded to be described as 'shabby chic' and a chandelier looked as if it hadn't been dusted for an age. Cathy saw him glancing at it with a slightly disbelieving expression and, to her horror, she noticed a froth of cobweb lacing its base.

'It's, well…it's a bit difficult to get to—even with a feather duster,' she said apologetically. 'I'd have had a go myself, only I'm slightly on the small side.'

Golden eyes assessed her from head to toe, lingering luxuriously on her petite frame. 'You certainly are. And presumably you're not actually the cleaner?' he questioned drily.

'Er, no—I'm not,' she said quickly. 'I'm…' She stared up into the man's gleaming eyes wondering if her next statement would make his interest fade. 'I'm…I'm the chambermaid actually.'

The *chambermaid*? Sweet heaven! Xaviero almost groaned aloud—because the image which sprang into his mind was of a bed. A large, soft bed. And her in it, rather than making it. That soft, voluptuous form sinking onto crisp sheets and him sinking right on top of her. It was the most powerfully erotic image he had experienced in years and he shifted his weight very slightly in a doomed attempt to relieve the aching at his groin.

'Really?' he murmured. 'That must be a very…*interesting* job?'

Cathy's eyes narrowed suspiciously. Was he making fun of her—flippantly discounting a very necessary job which carried with it zero status? And yet he *looked* interested. She gave him the benefit of the doubt. 'Well, it can have its moments,' she said truthfully and then smiled again. 'Honestly, you wouldn't *believe* some of the things the guests leave behind!'

'Such as?'

Primly, she locked her lips together. 'I couldn't possibly say.'

He laughed. 'A loyal chambermaid,' he murmured.

'Professional discretion,' she agreed. 'And at least it's a job which gives me plenty of free time.'

'I suppose there is much to be said for that,' he answered reflectively, thinking that she would not have dared speak to him in such a natural and unaffected way if she had been aware of his identity.

'Yes.' She opened her mouth to start telling him about the magnificent grounds which surrounded the hotel and all the secret places you could find to daydream in. About the scented haven she had created in her own little garden, but then she changed her mind and shut it again. *Just go,* she told herself. *Go before you make a fool of yourself. Because haven't you done overtime in the fool stakes recently? You've just been left by one man—so best not frighten away another.*

'Look, I've wasted enough time talking. I'd...I'd better leave you to get on with your work,' she said reluctantly, though she noticed that he hadn't produced a tape measure. Why, he didn't even appear to have anything to write with!

Xaviero studied her. The most sensible thing in the world would be to come clean—to disclose his real identity and tell her that he wasn't some painter and decorator at all. But he wasn't feeling in the least bit sensible. In truth, he was feeling reckless and more than a little wild—a feeling which had only been intensified by recent events on his island.

His mouth hardened. Except that it was not *his* island any more, was it? It lay firmly under the rule of his elder brother now—it was *his* domain. The moment the crown had been placed on Casimiro's head Xaviero had felt as if he no longer had any real role there.

The year of official mourning for his father had left him feeling strangely hollow and empty—and wasn't that one of the reasons he was here? To swap his bustling New York existence and make a new life for himself— by purchasing one of the most famous polo grounds in the world, and realising a long-cherished dream to build up a training school?

He stared down into the face of the blonde, mesmer- ised by her pale beauty. She was so tiny, so delicate and light that he thought he might be able to pick her up with one hand, and hold her—like a small trophy. He imagined his big, dark body contrasted against her pale fragility. Could a woman this small accommodate a man as large as him?

He felt the recklessness transmute into desire—and the sheer and potent power of desire after so long an absence took him off guard. His gaze drifted over her lips and their rose-pink softness only increased his sudden yearning. Lips as luscious as rain-swollen petals and slightly parted as she gazed up at him. Lips that were born to be kissed; begging to be kissed. Would she let him? No woman had ever resisted him—because there wasn't a woman alive who would refuse the advances of a prince. But he had never kissed a woman under the guise of anonymity before…

How would he fare as an artisan? Did small-town country girls let painter and decorators take immediate liberties whenever lust coursed through their veins? He saw her eyes darken. Saw the sweet, almost wary way she stared up at him. It seemed that they did.

'No,' he said suddenly. 'Don't leave.'

Cathy's eyes widened. For a moment she thought that she had misheard him. 'I'm sorry?'

'I don't want you to go anywhere,' he said unevenly, and his smile was complicit. 'Any more than you do.'

There was a split second before the fantasy she'd been nurturing ever since he'd walked in began to come true. As he began to move towards her Cathy felt she should protest, but no words came—despite the certainty that he was about to kiss her and that it was both inappropriate and unprofessional to kiss a man she had only just met.

But Cathy's ego was bruised—she had been left feeling bitterly hurt by Peter's rejection. The future she had imagined for herself was no longer an option and she felt empty and undesirable. When her fingers had tightened around her fiancé's letter, hadn't she imagined that no man would ever desire her again? And yet, now—out of the blue—came this.

'You don't want to go anywhere, do you?' he persisted, on a murmur.

'I'm…I'm not sure.'

'Oh, I think you are, *cara*. Just as sure as I am.'

Leaning forward, he brushed his mouth over hers and felt the corresponding tremble of her lips.

'You like that?' he questioned unsteadily.

'Yes,' she whispered back as the lips came back and this time lingered—and Cathy knew she was lost as he pulled her into his arms and began to kiss her in earnest. Because it felt as if her life had been on hold until that moment. Peter's letter had left her feeling empty and

aching and worthless. Yet all her fears and insecurities—
all that hurt and rejection—were wiped away by the
sheer, simple power of this man's amazing kiss.

Xaviero felt her instant capitulation—she gasped
when he deepened the kiss still further. He felt the
instant and glorious response of his own body, and his
mind began doing rapid calculations. How long before
his security bleeped him? Time to lock these doors and
push her to her knees and have her pleasure him with
those incredible lips of hers? She was too *easy*, he
thought despairingly as desire now became mixed with
disgust—for Xaviero freely admitted to having the
double standards of many men where women were concerned. But that did not stop him guiding her hand to
the hardness at his groin.

Several things happened at once. Firstly, an alarm
began to vibrate in the pocket of his jeans—a movement
which corresponded with the blonde snatching her hand
away with a little yelp. And somewhere in the distance,
a telephone began to ring.

Through a haze of humiliation and a terrible unfamiliar aching sensation in her breasts, Cathy took a step
back and stared up at the man in horror, her cheeks
burning as the memory of his hot, hard ridge seemed to
be imprinted on her fingers.

'Wh-what the hell do you think you're doing?' she
demanded tremblingly, though deep down she knew
she should have been asking herself the very same
question. *Why had she let this stranger take such liberties with her?*

Xaviero gave a scornful laugh as his gaze raked over
her swollen breasts—their tips now clearly outlined
against her ill-fitting overall, just crying out for the feel

of his fingers and his lips. Frustrated desire quickly became self-contempt. Was he so hungry for a woman that he should resort to behaviour like *this*? Like some teenage boy who had never known sex before?

'I should have thought that was obvious,' he grated. 'I was giving you what your body was clearly crying out for and still is, by the look of you. Sadly, I don't have time to oblige you, at least not right now—although, frankly, I prefer my women to put up a little more fight.' His mouth hardened with a mixture of derision and frustration as he fought the desire to start kissing her all over again. 'Did no one ever teach you that when something is given so carelessly it loses much of its appeal?'

Cathy felt a wave of injustice wash over her. He probably wouldn't believe her if she told him that she'd never behaved in such a way with a man before and yet why *should* she take all the blame for what had just happened? *He* had been the one who'd started it—who had begun to kiss her with such practised skill that she had melted in his arms like a piece of molten wax.

'I suppose you consider yourself to be blameless?' she demanded, wanting to slap him around his arrogant face. But he obviously saw the itching temptation in her trembling fingers, because he shook his dark head, the gold of his eyes almost completely obscured by twin circles of black fury.

'Don't even *think* about it, *cara*,' he warned.

The thinly veiled threat brought her to her senses as a sudden and acute sense of shame washed over her. But it was too late for redress because, with one final look of frustrated contempt, the golden-eyed man turned and walked from the room without another word.

For several disbelieving moments she just stood there

until, in the distance, Cathy heard the muffled sound of tyres squealing over gravel and she hurried over to the window to see two expensive black cars racing down the drive at high speed. Automatically, she registered the sound of their powerful engines, and frowned. Now where had they come from, and where were they disappearing to? she wondered dazedly.

Trying desperately to compose herself, she smoothed her hands down over her hair before walking back into the reception area—to find a plump middle-aged man standing by the desk, wearing paint-covered overalls and holding a large notebook in his hand. He looked up with a wide smile when she appeared.

'Can I…can I help you?' asked Cathy—though some chilling sixth sense began to clamour out a terrible warning in her head.

'I certainly hope so,' said the man, in a cheerful Irish accent. 'I'm the painter. Well, the foreman—to be exact. And I've come to measure up. So where would you like me to start?'

CHAPTER TWO

STANDING in the small bedroom of her cottage, Cathy stared into the mirror and shook her head in mute horror. How could she possibly go to work, looking like *this*? Like…one of those women you sometimes saw falling out of the pub late on a Friday and Saturday night. The kind of woman who poured herself into her clothes without stopping to consider whether they might be the right size. Yet surely the dressmaker couldn't have got her measurements wrong when she'd been for, not one, but *two* fittings?

She did a little swivel to regard her back view, and shuddered—because from the back it looked even worse, if that were possible. The material clung to her bottom and seemed to draw cruel attention to its over-generous curves.

Her nerves were already shot to pieces and picking up her new uniform from the dressmaker's had only made her precarious mental state seem a million times worse. She'd put it on with trembling fingers but it seemed unsuitable no matter what angle she came at it from. Too small and too tight—the man-made fabric strained over the lush lines of her breasts and made them look absolutely enormous.

She didn't want to wear clothes which made her feel self-conscious about her curvy figure, nor to plaster her face in make-up—which she hadn't a clue how to apply properly. But Rupert had read her the Riot Act and so she had reluctantly complied—just as she had agreed to jettison her normal comfy flat shoes and replace them with a pair of heels so high she could barely walk in them. Beneath the mascara and lip gloss, she felt like a fraud, but one who was not in any position to object—because how could she possibly do that when she had placed herself in such an unwise situation?

Her boss was ignorant of the fact that she had behaved like a complete fool who had allowed a complete stranger to kiss her in a way that still made her cheeks burn when she remembered it. Only in this case, the complete stranger had turned out to be a royal prince. A guest of honour who would shortly be arriving with all his royal entourage.

A lying and duplicitous prince, she reminded herself bitterly—and one who clearly found it funny to unleash his potent sex appeal and to amuse himself with a naïve and stupid woman who had fallen completely under his spell. Playing games with commoners—was that how he got his kicks?

After he had walked out of the hotel last week it had taken only minutes for Cathy to work out that the man with the golden eyes had not been a humble decorator—but Prince Xaviero himself. A fact which had been confirmed by her subsequent heart-sinking search on the Internet, where his official portrait had flashed up in front of her disbelieving eyes. Yet the sternly handsome face which had stared back at her from the computer screen had seemed worlds away from the denim-clad man who had kissed her with such careless sensuality.

On the official website of Zaffirinthos Xaviero had been pictured dressed in some sort of formal uniform—wearing a dark jacket with several medals pinned to the front of it. His black hair had looked tamed instead of ruffled and his lips had been hard and unsmiling. And try as she did to resist, Cathy hadn't been able to help drinking in his remarkable beauty—before reminding herself that he had deliberately deceived her.

Dragging her eyes away from his portrait, she'd clicked onto the history of the island instead. Zaffirinthos. A beautiful, crescent-shaped paradise set in the Ionian Sea—close to Greece and at no great distance from the southernmost tip of Italy. It was rich in gold and other precious minerals, and the di Cesere family was fabulously wealthy—with property and business interests in just about every part of the globe.

With one final fraught glance at the unfamiliar image gazing back at her from the mirror, Cathy realised that she couldn't keep delaying the inevitable. It was time to go and face the man she had kissed so impetuously and who, for one stupid and unedifying moment, had made her heart sing. And then what? Pray that he wouldn't inform her boss that she had behaved so unprofessionally—and leave her to fade into the background with her embarrassing memories.

It was a sunny summer's day and a pretty walk through green and golden lanes to the hotel. Although it was still early, she could see a big shiny black limousine parked in front of the entrance and a burly-looking man standing sentry at the doors.

'I work here,' she said in reply to the rather hostile gaze which was levelled at her as she approached.

'Identification?' he clipped out.

Fishing around in her handbag, Cathy produced her driving licence and gave it to him and stood while a pair of emotionless black eyes slowly compared her face to the photograph. Eventually, he nodded and stepped back to allow her through.

Bodyguards clearly didn't need much in the way of people skills, Cathy thought wryly as she made her way inside. But once she'd substituted her trainers for the dreaded high-heeled shoes and locked away her handbag she looked around—marvelling at what a transforming effect a little care and attention could have.

All the walls had been painted a pale sienna colour—so that the whole place looked bigger and cleaner. Cobwebs and dust had been removed from the chandeliers, which now cascaded from the ceilings like floating showers of diamonds. Huge bowls of flowers were dotted around the place, and they seemed to make the biggest difference of all. Blue irises and white roses added scent, beauty and focus to the downstairs rooms.

Yesterday, she'd made up the bed in the Prince's suite with the pristine Egyptian cotton sheets which had been sent down specially from London. Smoothing her fingers over their crisp surface, she had marvelled at how much money Rupert must have spent on his revered guest. Soft new velvet drapes hanging from the four-poster bed had completely changed the look of the room and all the lighting had been updated. Even the ancient old bathroom had been ripped out and replaced by a spanking new top-of-the-range version.

She was just tugging down at the too-short uniform when Rupert walked into Reception, a look of immense satisfaction on his face.

'Has the Prince arrived?' asked Cathy nervously.

'He's on his way. One of his people has just rung me.'

She felt the quickening of her heart in alarm. She didn't want to see him. *Liar. You've thought of nothing else other than his golden eyes and the soft promise of his lips.* 'I'd…I'd better go—'

'Wait a minute.'

Cathy realised that Rupert's attention was focused solely on her, his gaze slowly trailing from the top of her head to the tip of her toes. And she found herself thinking that when the Prince had looked at her—*no matter how much her conscience had protested that it was wrong*—she had felt an unexpectedly hot kick of awareness. As if his gaze had lit something deep inside her and she wanted it to keep burning. As if he had brought her to sudden life.

Yet when Rupert looked at her, all she was aware of was a faint sense of nausea and a slow creeping of her flesh.

'You look fabulous,' he said thickly.

She made to turn away, but he caught her by the arm.

'No. Don't move, Cathy. Let me look at you properly.'

'Rupert—'

'Very nice,' he said. '*Ve-ry* nice indeed. What *amazing* legs you've got! Who's been hiding her light under a bushel all this time?'

She was saved from having to answer by the sound of footsteps ringing out—and Cathy sprang away from the contamination of Rupert's touch. But not before she whirled round to see the look in the golden eyes of the man who was coming through the doors towards them. A look as hard and as cold as metal itself and she felt a shiver of apprehension shimmering its way down her spine as his eyes iced over her.

She had mentally been preparing for this encounter

ever since the Internet had confirmed his identity—but nothing could have cushioned her against the shock of seeing him in his true guise for the first time.

Today there was not a shred of denim or mud-spattered clothing in evidence. Today he could never have been mistaken for anything other than a prince as he arrogantly swept in. His towering height and awesome presence were both imposing and auto-cratic, with power and privilege radiating from every atom of his being.

And no matter how much she told herself not to stare, Cathy couldn't tear her eyes away from him. The dark grey suit fitted his body closely—its luxurious fabric skating over every hard contour and drawing attention to the muscular physique beneath. A snowy shirt em-phasised the soft olive glow of his skin and the jet-dark ruffle of his hair. But it was the golden eyes which dominated everything—gleaming and dangerous as they raked over her with predatory recollection.

Cathy's heart raced with fear and self-consciousness. Should she curtsey to him? She had only ever seen people curtsey in films and her attempt to replicate the crossed-leg little bob was a hopeless parody of the movement. She saw the Prince's lips curve in disdain and instantly regretted having made it.

'Don't curtsey—I don't want formalities,' Xaviero clipped out—but the quiet fury which was simmering inside him was not because she had breached some un-spoken code of conduct. No, it had its root in something far more fundamental than etiquette. The inexplicable had happened and Xaviero did not like it.

Because the tiny blonde had haunted him when he had not wanted nor expected to be haunted by such a woman. A *chambermaid*! A humble, low-paid worker whom he should have forgotten in an instant.

So how was it that ever since he had taken her in his arms last week for that laughably brief kiss, she had disturbed his nights and his dreams. Was it because she was the first woman he'd ever kissed under the guise of total anonymity? And, by responding to him so passionately, hadn't she somehow managed to explode one of his tightly held beliefs? That despite his undeniable physical characteristics it was the cachet of royal blood which provided his major attraction to the opposite sex. Yet the chambermaid had not known about his royal status and neither had she seemed to care. She had seemed to want *him*, and only him.

The memory of her hungry reaction had taunted him with tantalising images of how that pale curved body might respond if it were naked and gasping and pinned beneath him. And all too vividly he had imagined plunging deep and hard into her body. Night after night he had awoken, bathed in slick sweat and inexplicably aching to make love to her.

Was it simply a case of her having been in the right place at the right time to excite his interest? His jaded sexual appetite returning with an inexplicably fierce hunger and swinging at him with all the weight and momentum of a giant ball bearing crashing against him? How else could he possibly explain his sustained interest in her?

Hadn't there been a part of him which had felt the whisper of anticipation as his plane had dipped down over the English Channel this morning, knowing that he was going to see her again? Knowing that he only had to snap his fingers for the little blonde to give him exactly what he wanted? He had fantasised about her lips on his aching hardness. The plunge of that hardness into her molten softness. The idea of losing himself in a woman's body after such a long sexual drought had been almost too sweet to contemplate.

And yet all he was aware of was a crushing sense of disappointment because the woman who looked at him today was merely a caricature of the one he had held in his arms. Gone was her scrubbed and fresh-faced appeal—for she had changed completely. From being like a sweet, native flower plucked on impulse from the meadow, she was now the manufactured and forced bloom of the hothouse.

The lush breasts at which the ill-fitting blouse had merely hinted so alluringly were now displayed in a tight-fitting and too-short overall, which only just stopped short of vulgarity. Likewise, her petite charms had been vanquished by the wearing of heels as high as a skyscraper. And her eyes! He had thought them mesmerising in their natural state. But now they were ringed with make-up—their sooty outline somehow diminishing the effect of their clear, aquamarine hue.

She looked like a tramp!

He felt the dulling edge of disillusionment and yet surely he should have been used to it by now. Because this kind of thing happened all the time. People were never truly themselves in the presence of a royal personage. They dressed to get themselves noticed. They said things they thought you wanted to hear. They were puppets in awe of his powerful position and sometimes he tired of knowing he could jerk their strings whichever way he chose.

'Your Serene Highness,' said Rupert. 'May I suggest—?'

'You may not,' snapped Xaviero as his disdainful scrutiny continued, 'suggest anything.' He recalled the familiar way the Englishman had just been admiring her as he had walked in. Was she *his*? he wondered. Xaviero felt the steady beat of his heart, remembering how, on more than one occasion, men had offered him their women in their pathetic attempts to ingratiate themselves with him. Would this man do likewise?

His mouth hardened. And would he accept such an offer? Did not his ancestors enjoy the charms of the opposite sex if they were presented to them in the same way as they might be presented with a goblet of good wine, or a plate of delicious food? He flicked his eyes over the blonde—noting the small pulse which fluttered frantically at the base of her neck. 'Who is this woman?'

'This is Cathy. She's our chambermaid—among other things,' said Rupert, and then he lowered his voice. 'I can get rid of her if you like, sir, if you'd like to speak to me in private.'

Xaviero gave an impatient flick of his hand to silence him. The presumption! As if he, Xaviero, should seek the private company of such a man as this! 'And she has knowledge of the area?'

Cathy wanted to open her mouth and tell them to stop talking about her as if she weren't there.

'Yes, she has,' said Rupert, as if she were some kind of performing animal. 'In fact, she's lived here all her life.'

Xaviero turned to her then, registering the automatic dilation of her blue eyes in response to his stare, and he felt a slow beat of satisfaction. Yes, she would be his. And before the day was out, too. Because this inconvenient hunger must be fed if he was to be rid of it. 'Good. Then she will be my guide while I am here.'

Cathy's lips parted and she stared at him in horror. 'But…but I'm not qualified as any kind of *guide*,' she protested in a voice which suddenly sounded squeaky.

'So?' challenged Xaviero, on a silken drawl.

'Surely…' Cathy swallowed as she twisted her fingers together. *It mustn't happen. He can't* mean *it to happen.* 'Surely you should have someone who is properly specially trained in royal protection, Your Highness.'

Xaviero's suggestion had been carelessly made—it would have meant nothing for him to retract it—but her objection secured his determination to have her. By expressing a wish to make herself inaccessible, she had sealed her fate. For a man who had spent his lifetime having his wishes met, it was the almost unheard-of protest which always intrigued him. Suddenly, the eager little blonde was not so eager any more!

'How very thoughtful of you to be so concerned about my welfare,' he murmured sardonically, 'but I want a guide, not a bodyguard. And someone with local knowledge is always much more useful than one of my own people.'

Cathy flinched. *Useful.* He had called her *useful.* It was the kind of word you might use to describe the pair of rubber gloves you wore when you were washing up. A deeply unflattering description, but maybe that had been his intention. Had he chosen it with malice and care? She glanced over at Rupert. *Can't* you *do it?* her eyes begged him. 'And besides, I work here,' she said. 'I…I can't just disappear at the drop of a hat to be your guide.'

'Of course you can,' Rupert said, completely ignoring the silent plea in her eyes. 'The hotel is closed to other guests while the Prince is here—and I'm sure that someone else can sort out the linen! Cathy is at your service for as long as you need her, Your Serene Highness.' He smiled and an unmistakable warning was arrowed in her direction. 'And what the Prince wants, we must make sure the Prince gets, mustn't we, Cathy?'

Cathy felt slightly sick—because Rupert seemed to have reduced her job and her status down to something as basic as linen-sorting. How sycophantic he sounded. Didn't he notice the Prince curling his arrogant lips in response to his toadying attitude?

But there were more pressing concerns than the Prince's arrogance—because she had very real reasons for wanting to refuse to be his 'guide'. Fleetingly, she thought of his kiss and her response to it. A heady encounter which seemed the most highly charged of her life had been given an even more piquant edge once she had discovered his true identity. She thought of the danger of being in such close proximity to him and excitement warred with fear. What on earth was his motive in making such a request?

She risked another look, meeting the cool mockery lurking in the depths of his golden eyes, and realisation hit her like a velvet hammer. *He wants you and, what's more, he thinks he's going to have you.* Cathy bit her lip. *And in view of the way you acted with him—can you really blame him for thinking that?*

And yet, if the truth were known, didn't she want him, too—even now? Hadn't the touch of his lips and his tight embrace made her feel really *wanted*—her broken and rejected spirit erupting into life at the thought that such a man could desire her?

Willing the hungry clamour of her body to calm down, Cathy hoped that her shrug disguised the frantic pounding of her heart. 'What can I say?' she questioned flatly. 'That I'd be delighted?'

Xaviero's eyes narrowed. Surely that was not *resignation* he could hear lurking in the depths of her soft voice? Or was she merely playing a coy game with him? Trying to show a little decorum where last week she had shown precisely none? 'Excellent,' he murmured.

Rupert beamed. 'Well, if that's all sorted—perhaps you would like to come with me, Your Serene Highness, and then I'll show you to your suite.'

'No, no.' Xaviero's voice was soft as he flicked his hand dismissively at Rupert. 'Go and leave us,' he ordered. 'The girl will attend to my needs.'

Rupert hesitated for one slightly puzzled moment before he left the reception area like a small child sent out into the rain to play and Cathy was left alone with the Prince. For a moment, there was silence and she didn't know where to look or what to say. All she was aware of was the prickle of her senses and the wild thunder of her heart as he caught her in the crossfire of his gaze.

'You look wary,' he commented softly as he reacquainted himself with the aquamarine beauty of her darkening eyes. 'Are you?'

She swallowed. Wary as anything—and frighteningly excited, too. 'Why would I be wary, Your Highness?'

'That doesn't answer my question.' Dark eyebrows arched in arrogant query. '*Are* you wary of me?'

There was a pause. 'Not at all,' Cathy answered, but she lowered her gaze lest he read the lie in her eyes.

Xaviero's lips curved into a speculative smile. Didn't she realise that desire was shimmering hotly from her tense and voluptuous frame, no matter how much she tried to disguise it? And yet the fact that she was trying to resist him was proving to be an irresistible aphrodisiac.

From the cold, bleak space which seemed to have

inhabited his body for so long, he felt the answering tug of desire.

'Then show me to my suite,' he commanded softly.

CHAPTER THREE

'YOU look different today,' Xaviero observed.

His words whispered over her skin like liquid silk but for a moment, Cathy said nothing. Her thoughts were scrambled and her senses working overtime as she tried to come to terms with the fact that she was standing in the newly decorated bedroom suite *alone with a royal prince.* How disturbingly claustrophobic it felt—with his golden eyes searing into her as if they could see right through her tight uniform to the trembling body beneath. And close by was a giant, king-size bed. A bed she had made herself...

His bags must have arrived earlier, for as well as a whole sheath of official-looking papers littering the desktop there were lots of precious-looking things lying around the place. A pair of gleaming golden cufflinks stamped with an intricate crest, a beautiful silver-backed hairbrush inlaid with jewels. They looked priceless and ancient—but even more dauntingly they were his personal artefacts, reminding her of the intimacy of their surroundings.

A robe hung over the back of a chair—its rich, satin folds cascading down like liquid silver. White shirts glimpsed through the half-open wardrobe door—and a riding crop, with a worn leather handle which was leaning against a door. Cathy swallowed down her apprehension and wondered how soon she could decently leave. And yet if she was being honest—wasn't there a part of her which could have stayed close beside him all day?

'*Very* different,' he murmured as his eyes continued their unashamed scrutiny.

Her heart was beating out a frantic rhythm but at least *he* wasn't aware of it and that knowledge helped keep her face completely expressionless. 'Yes, Your Highness,' she answered matter-of-factly. 'I have a new uniform.'

He looked at the buttons which trailed so enticingly down the front—and which seemed to be losing the battle to keep those magnificent breasts contained. 'So what happened?' he questioned unevenly. 'Did you gain some weight while it was being made?'

Cathy suspected that Rupert had deliberately told the dressmaker to make the uniform tighter—but she could hardly turn round and admit *that*. Disloyalty to your boss was not an admirable trait—no matter how much he might have deserved it. And neither was answering back this insolently rude prince—no matter how much *he* deserved it.

'None that I'm aware of,' she said woodenly.

Xaviero found his gaze travelling over her undulating curves. No, if she'd gained any weight at all, then it had been a complementary gain, because there wasn't an ounce of flesh on her which shouldn't have been there. Hers was not a fashionable shape, he decided— much too rounded for modern tastes—but it appealed to the primeval sexual hunger which underpinned the desire of every man. The biological imperative which subliminally announced to the onlooker that soft hips and full breasts equalled fruitful and fertile.

He felt his mouth drying along in time with the increasingly sweet torture of his tightening groin. Those magnificent breasts looked as if they should never be sullied by the wearing of clothes—and maybe he should do them both a favour by removing them as quickly as possible. She looked like one of the naked women adorning his favourite painting in the Throne Room back in Zaffirinthos—the one he used to gaze at with surreptitious longing during his teenage years.

Yet this woman was not responding to him as he had anticipated she would. Xaviero studied her with interest. Today she wasn't sending out those delicious *come-and-kiss-me* messages which had made him pull her into his arms without thinking. Her eyes weren't telling him that he was at liberty to do so again—in fact, on the contrary, she was regarding him with the caution that she might use if she had suddenly found herself alone in a room with a rather terrifying snake. And why was that? Especially when this time they were not in a public place. Rather, one which conveniently had a bed in it—and his guards would not disturb him unless he gave them permission to do so. What the hell was holding her back?

Xaviero's eyes narrowed. Unless she really *did* desire the man she had thought him to be more than the man he really was! A woman more turned on by a painter and decorator than a member of one of the most prestigious royal houses in Europe. And, inexplicably, this thought excited him more than anything he could remember.

'So which is the real you?' he drawled softly. 'Did I catch you unawares the other day, all soft and natural. Or is this...*showgirl* appearance your usual look?'

Irresistibly, his eyes now strayed to the generous curve of her bottom. 'Maybe you thought that a prince would respond favourably to the rather *obvious* signals you're sending out today. Am I right, Cathy?'

He said her name quite differently from the way anyone else had ever said it—his tongue seeming to caress the first syllable as if he were kissing it. And even though she was dimly aware that he was insulting her with that sexy drawl of his, that didn't seem to stop her traitorous body from responding. It was as if she had no power at all over her reaction to him. As if she was helpless in her fight to resist him. She could feel the blood pounding at her pulse points and her throat seemed to have constricted so much that she could barely stumble out her answer. 'I…I would not dream of being so presumptuous, Your Highness.'

'Wouldn't you?' he questioned as he noticed the soft rise of colour washing over her cheekbones. 'That's a pity. Because maybe I'm in the mood for a little presumption right now. Maybe I'm bored with the people who always bow and scrape to me. Who act like puppets and tell me only what they think I want to hear.' He glittered her a look. 'Because, you know, I rather enjoyed the way you reacted to me the other day.'

'Sir—'

'I enjoyed the honesty with which you looked at me and the unashamed hunger you clearly felt for me. The way you gave yourself up to that kiss and melted into my arms—that delicious body promising untold pleasure.'

Her throat dried. Hadn't she been trying to put the memory from her mind ever since? 'Sir—'

'Why, if that infernal alarm hadn't gone off, then who knows where it might have ended?' His voice deepened, enjoying the way she was trying not to react to his verbal seduction. 'Except that we both know exactly where it would have ended, don't we, Cathy?'

Please stop looking at me like that, she prayed silently. A way which was making her blood move like thick, warm honey as it pulsed its way through her veins. Making her stomach feel as if it wanted to dissolve and her skin tremble as if she were standing in a snowstorm. She struggled to find something to say, but the only thing which came from her dry lips was a strangled little sound which was barely comprehensible. 'I—'

'And there's nothing I hate more than unfinished business,' he murmured. 'So I think we'd better do it all over again, don't you? Kiss me again, Cathy. Only this time without stopping.'

His words both shocked and excited her but Cathy could feel her body thrilling in eager response to the way he was looking at her. Wanting to feel the warm brush of his lips against hers once more. Was that so very wrong?

Xaviero's eyes narrowed, her hesitation surprising him as he reached out his hand and touched the smooth flush of her cheek. He couldn't remember ever having to ask twice before. 'Unless there is something preventing us? Some commitment you have made to another man perhaps?' But he spoke with the natural arrogance of someone who knew that there was not another man who could not be cast aside in the light of his own wishes. The Prince's desire overrode anything. The only thing was that meant he might have to wait…and he did not *want* to wait—not when his appetite felt so exquisitely and unexpectedly sharpened.

Cathy shook her head—her pulse racing erratically.

How could she think straight when he was looking at her like that? 'No. There isn't.' She bit her lip as she remembered the sense of aloneness and rejection which had flooded through her on receipt of Peter's letter. 'There was…there *was* someone. I was engaged to be married, but…but…'

'But what?' prompted Xaviero, eager to get this one last obstacle out of the way.

'He…he…well, it's over.'

Xaviero allowed himself a brief smile of satisfaction. Perfect. Absolutely perfect. A fiancé meant that she was experienced—but that she had been faithful, too. Had the man broken her heart? he wondered idly. And if that were the case—couldn't he, Xaviero, show her that there was life after the end of a love affair? And that she could enjoy the caresses of another man…

He traced the outline of her quivering lips almost thoughtfully, recognising that in a way she would be getting the very best and yet the very worst of a post-fiancé lover. Because he was undoubtedly the finest lover she would ever know—but she would spend her whole life searching fruitlessly for a man to equal him.

'So let's make love,' he said simply.

'Your Highness!' she breathed, even though she realised that her protest lacked any real conviction. The look of intent which had darkened his golden eyes was just too beguiling—the expectation that he was about to hold her too tantalising to resist. And the sense of burning hunger in her empty heart was like nothing she had ever experienced before. *Should she stop him? Shouldn't she even try?*

She would never know. Because now he was pulling her into his arms with a smile on his lips which made her desperately want to kiss him. To relive the amazing sensations he'd awoken in her the other day. Half-heartedly Cathy twisted in his arms but the movement brought from him a low and mocking laugh and she quickly realised why—as she collided with a rock-hard and very formidable groin. She felt the mad, frantic race of her heart and the intoxicating fizz of her blood—her body blindly reacting to the sweet sensation of his touch.

'Sir!' she gasped.

'Xaviero,' he corrected, on a groan. 'What is it? Tell me.'

What could she tell him other than that this felt like heaven itself? As if she'd never been properly alive before that moment—because no man had ever made her feel like *this*. He was so close that she could feel the warmth of his breath on her face and it felt so unbelievably intimate that she felt weak. Already she was way out of her depth—and every atom of common sense she possessed was telling her to get away from him before it was too late. But common sense was immediately scrambled into a hot and senseless desire as his lips came down to meet hers—and Cathy knew she was lost.

His last kiss had been lazy, almost careless—like someone dipping a toe into a pool of water to test the temperature. But not today. Today it was as if he had dived straight in. His lips were seeking. Expert. Driving down on hers with sensual insistence and making her gasp with pleasure.

Without preamble, Xaviero pushed her down onto the soft bed, seeing her eyes widen in surprise as he began to unbutton her dress. 'You thought perhaps we would—how do you say it—*pet* for hours? The struggle on the bed as we remove first one item of clothing, and then the other? No.' He smiled as her milky flesh began to be revealed to him. 'I like my women naked,' he murmured and touched his lips to the pulse which fluttered wildly at the base of her neck.

Her thoughts struggled to make themselves known over the clamour of her senses. *My women*, he had said. Which implied he had known quite a few. She swallowed as his lips began to graze over the line of her jaw. *Of course he has known quite a few—did you really think that a man like this wouldn't have done?* Another button popped open and Cathy closed her eyes as she felt the whisper of his fingertip skating over her belly. Should she tell him?

But now he was sliding her shoes off. And her tights. And his fingertip was sliding over the insole of her bare foot—tracing a tantalising circle there—and Cathy thought it incredible that such a sensation could come from so provocative and yet so innocent a gesture.

'Ooh,' she breathed, forgetting all her misgivings as she thrilled to his touch. Because in this setting all the pomp and circumstance surrounding him had dissolved. Suddenly he was simply the man in denim again. The man with the golden eyes who had so bewitched her. Who was bringing her to life beneath his expert, seeking fingertips. 'That's…that's just *gorgeous*…'

Briefly, Xaviero smiled as he peeled off the uniform dress, briefly assessing her underwear. You could tell a lot about a woman from her underwear—and he had experienced more than his fair share of it. Virginal white lace—never applicable—or sensual scarlet satin chosen to send out a very specific message about the wearer. He'd seen just about every variation on black—and garments where less was supposed to equal more. He'd seen bottoms clad in French knickers and bottoms almost naked in Brazilian thongs. He'd seen stockings, suspenders and hold-ups, which always seemed to slide down at the most inopportune moments. But he had never seen underwear like Cathy's before.

It was… His fingers moved around her narrow back to find the clasp of her bra. *Functional* was pretty much the only word you could use to describe it—because it certainly hadn't been chosen with eye appeal in mind. Flesh-coloured briefs and a flesh-coloured bra—but then the latter had quite a tough and supportive job to do, he acknowledged.

But when the catch sprang free, it was Xaviero's turn to moan with pleasure as her breasts tumbled out, glorious and unfettered and free.

'*Porca miseria!*' he groaned, staring at them in disbelief before eagerly taking them in his hands.

Cathy let her head fall back against the pillow, vaguely aware that perhaps she should be objecting—but unable to form a single coherent thought, because now his lips were trailing sweet fire over her breasts.

'Oh!' she gasped.

His tongue stilled for a fraction of a second and he dragged in a shuddering breath, feeling the jerk of his erection and the hot fever of his blood. She was as responsive as he could have hoped for—even more responsive than she had been in his dreams. And dreams were powerful things, he recognised—sometimes they intruded on your reality and altered it. So that for a moment he felt he *knew* this woman because he had met a version of her in the unconscious world he inhabited while asleep. Was that why he felt so intensely turned on? Or was it simply because his body was so hungry for a woman's touch?

Except she wasn't touching him at all—and maybe that was because she was clad in nothing but a pair of unattractive panties while he was still wearing his suit.

He lifted his head and brushed his mouth against hers. 'You will forgive me if I leave you for a moment?'

Cathy froze as the erotic bubble in which she had been losing herself suddenly evaporated. '*Leave* me?' she echoed.

Xaviero's lips curved into a satisfied smile. Did they not say that low-born women made the very best of all lovers—with their unaffected passion and disregard for the convention that a woman must never be *too* enthusiastic if she wanted to snare a man? He began to trail his finger over her skin and felt her shiver in response. Because she would surely be aware that nothing permanent could ever come from such a liaison. Unlike the socially ambitious beauties of his past, this voluptuous little chambermaid would have no expectations of a future with him. And how liberating was that?

'Just while I undress,' he qualified, one lazy fingertip skating irresistibly to circle the heavy warmth of her breast. 'I want to feel my skin next to your skin.'

'Oh,' she said softly. Cathy's cheeks flamed with pleasure, revelling in how those simple words could thrill her so—her lingering doubts banished by the glorious reality of what was happening. 'What a lovely thing to say.'

'Well, then.' Reluctantly he moved away from her pink and white body and stood up. She was so sweet—too sweet really. He couldn't remember a woman ever being quite so straightforward. Quickly, he stood up, kicked off his shoes and socks and shrugged off his jacket—seeing the aquamarine eyes watching his every move, making no attempt to hide her expression of enjoyment. 'You want me to perform a slow striptease for you?' he questioned unsteadily. 'Is that the kind of thing which turns you on?'

Her cheeks suddenly grew pink again. *Perform?* Have the Prince slowly remove his clothes and perhaps have second thoughts about what was about to happen? What she *wanted* to happen. And *would* happen, she thought fiercely—because she had never felt like this before. Never imagined that this kind of expectant joy could ever exist—and it had banished all her normal shyness. Why, she was lying on one of the hotel beds, wearing nothing but a pair of panties, and she didn't even care!

She swallowed as she watched the Prince unbuttoning his shirt and revealing a broad bare chest. Up until now she had lived her life as she'd been taught—and where had it got her? Precisely nowhere. *And yet she had never felt for Peter what she felt for the Prince. As if she would die if he did not quickly come over here and kiss her again.*

Firmly, she pushed her conscience away—losing herself instead in the molten gold of his eyes as he pulled off his tie and let it drop to the floor, where it lay coiled like a silken serpent. She shook her head in reply to his question. 'No,' she said. 'I don't want any kind of show. I...I just...want you here again.'

'Then you shall have me,' he promised softly. 'Just as soon as I get rid of these...' His hand moved to his belt and then gingerly he slid the zip of his trousers down over his aching hardness. And then, after removing something which glinted silver in the light—something which he put down on the bedside table—he stepped out of his trousers. And his boxer shorts...

Cathy gasped and he smiled.

'So big, mmm?' he questioned with soft satisfaction as he climbed back onto the bed beside her and guided her hands between his legs.

Even though Cathy baulked at such intimacy, she wanted to please him—and after that initial touch she did not feel in the least bit shy. On the contrary, she was longing to know him and to explore him. To acquaint herself with every centimetre of his glowing olive flesh. Eagerly, her fingers tiptoed over the taut silken length— but he jerked away as if she'd scalded him.

'No,' he said fiercely, and caught hold of her hand, pressing his lips against her wrist and feeling the wild fluttering of her pulse. 'Not yet. Not the first time.'

She wasn't sure what he meant, but by then he had moved over her and begun to kiss her—melting away all her questions—dissolving everything except pure passion with the power of his kiss. It was…it was the most wonderful thing which had ever happened to her— as if she hadn't lived properly until that moment.

'Oh,' she moaned, her body moving restlessly beneath his as she silently communicated her growing desire.

Xaviero reached down to test her honeyed warmth, feeling her buck beneath his fingers—thinking how passionate she was. Usually, he liked to run through an entire repertoire of his considerable sensual skills— something which completely captivated all his lovers. Women thought him unselfish, and in many ways he was—although he was always accused of holding back emotionally. But he was aware that giving them so much pleasure was also a kind of sexual boast—an innate need to surpass every other man that they might have known. For wasn't it the curse of the younger royal son to always feel the need to prove himself, in every sphere?

Yet as Cathy's fingers kneaded softly at his shoulders and she grazed her lips over his nipple he felt himself shudder and knew he could not wait. Her fresh eagerness was like nothing he'd ever felt before—like fasting for days in the fierce heat of the sun and then suddenly finding a long, cool drink of something indescribably sweet.

He reached for a condom and began to slide it on, aware that she was watching him. If there was one thing which had been drummed into him since he had first entered puberty—it was the precious nature of royal seed.

Cathy bit her lip. Should she tell him how gauche she really was—and that she was terrified of disappointing him? But who in their right mind would want to let reality intrude and threaten this delicate magic he had woven over her? And then he pulled her back in his arms and began kissing her again, and it was too late to say anything.

She felt herself shiver as his tongue slid inside her mouth and that irresistible heat began to creep over her body once more, dissolving all thoughts in its wake. It was as if something had taken hold of her. Some urge. Some desire. Some *need* to feel him closer than close. Something beyond her control, which was orchestrating her movements.

She felt him suddenly tense as he shifted his position, his fingers parting her legs, and Cathy trembled as his mouth continued its heavenly plunder. There was a split second where one final consideration struggled to make itself heard and her lips parted to tell him. But it coincided with a single thrust, the sharp sense of pain mingled with the sweet sensation of this beautiful man filling her. Her strangled cry. And then his.

What was he saying? Surely not, 'no'? *No?*

Something had changed. There was movement, yes—but the mood in that bedroom seemed to have shifted inexplicably from joy to anger. Yes, anger. Bewilderedly, Cathy struggled to chase the incredible feeling which had been so tantalisingly close, moving her hips in time with his.

'Keep *still*,' he bit out.

But it was too late. She writhed beneath him with an abandon which was driving him wild, and that—combined with her hot tightness—meant that he was lost. Completely lost.

It was the most intense orgasm he had ever experienced and yet he hated her for every gasping second of it, withdrawing from her just as soon as his body recovered its strength from those powerful spasms. Staring down at her as a heavy kind of blackness enveloped him.

'Why did you keep something like that to yourself?' he accused, getting off the bed and grabbing his robe, before knotting it viciously at the waist.

All she was aware of was the condemnation which was spitting from his eyes as he towered over her like some dark avenging angel. 'But...Your Highness,' she said shakily—still not quite daring to use his Christian name—and her sense of shame and confusion grew, 'what have I done?'

'Done? You know damned well *exactly* what you've done!' he bit out with quiet rage. 'What kind of game are you playing?'

'G-game?'

'Didn't you think it might be a good idea to tell me you were a virgin?'

CHAPTER FOUR

CATHY shrank back against the pillows, her heart sinking as she stared up at the darkened fury of the Prince's features. 'I've done something wrong?' she questioned, her voice shaking with bewilderment.

'Wrong? Oh, please don't play the innocent with me!' Xaviero snarled, until the irony of his words hit him. Because she *was* innocent, or, rather, she had been—until about five minutes ago. But now he realised that a woman could be innocent in the *physical* sense while having the most devious of motives. And there he had been—imagining that she was a sweet little thing who had desired him as a man more than she had desired him as a royal. As if!

How could he have been such a fool not to have seen through her? To have realised that he was being lured into the oldest trap of all. Because she had misled him, that was why. And so cleverly, too—those big aquamarine eyes clearly concealing a scheming brain, that voluptuous body luring him with its seductive promise. His fist clenched with impotent fury. 'Did you lie about having a fiancé?'

'No!' she protested. 'I did have one!'

'Then how can you still be a virgin if you were engaged to be married?' he flared. 'I know that nobody waits until their wedding day any more—well, certainly not in the world which *you* inhabit!'

Cathy saw the contempt which had twisted his sensual lips, and flinched at how little he obviously thought of her. Oh, what a fool she had been. What a stupid little fool. Her greatest gift and she had given it to a man who had thrown it back in her face as if it had been a dirty rag. Her virginity treated with the contempt with which he might have viewed the bargain-basket at the supermarket. Except that she doubted this man had ever been near a supermarket in his life.

'As a matter of fact, he said he thought we should wait until we were married!' she objected heatedly.

'And *you*—a woman who turns on as quickly as you do—you were *happy* to wait?' he demanded, in disbelief.

'Well, *yes*! Actually, I was.' With Peter waiting had never been a problem and in view of his job it had been more than appropriate. 'He wasn't like you,' she finished miserably.

'Nobody is like me,' he qualified arrogantly, before his features darkened even more. 'I have been duped,' he grated.

Cathy stared at him. Wasn't he forgetting something? 'And what about me?' she whispered. 'You duped me, too, didn't you? Pretending to be a painter and decorator! What was that all about?'

But he was not listening, his mind working overtime—until the realisation of what must have happened hit him like a dull blow in the solar plexus. He thought of the Englishman, Rupert. The way she had whirled away from him when he had entered the hotel that morning. Surely *he* was not the fiancé?

'It is this…this…*Rupert*?' he accused hotly.

For a moment Cathy stared at him in complete puzzlement. 'What is?'

'He was the man you were to have married?'

'No!' she protested, appalled. 'My fiancé was a trainee clergyman,' she added, though this added piece of information seemed to make him even angrier.

Xaviero's eyes narrowed. Then what the hell was going on—were she and the hotel owner colluding? Had he convinced this little chambermaid to seduce him for his own nefarious purpose? But there was no way he could possibly interrogate her when she was lying there so bare and so beautiful. 'Cover yourself up!' he demanded hotly.

Cathy wondered if he meant for her to start dressing and she went to get off the bed when something in her movement made his face darken again and he bent and picked up the silky coverlet which must have slipped to the ground during their love-making. *Love-making*, she thought in revulsion as she hastily caught the coverlet he tossed towards her, and hauled it over her body. The last word you could ever apply to what had just happened was *love*.

Xaviero drew a deep breath as he looked at her, at the pale hair beginning to fall out of the pins which constrained it—thinking that he had been so eager to possess her that he hadn't even got around to letting it spill over her magnificent breasts. A pulse flickered at his temple. 'Okay,' he said steadily. 'Let's just get it out of the way. Tell me what it is you want?'

'What I w-want?'

'You heard me!'

She stared at him. What she wanted was to be rid of this terrible feeling that she had just made the biggest mistake of her life. Or for the last ten minutes not to have happened and for him to come back and start kissing her again. But she suspected that neither of those options was going to happen. 'I don't understand what you're talking about.'

Xaviero looked at her disbelievingly. Had he believed those eyes to be so guileless, her passion to be so sweet, because he had *wanted* to believe it? But he came from a world where virginity was highly prized—an old-fashioned royal essential to ensure the pure continuation of his ancient bloodline. And he could not believe that any woman would have given it away so carelessly unless she had some kind of separate agenda.

'You must want something to have behaved so impetuously,' he snapped. 'Did you collude with your boss? Provide the irresistible bait with your too-tight uniform and your over-made-up eyes? Knowing all the obvious ploys which will hook in a man. Yet I *knew* all that, and *still* I fell for it,' he added bitterly. 'Because sexual hunger has made fools of men since the beginning of time.'

'I don't understand,' said Cathy again, beginning to grow a little bit angry now. Yes, he was a prince and yes, he seemed genuinely shocked that she had been a virgin—but everything was about *him*, wasn't it? Him, him, him! Didn't he stop to think for a moment about how *she* was feeling right now? Foolish and empty and aware that she had been carried away by a hopeless fantasy that there was a spark of something *real* between her and the golden-eyed man. Something which had begun the very first time she'd seen him. Inexperience had made her attribute the passion of his kiss to something more than mere lust. So hadn't *she* been the fool, not him?

Clutching onto the silken coverlet, she lifted her chin. 'Why on earth should I want to collude with Rupert?'

'To negotiate a better price?' he returned, golden eyes lancing into her.

For a moment the room seemed to sway and Cathy felt sick. 'To negotiate a better *price*?' she echoed in disbelief. Surely—oh, please, no—surely he wasn't implying that she was *selling herself*. She swallowed down the acrid taste in her throat. 'A better price for *what*?'

'For the hotel, of course,' he snapped.

There was an odd, debilitating kind of silence. A moment when it seemed to her that everything which was dark in the world had formed itself into a horrible, tight little ball and been hurled, hard—at her stomach. 'For the hotel?' she whispered.

There was a pause. 'He hasn't told you?'

'Told...told me what?'

'That he's selling?' His eyes narrowed as he saw her face blanch. 'No, clearly he hasn't.'

'To...*you*?'

Xaviero gave a grim kind of smile. 'Of course to me.'

Through the series of befuddled impressions which began ricocheting through her mind, Cathy's overriding thought was that she would have to leave now. She would *have* to. Prince Xaviero as her *boss*? How could she bear it? But then she met the cold, metallic gleam of his golden eyes and wondered who on earth she thought she was kidding. As if a man who had made his contempt for her so apparent would ever keep her on the payroll.

But something didn't make sense to her. She knew

that princes in modern times had 'normal' careers—but *this*? She tried to imagine him doing a stocktake of the cellar—or taking the chef to task when he had one of his periodical tantrums.

'You mean…you're going to be a hotelier?' she questioned, mystified.

There was a moment of stunned silence before Xaviero gave an arrogant laugh, knowing that he should have been outraged at her suggestion and yet, in a way, didn't it make walking away from her not just easy—but necessary? Because her ridiculous question had simply confirmed that he could not have picked a more unsuitable lover if he had searched to the ends of the earth to find one.

'You can see *me*—running a hotel such as *this*?' he mocked.

Now he came to mention it, no, she couldn't—but something in his contemptuous attitude stabbed even harder at Cathy's heart. It might not have been the most fashionable hotel in the country, but it was the only real job she'd ever had—and she felt a certain kind of loyalty towards it.

'Not really, no,' she said. Because some modicum of politeness and charm were necessary if you wanted to make a place a real success—and, unless he was actually trying to get a woman to kiss him, the arrogant Prince Xaviero seemed badly lacking in both. 'So why are you buying it, then?'

'Because I want a retreat—a beautiful, English country home, which this has the potential to be. Something with history which can be brought up to date with a little care and money injected into it. Somewhere that's close enough to London and the international airports—near enough to my polo club but far away enough to escape from it. Somewhere big enough to site a helicopter pad—and which will satisfy my security people. This place seems to fulfil most of the criteria—though obviously it needs extensive work before it can be made habitable.' He began to laugh softly. '*Me*? A hotelier? Can you *imagine*?'

Cathy stared at him. In a way, she had thought the worst thing that could happen was the Prince taking over the hotel—but now she saw that there was a far worse scenario. That soon there would be no hotel at all—it would revert to being a private home and not just she but all the other people who worked there would be out of a job. Dismissed as if they were of no consequence by a spoilt and selfish prince who thought of nobody but himself!

'No, now I come to think of it, I can't—it was a ri-ridiculous thing to say,' she agreed, her voice shaking with rage and hurt. 'I don't think you've got the people skills to run a hotel.'

There was a stunned silence, while he stared at her in a slow-burning disbelief. '*What* did you just say?'

Don't let him intimidate you, thought Cathy fiercely—because now indignation was taking over from the terrible hurt which seemed to have turned her body into a block of ice. Had she done something awful in a past life which meant that men felt they had a right to trample over her feelings like a herd of cows in a meadow? He had just taken her virginity and then turned on her as if she were nothing more than a cheap con-artist.

'I think you heard me.'

'How dare you?' he bit out dangerously.

'Why?' She didn't flinch under his accusing stare. 'Does the truth make you angry, Your *Highness*?'

Xaviero's eyes narrowed as her impudence almost took his breath away. 'This is completely unacceptable!' he hissed.

Didn't what they had just been doing give her at least *some* rights? Clearly not. Clutching the silken coverlet even tighter, Cathy thought that if someone had spoken to him like that more often in the past, then he might not be so overbearingly arrogant. 'Well, if you'll let me leave—then I won't need to bother you any more, will I?'

Still reeling from her insubordination, he paused to study her flushed face and the aquamarine eyes which were unexpectedly sparking blue fire at him. And even while her sudden defiance began to turn him on he remembered something else, too. Something which might account for her spiky rebelliousness.

'I'm not stopping you from leaving,' he said softly.

She stared at him—as a hungry mouse might stare at a piece of cheese while wondering what the glint of metal behind it could possibly be. 'You…you aren't?'

'Of course not.' He smiled, feeling himself grow exquisitely hard beneath his robe. 'Go. Go on, if that's what you want.'

Cathy swallowed, knowing that she could not move an inch while those eyes were melting into her like molten gold. 'Then…then would you mind turning your back?'

His lips curved into a mocking smile. 'Yes, I would, actually.' He reached out and hooked his finger inside the silk-satin rim of the coverlet which concealed the trembling rise and fall of her breasts. 'Isn't it a little late in the day for modesty?'

Her breathing was coming in short little bursts.
'N-no. I don't th-think it is.'

The finger slipped a little further down and sank into
the cushioned flesh. 'Sure?'

'Q-quite sure,' she breathed, wanting—no, *praying*
that he wouldn't stop touching her even while part of
her despised herself for letting him. *Push him away*, she
told herself. *Push him away and he will let you go.*
Because despite the dark look of predatory intent which
had made his features grow tense, some deep-rooted
instinct told her that he would stop immediately if she
wanted him to.

'You see, what just happened was not the best initia-
tion into sex you could have had, *mia cara*,' he
murmured as his finger dipped down and began to tease
at one tightly aroused nipple.

Cathy's grip on the coverlet loosened. 'It…wasn't?'

'No.' His palm now captured the entire heavy mound
of her breast and he felt the coverlet slither down uselessly to her waist. Leaning over, he bent his lips to one
rosy tip, feeling a convulsive shudder rack her tiny
frame as he flicked his tongue against it. 'If I had
known…' *If he had known, he would have run a million
miles away from her blue-eyed enchantment.* But
perhaps this wasn't the best time in the world to say so.
'Then I should have taken things more…slowly.'

Cathy's eyes fluttered to a close as she felt his tongue
now slide its way down towards her belly, and an unbearable flame of desire shot through her. 'Oh,' she
breathed as he slid a slow, moist trail over her skin and
her fingers drifted automatically to tangle themselves in
the dark silk of his hair. Sweet sensation sucked her
towards an unknown vortex as she struggled to hold

onto reality. She wanted to ask him what he thought he was doing—but it felt so good that she didn't want to risk him stopping by answering.

'Is that good?' he murmured as his mouth lingered against her navel—his tongue circling the neat little hollow.

Good? 'Yes,' she breathed.

Parting her legs with gentle fingers, he put his face between her thighs, his first slow lick producing a squirm of pleasure and a disbelieving intake of breath.

'Oh!' she gasped as his tongue began to move against her heated flesh. Cathy was on fire—as the growing hunger of her body demanded to be fed. And in a way, this felt even more intimate than what had happened before. The Prince kissing her there…there…how was that possible? But then she forgot that he was a prince, forgot the angry words and the accusations which had preceded this, forgot everything except the sensations which began to build and build, promising her some tantalising conclusion so perfect that she didn't dare dream that it might really exist.

But it did. It really did. She choked back a cry of disbelief, her back arched like a bow as it began to happen and she was hurtled, unprepared—into an entirely new stratosphere. It was like slowly falling off a cliff and into a warm and soaring sea—as waves and waves of warm pleasure began to wash over her.

Moving away from her, Xaviero watched her climax, unbearably turned on himself as he watched one hand stray to her neck, as if heating itself on the rose-bloom flush which had begun to flower there. For a moment he saw her naked body shift in lazy and uninhibited contentment, but when eventually her eyes fluttered open they fixed on him, suddenly becoming veiled, as if she was remembering exactly where she was, and with whom—and uncertain of what to do next.

There was a moment's silence.

'You liked that,' he observed eventually, swallowing down the sudden lump in his throat.

Still dazed and confused by the intense experience, Cathy shook her head.

'You *didn't*?' he murmured mockingly.

'Oh, yes, I did—of course I did.' She wanted to fling her arms around his neck. She wanted to cover him with a million little kisses of gratitude for making her feel that way, but she didn't dare. 'It was…oh, it was the most incredible experience of my entire life.'

He smiled. Her unqualified praise was rather touching, because all women thought it—even if few were gauche enough to express it so fulsomely. 'That is what was making you so…argumentative,' he observed reflectively. 'You should have an orgasm every time you have sex.'

Cathy cringed, the baldness of his statement shocking her—though not quite enough to pull away from his embrace—telling herself that at least nobody could accuse him of being a hypocrite. And then her attention was caught by the unmistakably hard outline which was apparent beneath the rich fabric of his satin robe and as their eyes met in silent acknowledgement she found herself blushing.

'Yes,' he agreed, as if responding to an unspoken question. 'I want you very much indeed—but I have to be at a meeting in…' he flicked an impatient glance up at the clock which hung over the beautiful marble fireplace '…just under an hour…' his voice lowered '…which means there won't be enough time.'

He thought that if she had been more experienced there would have been plenty of time. By now she would have taken the initiative and he would have loved nothing more than to see her on her knees in front of him. Pleasuring him with her lips while he tangled his fingers in the pale silk of her hair and fulfilled the very first fantasy he'd ever had about her.

And that was when a solution presented itself to him—a solution so perfectly simple he was amazed he had taken so long to getting around to it. One which would please and satisfy them both—but would also wipe the slate clean.

Because in a crazy way, he felt responsible for what had just happened. He would never have taken her so swiftly and perfunctorily if he had known she was an innocent. To be truthful, he would not have taken her at all. But he had and—while he had just shown her how pleasurable certain aspects of sex could be—she still had a lot to learn. And shouldn't he be the one to teach her? Might that not more than compensate for the fact that he had unwittingly taken her virginity?

Abruptly, he turned his back on her—went to look out over the sweeping grounds. He noticed that the lawns which swept down to the lake were ragged at the edges, and that the lake itself looked clogged with debris. Encroaching weeds had made a mockery of the flowerbeds and some had even disappeared completely.

Had he been crazy to come up with this scheme—to uproot his New York life and establish himself in a brand-new part of the world? Yet his father's death had unsettled him—made him aware of the impermanence of life and the need to chase your dreams.

Turning back to face her, he was aware that at least

his arousal had subsided and was grateful for the fact that she had grabbed the coverlet and had slithered it over the enticement of her curves.

'I need to get showered and dressed,' he said shortly.

Hearing the abrupt note of dismissal in his voice, Cathy eyed her discarded uniform doubtfully, realising that she was going to have to leave here in a completely dishevelled state. What if she bumped into one of the other staff—how on earth would she be able to explain her appearance? 'I'll—'

'You can use the bathroom after me,' he said. With an effort, he flicked her a glance—barely able to look at her tousled golden beauty lest it make him break his resolve and go over there and ravish her. He smiled with predatory pleasure. 'And I want you to be ready at eight tonight,' he added softly.

Cathy's heart missed a beat; she thought she must be imagining things. Was he asking her out on a *date*? 'Tonight?'

'That's right. There's a party at the polo club—what they're calling a low-key celebration of my successful takeover—and you're coming with me.'

She stared at him incredulously. 'B-but, why? I mean, why me?'

His eyes narrowed. Was she really as disingenuous as she seemed? Didn't she realise that even a man of his calibre found her tight, lush body irresistible? Up until now those sinful curves had been woefully underused—but not for much longer.

'These occasions are always easier if you have someone beside you to deflect some of the inevitable attention—and also, I intend taking you to bed afterwards,' he drawled, and his eyes glittered her a silent, sensual message. 'But neither of us should forget that you are completely untutored—and royal princes expect their mistresses to be skilful.'

Cathy's pulse rocketed as one word reverberated over and over again. *'Mistress?'* she gasped.

'I rather think what we've just been doing qualifies you for the role, don't you, Cathy?'

'I...I don't know what to say,' she breathed.

'Then say nothing. Women usually say far too much when they would be better remaining silent and simply looking beautiful.' He glittered her a look. 'And beauty is marred by too much make-up—so please don't wear quite so much in future because I can assure you that I don't find it attractive.'

'That was...that was Rupert's idea,' she blurted out.

'Oh, was it?' he questioned thoughtfully as he studied the too-sooty eyes and suddenly her tarty transformation began to make sense. What a creep the Englishman was! 'Well, from now on—you will take instruction only from me in the best way to present yourself as my mistress. You show great potential for the position, *cara mia*. I should never have taken your virginity—indeed, you are the only virgin I have ever bedded—and that cannot now be undone. But perhaps I can in some way redress the balance.'

Cathy stared at him, her heart pounding wildly, her mouth drying. 'What are you talking about?'

'Why, in return for having robbed you of your innocence, I intend teaching you everything I know about the art of love-making.' He gave a slow and provocative smile. 'And that way, we can call it quits.'

CHAPTER FIVE

THE violet shadows of evening were lengthening and the fading light seemed to pick out the brightness of the flowers which were packed so tightly into the small garden. Xaviero paused, his eyes narrowing as he took in the unexpected kaleidoscope of colour which appeared before him.

The path leading to Cathy's cottage was lined on either side by the purple haze of lavender and tall delphiniums which stood like cobalt arrows against the grey flint of the garden wall. Creamy-pink roses scrambled over a trellis—while blooms which looked like bells and others which resembled stars all jostled and billowed for space in the flowerbeds. And everywhere there were drifts of scent—some subtle, some powerful but all of them beguiling to his senses. It was a place of real beauty, and of calm.

For a moment he lingered there, his senses drinking in the extraordinary peace of the place as he realised that his expectations had been confounded. Hadn't he thought that the little chambermaid might live in some faceless and featureless little apartment in the nearby village? A humble abode whose very modesty would reinforce her subservience to him.

Yet this place was nothing like that.

At that moment the front door opened—she must have been watching him from inside—and there she stood, framed in the doorway and staring at him, as if she couldn't quite believe he was there. Truth to tell, he couldn't quite believe it himself.

But the fire Cathy had lit within him still burned. It had been burning all day, all during the dull, dry lawyers' meetings and his subsequent sessions with a local horse-breeder. He hadn't been able to get her out of his mind, remembering with painfully acute clarity just how good it had felt to thrust into that hot, virgin tightness of hers. Maybe he had underestimated the primeval pleasure that her innocence had given him.

Subduing the aching response to his thoughts, he raised his black eyebrows. 'Ready?'

Although she registered the fact that it wasn't the most affectionate of greetings, Cathy's smile was nonetheless wide and genuine—because hadn't she been dreading that he might have had second thoughts and changed his mind about taking her out? But no, he was here to take her to some fancy polo-club do and it hadn't been some kind of wild and crazy dream, after all. Prince Xaviero of Zaffirinthos really *had* taken her bed and then announced that she was to be a royal mistress and he was to instruct her in the things which pleased him!

Could she have said no?

She thought of his cold-blooded reasoning. *That way, we can call it quits.* In view of that, then *shouldn't* she have said no? But the truth of the matter was that her heart felt a bursting kind of happiness that he was here at all— and wasn't her body eager for more of his expert touch?

She looked up at him uncertainly, fingers fluttering

over the black dress which skimmed her hips. 'Is this…okay? They say you can't go wrong with black but I wasn't sure if it would be suitable for a polo club? You see, well—I've…well, I've never actually been to one before.'

Golden eyes swept over her. The dress was unremarkable—a cheap creation which neither emphasised nor concealed her figure, while the glorious sun-ripe hair was tied back in some sort of ribbon. But at least she had heeded his words about not plastering her face with make up—the lightest touch of mascara and lipstick now emphasised her subtle beauty rather than parodying it.

'The dress is fine—although in future I may buy you dresses more pleasing to the eye. But there is one thing about your appearance which jars.' He walked towards her and, without warning, reached for the band which constrained her hair, slithering it off with an impatient jerk so that her hair tumbled wildly all over her shoulders. For a moment, he stared down into aquamarine eyes so wide and so deep that he felt as if he might drown in them. 'Don't ever wear your hair like that when you're with me,' he said unevenly. 'I like it loose. Understand?'

Cathy felt the tendrils falling around her face, acknowledging the dark mastery of his command even while a squeak of protest demanded to make itself heard. It was outrageous that he should come out with something as old-fashioned and bossy as that, she thought weakly. Prince he might be, but did he have the right to speak to her in that way?

'Understand?' he repeated.

Yet, dazed by his proximity and the sensual recall of his touch, all she could do was nod. 'Yes,' she whispered.

For a moment the sight of her wide eyes and trembling lips tempted him into ringing up the club and telling them he'd changed his mind. But something was stopping him and he wasn't sure what it was. Perhaps the faint air of insecurity about her which, infuriatingly, made him feel that he ought to spoil her. Take her out and give her a taste of the high life—as if in that way he could repay her for what he had already taken and would later take from her again.

His mouth hardened, because the last thing he wanted to feel was any kind of *conscience* about her. She had wanted him just as badly—and every woman had to lose her virginity *some* day. So why not lose it to the best? 'My car is parked at the end of the lane,' he said.

It felt odd to be walking down a dusty summer lane with the golden-eyed Prince and odder still to remember what had taken place between them. Cathy was conscious of the chauffeur's curious looks as he held the door open for her. Was he wondering what the Prince was playing at? Or maybe this was the kind of thing he did all the time and she was only one in a long series of women who had climbed so meekly into the back of the luxury limousine.

That thought sat uncomfortably with her and she waited for—and wanted—Xaviero to take her in his arms once they were enclosed within the tinted luxury of the car. To blot out all her misgivings with the power of his kiss. But he didn't. Instead, he simply leaned back against the soft leather seat, his long legs spread out in front of him while he surveyed her from between the narrowed golden eyes.

'Your house is not what I was…expecting,' he observed slowly.

It sounded more like a question than a compliment and Cathy knew exactly what he meant. 'On a chambermaid's salary, you mean?'

He shrugged. 'How the hell should I know? I have no idea what chambermaids earn.'

No, of course he wouldn't. Princes didn't draw salaries like ordinary folk, did they? What must it be like to exist inside a great, privileged bubble which separated you from the rest of the world? she wondered. 'My great-aunt left it to me. She brought me up when my parents died. It's…' Her words trailed off. Wasn't *he*, as the Prince, supposed to initiate all conversation—so maybe that meant just answering his questions and not bothering to elaborate on them. She clamped her lips shut.

'It's what?'

'You aren't really interested.'

He felt a mixture of amusement and irritation. 'Oh, aren't I?' he questioned silkily. 'One session of sex and already you can predict what I'm thinking? I know that all women like to think they're mind-readers—but that really must be breaking some kind of record.'

Cathy blushed. How *cynical*. How *hard-bitten*. What had he said? *One session of sex.* It was a hateful way to describe what had happened between them.

'The cottage is one of the reasons I stay round here— well, the garden mainly,' she said stiffly. 'I can't imagine ever finding anywhere else as beautiful. And…well, gardening's my hobby—though it always sounds so tame when someone my age admits that they like it.'

'Or elemental,' he amended surprisingly. 'Some people might consider it sexy to think of a woman bending over a flowerbed, with mud on her hands.'

'Really?' she questioned, not believing him.

'Yes, really.' Hearing the wooden quality of her tone, Xaviero studied the way her little teeth were digging into the cushioned curve of her lower lip, and he smiled. 'You look disappointed,' he murmured. 'Are you wondering why I haven't yet kissed you?'

'Not at all,' she lied.

He laughed. 'Ah, but you must learn not to blush when you tell an untruth,' he murmured and saw her colour deepen even more.

'I wasn't—'

'Yes, you were. There should be few secrets between lovers. If you're wondering why I haven't yet kissed you, can't you think of a reason why that might be?'

Like the class dunce who had been unexpectedly picked out to answer a question by the teacher, Cathy was eager to please. 'Because you don't want your driver to see us?'

Xaviero clicked his tongue. How very mundane of her—but then what could he expect? She *was* a very ordinary woman. Impatiently, he shook his head. 'You think I would leave that to chance?' he mocked. 'The back of the car is completely soundproofed so the driver hears nothing. At the touch of a button, blinds will float down over all the windows, concealing us from the prying eyes of the outside world. Why, I could make love to you now and nobody but us would know.'

'Oh,' said Cathy, aware of an aching feeling of disappointment.

His impatience fled as he registered her unashamed frustration. 'Yes, I know. You want it and I want it, but it will be a rushed encounter—and what is more, we will both arrive at the club in a state of disarray which will not be particularly good for my reputation.'

And what about mine? Cathy wanted to ask. 'Oh, I see.'

'No, I don't think you do.' He reached over to take a silken lock of hair between thumb and forefinger and twisted it. 'The sexual appetite is like any other, Cathy—its needs are many and must be tempered accordingly. Sometimes—like what happened between us today—the hunger is fierce and urgent and must be instantly assuaged. And at other times, well—the anticipation of the feast to come sharpens the taste buds and heightens the pleasure.' His eyes gleamed. 'This evening may be tedious—as so many of these functions are—but rather than sinking into the torpor of that tedium, I shall instead allow my senses to tingle with the thought of just what I am going to do with you later.'

Cathy's mouth dried—partly with desire and partly with shock as she registered his arrogant statement. *Just what I am going to do with you later.* Why, he made her sound so malleable! 'That's if I let you,' she retorted.

Xaviero tensed and then gave a slow smile. 'Oh, you'll *let* me,' he vowed softly. 'Now come over here and kiss me, little chambermaid.'

'But I thought—'

'Mistresses aren't required to *think*—their talents are of a far more practical nature,' he amended silkily. 'So come over here. Now. And kiss me.'

For a moment Cathy sat there. His words made her feel more like a doll than a person and she suddenly realised that this man could easily hurt her. *So wouldn't it be sensible to get out now—before it was too late?* She could feel his eyes on her—that distinctive golden gaze raking over her. He was sprawled back against the seat, eyeing her with lazy amusement as if sensing her inner struggle.

So did he feel triumph over the way she lost the battle

she had half-heartedly been fighting? Leaning over him instead and eagerly pressing her lips to his—not caring about pride or conscience or reputation or getting hurt. Not caring about anything—other than the urgent need to find herself tightly in his arms once more.

She heard him give a little murmur of approval as he drew her against him, before she felt him take control—expertly coaxing her lips open and letting his tongue slide inside her mouth.

Cathy gasped as, in an instant, all those new feelings he had ignited earlier came flooding back in a thick, sweet wave and she clung to his broad shoulders as if she could never bear to let him go. Pressing her body closer, she heard his shuddered little groan and that felt like some kind of small victory.

But if it was Cathy who initiated the kiss, it was Xaviero who demonstrated his mastery by terminating it, gently prising her fingers from his shoulders and placing them firmly in her lap, leaving her breathless and aching as she stared up at him in mute disappointment.

'You must learn to control your appetite, my eager young pupil,' he chided softly, though he felt the wild thunder of his heart as he steadied his breath. 'There is a time and a place for greed, and that time is not now.'

In an effort to distract himself, Xaviero turned to glance out of the window as the car passed through wide gates and up a long gravelled drive. At its end stood an imposing brightly lit and colonnaded white house with a whole fleet of top-of-the-range cars and several chauffeurs standing in a little huddle beside them. He saw one of them glance up and spot the car approaching and it was as if they were all suddenly galvanised into action. Inside the illuminated building he could see figures beginning to hurry around and mentally he prepared to deliver the image of himself the public always expected.

'We're here,' he said, raking his fingers back through his hair. 'And they've seen us.'

Cathy glanced at the sudden cool mask which had replaced the dark passion on his face. 'You don't sound very…keen.'

He should have been irritated by her intrusive observation—but the appeal in her wide blue eyes meant that he was momentarily disarmed. Couldn't he relax his guard for once, just a little? This little chambermaid would never make the error of attaching any significance to any confidences he might share with her—and if she tried, he would merely point out her error so that she would not repeat it. 'I'd much rather be making love to you,' he admitted softly.

And that one murmured comment, along with the sizzling golden look which accompanied it, was enough to make Cathy feel as if she were walking on air as the car door was opened for them.

'And so would I,' she whispered shyly, but her momentary pleasure was eclipsed by nerves as she saw the glamorous women who were assembling to meet them. They were decked in glittering jewels, their skin faintly tanned, pampered and massaged—she felt anxiety flood through her. How could she possibly compete in her cheap little chain-store dress when they all looked like expensive birds of paradise?

Uncomfortably, Cathy followed Xaviero into the banqueting hall, where every table setting seemed to contain a whole canteen of cutlery—but at least she'd helped out at enough formal banquets at the hotel to know which was the correct knife and fork to use.

Picking at her meal, Cathy noticed that everyone waited until Xaviero had begun to eat before they, too, followed suit. How wearing that must get, she thought. She found herself seated in between two very wealthy landowners who wouldn't have given her a second glance if she'd been changing their duvet cover.

But Xaviero had, hadn't he?

Cathy swallowed. He might be arrogant, and proud. He might have taken her to bed and she might have foolishly let him—but nothing could detract from the fact that he had wanted her, just the way she was. And she had wanted him. In fact, if only he really *were* that man in denim and not a prince, then they wouldn't have to be sitting here, having to endure these stilted conversations. They could have been snuggled up under their own duvet—making love and maybe making some kind of future together.

'I'm sure I've seen you somewhere before, Cathy,' one of the landowners was saying to her.

Cathy felt her heart begin to pound with trepidation. 'I...I don't think so—'

'Good heavens—you're not...' The man pushed his scarlet face closer and frowned. 'You don't by any chance work at Rupert Sanderson's hotel, do you?'

Cathy froze and looked across the table in alarm—to find a pair of curious golden eyes fixed on her. Obviously Xaviero had heard every word and was watching her, waiting to hear what she would say.

For one tempting moment she thought about the reaction she'd get if she told the truth. That she was the chambermaid at the hotel he was currently buying and that she'd tugged Egyptian cotton sheets over the Prince's king-sized bed before letting him make love to her on it?

She realised that the landowner was still waiting for her answer and she looked into Xaviero's eyes as if seeking an answer there and, to her astonishment, he gave her a slow smile.

'Yes, Cathy works locally at the hotel—and has kindly agreed to be my guide while I'm here. Aren't I lucky?' he murmured, noticing that the redhead who had been flirting with him all evening was now flicking the little chambermaid a superior glance. Thoughtfully, his eyes narrowed, as he realised that he had not done Cathy justice. 'It helps that she's very beautiful, of course,' he added softly.

Cathy felt the rush of colour to her cheeks at the faint ripple of surprise this remark produced—before the chatter resumed around the table. And although she was pleased that Xaviero had come to her rescue, she wished he hadn't felt the need to tell a blatant lie like that.

Under his mocking stare she noticed the fractional dilation of his eyes. Saw the way the tip of his tongue had touched one corner of his lips as if deliberately reminding her of the sweet delight those same lips had brought to her earlier. And suddenly she didn't care if he'd lied about her being beautiful. When he looked at her like that, she actually *felt* beautiful. Just as she'd felt when he'd gazed down at her naked body as if he couldn't quite believe his eyes.

Was she alone in feeling the tension which fizzed across the table between them? Was he aware that every time his lips curved into a slow and speculative smile she experienced the warm pooling of desire at the pit of her stomach? The impatience to be alone with him and away with these people who fawned over every word he said. The women on either side of him might have been flirting outrageously—but *she* was the woman he had chosen to be his lover!

Her pulse skittered as he stood up and made a brief speech, telling the enthralled audience how delighted he was to have purchased such a prestigious club and his plans to create a world-class polo school there. But Cathy watched the faces of the other diners as they listened to him and laughed conspicuously loudly at his jokes. Rapt and rapacious—the women surveyed him with open hunger while the men regarded him with a kind of grudging envy. What a strange world this was, she thought. One where everyone wants something from him.

And don't you? taunted the voice of her conscience. *Don't you want most of all?*

No. She was modest by nature and modest in her expectations. All she wanted was to feel his arms around her again. To feel the warmth of his skin and the thunder of his heart against her heart. She felt her mouth drying as he finished his speech and looked straight into her eyes as the applause rang out through the vast room.

Needing the washroom, she rose to her feet and saw that Xaviero had mirrored her movement—which in turn caused the entire table to stand up! How awful, she thought. You could never just sneak out if you were a royal. In the restroom, she splashed some cold water over her heated cheeks, battled a brush through the thick hair, and when she emerged it was to find Xaviero standing by the entrance to the ballroom. It took a moment or two before she registered that he was waiting for *her*.

In that moment she felt nervous and slightly out of her depth—but she had to say *something*. 'Thank you for coming to my rescue back there,' she said quietly.

He shrugged and gave a dismissive wave of his

hand. 'No thanks are required. The man was nothing but a crashing snob and I'm sorry you had to be subjected to him.'

Cathy glowed with pleasure at his kindness, wanting to compliment him—just as he had complimented her. 'And I…I really liked your speech,' she ventured softly.

It was the most straightforward thing anyone had said to him in a long time and she sounded as if she really meant it. For a moment Xaviero looked down into her upturned face, thinking how simple her life must be. How unlike those glittering and bejewelled women with their bony shoulders who had vied shamelessly for his attention all evening. And suddenly, the memory of her smile the first time she'd seen him stirred in him a distant memory. Sunny and uncomplicated and full of innocent promise.

'Come on, we're leaving,' he said suddenly.

She glanced down the corridor into the still-packed ballroom and thought about their two glaringly empty chairs. 'But won't…won't people mind?'

'Mind? I don't care if they do,' he murmured, meeting her wide-eyed question with a smile. 'It is time for your next lesson, my beauty. It's going to be a very long and extensive lesson—and I, for one, can't wait for it to begin.'

CHAPTER SIX

'GOING out somewhere tonight, are you, Cathy?'

Momentarily, Cathy froze in the act of picking up her handbag as Rupert's words stopped her in her tracks. Composing her face, she turned around, preparing to face him—remembering what Xaviero had told her when she'd worried aloud about people finding out that they were lovers.

'So what? You have nothing to hide, *cara*,' he had murmured casually. 'And neither do I. Every man is entitled to a mistress.'

It had made her briefly wonder why he had used the term 'mistress' instead of 'girlfriend', when he wasn't even married. But maybe that was what princes did when they acquired a lover who was also a commoner. They erected boundaries—so that the lover wouldn't ever make the mistake of thinking that there might be some kind of future in their affair.

Trying to hide her nerves, she gave a slightly wobbly smile because Rupert was still standing in front of her, blocking her way and clearly expecting some kind of answer to his question.

'Actually, I'm staying home tonight,' she said,

noticing her boss's eyes straying to the bulging carrier bags at her feet. She'd rushed down to the village at lunchtime and had bought crusty wholemeal bread and some thick slices of ham from the butcher.

'Cooking dinner for lover-boy, are we?' he sneered.

Cathy swallowed and then drew her shoulders back. If Xaviero liked her enough to want to spend time with her, then there was no way she was going to let Rupert Sanderson look down his nose at her! 'No, we're having salad tonight,' she answered calmly.

Rupert looked irritated. 'He could have a silver-service dinner any night of the week right here and yet he seems to prefer slumming it with you! And we all know why that is, don't we?' His petulant voice lowered to a kind of hiss. 'But better not get *too* used to it. You may have managed to entice a prince into your bed, Cathy—but he'll drop you like a hot potato once the novelty has worn off.'

Cathy froze—because wasn't her boss only articulating thoughts she'd had a hundred times herself since she'd become Xaviero's lover? Heart pounding, she lifted up her chin and looked him directly in the eye. 'May I please pass?' she questioned politely.

'Feel free.' He fixed his gaze on her breasts. 'Nice blouse, Cathy—is it new?'

As she passed by Cathy blushed—because yes, it *was* a nice blouse. In fact, it was an extremely beautiful blouse—made out of the softest silk chiffon imaginable, and covered in lots of tiny little flowers so that it resembled a summer meadow. And Xaviero had bought it for her.

It had arrived in a fancy box, which she'd had to collect from the village post office. Cathy had no experience of costly clothes, but even with her untutored eye she immediately sensed that the blouse was worth a small fortune. It transformed an old pair of jeans into an eye-catching outfit and had made Xaviero's eyes narrow with appreciation.

Next, a large box of fine French lingerie had been delivered—and the Prince had waved her protests aside with a careless gesture of his hand. He didn't care that she was reluctant to accept gifts from him, he told her—*he wanted to give them to her, and his wishes were paramount.*

'I don't want you in cheap underwear,' he had murmured as he'd slowly peeled off a pair of sheer lace cami-knickers and watched her squirm with delight. 'My mistress must be clothed in silk and satin.'

It had made her feel rather odd. A bit like an object. But then his expert lips and seeking fingers would get to work and dissolve any lingering doubts—replacing them with a sense of wonder that he should desire her as much as he did.

As she walked down the flower-banked path to her cottage Cathy reflected that her weeks with the Prince had been everything that any woman could ever have wished for.

Well, maybe *some* women might have objected to the fact that they didn't go out very much—though he had certainly offered to take her. The trouble was that going out with a prince was beset with difficulties. A supposedly incognito visit to the cinema had been spoiled when word had got out that a European royal was present. Maybe it had been the attendance of his bodyguards who had given the game away, no matter how discreet they had tried to be. And consequently, the staff had made a fawning kind of fuss of him.

Cathy had noticed how much he hated being recognised; she hated it, too—and not just because she was thrust aside into the shadows. Understandably Xaviero was much more uptight when he was being observed by other people. So she had suggested that they stay at home, in her little cottage. They could eat supper outside if the weather was fine—in the seclusion of the small garden. And if it rained, then they could watch DVDs while cuddled up on the sofa, just like any other couple.

To her surprise, he had agreed—and to her even greater surprise, he hadn't grown bored with the arrangement. On the contrary, Xaviero seemed to love the simple life, which was all she could offer him. And it gave Cathy almost as much pleasure as his love-making—to see her prince relax in the relative anonymity of her little home.

He's not your *prince*, she reminded herself fiercely as she dumped the two carrier bags on the kitchen table and went out into the garden to pull some potatoes from the ground.

She was so busy tugging at the tiny little vegetables that she didn't hear anyone come into the garden. In fact, the first she knew that Xaviero was present was the touch of his hands at her waist. Such an innocent touch and yet it had the power to make her feel weak with wanting.

'Xaviero,' she breathed.

'You were expecting someone else?' came his wry reply as he turned her round to face him.

'I'm all muddy!'

He stared down into her flushed and healthy-looking cheeks—at the bright aquamarine eyes which sparkled like blue stars. She was…enchanting. Completely without guile or affectation. 'Who cares?' he murmured as he lowered his head to kiss her.

The kiss became breathless—and the potatoes scattered around their feet. Inside, she quickly washed the mud from her hands and then her lover carried her to bed, where they made love with an urgent kind of fervour which suggested that they might have been apart for weeks, rather than mere hours.

And afterwards he pulled her up to lie against his warm body, kissing the top of her head and breathing in the silky scent of her hair.

'That was...*amazing*,' he murmured, his fingers settling over one soft breast. 'Who taught you to do that?'

'You did,' she whispered. Just as he had taught her everything. Tightening her arms around him, Cathy felt the powerful body relax against hers and wished that the world outside this cottage didn't exist. That they could stay marooned in here in a world of make-believe, where she could pretend that he was simply Xaviero—the man whose golden-eyed beauty had grown to dominate her world.

He began to drift off to sleep beside her and she could hear nothing but the steadying of his breathing, and the ticking of her bedside clock. Oh, how she hated that little clock which ruthlessly whittled away the minutes they spent with each other. Hands which crept round so agonisingly slowly when Xaviero was absent that they seemed almost stationary. But when he was here...well, that was when time would play cruel tricks—greedily running away with itself until the alarm on his cell phone reminded him that it was time to leave.

Then, in the early hours he would prise himself from her warm embrace, pulling on his clothes to slip out into the balmy summer air where his chauffeur was waiting patiently at the end of the lane, ready to drive him the short distance to the hotel.

'Why don't you…stay?' she had ventured, on that blissful first night in his arms—when she had lain there dazed in the sweet aftermath of his love-making.

'I can never stay the night with you, Cathy,' he had stated, his voice suddenly hard and resolute.

Too full of emotion and pleasure to heed the unmistakable caution which smouldered at the depths of his golden eyes, she had looked up into his face with innocent bewilderment. 'Why not?'

'Because staying a whole night is a statement. It implies a commitment which is not present—and to do so will compromise both of us.' He had lifted her chin then. Stared hard into her eyes. 'And you know that this is nothing but a very temporary affair, don't you—because I made that clear from the beginning?'

'Yes. Yes, of course I do,' she'd said, trying to keep her voice from trembling. Telling herself that at least he wasn't lying to her—or keeping false hopes alive by pretending that there might be some kind of future in it. Because she had known from the outset that there wasn't. Far better to simply revel in every glorious and unbelievable moment than try to hang onto a hopeless dream.

Beside her, Xaviero stirred from his brief sleep. 'Cathy?'

She rolled over to face him, their gazes meeting in the confined space of her bed, and her heart turned over with longing. 'What?'

'This.' He slid her hand between his thighs until her fingers collided with his hotly aroused flesh and Cathy's lips parted.

'Again?' she whispered breathlessly.

'*Sì*, again,' he agreed unsteadily.

She swallowed as the familiar heat of desire began to unfurl in her stomach. 'So…soon?' she managed huskily.

'Always. Always! Because you drive me crazy!' he said fiercely. 'Crazier than any woman I have ever bedded!'

Feeling his hands encircle her waist, Cathy drifted her lips to his neck and trailed her mouth lightly over his silken flesh. 'Do I?'

'*Oddio*, I think I have taught you a little too well,' he said unsteadily as he lifted her up and then brought her slowly down on top of him and she gasped as she felt him fill her.

She didn't have the time or the inclination to question him—not then, when he was moving her up and down on his swollen shaft like that. Taking her to that sweet place of release where the rest of the world and all its nagging doubts could be forgotten. When she could cry out his name with uninhibited joy and he would think it was simply the orgasm speaking and not a shout of fervour from her heart.

Much later, they clambered back into their clothes and Cathy concocted a meal, while Xaviero opened some of the wine he'd brought with him. Tipping the ruby liquid into the chunky little tumblers she kept in her kitchen, he smiled.

'One of the finest wines in the world,' he murmured. 'And here we are drinking it from tooth-mugs!'

Cathy put a little bowl of cherry tomatoes on the table and turned to look at him. 'You want me to get some proper wine glasses?'

He looked at her, and at that moment Xaviero felt a sharp longing for a world he would never really know—where every purchase had to be calculated and assessed.

Where things were bought for necessity and governed by cost—without bringing elegance or beauty into the equation. He would no more have drunk from glasses like this in his own home than he would have lapped wine from a saucer—but for now they seemed to symbolise a sense of simplicity he had never known.

'I don't want you to change anything,' he said.

Cathy bit her lip as she went back inside the cottage to get the butter dish—afraid that her sudden fears would show on her face, and scare him. The very real fear of how on earth she was going to cope with life once Xaviero had left it.

But doubts could grow in your mind—even if you didn't want them to—and Cathy barely touched her meal, though she drank deeply of the rich Italian wine. Xaviero had shared her life these past weeks and yet she realised that she knew very little about him. Or at least about his other life. His royal life.

'Tell me about Zaffirinthos,' she said suddenly.

'Not now, Cathy.' He yawned.

'Yes, now,' she said stubbornly. 'Why not?'

His lips curved into a reluctant smile as he watched her push a stray strand of thick blonde hair from her flushed cheek, recognising that she was a beguiling mixture of innocence and outspokenness. She was a complete *natural*, he realised—and it was still enough of a novelty not to irritate him. And yet wasn't one of her most appealing qualities the fact that she was so biddable—so willing to be taught? Why, if he'd told her that it increased his sexual pleasure to have her dance naked around him beforehand, she would have gone about it in an instant!

His smile was one of rare indulgence. 'And what—specifically—do you want to know about Zaffirinthos?'

'Everything,' she answered, wondering if she had imagined that faintly patronising tone.

'But surely you must already know something? Some facts you picked up on the Internet. Because I can't believe you didn't look me up when you discovered who I was,' he drawled. 'People always do.'

Cathy found herself colouring, like a child who had been caught with her fingers in the cookie jar. Or some stupid little royal groupie. 'Obviously I found out some things—'

'Of course you did.' His smile was faintly cynical. 'What things?'

'Not the kind of things I'd really like to know.'

'And what might they be?'

'Oh, I don't know.' She screwed the lid back on the mayonnaise. 'Like what kind of childhood you had?'

If anyone else had dared quiz him about something so personal, he would have dismissed it as an outrageous imposition—but Cathy had a soft way of asking which was hard to resist. 'It was a childhood in two halves,' he said thoughtfully. 'The first bit was idyllic—and then my mother died.'

Her heart went out to him—because didn't she know only too well the pain of *that*? 'And everything changed?' she prompted quietly.

'Totally. My father was utterly bereft.' He stared at the ceiling. The depth of his father's grief had taught him the dangers of emotional dependence as well as the temporary nature of happiness. 'And then he turned all his attention into grooming my older brother to succeed him, as King. It meant a lot of freedom for me—so I was able to concentrate on my riding. That's when I first started to learn about polo.'

Cathy experienced another wrench of sympathy—because too much freedom for a child could sometimes mean loneliness. She tried to imagine Xaviero as a little boy, doubly bereaved in a way—first by his mother's death and then by his father's withdrawal. And while she knew all about bereavement, at least she had enjoyed a close relationship with her great-aunt. 'And your brother is now King,' she said.

'That's right. My father died last year and big brother is now in charge,' said Xaviero, a sudden edge to his voice. 'Busy modernising Zaffirinthos with his sweeping reforms.'

But Cathy wasn't interested in sweeping reforms—she wanted to see the island through her lover's eyes. 'And is it very beautiful?' she asked. 'Zaffirinthos?'

'Very beautiful,' he murmured. But somehow her questions made him realise how long he'd been away—and reinforced his sense of exile. He had not returned since his brother's coronation, for reasons which were essentially primitive and guilt-inducing. Boyhood rivalries ran deep as blood itself, he thought grimly—and hadn't there been a part of him which had always resented the accident of birth which had ensured that Casimiro would inherit the crown? Power was easy to come by, and Xaviero had built up his own power-base through his own hard work—but no one could deny the lure of ruling a country…

He realised that Cathy was still looking at him, her aquamarine eyes searching his face as she waited for him to paint the perfect, holiday-brochure picture of his paradise home.

He shrugged his shoulders. Well, he would give her the brochure version. Why not? He would be her fantasy prince in his fantasy land and that could be the memory she would keep of him. 'It has forests so green that, like Ireland, it is known as the emerald isle. And the best beaches in the world, with sand as pale as sugar. And we have a bay with the bluest water—even bluer than your eyes, *cara*—where the rare caretta-caretta turtles come to lay their eggs on summer nights so still that you can almost hear the stars shooting across the sky.'

Cathy looked at him and couldn't suppress a little sigh of longing. His lyrical words painted pictures, yes—but also helped create an image of the man she wanted him to be. One who was romantic, and caring. Would it be too much to hope that he cared a little bit about her? Hadn't he just compared her eyes to the bluest sea and then called her 'darling' in Italian? How easy it would be to read too much into a simple remark like that—perhaps imagining that he wanted more from her than just being his willing bed-partner. 'It sounds…it sounds like paradise,' she said wistfully.

'Oh, it is,' he agreed evenly, because he knew exactly what she was doing. She wanted him to say that he would take her there. Was she building little fantasies about visiting the magnificent palace, perhaps—mistakenly imagining that she might have some place there? In which case, she should be very careful not to confuse fantasy with reality.

'But you know, of course, that I can never take you there,' he said softly, and, reaching out, he pulled her down onto his lap.

On one level, of course she had known that—but on another, she had hoped… Cathy bit her lip. She had hoped for what every woman in her situation would hope for—no matter how foolish that hope. And why had he made that completely unnecessary statement, which necessitated her asking a question she didn't really want to ask? Suddenly, she found herself on the defensive.

'Why not?'

He lifted her chin with the tip of his finger. 'Because my people would never accept me openly flaunting a lover there. They are less accepting of modern sexual manners than you are here.'

'They would look down on me, I suppose?' she questioned shakily.

'Cathy,' he appealed. 'Don't do this.'

'Because, of course, it's always the woman who takes the blame, isn't it? They would never dare to think that their darling Prince might have something to do with it.'

'That,' he said warningly, 'is enough.'

Her lips were trembling. 'All right, it's enough. And actually, I'm pretty bored with the subject myself!'

'Well, you're the one who brought it up.'

'And you're the one who spoilt it.'

'Are you aware,' he questioned silkily, 'that if you spoke to me in such a way in the presence of others you could be accused of gross insubordination?'

Pull yourself together, Cathy told herself fiercely, banishing her foolish longings and pressing her lips hungrily to the base of his throat instead. 'You could—but only if I were your subject,' she objected as she inhaled his raw, masculine scent. 'Which, of course, I'm not.'

As he laughed Xaviero felt his irritation dissolve, acknowledging that her native intelligence was surprising. And in a curious way she could have almost held her own when compared with other women he had bedded—all of them more high-born than her.

He had slept with heiresses whose own fortune could

almost have matched his and he had slept with super-models whose rangy bodies and exquisite features had graced countless glossy magazines.

Once, he had even dated an Oscar-winning English actress and had watched from his hotel suite while she had tearfully—and rather embarrassingly—accepted the award and dedicated it to *'the only man I have ever loved. The other man with the golden eyes.'* The press had gone crazy when they had worked out just who she was referring to. Later that night, they had made love beneath the metallic gaze of the statuette and a week later he had told her it was over—that public declarations of love had never been on the agenda.

But, out of all those confident and accomplished women, none had spoken to him with quite the same sunny simplicity as Cathy. It perplexed him—and he was not a man who did perplexity. Was it because her whole life had been spent in service that she seemed totally without guile or expectation? Or was it because she had been a virgin, and he had taken her innocence that she was so eager to be moulded by him?

He could see her looking at him questioningly, and he stroked at her silken hair. 'Who'd have thought,' he murmured, 'that a couple of weeks of intensive sexual tuition could make a humble little chambermaid such a perfect partner in bed?'

Cathy's smile didn't slip. She told herself not to react. That he probably wasn't *intending* to insult her. To concentrate instead on the way he made her feel when his fingers were stroking sweet enchantment over her skin. Anyway, perhaps he couldn't help it—maybe that arrogance was inbuilt and part of his unique royal make-up. Maybe princes from Zaffirinthos were *expected* to be arrogant. Far better to accept him for who he was and not try to change him. Why spoil what was never intended to be anything other than a brief, beautiful liaison? 'Who'd have thought it?' she agreed.

'So how do you do it?' he persisted.

'Oh, Xaviero—'

'No, I'm interested. It's more than a learning of sexual technique—though you are a surprisingly fast learner and a very satisfactory pupil. What's your secret, Cathy? Did you back up your practical skills with a little theory? Maybe you quietly read up one of those self-help books which advise women on the most effective way to deal with a powerful man?'

Leaning on her elbow, she looked at him. His arrogance was breathtaking—but sometimes even *he* overstepped the mark. Yet what could she say? Wouldn't he laugh in her face if she told him that her 'secret'—if that was what you could call it—was that she had schooled herself to *forget* that he was a prince? That at least in his arms she could pretend that he was the uncomplicated flirty man in denim she'd been so powerfully attracted to—the man with the golden eyes. And maybe he would take it the wrong way—because he *wasn't* that man, was he? Not really.

'Actually, no—I haven't. Those books aren't really directed at chambermaids,' she answered, deadpan.

'No. I don't suppose they are.' He surveyed her thoughtfully, and realised he couldn't keep putting off the inevitable. 'You know, I've been thinking…do you want me to help you find some other kind of job? Something different to do when…'

Cathy stilled as his words trailed off, the unusual hesitation alerting her to trouble. 'When…*what*, Xaviero?'

His eyes narrowed as he watched her, sizing up her reaction and preparing for tears, maybe hysteria. 'When all this is over.'

The silence grew like a gathering storm cloud while Cathy tried to dampen down the terrible feeling of fear which was clutching at her heart. Telling herself that she had known this was coming. It was just she hadn't been expecting it. Not now. Not yet.

'And…and is it all over?' she managed at last.

Xaviero relaxed a little. No tears. That was good. 'Not yet. But soon,' he murmured as he kissed the curving line of her jaw. 'Probably sooner than I thought.'

'Oh.'

'You've known all along that I've been planning to go to South America for the winter to look at horses?'

'Yes, of course,' answered Cathy, marvelling at the way she could make her voice sound so bright when inside her heart felt as if it were breaking in two.

'Well, a stallion I've had my eye on may be coming onto the market and it makes sense to go out there to look at it within the next few days. I complete on the hotel next week and I've been meeting with architects. The whole building is going to be remodelled to my specifications while I'm away—and I'm planning to keep on any existing staff who may wish to stay once it reverts into being a private house again.' He looked into her wary blue eyes. 'I'm just not sure how appropriate that might be, in your case.'

In the pause which followed, Cathy felt as if someone had taken a jagged shard of glass and speared it hard through her heart. She felt faint, dizzy, as his words had sent a chill of fear icing down her spine. 'I'm not sure I understand what you mean,' she said slowly.

Xaviero sighed. He had hoped that she might make this easy for him—without him actually having to spell out the gulf of inequality which would make any further liaison impossible. 'You know we can't continue being lovers when I return,' he said softly. 'I'll be building a settled life here, and it won't look good—not for either of us.'

'But especially not for you?'

He saw the hurt in her eyes which she was doing her best to disguise, but he knew he had to be honest with her. With a sudden sharp pang, he remembered how the doctors and even his own father had prevaricated when he had asked them whether his mother would live. They had given him hope. Stupid, misplaced hope. So that Xaviero had learnt there was only one solution to misplaced hope—and that was to kill it.

'No,' he agreed heavily. 'You may find it uncomfortable if you stay here, Cathy. One of these days I may get around to looking around for a suitable partner,' he said, and then added, just so that there could be no possible misunderstanding, 'A bride. Because sooner or later I'm going to have to think about settling down.' He felt her stiffen. 'And I'm not sure how easy you might find that, either. If you were still employed here in some kind of chambermaid capacity, and I was bringing a woman back here and—'

'Asking me to change your dirty sheets?' she questioned bluntly.

'Cathy!'

'Well, it's true, isn't it?' Because he had sketched out the possible scenario and now wasn't it up to her to colour in the blanks? To imagine the whole ghastly reality of what he was saying to her. And that way, surely, there would be no space left for illusion or any more hurt?

'And, yes, you're right, Xaviero. It really would be very awkward for both of you if I were still around.'

'Well, there isn't any *both*, is there? At least, not yet there isn't.' He traced the trembling line of her lips with a questing fingertip but she did not clamp her little white teeth around it and suck on it, as usually she would have done. 'Though I don't want you to feel you *have* to leave, just because of me.'

She stared at him, his royal status now forgotten— because in the circumstances it was irrelevant. This was her life, she realised—a life so very different from his. And it was where their two lives had merged and were now about to divide again, propelling her towards a scary and unknown future. 'Oh, of course I have to leave, Xaviero. There's no other alternative.' Or did he imagine that she would hover in the background of his life—some pale-faced little ghost of a woman he'd once known, while he made a new life and a family with his suitable bride?

Desperately, she tried to scrabble back a little dignity. 'But please don't feel bad about it, when we both know it's inevitable—we've known that all along. It's probably just the kick-start I needed. I've been telling myself I've been in a rut for ages and kept meaning to change—I just never got around to it before.'

His eyes narrowed as they studied her. 'If you want— I could perhaps help.' He saw the confusion in her face. 'You know—set you up in something, somewhere else.'

She recoiled. 'You mean…like…*pay me off*? What's that for—services rendered?'

'That isn't what I meant at all!' he snapped.

'Well, that's what it sounded like!'

For a moment he was tempted to leave her right then,

to storm out of her little cottage and its surprisingly beautiful garden. A place where he had been able to shrug off privilege and position with his biddable little virgin whom he'd transformed into a near-perfect lover. And another man would one day benefit from all his tuition, he thought—with a sudden and unexpected spear of jealousy.

'Cathy, don't let's fight—not now,' he said, in as placating a tone as he had ever used, pulling her face towards his.

And to Cathy's everlasting shame, she let him begin to kiss her. Even after all the things he had said to her, she just let him. All those stark statements he'd made which had hammered home her rightful place in the Prince's life. Which was nowhere. What woman with a shred of pride could sink back and revel in his expert caresses like this? But she wanted one more taste of him. One more erotic coupling with a man she recognised would never be equalled—not in anyone's life, but certainly not in hers.

He lifted his head and looked down into her wide aquamarine eyes and saw in them the telltale glimmer of tears. But for once he accepted the unnecessary intrusion of emotion—knowing that his biddable little pupil was about to learn that saying goodbye was the hardest lesson of all.

CHAPTER SEVEN

WITHOUT Xaviero, life suddenly felt lonely and scary—but Cathy did what all the advice columns suggested as a way of trying to forget him. Instead of sitting around and moping, she changed her life completely—deciding to grab every opportunity which came her way instead of just sitting back and going with the flow. Her Prince had gone, yes—but she had known from the beginning that he would. He had gone and he wasn't ever coming back and so she had better start learning to live with that and hope that this gnawing pain in her heart would some day lessen.

The first step in her recovery was leaving Colbridge—though really she didn't have much choice. Hadn't Xaviero himself spelt out in cruel and accurate detail just how difficult it would be if she were still there when he returned from South America?

Saying goodbye to friends and colleagues was harder than she'd thought, though it was no hardship leaving an openly curious Rupert, who had spent some of his profit on a red Lamborghini and was planning to open up another hotel in the south of France.

This time he *did* come right out and ask her if she'd

been sleeping with the Prince, but although Cathy blushed she remained tight-lipped and told him it was really none of his business.

'I think your response speaks for itself,' he drawled.

'You can think what you like, Rupert.' Her cool reply clearly startled him—but, while Xaviero might have taught her about the pain of love, there was no doubt that sleeping with a prince had given her confidence.

It was harder to leave her little cottage where she'd lived for much of her life, and harder still to walk away from the garden on which she had fostered so much love and attention. But she rented it out to a plant-lover who promised to look after it, and moved to London, where she got a job in a famous bookshop situated right on Piccadilly, just along the road from Green Park. In a big, noisy capital city a bookshop seemed a warm and friendly place to be, and when they discovered her passion for plants and flowers she was quickly assigned to the Gardening, Cookery and Sport section of the store.

With the money she made from letting out her home she was able to rent a modest little studio flat just down the road from the bookshop. It was small, the heating was haphazard and it took a hundred and eight rickety steps just to reach it—but once you did, the view over the city was worth...

Worth what? mocked a voice in her head. A prince's ransom?

Heart racing, Cathy tried to shift the taunting thoughts her mind seemed determined to hang onto—but it was far from easy. She *missed* Xaviero. Really missed him. This felt like a broken heart. Like the real thing—while her break-up with Peter had been forgotten in a couple of days. This felt uncomfortably like love—even though she tried to tell herself again and again that she couldn't possibly have been in love with the golden-eyed Prince. It had just been a wonderful sexual awakening, she reasoned—and all she was doing was seeking to put a respectable label on the way she'd behaved.

And Cathy soon realised that being the spurned lover of a prince was a hopeless situation to be in. People always said there was no point in bottling things up—but she had little alternative. She couldn't *tell* anyone what had happened; quite apart from anything else—who in their right minds would ever believe her? Maybe the healing hands of time would help the vivid memories fade. And even though she enthusiastically threw herself into her new life, each night she cried softly into her pillow for the man who had captured her heart and her body so profoundly.

Autumn was approaching and she took to walking round Green Park in her lunch-hour and watching as the leaves began to turn golden brown and scrunched beneath her feet. And she drank her morning coffee in the dark staffroom at the very top of the building, and tried to make friends with the rest of the staff. There were all kinds of people working there, because bookshops seemed to attract a strange mixture. Lots of them were would-be writers, but there was also an ex-soldier, a hand model and a man who had once trained in Paris as a clown. And a part-time girl called Sandy who painted portraits of cats, which then went on to grace the covers of greetings cards.

It was Sandy who was beside her on the day Cathy turned on the Internet, and—when she thought nobody was looking—typed 'ZAFFIRINTHOS' into the search engine the way she did every morning. And Sandy who gripped her by the elbow as the world swam horrifically before Cathy's eyes and the large London bookshop became a blur.

'Cathy? For heaven's sake—what's the matter?' Sandy demanded. 'Cathy, are you *all right*?'

But Cathy barely heard the voice, which seemed to come from a hundred miles away; she was too busy waiting for the dizziness to clear from her eyes and she uttered a small, disbelieving whimper as she took in the words which leapt out at her.

'*Young royal fights for life: Zaffirinthos waits.*'

'No!' she whimpered, shoving her fist into her mouth and feeling her knees begin to sway.

'Sit down!' urged Sandy.

Her head was placed between her knees and water was fetched for her to drink—and when the colour returned to her cheeks the section manager insisted that she go home for the rest of the day. She wanted to read the rest of the article but she could hardly start browsing the Internet in the store if they thought she was sick. Better get outside and buy a paper, or go to an Internet café or *something*.

'Are you pregnant?' muttered Sandy.

Cathy flinched at the unwitting hurtfulness of the remark. Actually, no, she wasn't—and hadn't *that* discovery proved unbearably poignant? For hadn't there been some crazy little part of her heart which had longed to hold onto some precious part of him, and to feel his child growing inside her belly? A hope banished when she'd stood in her tiny bathroom looking at a trembling stick which had stubbornly refused to turn blue.

'No, I'm not pregnant,' she said flatly.

Outside, the autumn wind was blustering in a cold funnel along the street, turning the newspaper she bought into a wild, flapping creature. She took it into a little café and ordered a cappuccino and then raked her way through the windblown pages. Zaffirinthos was a relatively small principality which was rarely newsworthy, but a young prince hovering between life and death would always make the international pages.

Her teeth chattering, she read:

King Casimiro of Zaffirinthos was today fighting for his life following a violent fall from his horse.

Cathy began to shake as the first thought which washed over her in a wave of intense relief was that…it wasn't Xaviero. But this was quickly followed by a second—a lurch of terrible guilt and sorrow—to realise that his brother should be lying stricken.

Poor Casimiro. Poor, poor Casimiro, she thought painfully as she read on.

The dashing royal, 34, who recently acceded to the throne of the tiny island kingdom, has been airlifted to the capital's hospital, where he remains in a coma. Doctors are refusing to comment on claims that the King is near death. His younger brother, Xaviero, 33 (pictured, right), is tonight on his way from South America to be at his stricken brother's bedside. This is not the first time that tragedy has struck the fabulously wealthy di Cesere family. In a cruel twist of fate, Queen Sophia—the King's mother and a noted beauty—died of a brain haemorrhage a quarter of a century ago.

Instinctively, Cathy began to examine the snatched photo, taken at Bogotá airport. Xaviero looked grim-faced and ravaged—his hand raised as if to strike the camera from the hands of the person taking the photograph. He looked *haunted*, she thought—and her heart went out to him.

Staring blandly at her now-cold coffee, she wondered if there was any way she could help. But Xaviero would be home by now, surrounded by advisors and guided by protocol, no doubt—what on earth could *she* possibly do?

Until she remembered that he had given her his cell-phone number—though possibly it was the only time a number had been handed out with the instruction *not* to use it.

'Only if it is absolutely necessary,' he had told her, his stern face leaving her in no doubt that he meant every word. 'If, for example, you were to discover that you were pregnant.' He had acknowledged her shocked little intake of breath, and had nodded, his face grim. 'And yes, I know we have taken every precaution, but accidents can and do happen—though, obviously, we both sincerely hope that this is not the case.'

Cathy bit her lip. What would she do if it were anyone else? If it were a friend or a colleague, someone she cared about or even someone she *had* cared about? Why, even if it were Peter—her errant fiancé—she would send him a message straight away, telling him to hang on in there and that she was thinking of him. But this was different. Imagine the amount of people who would be trying to get in touch with a man as important as Xaviero. She was crazy to even think of trying.

As the days dragged by she couldn't settle. She kept thinking about Xaviero and wondering how his brother was faring—but even though she scoured the newspapers and the Internet for news there was no new update on his condition.

But one evening her conscience got the better of her and she knew she had to contact him. Who cared if it was the wrong thing to do, or if it was some diplomatic no-no? Or even if he thought her a fool for doing so? This wasn't about *her*—it was about *him*.

Sitting down on the rather scruffy sofa, she carefully composed words of comfort in her head before she dared translate them into a text message—terrified that he might think she was writing to him simply because she had an ulterior motive. In the end, she simply wrote: 'DESPERATELY SORRY TO HEAR YOUR BROTHER SO SICK. MY THOUGHTS WITH YOU. CATHY.' She hesitated before adding a single 'X', and then she pressed the 'send' button before she could change her mind.

She didn't expect to hear anything and when the phone began to ring a bit later on she thought it was probably Sandy, who'd been trying to persuade her to go to a comedy stand-up evening in town. But a quick glance at the screen of her cell phone set her heart racing in disbelief. It said…it said…

Xaviero?

Heart pounding, Cathy snatched up the receiver. 'H-hello?'

'Cathy?'

'Yes, it's me. Oh, Xaviero, I'm so s—'

His words cut across hers. 'Are you alone?'

'Yes. Yes, I am. Xaviero—how's your bro—?'

Again he interrupted. 'I can't talk for long and I can't guarantee the security of the line. I need you to listen carefully, Cathy—and then to answer me. Can you come out to Zaffirinthos?'

'Wh-when?'

'Tomorrow.'

'*Tomorrow?* But, Xaviero—I don't understand—'

'I told you.' His voice sounded strained. 'I can't talk now—all I need is your answer—a simple yes, or no?'

Her mind was spinning as she tried to take in his extraordinary request, but on another level she registered the harshness of his tone. Her acquaintanceship with Xaviero might not have been long but it had certainly been intense and she knew that a tone like that brooked no argument.

Which meant that if she went, she would be going into the unknown…

'You hesitate, Cathy,' came the cool interruption to her swirling thoughts.

His words brought Cathy snapping straight back into reality. Why on earth was she hesitating for more than a second? This was the man who had haunted her dreams and her waking hours. The man who had made her feel like a woman for the first time in her life. Who had made her realise what glorious highs there could be in life…and what crashing lows, too. But he had taught her how to feel *alive*.

Yes, he was a prince, but in a way that was irrelevant—for the man with golden eyes had a power which he had exerted over her from the very start. Did he *need* her and wouldn't that be the most glorious thing in the world—to be needed by Xaviero? Cathy swallowed. He wasn't telling her anything and if she went to Zaffirinthos it would be on blind faith alone—a faith which might easily be misplaced and leave her as empty as a waterless well.

But there was no choice. Not when you felt the way she felt about Xaviero—no matter how many times she'd tried to tell herself that it was a complete waste of time. Sometimes you just had to follow your heart—to take a risk and leap into the unknown.

'Yes, I'll come to Zaffirinthos,' she said.

Standing in the ornate splendour of one of the palace's private offices, Xaviero expelled a long, low breath.

'Have your passport ready,' he instructed softly. 'A car will be sent to pick you up at ten tomorrow morning—'

'Xaviero, I have a new job.'

'Yes, I know that,' he said impatiently as he saw the red light of another phone begin to flash on his desk. 'I've had my people check it out.'

My people? For some reason the words jarred. It sounded scary—and more than a bit *controlling*. 'I can't just walk out and leave them in the lurch.'

'Don't worry—all that will be taken care of. The store will be adequately compensated and a replacement found for you, if necessary.'

He barely even needed to think about it, she realised. Such was his power and his influence that he could simply shift people around like chess pieces. He had done it first with Rupert and now he was doing it again. Could that be *good* for a person? Was it good for her to be at his beck and call like this? 'And I've moved. I'm not living where you think I'm living any more.'

'I know that, too. Cathy, these are just minor details which can easily be resolved.'

Minor details? These minor details were her *life*! Cathy swallowed. It sounded so humdrum to ask—but she needed to know, or risk making a fool of herself. 'And what…what shall I bring?'

'Bring very little.' There was a pause. 'All that will be taken care of as well.'

Again, that sense of utter influence and dominance—that newly emphatic timbre to his voice. Surely he had not sounded quite that oppressive in the past? Did that mean her stay was to be short? 'Xaviero, I—'

'Look, I told you—I can't talk now. It's… I'll see you tomorrow—there will be time enough then.' There was a pause. 'Goodbye, Cathy.'

She was left holding a buzzing receiver as he terminated the connection and when she'd replaced the receiver she didn't move for a moment or two. As if expecting her phone to ring again and for someone to say that it had all been a mistake. That the Prince had temporarily taken leave of his senses.

But no such phone call came, and instead Cathy realised that what he'd said must be true. Pulling herself together, she went into her bedroom and packed a small suitcase—hideously aware of the shortcomings of her meagre wardrobe.

She spent the rest of the evening cleaning the apartment and the following morning she was up pacing the floor, her stomach a knot of anxiety, when the car arrived. It was the same dark, bullet-proofed limousine which she'd ridden in with Xaviero on their one proper 'date' to the polo club. It seemed like an age ago. Another life.

They sped with miraculous ease through the traffic—never seeming to be challenged until Cathy noticed the diplomatic flag fluttering on the vast and shiny bonnet and realised why. And then on to an airfield where a private plane was waiting, along with several hefty-looking officials who scanned her passport—was it her imagination, or were they looking at her askance?—before whisking her aboard the luxury jet.

She refused most of the fancy foods and drinks offered by two sleek female cabin crew, and the journey passed Cathy by in something of a blur. She felt a bit as she'd done after a general anaesthetic when she'd had her tonsils removed—all whoozy and disorientated—and it wasn't until the plane began to descend towards a crescent-shaped island set in a sapphire sea that apprehension began to set in once more.

Her heart began to pound as the aircraft passed over deep green cypress forests towards a small airport. Would Xaviero be waiting there to meet her with some kind of explanation about why she had been rushed out here like this? She peered out of the porthole window at a small cluster of people who were assembled on the tarmac, presumably waiting for her to land. But she couldn't see any sign of him—just a large car with dark-tinted windows at the front of several other similar, assorted vehicles.

Warm, scented air washed over her as she walked carefully down the steps and onto the tarmac where a smart woman of around forty, dressed in cream linen, detached herself from the group and came towards her, hand outstretched in greeting.

'Catherine?' She smiled. 'We are delighted you are here. My name is Flavia Simoni and I am the wife of Prince Xaviero's political secretary. Did you have a pleasant flight?'

Cathy wanted to say to the woman that she was *never* called 'Catherine'—but maybe now wasn't the right time.

'It was fine. Thank you. How's Casimiro?' she asked, wondering if she'd imagined the momentary look of disapproval which crossed the woman's face.

'I am sure that the Prince Xaviero will wish to speak to you in person about his brother, the King,' Flavia replied coolly.

Yes, definitely disapproval. Cathy felt slightly desperate now—aware of the beads of sweat which were prickling her forehead and the sudden dawning that she hadn't realised how *hot* it would be. Surreptitiously wiping the back of her hand over her brow, she looked around. Surely he was here to meet her? Perhaps sitting in the back of one of those dark-windowed cars. 'And is he here? Xav—Prince Xaviero, I mean,' she amended hastily.

'Unfortunately, he is not. The Prince is tied up with affairs of state,' said Flavia. 'Which is why he asked me to accompany you to the palace. So if you would like to come with me, we'll waste no more time.'

As she slid onto the back seat Cathy tried desperately to smooth down a floral dress which looked so cheap when compared to Flavia's cool, creamy linen. A million questions warred in her head, but the one which screamed out with utter clarity was the most fundamental of all. Having flown her out here without any kind of explanation—*why on earth wasn't he here to meet her?*

She stared out of the window, trying to take in the beauty of this foreign land. Thick palm trees lined a surprisingly wide road—their succulent fronds outlined against a sky of breathtaking blue and the air was light from the glitter of sun on the distant sapphire sea. After a while, she could see the cluster of buildings in the distance and she leaned forward to get a closer look.

'We are approaching our capital city of Ghalazamba,'

said Flavia, with a note of unmistakable pride in her voice. 'A city which has been ruled by the di Cesere family for centuries.'

Flavia's statement only served to increase Cathy's growing sense of unease. Yes, she knew that Xaviero was a prince, but, despite the fancy car and the discreet presence of his bodyguards, his royal status had not really intruded on the time they'd spent together in England. But *here*…why, it was as if the sheer magnitude of his royal inheritance had hit her for the very first time.

As they passed through the city walls Cathy thought the beautiful buildings looked like pictures she'd seen of Venice—while the dark, labyrinth lanes emphasised that she was essentially in an unknown and secretive place. But then everything became greener—she could discern a verdant sweep of unexpectedly lush grass through the tallest gates she had ever seen. Gates which gleamed a gold as bright as Xaviero's eyes and which swung open to allow the car through.

'And this, the royal palace of Zaffirinthos,' announced Flavia quietly.

The palms of her hands growing clammy with nerves, Cathy stared up at a huge, stately white building with tall columns and elegant, arch-shaped windows. She was aware of unfamiliar trees and plants—flowers she'd never seen before—and the scent of their perfume was overpowering. There was a stately statue of a nymph standing in the centre of a fountain—a small globe held in her hands, over which cool water flowed, and Cathy wished she could go and splash some over her heated brow.

Gesturing to a sweep of marble stairs which lined the main entrance and was guarded by a row of solemn-faced men in uniform, Flavia indicated that Cathy should follow her. 'The Prince has requested that I take you immediately to his private office,' she said.

Cathy's heart began to race as, suddenly, a wave of uncertainty swept over her. *What was she doing here in this mighty and magnificent palace where, all around, inscrutable guards failed to meet her eyes?* But there was no time to think or to wonder because long marble corridors were echoing to the sound of their footsteps and minutes later she was being ushered into a room so elaborate and glittering that it momentarily took her breath away.

But only momentarily—because her attention was immediately drawn to the tall figure who stood by one of the long windows. His face and powerful body were shadowed by the light behind him, but just seeing him again made Cathy realise how much she had missed him and how she had longed and craved to feel his embrace.

'Xaviero!' she cried, and impetuously started to move towards him until the brief elevation of an imperious palm stopped her in her tracks and the words dried on her lips.

He stepped out of the shadows then and, with a shock, she could see that he had lost weight. The flesh was stretched tightly over the autocratic bones of his face and his golden eyes were darkened by lack of sleep. But more than that—they were cold and distant. Gleaming out a warning so distinct that he might as well have held up a placard saying: *Do not come near me.* The only thing she could compare it to was that time when he had told her that their affair was over and he was going to South America. Back then, as now, it had been as if he'd flicked a switch to make himself icily inaccessible—and a sudden feeling of foreboding made her heart miss a beat.

'It is good to see you again, Catherine,' he said, in a voice she'd never heard him use before. Cool and diplomatic—it made her feel as if she were little more than a stranger to him.

And Catherine? What was it with all this 'Catherine'? First Flavia and now him. Dazed by the sheer magnificence of her surroundings and more than a little intimidated by Xaviero's daunting presence, she stood before him mutely and waited for some kind of explanation which might clear this confusing fog she seemed to be standing in. 'It is good to see you too, Your Highness,' she said, echoing his formal tone.

Xaviero looked at her. Wearing some crumpled and cheap little dress, she could not have looked more out of place in the splendour of the palace setting and for a moment he wondered if he had undergone some kind of temporary insanity by bringing her out here.

But what choice did he have in a situation which showed no sign of ceasing? What was it they said? he thought bitterly. *Be careful what you wish for…*

'Flavia,' he said steadily, with barely a glance at the middle-aged aide. 'I wonder if you might give us a few moments?'

'Of course, Your Highness.' Flavia bobbed a smooth curtsey before exiting the room and quietly shutting the massive doors behind her.

And it was the curtsey which stirred a distant memory and shook Cathy out of her torpor. 'I thought you didn't like formality,' she said slowly.

He gave a grim kind of smile. 'Unfortunately, it has become a necessity I am fast learning to deal with.

There are fairly rigid definitions of acceptable behaviour here—and you running across the room and hurling yourself into my arms in front of an aide isn't really one of them.'

The criticism stung—but how had she been expected to know the rules of royal protocol when all she had been trying to do was console him? 'How... how is your brother?'

The golden eyes seared through her. Could he trust her? *Really* trust her? And yet would he have brought her out here on this crazy mission if he did not? 'What I tell you is in strictest confidence.'

'Of course.'

'His condition remains unchanged. The King lies in a coma, unresponsive to all stimuli.' Xaviero's mouth thinned into a bleak line. 'He is alive and yet not alive—for he can engage none of the senses which really constitute living.'

She heard bitterness mixed with sadness in his voice and something else, too—something she couldn't put her finger on. 'I'm so sorry.'

'Yes. We're all sorry.'

She lifted her eyes to his, realising that he still hadn't touched her—and that something in his body language was deeply forbidding, as if daring her to touch *him*. And she didn't. How could she after everything he'd just said? She stood there feeling as if he were nothing more than a distant stranger. He seemed like a man she had known briefly in another life—and yet she couldn't even imagine it now. It seemed impossible to think of him in her arms and in her little bed, making love to her and teaching her how to pleasure him. He looked cold, untouchable—like some gleaming golden statue.

'Xaviero,' she whispered. 'Why have you brought me here?'

By the shafts of his powerful thighs, Xaviero's fingers briefly flexed—a split second of unfamiliar indecision making him hesitate. Because the repercussions of what he was about to say were enormous. He regarded her steadily. Should he go through with it? *Could* he go through with it? And yet, did he really have any choice in the matter if he was to live any kind of tolerable life here on an island where his every move was watched and analysed? Drawing a deep breath, he stared down into the wide-spaced aquamarine eyes.

'I want you to marry me,' he said flatly.

CHAPTER EIGHT

CATHY suddenly experienced the strangest sensation—almost as if she had moved outside her body, and were now looking down on it. As if she were distanced and removed from the moment.

She could see the imposing physique of the Prince radiating power and privilege—and that slightly hunched woman in the crumpled floral dress must be her. She was staring up at him, an expression of disbelief on her face—as if she couldn't believe that such a man had just asked her to marry him. Her lips were dry and she couldn't utter a word—even if she'd had a clue how to reply.

'Cathy? Did you hear what I said?'

His voice interrupted the swirling confusion of her thoughts and brought her telescoping back into her own body with a shock. Swallowing down the sudden clamour of fear as her senses returned, she felt the cold prickle of sweat at her brow and prayed that she wouldn't do something foolish, like slide to the ground in a faint.

Yet her heart wasn't beating wildly with the exultant joy she might have expected. Wasn't it strange how something you'd longed for only in your wildest dreams could have the ring of the nightmare about it when it actually came true? This man—no, this *prince*—had flown her out to his Mediterranean island and just proposed marriage to her. Cathy's eyes searched the hard contours of his face, wanting him to repeat it—no, *needing* him to repeat it, for fear that she might be quietly going insane.

'I'm not sure that I did,' she said. 'Say it again.'

'I want you to marry me.'

Her voice was now little more than a hoarse whisper. 'But...*why*?'

'Because...' He knew the words she wanted—the words were traditional at such a time. Words of love and hopes for a shared future. But he couldn't do that. Xaviero wasn't blind to his faults—though the power afforded him by his position in society meant that they were always tolerated, even indulged—but he had never been a hypocrite and he wasn't going to start now. 'Because I need a wife.'

Need. It was an interesting choice of word and usually it implied some kind of emotional dependence—but Cathy suspected that it didn't mean the same for Xaviero as it did for other people. His face was nothing but a cool, dark mask of near-indifference. He wasn't exactly flinging his arms around her and telling her that she was the only woman in the world for him, was he? That his life would never be the same unless she said yes.

'Why?' she questioned again. 'I don't understand.'

Again, he chose his words with care. The truth was vital, yes—but how much of it could she take? And yet if he were anything other than completely candid with her—might she not in future turn round in that hysterical way that women sometimes had when life didn't turn out the way they wanted it to, and accuse him of having tricked her?

'Because…' The lump in his throat momentarily restricted his speech. 'Because my brother lies insensible in his hospital bed and thus is powerless to act in the interests of his people. It is an impossible situation which cannot continue and I have been charged to govern my country as Prince Regent until he recovers.'

'*Until?*' Cathy seized on the single word. 'You mean there's a chance he *will* recover?'

His eyes narrowed. He had forgotten her native intelligence which seemed to shine through despite her formal lack of education. Had he implied that Casimiro's prognosis was hopeful? '*If* he recovers,' he allowed unwillingly and then met the question which clouded her brilliant aquamarine eyes. 'The doctors think it unlikely. They say that he could lie in this vegetative state for years. I am to be sworn in as Prince Regent—and if I am to rule, then I need a woman at my side.'

To help and support him? she wondered—as her heart gave a sudden leap of hope. To be his solace and his comfort in times of need? Wouldn't she gladly do all that—and more—for this complex and compelling man? Wouldn't she be honoured and thrilled to stand by his side? Trying not to let the sudden rise of happiness show on her face, she clasped her hands together. 'Do you?'

He nodded. '*Sì*. The people are obviously unsettled by what has happened. But a new Princess would give them hope—something bright to lighten the gloom of the accident and the dark days which have followed. Someone to open their hospitals and visit their schools.'

There was a pause while his golden eyes gleamed out a different message entirely. 'While I cannot live without the physical comfort which only a woman can provide. A comfort which you provide so exquisitely,' he said, his voice growing husky with memory. 'As we both know only too well.'

Somehow Cathy kept her face from crumpling. What had she been expecting—words of *love*? Or at least words which contained *some* kind of affection, along with hope for a shared future. Instead, he had presented her with the option of visiting schools and warming his bed at night! Was he expecting her to eagerly snatch at his offer—the way she had greedily fallen into bed with him? Well, she would match his cool words with her own response.

'But why me?' she queried. 'Why not a woman more suitable for a prince—someone high-born and not a humble chambermaid?'

Xaviero nodded, pleased with the dispassionate nature of her question—because surely that boded well for the future. 'Because I know the identity of every eligible woman on the island—and have no wish to marry any of them. But neither do I have the time to go trawling the world in search of a more...' He shrugged as he met her eyes, but he would not shrink from what was, essentially, the truth. 'A more *suitable* candidate of aristocratic breeding. And of course you have one essential qualification for the role, Cathy—one which I can vouch for myself.'

'My virginity?' she guessed slowly.

'Of course.' Remembering the afternoon she had lost it, he felt the beat of desire and longed to take her in his arms right then. To lose himself there in the sweetest way possible and to temporarily rid himself of some of the dark weight of expectation which now fell on his shoulders. But he dared not touch her. Not yet. 'So...' He raised his dark brows. 'Your thoughts on the matter?'

If only he had kissed her or hugged her instead of asking the question in such a cold-blooded way. If he had let physical affection masquerade as love—then wouldn't it have made everything easier? But he was still standing away from her—only a few feet, it was true, but it might as well have been a million miles. *Think straight, Cathy*, she urged herself. *Because this is very important—for both of you. And if you are to give his unbelievable proposal any serious consideration, then you must be in full possession of the facts.*

And that meant remaining as detached as he was.

'So my innocence is the sole reason for this fairy-tale proposal?'

Xaviero gave a quick smile. Was she trying to shock him with her sudden bluntness? 'I think you underestimate your petite, blonde beauty, *mia tesoro*,' he demurred softly. 'Though our marriage would of course be impossible if you had been intimate with other men. But it is your biddable nature which was equally important in helping me come to my decision.'

Cathy stilled. 'What...what are you talking about?'

'It is one of your most commendable qualities—the fact that you are so wonderfully compliant,' he murmured and he began to walk across the room towards her. 'Such a wonderfully old-fashioned trait and it is *because* you are not from aristocracy that you are in possession of it. I watched you begin to learn about sex with an enthusiasm and an aptitude which was thrilling to behold. Your eagerness to please and to improve bodes well, Cathy—and can be applied to other fields outside the bedroom.'

'Compliant?' she repeated weakly, because now he was before her—his glorious face in close-up, his own distinctive scent invading her senses.

'Yes—compliant. You are like a blank canvas on which I can paint whatever I like. Someone who will learn to be the perfect Princess, just as you have learnt to be the perfect lover. Few women are as teachable as you, *mia bella* Cathy. Now come here—'

His voice had dipped and Cathy heard the raw hunger in it—but she stood stiff and unmoving when he took her into his arms. *Say no*, she silently urged herself. *Tell him what he can do with his insulting request. Tell him that you're more than just an ex-virgin who learns quickly and will grab at anything he offers you.*

'Cathy,' he murmured, touching the tousled fall of her hair as he had been longing to do from the moment she had entered the room, tangling his fingers in its silken spill. 'Sweet, sweet Cathy.'

She tried to fight it, but desire was proving far stronger than pride—and hadn't she hungered for his touch for so long? Hadn't he hovered on the periphery of her every waking thought for each moment they'd been apart—reminding her of how totally he could captivate her?

She had thought that she had tasted the last of him, and couldn't ever have envisaged that she would be in his arms again. But now she was, and it was even better than she remembered—obliterating everything but a hot and urgent desire. He was smoothing his palms down the side of her head, stroking her hair as if she were a cat. Each of his thumbs was now tracing an outline on each side of her lips, sending them into a helpless tremble. It was a fervent and curiously innocent gesture and it was almost her undoing. 'Xaviero—'

'Kiss me,' he urged, his voice suddenly raw. 'Kiss me as you've been wanting to kiss me since you walked in here. But do it now for we do not have long—and then I must have your answer.'

Pride made her ask and she prayed that her eagerness didn't show. 'You still haven't told me wh-what's in it for me.'

Should he tempt her with diamonds and palaces? Or something more potent still? The inexplicable something which had sizzled between them right from the start. 'This,' he said roughly as his mouth drove down to meet hers.

Later she wondered that if she'd had the strength not to let him kiss her, whether her answer might have been different. But she was too weak to resist and just one touch was like lighting the touchpaper on her dormant passion. And hadn't he had that power over her from the very moment he had first walked into her life—the man in denim with the lazy smile? Hungrily, she clung to him as his lips began to plunder hers and she gasped as he pulled her roughly against him so that she could be in no doubt about the powerful strength of his arousal.

Cathy moaned softly. If he had stripped her bare and taken her there, without formality on the marble floor of the elaborate room, she would have let him— welcomed it even, for then he would have been simply a man again, without all the trappings of his royal title. But he suddenly terminated the kiss, his golden eyes almost black as they scoured her face, his breathing as ragged as if he had just been running a race.

'You will be my bride,' he stated, necessity forcing him to swallow down the urge to quickly join with her sweet, supple body, and then he put his lips to her ear. 'Won't you?'

And despite the misgivings which ran as deep as her desire, Cathy knew that she couldn't say no to that soft, urgent entreaty. This renewed contact with him had made her realise just what she'd been missing, how much she had ached for him during his absence—and the thought of leaving him tore at her heart like a rusty nail. It was true, he wasn't offering her what men usually offered when they asked a woman to marry them—but he was offering himself.

And wasn't that enough?

Couldn't she make it enough?

'Yes, Xaviero,' she said slowly, her heart thudding beneath one swollen breast. 'I will be your bride.'

CHAPTER NINE

IT WAS, by necessity, a quiet and hasty wedding. With the young King lying hovering between life and death in a hospital bed, any lavish display of celebration would have been seen as being in extremely bad taste.

In the event, Cathy found the low-key tone of the event a relief. Imagine if it had been a full-blown royal wedding, she thought—attended by all the world's top dignitaries and politicians? The kind of nuptials which had apparently been enjoyed by Xaviero's own parents and which had been splashed over glossy magazines the world over. How on earth would she have managed to pretend that her own union was all for real—and that her royal groom was madly in love with her—if there were battalions of cameras around? Until she reminded herself that she wouldn't *be* here if it were a 'normal' royal wedding—because Xaviero wouldn't have needed a bride in such a hurry.

Flavia was assigned to help Cathy settle into the beautiful and closely guarded house within the palace compound which was to be her home until the marriage—and to school her in the automatic changes which the ceremony would bring.

'You understand that with the making of your vows, you will automatically become a princess?' the older woman asked.

'Yes.'

'And that in future, you will be known as Catherine.'

Cathy smiled. 'I prefer Cathy, if you don't mind.'

Flavia's expression hadn't changed. 'Actually, that won't be possible,' she said apologetically. 'The Prince Regent has ordered all your stationery to bear the name Catherine.'

For someone whose identity had already been in crisis, this was the final straw—and Cathy went marching off to the Prince Regent's room. And then was humiliatingly forced to endure an hour-long wait while Xaviero finished off with some government business before he could see her.

When she was eventually ushered into his office, he took one frowning look at her and then dismissed all his aides until they were alone together—something which had not happened since the day when he had proposed marriage to her.

His eyes narrowed as he indicated the seat in front of him, knowing that he had a meeting with the transport secretary in half an hour and a whole stack of reading to get through before then in order to get his head round the new road plans. For the first time in his life, he was realising that he couldn't use his immense wealth to delegate—that the buck really did stop with him. And that maybe this kind of power wasn't all it was cracked up to be… 'Sit down,' he said.

Distractedly, she shook her head. 'I don't want to sit down!'

He let that go. For now. Was the frustration of being

apart so much getting to her as much as it was to him? If that were the case, then he would forgive her discourtesy—but she would have to learn soon enough that he would not tolerate being spoken to like that. Not even by his wife. 'Something has upset you?'

'I won't change my name!'

He laid down his fountain pen and studied her, a nerve beginning to work in his cheek. 'You have interrupted my busy morning schedule to talk to me about a *name*?' he questioned in disbelief.

Couldn't he see that it was more than just the matter of a name? That she was left feeling like a puppet which was having its strings jerked—and that now even her identity had been torn from her? 'I won't change it, Xaviero.'

'It is not a question of choice. You must.'

'Must?'

Compliance had been one of the main reasons he had selected her as his wife—but she was displaying none of that compliance now. Xaviero's mouth hardened. If she was to learn the hard lesson of obedience to her royal husband, then was it not better she did so as soon as possible?

'Yes, must,' he bit out, ignoring yet another phone sending out its silent, flashing demand. 'Which part of the word don't you understand?'

Cathy flinched. 'Am I...?' She was aware that her voice was trembling—but that was less to do with her sudden sense of powerlessness and more to do with the gleam of quiet fury which was emanating from the golden eyes. 'Am I allowed to know why?'

He didn't want to hurt her, but she had pushed him into a corner and she would learn not to do so again.

'Because Catherine is the name of a possible future Queen, while "Cathy" is the name of a—'

She swallowed as the great gulf of inequality stretched between them like a black chasm. 'A chambermaid?'

'Precisely.' He saw the aquamarine eyes begin to take on a suspiciously bright glitter and he felt a momentary wave of irritation. His brother might be dying and she was making a fuss about a damned *name*? Appeasement did not come easily to him, but with an effort he sought to embrace it now. 'Look,' he said, in as placating a tone as he had ever used. 'Catherine is a very pretty name. It suits you. Is it such a big thing to ask?'

Maybe it wasn't—but Cathy was already reeling from the list of 'dos' and 'don'ts' she'd been given by Flavia. Don't stand up unless you want the entire room to follow suit. Don't spend too long in any line-up. Don't forget that everyone who tries to make your acquaintance will have their own agenda—and will try to use their royal connection to better themselves. But the one which had scared her the most was: *Don't trust anyone without first running it past the palace.* No wonder Xaviero was so cynical.

She had spent the morning with a dress designer who had been unable to hide her faint surprise when she'd seen Cathy's existing clothes—before revealing her planned designs for her new, royal wardrobe with the air of a magician producing a rabbit from a hat. And Cathy had looked at all the different clothes she was going to need with a sense of wonder. The brand-new outfits she would require when she took her place in royal life would have excited the heart of most young women. But she was left wondering whether all traces of the real Cathy were going to be completely eradicated by her makeover. And now this.

'Maybe I would have liked to have been consulted about the name change *before* it was decided,' she said, in a small voice.

'And you will be in future,' he assured her suavely. 'I promise.'

She felt like a child being placated with a spoonful of sugar after an unexpected dose of particularly nasty medicine. It seemed so long since Xaviero had actually *touched* her. And wasn't that part of the trouble—that she was left feeling insubstantial, as if she didn't really exist any more?

'And I really want to kiss you,' she said boldly.

He felt the hot jerk of arousal as he got up from behind the desk and advanced towards her, his face darkening with frustration. 'You think I don't? You think I don't lie awake at night realising that you're on the other damned side of the compound surrounded by guards? Why, I am so hot for you that I hardly dare trust myself in your company,' he groaned, before pulling her into his arms and kissing her with an intensity which made him think very seriously about locking the door.

Instantly, she began to melt beneath the seeking heat of his lips—feeling the warm pooling of her blood, the faint tremble of her knees. 'Xaviero,' she breathed against his mouth. 'I want you.'

Splaying his hand greedily over the curve of one magnificent breast and feeling its bursting tightness, he found himself wondering whether there would be time to…to…

And then one of the phones on the desk began to ring and silently he cursed her for inflicting desire on him before so vital a meeting. This was madness! For a moment back there, he'd actually been contemplating…

'You see?' he demanded heatedly. 'Now you have driven me into a state of intense longing!'

'And that was wr-wrong?'

'Of course it was wrong!' He looked down into her darkened eyes and saw the way her lips now quivered with uncertainty. For a moment his voice softened as he traced a featherlight outline over their trembling surface. 'You must learn that duty always comes before desire and we can't do this, *mia bella*. Not now—and certainly not here.'

His soft censure sliced through her like a knife and Cathy's hand reached out to a nearby chair to steady herself on its gilded support. Had she made a complete fool of herself—trying to seduce him away from his frantic workload? 'I'm sorry.'

He shook his head impatiently. 'It's forgotten—but if you embrace the rule from the beginning, then there won't be any need to apologise. There are certain protocols to be observed and one of them is that it is unwise for us to be alone together before the wedding. We certainly can't make love without causing a national scandal and that is something I am not prepared to do in the current circumstances—no matter how much I want you. The wedding takes place the day after tomorrow—so you won't have much longer to wait. Do you think you can hold out until then?'

Cathy felt the sting of colour to her cheeks. 'There's no need to make me sound like some kind of…of…sex maniac.'

Softly, he laughed. 'Oh, I'm not knocking it, *mia bella*. Your unashamed eagerness is one of the very things which makes you so very irresistible. It's just a question of timing.' His eyes glittered as they raked over her flushed face. 'And think about how good it's going to feel, mmm?' He went back behind the sanctuary of his desk and picked up the golden fountain pen before flicking her another quick glance. 'Oh, and in the future, you are to be known as Catherine—is that understood?'

He had waited until she was soft, vulnerable—and then he had driven his point home with ruthless disregard for her feelings. Cathy bit her lip. But what could she do, other than agree?

Because by then a whole train of events had been set in motion and she knew that it was too late to stop them, even if she wanted to. And when it boiled down to it— did she really want to escape from all this, and, more importantly, from Xaviero himself? To do what? Go back to London and her job in the bookshop? Deep down she knew that there was no contest—even if instinct told her that she was laying herself open to possible heartache.

And so it was that Catherine Helen Burton married the Prince Xaviero Vincente Caius di Cesere in the exquisite chapel within the palace compound and became his Princess. The only people present were the Prime Minister, the Chief Minister of Justice and their partners as well as Flavia and her husband, Marco—the Prince's aide.

Naturally, there was no one from Cathy's side and it seemed that this was another point in her favour—that she arrived unencumbered by any emotional baggage. Thus there was no chance of potential embarrassment from loud-mouthed relatives—because she didn't have any. No kiss-and-tell stories or embarrassing photographs dredged up from the past. In fact, no press were present, either—although a brief statement was to be issued to the world's media afterwards.

Cathy wore a pearl-coloured dress of silk chiffon, ornamented by a short, lace bolero jacket worn during the service, which added a touch of formality. She had wanted something knee-length and more relaxed—something which seemed more appropriate for the occasion. But in this, as in so much else, she was overruled. As Flavia crisply informed her—princesses didn't wear day-dresses when they married. They wore fairy-tale dresses which little girls would drool over when the photos appeared in the island's newspaper the following day.

So Cathy tried to appreciate the thousands of tiny seed pearls which had been sewn into the bodice and filmy skirt of the dress and which gleamed as she moved. And to acknowledge that the pearls and diamonds which glittered in the tiara which adorned her carefully coiffured hair were *real* jewels. How many women would long to wear something this magnificent? Yet their cold brilliance was slightly intimidating as well as beautiful—their weight as heavy as the burden of expectation which she knew hovered over her.

But she would be a *good* Princess, she told herself fiercely. She would care for her Prince in any way that he would let her—and she would use whatever talents she had to try to make the people of Zaffirinthos happy.

There was no triumphant peel of bells as they emerged from the chapel into the bright sunshine and she wondered whether there might be a public kiss to seal the union. But there was not. Just the golden gleam of his eyes as he looked down at her.

'So, Catherine,' he said softly. 'Princess of Zaffirinthos. How does that feel?'

'It feels unreal,' she admitted with a whisper and saw the brief shuttering of his face.

'All royal life is unreal.' He gave a short laugh. 'That is both its attraction and its danger.'

'Its *danger*?' she questioned shakily.

Lifting one olive-skinned hand, he gestured at the splendour which surrounded them. 'Of course. Sometimes people who are not born to it find it incredibly restrictive. Or they fall in love with the heady sense of power it bestows. Few remain immune to its lure. Can't you see the danger in that, Cathy?'

'I…suppose so.' She wanted him to tell her not to worry, that it was all going to be okay—especially today, of all days. She wanted to feel part of everything—but most of all she wanted to feel part of *him* in the way that all new brides were supposed to. Her fingers dug into the tight white roses of her bouquet. 'But I'd prefer to think about happier matters on my wedding day.'

He looked down at her. With her pale hair caught up in a sophisticated chignon and threaded with glittering jewels, she looked incandescent. Already, the image of the simple little chambermaid she had once been was fading—though her naïve statement reminded him that, essentially, she was the same woman underneath. 'Yes, of course you do. So come on. Big smile—and then let's go and say hello to the staff.'

All the palace personnel were lined up along the marble steps to greet the newly-weds and Cathy was grateful that Flavia had told her to stop and chat only every few places—otherwise they would have been there all day. But she saw a couple of crestfallen faces from the younger maids she didn't actually get to speak to—and she determined to make their acquaintance on another occasion. Because hadn't she been there, where they were—a small, anonymous face looking out at all the splendour as the moneyed people went by?

Suddenly, Cathy felt a pang for the old life—the life she had left behind. One where feelings were allowed precedence over rules, and where it would have been perfectly acceptable for a new bride to fling her arm around her husband's neck and to kiss him.

The wedding breakfast was held in what she had learned was the smallest and most intimate of the three dining halls—though intimacy was not a word which married well with such a room. How could it when every piece of cutlery they used was made of solid gold and studded with rubies? Even the crystal glass containing priceless wine was so heavy that she needed to use two hands to pick it up.

And Cathy suddenly realised that she had nothing to say! Not unless she started advising the noble assembly how to make a bed—or the best way to fold sheets—and Flavia had tacitly advised her not to dwell on her former life. Her words and her thoughts seemed to have dried up, leaving her feeling empty. Not that anyone seemed to mind. It was clearly Xaviero who was of prime importance. Xaviero whose jokes they laughed at and Xaviero whose observations were met with nodding interest.

Cathy sat listening, absorbing everything she heard—trying to learn as much about her new royal life as she could. But the meal seemed to drag on and on—course after course of it—all amazing little delicacies, most of which she'd never tasted before and were much too rich to lay comfortably in a stomach already churned up with nerves. Especially when all she really wanted was for Xaviero to take her in his arms and to kiss away all her fears and insecurity.

Yet despite the fact that they were newly wed, they were still surrounded by onlookers and protocol. She tried sending him looks of appeal across the glittering table—and was it her imagination, or did he simply ignore her silent entreaty?

By the time the meal was finished she was a mass of insecurity, but consoled herself with the sight of her new husband as he stood up. In his dark naval uniform awash with medals as golden as his eyes, he looked so tall and so handsome. And in that moment Cathy simply felt an immense and quiet pride that she had married such a man.

It didn't matter what had gone before—it was the now which mattered, and soon she would be locked in his arms again. Her bare skin would be close to his in a way she had hardly dared remember, for fear that it would never happen again. But tonight it most definitely would. Hadn't they always been magic in bed together—and wouldn't her pleasure only be enhanced by knowing that she was now legally his wife? She could show him love in the privacy of their bedchamber and Xaviero would learn to accept it—maybe even one day to return it.

Slanting him a demure smile, she rose to her feet— smoothing down the silk chiffon of her wedding dress and imagining him peeling it from her body very soon.

He walked over to her side and offered her his arm as he took her over to the window, for he had not been oblivious to her pale fidgeting throughout the meal. 'You seem a little distracted, Catherine,' he murmured.

Unseeingly, she gazed out at the perfectly manicured palace gardens and told herself not to react. If Catherine he wanted her to be—then Catherine she would be. Hadn't she learnt her lesson over *that* particular quibble?

'Do I? Well, it's been a pretty overwhelming experience,' she answered truthfully, and then lowered her voice so that only he could hear her next remark—because surely a new bride was allowed a little coquetry with her husband, no matter how exalted his position. 'And I just can't wait to be alone with you.'

'Neither can I.' He didn't miss a beat as he saw her lips part. 'But you must be patient for a little longer.'

'P-patient?' She turned her eyes up to him in bewilderment. 'You mean there is some other sort of c-celebration we must attend?'

'Hardly a celebration,' said Xaviero, his voice hardening. 'Now that you are my wife, protocol demands that you must meet my brother, the King. When the meal is ended, we will be driven to the hospital.'

'Y-your brother? But…'

He raised his dark brows. 'But what?'

'Your brother's in a coma, Xaviero.' Tiredly, she shrugged her shoulders—aware of the weight of the pearl-encrusted bodice and the tiara still in her hair. 'Does it…does it have to be today?'

'You mean, he won't know or won't care *when* I introduce him to my new bride—that we could wait a year and he wouldn't notice?'

Hearing the condemnation in his voice, she lowered her own. 'I didn't mean that at all. It's just that you look exhausted—it's obvious you've been under a lot of strain since you came back and took over. Would it be so very wrong if we spent a little time on our own tonight—and went to see Casimiro tomorrow?'

Didn't the guilt which was churning inside him make him want to lash out? 'Is it too much to ask,' he questioned, in a voice of silken danger, 'that you wait a little longer to satisfy your sexual appetite?'

She wanted to gasp out her outrage, to vehemently deny his softly uttered accusation—but, of course, she could not. Not when there were the island's most important dignitaries on the other side of the room, no doubt trying to ignore the fact that the newly-weds seemed to be having some kind of disagreement.

'I wouldn't have put it quite like that,' she said, her calm voice belying the painful scudding of her heart. 'And you know I'm longing to meet your brother.'

'Then why make all this fuss?' he questioned softly.

Somehow he had managed to twist her words and leave her feeling inadequate—as if she had failed him on every level. The first test of royal life, and she had somehow flunked it.

Pausing only to change from her wedding gown into something more suitable for hospital visiting, Cathy joined Xaviero in the back of the limousine for a tense journey across the city as she nervously twisted the new gold wedding band round and round on her finger.

But all her own insecurities were banished when they were ushered into the intensive-care room at the top of the high-tech building, to a room dominated by a white bed which for one awful moment almost resembled a bier. Her fingers flew to her lips and she bit back a little cry of distress.

For there lay the King. His eyes were closed and his muscles wasted through inactivity—but he was still recognisably a formidable figure with the same high slash of autocratic cheekbones as his brother. At well over six feet, he seemed to dwarf the narrow bed on which he lay and the deep, hoarse sound of his breathing echoed heartbreakingly through the room. Cathy looked at all the medical paraphernalia of tubes and resuscitation equipment which surrounded him and had never felt so helpless in her life. That a fine, fit young man could be struck down like this…

And then she glanced over at Xaviero, and as his tortured features burnt themselves into her vision her heart clenched. He looked *haunted*, she thought guiltily. No wonder he had been so tetchy and so ill at ease with her. How must it feel for him to see his brother lying there like that and to be unable to do anything to help him, for all his power and his position? And there she had been—petulant about a name-change and because she'd barely had any time alone with him. A shudder racked her slender frame and for a moment their eyes met in a shared moment of silent pain.

'Casimiro,' said Xaviero heavily. 'I would like you to meet my wife.'

And Cathy went through the motions of sinking in a low curtsey. The head nurse had advised her that the King might be able to hear her, and that she should talk to him. And so, shrugging off any feelings of self-consciousness, she sat and told the stricken monarch how happy she was to have married into his family and how she would do everything in her power to be a good princess. She found herself searching his inert, cold features for some kind of reaction—*any* kind of reaction. Could he understand anything she was saying to him? How terrible if his mind was locked in some frustrating prison—hearing everything and yet unable to respond.

By the time they left, a small crowd had gathered outside the hospital and Cathy was aware of the flash of a camera exploding in her face as Xaviero's security ushered them through to the car.

But once the powerful vehicle had moved off, her new husband reached out and pulled her close to him, staring down into her too-white face. 'I have been harsh with you, Cathy,' he said bitterly. 'Can you forgive me?'

'It…it doesn't matter.'

'Oh, but it does.'

'No, I have been putting my own concerns first,' she whispered. 'Instead of realising all the responsibilities which have been pressing down on you.'

He pushed her hair back from her cheek. 'Having you so close—and yet unable to touch you—has been driving me half crazy with desire.' His mouth softened into a smile tinged with sadness. 'And you were brilliant with my brother.'

Basking beneath the unexpected compliment and sinking into the longed-for warmth of his embrace, Cathy found herself wanting to smooth away those hard lines of strain from his formidable features. 'Does he get many visitors?'

All Xaviero wanted to do was to block out the nightmare image of what they had just seen, but her eyes were dark with a question he had no right to ignore. 'We have no other living relatives.' He shrugged. 'I go, when I have time…although every second is now planned out for me, as you know, so it is not as often as it should be. And, of course, I do not find it as easy to talk to him as you just did.'

'That's because women are better at that kind of thing.'

'Are they?' He allowed himself a brief smile. 'And naturally, the King's security and privacy is paramount, which means that no other visitors are permitted—not even his aides.'

Cathy thought about Casimiro's terrible loneliness and isolation, lying there with only the nurses going about their daily duties of helping keep him alive, and she bit her lip. 'Could I...could *I* go and visit him—would that be all right? I mean, I'm a relative now, aren't I?'

Xaviero looked into her shimmering blue eyes, taken aback by her tentative request—since a desire to visit the sickbay would not have been a request made by any of his past lovers. 'I don't see any reason why not,' he said gruffly.

'Then I'll ask Flavia to sort it out.'

He pulled her properly into his arms at last—and the sweet, fresh smell of her after the sterility of the hospital bay made him want to weep for all the joys his brother had lost. 'Oh, Cathy,' he said as he stared down at the uncertainty written on her trembling lips, wanting her to wipe some of the pain away with the tenderness of her touch. 'Cathy, Cathy, Cathy.'

Trembling with the pent-up emotion of all that had happened, she paid no heed to the fact that he had rebuffed her more than once. She was just empowered by a need which matched the naked hunger in his eyes and her arms reached up to lock themselves around his neck while their lips collided in a kiss. She heard the small ragged sigh which escaped him and felt the beat of his heart so close against her own. 'Xaviero,' she whispered.

'I want you,' he declared unevenly.

And, oh, how she wanted him. Back in a suite decorated with fragrant white roses, Cathy let him carry her straight to the bed, where he began undressing her with a sudden urgency.

'You haven't carried me over the threshold,' she teased.

'You want to go outside and come in again?' he demanded, lifting his head from her breasts, which he was baring—button by button—his eyes almost jet-black with desire.

Terrified of tempting a fate that had kept them segregated since she'd arrived and too transfixed by the shivers of desire which were skating inexorably over her skin, Cathy shook her head. 'No,' she whispered. 'I just want you.'

'Then you shall have me, *mia bella*. All night long, I am yours.' Making a sound a little like a low growl, Xaviero stripped the clothes from her body almost ruthlessly, his fingers and his lips reacquainting themselves so deliciously with her flesh that she immediately choked out a little gasp of pleasure.

But that first time of making love as man and wife was not the slow coupling she might have hoped for. It was wild, almost primeval—though no less thrilling because of that. And the pleasure was exquisitely sharpened by abstinence. Yet it felt as if he was using the sex as some kind of catharsis to exercise unknown demons. Sobbing out his name as Xaviero shuddered inside her, Cathy clung to him as he breathed something in Italian against her damp skin.

'I've…I've missed you,' she said eventually.

Lazily, he turned onto his side, his finger tracing an undulating line from hip to breast, where it lingered and teased the rosy little tip until she gave a moan of pleasure. 'And I have missed *this*…' Letting the hand now splay luxuriantly over the silken globe of her bottom, he felt much of the strain and tension dissolving in that soft, sensual touch. 'You are…*sensational*,' he breathed.

'Am—am I?'

'I'd forgotten quite how much,' he declared unsteadily.

Wordlessly, they made love again and when it was over Cathy lay there staring up at the ceiling as her heartbeats gradually began to slow—not wanting to disturb a moment of the perfect harmony she felt. But as her own pleasure began to fade she felt a strange foreboding creep in to replace it. They were close, yes—but only physically close. The sense of oneness she had longed for had so far failed to materialise. Was she being greedy or unrealistic in expecting it to happen so soon? Or was she foolish in hoping that it might happen at all?

All night long, I am yours, he had said.

And for the rest of the time, what then?

CHAPTER TEN

THE next weeks were spent immersing herself in the art of being a princess—and Cathy was endlessly grateful for the adaptability she'd learnt while working at the hotel. Seamlessly slipping between chambermaiding and receptionist duties, she had been able to turn her hand to just about anything—and these were skills which proved invaluable in her new life.

And didn't throwing herself into her new role help her paper over the cracks in her marriage?

Busying herself with tasks befitting a brand-new royal helped Cathy forget that her worst fears were being realised, day by day. And that the ice-cold heart of her new husband could not be thawed, no matter how much tenderness or passion she showed him in their bed. Only at night did he let his guard down—but the ardent lover he became crumbled into nothing but a memory by morning. The mask of his regency was assumed as soon as his valet began laying out his clothes and he became a distant stranger once more.

It was as if she had no real part in his daily life—when he treated her with the undemonstrative civility he might show one of his aides. She was never allowed to show affection, nor to disturb him—and if she wanted to speak to him, she had to make an appointment like everyone else! Reminding herself that she had been chosen as his wife primarily because she would accept such conditions, she resolved to say nothing. And, like generations of women before her, Cathy played down the shortcomings in her relationship by reaching outside it for fulfilment.

Her days were spent organising her new office and deciding on what staff she would need to help her. There were posts for a private secretary, assistant secretaries and ladies-in-waiting as well as a hairdresser and a language coach. Although English and Greek were taught in all the schools, Cathy had started to study Italian, which was the main language spoken on Zaffirinthos. From being a non-academic child herself at school, suddenly she could see the point in learning, if it actually had some kind of *purpose*.

And Xaviero's aides were proposing a grand joint tour of the island to introduce her to the people—even though the dark cloud of Casimiro's continuing coma meant that they were reluctant to pin down a date. But by then Cathy had started to visit the King on a regular basis and found that increased exposure to the inert figure on the white bed made his incapacity seem far less shocking than it had done at first.

She found herself actually looking forward to the visits—at least they made her feel as if she was being properly useful. She soon got to know all the nurses, who—once they'd stopped viewing her with a certain suspicion—soon started to warm to her. Because here, in this stark and bleak setting, all status and privilege seemed completely irrelevant.

Each day Cathy would sit with the King, while a bodyguard stood keeping his own vigil behind the bullet-proofed glass which had been specially installed. She found herself telling him about her blundering attempts to learn Italian and about how much all the staff at the palace talked about him and missed him. She described her little garden in England and how she hoped her tenants were looking after it properly.

And despite her own increasing loneliness, she tried to do what she had promised herself from the very beginning—to be a good wife to Xaviero, even though their time together was so restricted. Her foolish heart leapt with pleasure whenever they had a joint meeting scheduled, when they would sit at opposite ends of a long, polished table while their aides tossed out subjects for discussion. Or, briefly, they might exchange smiles if their respective retinues happened to pass each other along the wide, marble corridors of the palace.

They were rarely alone, except in bed when they would fall into each other's arms as if their lives depended on it. And in the pleasure that followed, Cathy couldn't bring herself to spoil the moment with a litany of complaints about how little they saw of each other. Maybe it was the same for every royal wife—one of the downsides behind the supposed fairy tale of privilege. In a way, with her limited access to him, she still felt a bit like a mistress—despite the bright band of gold on her finger and the royal crest which adorned her notepaper.

At meal times, there were always members of staff hovering silently in the background, pretending not to listen but watching carefully for any sign that the royal couple might require something—leaving Cathy to eat rather self-consciously, worried that her table manners might not be up to scratch. Perhaps that might explain why the waistbands on some of her dresses had become a little loose of late.

'You've lost weight,' said Xaviero one evening as she was dressing for a formal dinner arranged for a visiting Italian dignitary.

'Have I?' she questioned. And if her voice sounded a little dazed, it was because she was still reeling from the fact that Xaviero was here—in her dressing room. He had wandered in to ask her to fix his cufflinks—a ridiculously simple and yet oddly intimate request which had left her feeling slightly flustered, until she had gathered her thoughts together enough to realise why.

Because they didn't *do* intimacy—not unless it was in the purely sexual sense. Xaviero had a valet to do his cufflinks. A tailor to measure his clothes. Aides he could confide in, and question about current affairs. Chefs to prepare his meals. He didn't need a wife in the way that other men did. His wife was an accessory—a compliant woman who was fast learning to be a competent princess.

'You know you have,' he said as he slowly circled her, like a predator eyeing up his victim. 'That dress fitted you perfectly the last time you wore it.'

'Only a few pounds,' said Cathy. 'And I'm…I'm surprised you noticed.'

Xaviero's eyes narrowed, allowing his gaze to drift over the creamy décolletage which was displayed to perfection by the soft sheen of the scarlet gown she wore. His voice thickened and he felt the familiar kick of lust. 'I notice everything about your magnificent body, *mia bella*—and you certainly don't need to lose any weight.'

'I wasn't trying to.'

She looked strained, he thought. The slight weight loss had made her cheekbones appear sharp and slanted, so that her face looked all eyes. Was she doing too much? Driving herself too hard in her attempts to fit in—attempts which hadn't gone unnoticed. Hadn't the court already expressed approval of her induction into the di Cesere family—despite initial misgivings about the wisdom of his hasty marriage to such a woman?

'Would you like a weekend away?' he questioned suddenly.

Cathy finished clipping in a diamond earring and met his eyes in the mirror, her heart beginning to thud with hope. A weekend away? Maybe like the honeymoon they'd never had? She turned round in the chair, a smile on her face as she beamed up at him. 'Oh, Xaviero—I'd love it! Do you really mean it?'

'Why not?' His lips curved into a speculative smile. She had been remarkably modest in her outgoings—in spite of him giving her carte blanche to spend his fortune as the mood took her. In fact, as far as he knew she had asked for nothing. If she had been trying to impress him with her restraint, then she had succeeded admirably— and maybe now was the time to reward her. 'You and Flavia could fly to Milan,' he suggested softly. 'Buy yourself something from the latest collections.'

It felt like a slap to the face but Cathy's smile didn't waver. How quickly she had become skilled at the royal art of never giving away your feelings by your facial expression. 'Flavia?' she echoed.

'*Sì*. The two of you get on well, don't you?'

'Well, yes, we do—but that isn't the point. I thought you meant us…the two of *us*.'

He frowned. 'And how precisely would that happen,

Cathy?' he questioned drily. 'Would someone magically step in to fill my shoes while I'm away? I am a busy man.'

With fingers which were trying not to tremble, she turned back to the mirror and pretended to fuss with her hair. She *knew* he was busy—that his diary was jam-packed—but surely even Prince Regents were allowed a holiday sometimes?

'Of course you're busy.' She swallowed. 'You're always busy. I'm sorry. It was a stupid assumption for me to make.'

Something in the resigned tone of her voice stayed him, and he came up behind her, his fingers slipping to her bare shoulders and beginning to massage them. 'No, it was an easy assumption to make...but there aren't going to be any holidays, *bella*—at least, not for a while.'

'Oh, well,' she said brightly. 'I guess it'll be all the better when it happens.'

Frowning, he felt the tight tension in her shoulders as he attempted to explain something of his dilemma—he who had never had to offer anyone an explanation in his life. 'Taking over a monarchy like this is a bit like being brought in to head up a powerful organisation—except much of this I cannot delegate, because the buck stops with me. And yet because, ultimately, mine is only a *substitute* authority, I must run every decision past the government to ensure that I am acting in the country's best interests. *Porca miseria*—but your muscles are tight, *mia bella*.' Gold seared into aquamarine as their eyes locked in the looking glass. 'Perhaps I should take you to bed and help you relax in a way which would please us both,' he said softly.

For a moment, she allowed herself to dream. 'Wouldn't that be lovely?' she whispered.

His hand slipped beneath her gown to tease a nipple between thumb and forefinger, a smile curving his lips as he felt its immediate response. 'Mmm. It would be *perfetto*.'

She felt like a child who had been offered an ice cream, only to discover that the store had just closed. 'But…but there isn't time, is there?' she said, jerking away from the temptation of his touch. 'Not with forty people waiting to have dinner with us.'

Reality intruded like a cold shower—washing away the soft heat which always suffused his skin when she was near. What a distraction she was, with her pale hair and her trembling lips and that way she had of looking up at him. Swallowing down his frustration, Xaviero said something harsh and raw in Greek—in a tone she had never heard him use before—and Cathy held his gaze as she put her hairbrush down, with a hand which wasn't quite steady.

'Why don't you say it in English so at least I can understand?'

His mouth hardened. 'You don't want to hear it.'

'Oh, I think I do. Aren't wives supposed to know what's troubling their husbands, even if they're Prince Regents?' she questioned, her heart suddenly beginning to thump with a cold dread which made the palms of her hands grow clammy. 'And…and something is troubling you, isn't it, Xaviero?'

There was a split second of a pause. Because didn't articulating something make it real? And yet if he didn't tell someone he thought he just might explode. He shrugged, and then let out a ragged sigh. 'I just said how much I hate this life.'

Quietly spoken, his words ripped through her: …*how*

much I hate this life. Powerful words which laid bare a dissatisfaction she had suspected from the moment she'd arrived on the island. Was she implicated in that unhappiness? she wondered painfully. *Yet how could she not be—for wasn't she part of the whole package?*

'Anything specific?' she questioned, in a light tone. The kind of tone she'd once used to ask people if they'd like an extra blanket or not.

'Oh, I don't know—*everything.*' The words left his mouth with soft, explosive savagery, a torrent he'd been trying to deny for too long—even to himself. 'I hate it all. The demands. The lack of freedom and privacy. The way that everyone wants something from you. Everybody has a damned agenda.'

'But surely that was always the case? You've been royal all your life, Xaviero.'

'Only when I had to be.' He lifted his hand up to rake it back through the ebony hair, the light glinting off the pale gold of his crested cufflink. 'Why do you think I went to live in New York, where I was able to live a reasonably anonymous life? Because I didn't want to stand out. It's why I picked the isolation of the countryside, when I decided to settle in England.'

'Then this happened, out of the blue,' she said slowly, praying that his valet or her lady-in-waiting wouldn't come in and disturb them—because Xaviero had never talked to her like this before. 'And there was absolutely nothing you could do about it.'

'No. My fate has been sealed,' he said, with an air of finality, and then his face darkened. 'And yet I have no right to express any kind of dissatisfaction with my lot. How can I—when my brother is lying insensible in what seems like a cruel enactment of our mother's demise? And if I'm honest—really honest—weren't there times in our childhood when I *wanted* the monarchy? When I wished it was *me* being prepared for the kingdom, not Casimiro. What is it that they say,' he added bitterly. *'Be careful what you wish for.'*

Cathy flinched, praying for the right words as she saw the deepening of the painful lines etched in his face. Something which could lessen his grief and his guilt and might make him see the positives in a life he would never have chosen for himself. Couldn't she persuade him that together they could learn a different way of living—if he was prepared to give it a try? But before she could speak, there was a gentle tap on the door and Xaviero opened it himself to find one of the butlers standing there.

Black eyebrows were arched in impatient query. *'Yes, what is it?'*

'Highness, your guests have arrived.'

Xaviero nodded, wishing for a brief and crazy moment that he were back in her tiny cottage, sitting in the soft, scented oasis of her garden, drinking wine from those ridiculous cheap little tumblers she used to use. But there was no use yearning for the impossible— because hadn't he learnt by now that duty always came first? And how could he expect Cathy to adhere to that principle if he found he was trying to shirk it himself? 'We'll be right down.' He turned to her. 'Ready?'

'Yes.' She hesitated. 'Xaviero, there must be some- thing you could—'

'Forget it.' Although soft, his tone was emphatic. 'It doesn't matter.'

She wanted to say that it *did*—but her heart sank as she saw the now familiar cool mask back in place and she sensed his confidences of just a moment ago already being erased from his mind. And yet his disclosures— far from bringing her closer to him—had left her feeling distinctly unsettled. Insecurity flooded through her as she realised she hadn't been imagining his frustration at his life here at all. And what would happen if that frustration built and built?

Side by side they walked into the ante-room where the assembled guests were waiting and Cathy carefully composed her face to prepare herself for the inevitable scrutiny. She was used to this by now—the way the women always looked her over and sized her up, as if trying to decide whether she was fit to be married to such a devastatingly handsome and eligible prince.

This was the part of the evening where she and Xaviero again went their separate ways—she to chat to the wives of the visiting delegation and to sip at a glass of water. She had given up taking wine before or during the meal—it made her grow too pink and uninhibited and sometimes she had to bite back things she really wanted to say.

It's as much a prison for me as it is for Xaviero, she realised suddenly as they were led into dinner, to opposite ends of the formally decorated table.

She watched Xaviero during the meal, her eyes straying to him despite her determination to respond enthusiastically to the man seated next to her. From time to time he would look up, his golden eyes sparking out a silent question—occasionally, he would even toss her a slow smile. And Cathy was aware that she seized on these little crumbs of affection as a starving dog would a piece of meat.

She saw the sultry woman at his side slant him a beguiling smile—and, to be fair to Xaviero, he didn't respond to it at all. No telltale silent flirtation in return. But that was because they were newly-weds—when she was still completely captivating to him in the bedroom and he couldn't seem to get enough of her. What would happen when that wore off—as people always said it did?

Trapped within the confines of their largely separate lives—might not Xaviero choose to dabble a little elsewhere, as royal men throughout history had been inclined to do? The opportunity was always there for them—they could have their pick of women so eager to bed a prince that discretion would be guaranteed. Why, didn't weak and ambitious men sometimes even offer up their wives as some kind of noble sexual sacrifice?

Maybe that was another reason why he had chosen a compliant wife—one so grateful to be married to him that she would put up with just about anything. Was he expecting her to turn a blind eye to his indiscretions as royal wives were famous for doing? She shuddered, quickly putting her heavy fork down before she did something unforgivable—like dropping it on one of the porcelain plates.

But it was like finding a tiny tear in an old dress and poking your finger inside it—only to discover that you were making the hole much bigger. It was as if tonight had opened the floodgates on all the inadequacies in their relationship—or had Xaviero's own words of dissatisfaction about his life helped to crystallise her own?

We've never even talked about children, she realised. Quickly, she gulped down a mouthful of water and felt it refresh her parched lips, but underneath the table her knees were trembling. Xaviero had continued to use protection after their marriage and she hadn't even questioned it—just tacitly accepted it as she had done so much else. Oh, she was certainly compliant! Did he *want* children? And could she bring children into this kind of peculiar marriage—or was this a 'normal' marriage in the royal world?

I'll ask him, she thought—though a wave of dark misery swept over her. *I'll ask him tonight.*

Dessert appeared—an extravagant confection of lemon cream and spun sugar—and Cathy was eyeing it unenthusiastically when one of Xaviero's aides entered the room and went immediately over to his side to speak softly in the Prince's ear.

Even without her crash-course in protocol, Cathy would have known that it was rare indeed for the Prince Regent to be interrupted when he was in the middle of an official dinner. And rarer still for Xaviero to suddenly rise to his feet, his face growing ashen.

Something was wrong. Helplessly, her fingers clutched at her napkin. She wanted to ask him what was happening but, of course, she couldn't do that for he wouldn't dream of telling her before an audience.

And then another aide entered and Xaviero quickly joined him at the side of the room, bending his dark head as the man spoke in a low, urgent tone in his ear. By now all the guests had abandoned any pretence at continuing with their dinner—as everyone seemed to sense that something momentous was happening.

What the hell was going on?

Xaviero's face grew suddenly taut as he spoke in a low voice to the assembled company. 'I regret to say that urgent matters of state mean that my wife and I must now leave you,' he said, and then paused before the golden eyes seared into her. 'Catherine, you will please join me?'

It felt like a summons, it most definitely *was* a summons, and never had a walk seemed so long as Cathy found her feet and slowly walked down the long dining room towards him. Searching his face for some sort of clue for the reasons behind this extraordinary break with protocol, she found none. Just a bleak and unfathomable countenance, but then, wasn't that Xaviero all over—because since when had she ever been able to read anything in his shuttered face?

In silence, they left the room—the aides following at a discreet distance—and once they were out of earshot of the assembled dignitaries she turned to him in perplexity.

'Xaviero, what on earth is going on?'

He seemed to struggle to find the right words. 'The hospital has just rung—'

Her heart missed a beat as she held her breath, sensing tragedy. 'And?'

He swallowed. 'My brother has tonight awakened from his coma.'

CHAPTER ELEVEN

THE car drove them straight to the hospital—but Cathy was still reeling from her husband's shock announcement and his inexplicably bleak response to it.

'I thought…I thought you'd be overjoyed about your brother's recovery, and yet…' she said slowly, registering the sombre set of his features in the dimmed light of the limousine. 'What exactly have they told you?'

'That he suddenly opened his eyes and began to speak. They're running tests now—but they say…' His voice thickened. 'They say he's going to make a full recovery.'

'So why…?' Dared she? *Dared* she? 'Why your restrained response?'

'I'll believe it when I see it for myself,' he said harshly as the car drew up outside the brightly lit and modern hospital, where the medical director was waiting for them.

The news was good. In fact, the news was pretty unbelievable, Cathy thought as she sat in the big, airy office and listened while the doctor explained that every test they'd run had been favourable. That every system was functioning and that the King was demanding physiotherapy as soon as possible because he wanted to—as the doctor relayed with the hint of a smile—'get the hell out of here'.

Xaviero felt a pulse working at his temple. 'That sounds like Casimiro. So when can I see him?'

'I can take you to him now, Your Highness.'

He turned to her, but the golden eyes were shadowed, distracted. 'Come, Catherine.'

Cathy was suddenly acutely aware that she was dressed in a scarlet evening gown—even though her shoulders were covered in a pashmina which had been thrust at her by an aide before their hasty departure. And aware too that her presence was superfluous to what would—and should—be an emotional reunion between the two brothers. She shook her head. 'No. Better that you see him alone,' she said quietly.

Eyebrows arrowed together in a frown. 'You're sure?'

'Quite sure.'

She sat drinking coffee while she waited, unable to stop the stream of thoughts pouring into her mind—no matter how much she tried to stop them. But shamefully the one which dominated all others was purely selfish. And while Cathy's heart felt fit to burst for joy that the young King should have come back to life, she wouldn't have been human if a deep dark wave of fear hadn't washed over her.

Because my place here is now redundant.

Xaviero didn't need her any more. He didn't need a wife by his side to ease the burden of unwanted duty thrust upon him by circumstance. He didn't even need to be here himself—not now. Judging by what the doctor had told them, the King was well on the way to recovery and would soon resume his rightful place on the throne.

She was so caught up in her troubled thoughts that when Xaviero appeared in the doorway for a moment she scarcely recognised him. Because this was a man she had never seen before—one transformed by a sudden sense of joy. It was as if he had been carrying around with him an impossibly heavy burden—and someone had suddenly lifted it from his shoulders and the weight had vanished. He was free, she thought—with another shiver of foreboding.

'How…how is he?' she asked.

'It's *unbelievable*.' Xaviero expelled a ragged sigh—because hadn't the past come back to haunt him as he had stood beside his brother's bed? Didn't he know better than anyone that doctors sometimes raised hopes when those hopes were better to let wither, and die? But the spectre of his mother's own failed recovery had been banished by the first sight of his brother's smile. 'He's…'

He had been about to say that Casimiro was the same as he'd ever been, but that would be a lie. His brother had changed—Xaviero had sensed that from the moment he had walked into the intensive care unit. And when you stopped to think about it an experience like that was bound to change you profoundly—for didn't death's dark shadow throw the rest of your life into focus and force you to reevaluate it?

'He's going to be okay,' he said, in a shaky voice which didn't sound like his own voice.

Her own fears forgotten, Cathy went to him then—putting her arms very tightly around him and resting her head against his shoulder, breathing in the raw masculine scent that was all his.

'Oh, Xaviero,' she whispered. 'I'm so very happy for you. So happy for him.'

'Not as happy as I'm feeling right now,' he whispered, his arms snaking round her waist as he buried his face in the silken tumble of her hair.

The car took them back to the palace, and, after telling the assembled staff the news, they hurried to their suite with matched and urgent steps. Xaviero was on fire, and so was she—he barely waited until the door was shut before impatiently sliding the soft silk-satin up over her hips. Questing fingers found her searing heat and he didn't even bother to remove the delicate lace panties—just hurriedly thrust the panel aside, as he unzipped and freed himself and pushed her back against the wall.

Cathy gasped as she felt the tip of him nudging intimately against her—wanting to squirm her hips to accommodate him—longing to feel his hard power filling her and completing her. But as he prepared to thrust into her—it was she who realised what was about to happen. Who cried out a little protest before firmly pushing against his chest before it was too late—before he risked trapping himself again, only this time by something which was preventable.

'C-c-contraception!' she gasped out.

Xaviero's mouth hardened as he haltingly complied with her wishes—the mood not exactly broken, but certainly changed by her shuddered command. And something in the act of putting the barrier between them distilled some of the jubilant wildness which had been heating his blood. His thrust was still deep, but his movements were more measured. Instead of the fiery, fast consummation he had sought, he now controlled the pace almost cold-bloodedly—nearly bringing her to fulfilment over and over again until at last she sobbed out his name in a helpless kind of plea.

Only then did he let go, feeling her convulse about him before allowing his own—strangely bittersweet—orgasm to follow. Afterwards he carried her over to the bed and ripped the silk gown from her body—thus ensuring she would never wear it again, for its associations were now too strongly linked to powerful emotions he would prefer not to remember.

It was a long and erotic night. He made love to her over and over again and, even while Cathy revelled in the incredible sensations he evoked in her, it felt almost as if he were trying to prove a point. What point was that? she wondered distractedly. To establish that he could reduce her to boneless longing any time he wanted to?

She woke to find him already dressed, and realised that it was the first time she had seen him in jeans since she'd arrived on the island. It was a strange moment—as memories fused and became tangled. It reminded her of the first time she'd seen him, when she had been crazily convinced that he was an itinerant worker!

Was he dressing down and reverting to the old Xaviero now that he had been freed from the burden of responsibility? And were his shadowed eyes an acknowledgement that perhaps he had been a little too hasty in acquiring a bride—that maybe he should have waited a little longer before encumbering himself?

She sat up in bed, pushing back her tousled hair—aware of the aching deep inside her body and the soft glow of her flesh. 'You're—you're up early.'

Golden eyes flicked over her. 'An emergency meeting of the government has been called.' The sight of her rosy-tipped breasts was making him want to tumble her back down among the already-rumpled sheets and Xaviero walked over to the safe distance of the window. 'We have to discuss what kind of statement we need to issue to the press,' he added tersely.

'Oh. I see.' He was standing in the shadows—she could barely read the expression on his face, but that wasn't such a new thing, was it? Wasn't his face fathomless even in brightest sunshine—the man who never gave anything of himself away? *Tell him now. Tell him while you have the courage.* 'Xaviero…this…changes everything.'

'I know it does.'

His instant confirmation added yet another brick to the fast-building realisation that what they had between them was as fragile as one of those flowers which bloomed in the desert. Glorious for one short day—and then gone for ever.

'You won't want to stay on the island once Casimiro is fully recovered.'

'I think I might cramp his style somewhat,' he observed drily, and sent her a sarcastic glance. 'Don't you?'

Don't be swayed by that glimpse of mocking humour, she told herself fiercely as she pulled a silken nightgown over her head—feeling less vulnerable now that her nakedness was hidden. *Concentrate on what is real and what is not. You can't trap him—it isn't fair. And you can't hold him to a union which was made in haste for all the wrong reasons. So set him free, Cathy. If you really love him—you'll give him his liberty.*

'I think we should dissolve the marriage,' she said bluntly.

Perhaps it was the shock of a woman actually suggesting they *end* it which surprised him more than anything—for Xaviero had never been dumped by anyone. But an innate sense of his own self-worth meant that he couldn't quite believe it. He stared at her with a sense of growing disbelief in his eyes. 'You want that?' he queried incredulously.

She remembered what he had said to her just yesterday, when she had been dressing for dinner. *How I hate this life.* Well, now he didn't have to live it any more, did he?

'I think it would be for the best,' she answered carefully, praying that her voice wouldn't tremble and give her away. 'You've just said you aren't going to want to stay here.' The face he presented her was a cold, dark mask as she strove to make him understand. 'So what will happen? Imagine it, Xaviero. You'll go to South America to look at polo ponies as planned—taking with you a wife you only married because you envisaged that circumstances would be entirely different? And then what? You return to Colbridge and start up your polo school with the hotel all tarted up and me, the ex-chambermaid installed as its new chatelaine? Come on—it's a crazy idea. Laughable. Why, the press would have a field-day!'

He couldn't deny the essential truth in her words but what struck him was how ironic life could be. How determined and how level-headed her argument! His compliant little chambermaid sounding so quietly confident as she told him that their marriage should be dissolved. *Her* telling *him*?

Pride made him shrug, telling himself that it was ego causing this sharp pierce of blistering pain. What did she think he was about to do—start begging her to stay? Had she overdeveloped a sense of her own importance since she'd been using the title 'Princess' before her name? Well, she would soon learn another lesson—that Xaviero di Cesere was dependent on no woman!

He nodded. 'We'll need to think about how best to go about it.' Dark lashes shaded the golden gleam of his eyes as he set his lips in a cynical line. 'In fact, I'm wondering if maybe we might be able to bury the story in the good news about Casimiro's recovery.'

Didn't part of her crumple then, because hadn't she—against all the odds—been holding out for more? All he had needed to do was to show her *something*— some sign that she meant more to him than compliance and passion. But there was nothing. That icy inaccessibility was back and all that concerned her husband was the most diplomatic way to announce their divorce to the press!

'Perhaps you could let me know what you decide is best,' she said as she pushed aside the sheets and got out of bed. 'I'll stay on the island for as long as you think I should—though, obviously, I'd prefer it if that time was as short as possible.'

'Obviously,' he echoed sarcastically, but the sight of the buttery fabric clinging to her voluptuous curves was a temptation beyond endurance and he swiftly turned his back and slammed his way out of the bedroom.

CHAPTER TWELVE

'CASIMIRO wants to see you.'

Cathy looked up from where she'd been studying the drawer lined with soft pastel piles of silk lingerie and debating how many of the sensual little sets she could reasonably take back to England with her. Or maybe she should leave the whole lot behind. Wouldn't it be easier that way? Easier to forget…

'Cathy?' Xaviero's voice cut into her thoughts. 'Did you hear what I said?'

Sitting back on her heels, Cathy forced a smile. 'He wants to see *me*? Why?'

Xaviero's mouth hardened. 'How the hell should I know? I'm not privy to his thoughts. He just said he'd like to see you before you leave.'

'Oh, right.'

Xaviero glanced at his watch. 'Everything's all been arranged. A car will be here to pick you up just after two. If there are any problems, then just speak to Flavia.'

She stared at him. 'You mean…you mean, you aren't going to *be* here?'

'To wave you off as the car drives away?' His lips

curved into a cynical smile. 'No, Cathy, I am not. I don't do goodbyes—I don't find them particularly palatable.'

Who did? She swallowed down the sudden lump which had risen in the back of her throat along with the telltale taste of tears. 'So…so this is *it*?'

'Yes, this is it,' he said implacably, doing his best to ignore the bright glitter of tears in her eyes which made them look as blue as a Californian swimming pool. 'This is what you wanted.'

'What I thought was best.'

'And you're right,' he agreed steadily. 'It is. Every single reason you gave as to why we shouldn't be together made perfect sense. And there are positives, of course. You'll leave this marriage a considerably wealthy woman—'

'I *don't want* your damned money!'

'Well, you're going to get it whether you like it or not! No ex-wife of mine is going to go back to being a chambermaid!' he bit out.

'You can't stop me!'

'No,' he concurred. 'I can't. What you do when you leave here is up to you. You're on your own. But what I can do is to make over a house and an income for you to do with as you see fit—because I will not be accused of having married a woman and then leaving her in penury!'

Cathy closed her eyes. Of course. This was all about *image*, wasn't it? And ego. *His* ego. How he would be perceived and judged by the rest of the world. If ever she had needed convincing that her decision was wise, he had just reinforced it with that damage-limitation statement of his.

'Now you'd better go to see Casimiro,' he continued, hardening his heart to the sudden chalky whiteness of her face. 'He may be grateful to be alive, but his old monarchical attitude has set in—and he doesn't like to be kept waiting.'

'So this really is *goodbye*?' Her voice was a tremulous little whisper, the realisation driving a sharp twist of pain through her heart.

'Yes, Cathy—it really is.'

His hand reached out—and for one moment Cathy thought that he might be about to pull her into his arms. And if he did that—she would be lost. Completely lost. As lost as she had been when he'd proposed this farce of a marriage. *So do it*, her eyes begged him silently. *Make me feel you need me.*

Instead, he merely caught hold of her own inert fingers and slowly brought them up to his lips—his mouth brushing against their unmoving tips in a parody of courtly manners. She could feel the warmth of his breath and could do nothing to stop the involuntary shudder of longing which shivered its way down her spine.

'Goodbye, Cathy.' Their eyes met in a long moment and then he let her go. 'Now run along and find the King,' he said softly.

Somehow she managed to leave the room without stumbling—but the tears had started spilling down her cheeks and she took a couple of moments' refuge in one of the out-of-the-way cloakrooms before she dared head for the King's quarters.

A quick glance in the mirror at her deathly pale face and the shadows beneath her eyes bore testimony to the strain she'd been living under in the days since Casimiro's recovery.

During Casimiro's convalescence, her husband had spent much of his time with his brother—being close to hand as the King's health and strength had rapidly returned. He had also been making arrangements to travel to South America—and for a trust to be set up in Cathy's name, as well as a house in London which was to be hers. Her threats to immediately sell the pretty Georgian property and donate all the money to charity had been met with a careless shrug.

'I don't care *what* you do with it,' he had drawled.

And why should he? Her decision to leave had been made and Xaviero had accepted it. In fact, to Cathy's horror, he seemed to have compartmentalised her—it was as if she were already in his past. As if she had ceased to exist.

Only in bed at night was there a temporary type of truce when they came together for some pretty explosive sex. And, while Cathy had no real experience of other men, she had learned enough to realise that they viewed sex in an entirely different way from women. Xaviero could still enjoy her body and give her delirious amounts of enjoyment in return—it didn't actually *mean* anything, not to him. Whereas for *her*…

For her it was something else entirely. Every poignant and exquisite caress entranced her. As she gasped out her orgasm beneath his hard, powerful body she was haunted by the terrible knowledge that she would never know pleasure like this again. But she also knew that deep down her reasons for leaving were sound—and that Xaviero had made no attempt to talk her out of them.

Brushing the last rogue tear from her eye and realising that she was keeping the King waiting, Cathy hurried from the cloakroom to his offices at the far end of the palace, where an aide showed her straight in.

Casimiro was seated at a huge desk and he looked up as she walked in.

'Catherine,' he murmured. 'At last.'

She sank into a deep curtsey. 'I'm sorry I'm late—'

'It isn't something which happens very often,' he said drily. 'Come in, and sit down.'

She slid onto the seat opposite him and, even though it was probably discourteous to stare at the monarch, Cathy simply couldn't help herself. Because his recovery was like a miracle. Like something you might see in a film but could never imagine happening in real life. The pale and unmoving figure who had been hooked up to all those wires and tubes in Intensive Care was now looking as vital and as vibrant as life itself.

The ebony hair, which had been shaved during his time in hospital, was fast growing back, showing the hint of a recalcitrant wave. Regular exposure to the sun meant that his olive skin had lost its pallor and now glowed with good health. He had been receiving physiotherapy, too—and had hit the gym with his trainer, so that lean muscle had returned to bulk out a fairly formidable physique.

He was an amazingly handsome man who looked, Cathy thought, very like Xaviero. But Casimiro's eyes were a much darker gold than his brother's and, curiously, his lips—although innately arrogant—were not nearly as cynical.

'So, Catherine,' he said, in a voice which sounded faintly amused. 'You study the King very intently today. What is your verdict?'

'You are looking very well, Your Majesty.'

He smiled. 'And I am feeling very well,' he said in a satisfied voice before his eyes narrowed and his voice grew thoughtful. 'Such praise is praise indeed from you, who saw me at my very sickest.' He looked at her and gave a soft sigh. 'You know I have a duty to thank you.'

'You don't have to thank me, Your Majesty.'

'Oh, but I do,' he demurred, his voice now underpinned with a stubborn quality which reminded Cathy painfully of Xaviero. 'The doctors don't know why I came out of the coma—and perhaps they never will—but they said I should never underestimate the healing power of another human voice. And your voice was the one I heard most of all during my time in hospital.' His voice grew even more thoughtful. 'In fact, the only one I heard so consistently.'

'Well, Xaviero was too busy with affairs of state—'

'How faithfully you defend him!' he murmured. 'And women are better at talking than men. Yes, he told me.'

For some stupid reason, Cathy found herself blushing. 'He told you that?'

'Yes.'

There was an unmistakable question in his dark gold eyes but Cathy clamped her lips tightly closed and knotted her fingers together in her lap. The last thing she wanted to do was to break down and dissolve into tears in front of the King.

'Catherine, why are you leaving?'

She swallowed. *Act normal. Stay calm.* 'Because there is no need for me to stay now that you are returned to health, Your Majesty. You have resumed your rightful place on the throne and Xaviero will soon be leaving the island.'

'That wasn't what I mean and you know it,' he said.

Cathy could hear the impatience in his voice, but it wasn't really his place to get impatient, was it? 'Wasn't it?'

For a moment he studied her impassive face. 'Xaviero told me how you met,' he said suddenly.

'He…he did?'

'He did. He said he was playing at being ordinary. It was something he used to do all the time when we were younger—a game he used to play.'

Cathy swallowed. A *game*? 'Really?'

'Yes.' His eyes narrowed and he leaned back in his gilded chair, the fingertips of each hand meeting to form a spire. 'You know, most people think that the younger son always has it easy.'

He was looking at her as if he wanted her to make some kind of comment and Cathy shrugged. 'But not when you're royal, I suppose?'

'No. Not when you're royal. It's the heir who always gets the attention. My father spent most of his time with me—instructing me about my inheritance—and Xaviero was pretty much left to his own devices. He was adored by our mother, of course.'

Casimiro paused for a moment and this time Cathy said nothing.

'Nobody told Xaviero just how sick she was,' he continued slowly. 'They led him to believe that she would recover. I think it was the way they dealt with children back then—never acknowledging the darker side of life. He wasn't even allowed to go to the funeral—it was decided that it would be too distressing for him. And after her death, my father turned all his attention on grooming me to succeed him, so that in a way it was as if Xaviero had lost both parents.'

Cathy bit her lip. 'Why…why are you telling me all this?'

'Because you told me about your life while I lay in

a coma, Catherine…and some of those words have remained fixed in my mind—they must have done, else how would I have known them when I awoke?' His mouth curved into a fleeting smile. 'About your tenants and your beautiful garden in England. The same garden in which you and Xaviero used to sit on long summer evenings and drink wine from cheap glasses.'

'But I didn't tell you about *that*,' she breathed.

'No. Xaviero did. My brother and I have talked long and often since my recovery.'

She stared at him. 'I don't understand where this is going,' she whispered.

'Don't you? Listen, Catherine.' Casimiro leaned forward, the spire dismantled as he placed his palms on the desk, almost in a gesture of supplication. 'If you were prepared to go to him. To seek his understanding and explain that you acted with undue haste in telling him you wanted to leave. If you were suitably contrite…' there was a moment's pause '…then I think he may be prepared to give you a second chance.'

Cathy froze. 'Excuse me?'

'I think he may be prepared to overlook your—'

'No!' She felt the colour blanch from her cheeks as she saw his startled expression, but suddenly she didn't care if her interruption had been an outrageous breach of protocol. 'I am not having this conversation,' she said, in a low voice. 'Has Xaviero picked you out as some sort of broker—to say to me what he hasn't got the nerve to say himself? To ask me to make some kind of unnecessary apology in order to pander to his pride?'

'He doesn't know *what* I'm saying,' Casimiro ground out.

'Well, my mind is made up.' Because a lot of people

had dud childhoods in some sort of way, didn't they? But that didn't mean they should behave like emotional ice cubes for the rest of their lives. And deep down Cathy knew that it didn't matter what Casimiro said. The only person who might have persuaded her to stay was his brother—and he had walked away as if her going had meant nothing to him. Because *she didn't mean anything to him*. And it wasn't enough. It wasn't enough now—and time would only make it worse. The balance of love was completely unequal—and she could not imprison him in a marriage which was no longer necessary. She would be living on tenterhooks, waiting for him to tire of her—before seeking a royal mistress and leaving his grieving and unloved wife at home. She rose to her feet. 'I'm sorry.'

'So you are both as proud and as stubborn as each other!' Casimiro snapped.

'So it would seem,' said Cathy. 'And now I must beg your leave, Your Majesty. The car will be arriving for me shortly. I am so happy that you are well again, sire.' Her voice wavered a little at this. 'And I wish you a long and glorious reign.'

With this she gave a quick curtsey before hurrying back to her rooms, but inside she could feel a mixture of anger and indignation bubbling up. The King expected her to go and seek forgiveness from his brother, but for what? For trying to love a man who had no love to give her in return.

Her hands were trembling as she threw a few ill-chosen items of clothing in her case before slamming it shut, but at least the fury she now felt helped dull some of the pain.

But there was no formal line-up of staff as she went

down the sweeping marble staircase into the lavishly tiled marble entrance hall. Just Flavia, whose own smile of farewell was as cool as if Cathy had been introduced to her only minutes before. But Flavia was an aide who had spent all her life defusing emotion—because that was what royal life demanded of its players. Cathy knew that. It was the downside to all the jewels and fawning. *And I never wanted that*, she told herself fiercely. *All I ever wanted was Xaviero—and he comes at too high a price.*

Outside sat the limousine, its powerful engine giving a soft roar of life when she appeared, and Cathy gave one last look around the beautiful courtyard, trying to imprint it on her memory. The succulent plants. The bright, fragrant blooms. The fountain which plumed out its rainbow spray. And always the bright blue sky and soft heat of the sun—as golden as the eyes of a man she would never forget.

Grateful for the sunglasses which shielded her brimming eyes, Cathy slid into the back seat as the car pulled away. She could just sink back into its air-conditioned luxury and say nothing until they reached the airfield and the plane which would take her back to England.

And then?

She didn't know and, at this moment, she didn't particularly care. She felt like a small animal which had wandered into a trap and escaped with wounds which might never heal.

Painfully, she watched the city walls retreating, the wide roads leading to the airport growing suddenly narrower, and she frowned. The driver was obviously taking a different route from the one by which she'd arrived.

She didn't know when exactly it was that she began to get alarmed—maybe when the car began to bump its way up a dusty road which looked as if it led to nowhere, and then stopped completely. What was going on?

Pressing the intercom connecting her with the driver, she found herself hoping that he spoke English—though surely even with her rudimentary Italian she could manage to convey that she was supposed to be catching a plane.

'Scusi, signor...' But then the words died on her lips as she saw the driver getting out of the car and opening her door. This was completely unprecedented! Her heart gave a leap of fear—and then a leap of something else entirely as she removed her dark shades. Because he was now pulling off the peaked cap which had hidden his ebony hair and shaded the remarkable gleam of his golden eyes.

And she found herself looking into the oddly forbidding face of her husband.

CHAPTER THIRTEEN

'XAVIERO!' Cathy gasped out. 'What…what on earth are you doing here?'

Dropping his chauffeur's cap into the dust, he moved towards her with sinuous grace. 'I am stopping us both from making the biggest mistake of our lives.'

'You mean you're playing another of your games of pretending to be ordinary? Today, a driver—tomorrow, who knows? A painter and decorator again?'

'This is no game—this is the real thing.' But a note of admiration had entered his voice. How feisty she was! 'My brother is still reeling from the fact that you marched out of his office without being given permission! He said that it was the most imperiously royal gesture he had ever witnessed!' His golden eyes raked over her face as if he had never quite seen it before. 'Oh, Cathy, what have I done?' he groaned, and then pulled her into his arms and started to kiss her.

For several sweet moments she gave into that kiss, feeling herself begin to melt beneath its sensual onslaught before summoning up every ounce of power she possessed to tear her mouth away from his and to push uselessly at his chest. 'Don't,' she whispered. 'Just don't.'

Something in the defeated little tone of her voice stilled him. 'But you want me to.'

Frustratedly, she shook her head. 'Of course I want you to! I've always wanted you to—that's been part of the problem. But the attraction I feel for you has blinded me to the truth. And it's no good, Xaviero. Not any more.'

Lifting a finger, he caught hold of a bright golden strand of hair which had fallen over her eyes and pushed it away from her flushed face. 'Why not?' he questioned softly.

'Because it's just…just sex.'

'I thought you liked sex.'

'You know I do.' She looked up at him. 'But it's not enough. I thought it could be, but it can't. You wanted me compliant—and maybe I was, but not any more. I seem to have changed—when you think about it, I suppose it was inevitable I would. And I can't just *be* what you want me to be—not any more. Can't you see that? I am not the same person. I'm no longer just someone you can mould—so I no longer fit the bill of what you really want from a wife.'

Xaviero's heart twisted and his breath felt hot and harsh in his throat. He knew what she wanted from him—but couldn't she at least meet him halfway? Because there was a sense that if he let go—really let go—and told her what he knew deep down she needed to know, he would make himself weak in the process. That he would lay himself open to all that terrible pain he'd experienced when he'd discovered that love made you vulnerable.

And yet, did he really have an alternative? Because hadn't the pain of knowing that she was going to walk out of his life been more than he could bear? He had tried to ignore it and then to block it—but it had kept coming back at him like a persistent mosquito in the dead of night. Did he somehow think he was immune to all the emotional stuff that other people had to deal with—that he could get away with behaviour which would be tolerated simply because of his royal status? Yes, he did. And up until now, he always had.

But then he had discovered that, for all his protestations about wanting to be treated like any other man—the truth was that he wanted it both ways. All ways. That he donned the protection of his royal mantle whenever it suited him.

'And if I told you that I think I was fooling myself all along?' he grated. 'What then?'

'That kind of admission doesn't sound like the Xaviero *I* know,' she answered quietly.

'No. It doesn't feel like the Xaviero I know, either. Maybe you aren't the only one to have changed, Cathy.' He gave a short, bitter laugh. 'When I gave you that cold-blooded list of requirements for a wife I thought I was being completely honest with you—and I've since discovered that honest was the very last thing I was being.'

Cathy frowned. 'You mean you didn't want someone—'

'I mean that there were a million women out there who would have fitted the bill for a marriage of convenience—even at such short notice. Pure women. Aristocratic women. Heiresses who would have found royal life no great challenge. I could have picked up a list of my ex-lovers and any one of them would have come running.'

'But you didn't do that,' said Cathy slowly.

'No. That's right. I didn't. I chose the most unsuitable woman of all—but she was the one who happened to make me *feel* stuff. The one who provided an oasis of calm in her simple little home. The one who had wanted me just as much when I walked into the hotel covered in mud and sweat from a hard morning's riding as when she discovered who I really was.' He looked at her, his eyes full of question.

'Sometimes I wanted that man more,' she admitted. 'I wanted you without all the trouble of the trappings.'

'I know,' he said simply. 'And can you understand how much that means to me? To be wanted for who you are, rather than what you are? I've never had that before. It made me feel...*emotion*.' He shrugged his shoulders. 'And that's why I fought it, just like I'd fought it all my life.'

When, as a lonely and bereaved little boy, he had sought comfort in his horses. She pictured the isolated little figure he must have been—brave and handsome and lonely as hell. 'Xaviero,' she whispered.

'No.' His voice was husky, thick with emotion. 'Say nothing. Just hear me out. What I have given you and what I have offered you has not been enough—not nearly enough. In fact, it makes me ashamed to think of how little I was prepared to give you. I know you're not into jewels or palaces, or fast cars or fancy planes, but I wondered if there was something else which would win your heart and persuade you to stay with me?'

Cathy held her breath as she stared at him, her heart missing a beat as she dared not hope. But her fingernails dug painfully into her palms all the same. 'Th-that depends what you're offering,' she said shakily.

'I'm offering love,' he said simply. 'How does that sound?'

Cathy couldn't speak for the lump in her throat, trying to swallow it down, trying to tell herself he was still playing games with her. Yet the look of intensity blazing from the golden eyes suggested the very opposite—she had never seen such a blaze of burning emotion on Xaviero's face before. Those hard, stern features had softened into the expression of a man who was feeling something, who was calling out to her. And she felt the answering call of her own heart.

But she was scared. Too scared to clutch at something and then find that it had all been some ghastly mistake. And now she needed to be brave—because she could no longer hide behind *her* feelings, either. She needed to know exactly where she stood—and if the foundations weren't solid enough, then she would move on. 'L-love would be enough,' she said shakily. 'If…if it was meant.'

He drew a deep breath. He spoke three languages fluently, but in that moment he felt like a child uttering its first words. And he knew that he must make his intentions unmistakable, because this might be his last chance to hold onto the most precious thing in his life.

'I love you, Cathy,' he whispered. 'I love you so much that if you leave me now I don't know if I could bear it. I love you in a way I never thought I could love—and it's scaring the hell out of me.'

Xaviero *scared*? She looked into his golden eyes, and her heart turned over—because wasn't she scared herself? Terrified. Maybe it was the same for every couple who were teetering on the brink of love, no matter who they were or what their circumstances. Instinct told her to believe him—and something else reinforced that instinct. The same something which had brought her out to his Mediterranean island in the first place.

Faith. But not blind this time—because she could read

in his eyes the only thing she wanted from Xaviero. The only thing she had ever really wanted from him. Just love.

Her smile was tremulous but she was having to blink back the sudden onset of tears. The first time she had ever tasted the tears of joy.

'I believe you and I love you,' she said softly, and then her head fell to his shoulder and she began to cry.

EPILOGUE

THEY honeymooned in South America, where the lush green foothills of the Andes took Cathy's breath away. On a sleek white yacht which drifted from island to stunning island off the coast of Brazil, they basked in the sun and sipped caipirinhas as potent as they were delicious. And once, in glorious anonymity, they daringly tangoed on the streets of Buenos Aires, while their security mingled with the crowd, having nightmares.

Then they criss-crossed across vast sweeps of land to track down some of the very finest horses in the world. Cathy had decided that if she was going to live a fulfilled married life with her darling Xaviero—then she wanted to learn all about his passion.

Just as he wanted to learn about hers. For when they returned from their six-month idyll to England, it was to find the hotel transformed into a beautiful home—exquisite in every way except for one thing.

'They haven't touched the gardens!' said Cathy as she stared in dismay at weeds which had encroached even further onto the neglected flowerbeds.

'That's because I want you to redesign them,' said Xaviero softly.

'Me?'

'Absolutely you.'

'But I don't have any formal training,' Cathy protested.

His fingers tangled themselves in the golden silk of her hair. 'Maybe not—but you have a natural instinct and an eye for beauty which no amount of teaching could provide.' Briefly he touched his lips to hers. 'I want my polo school to offer scholarships to talented youngsters from all backgrounds, all over the world, Cathy. But I want more than to make them talented riders. I want to bring them here, where they can experience the kind of calm which you weave around you wherever you go. So create a beautiful oasis of a garden, my love,' he urged softly. 'A place where people can come and be at home with their senses.'

Cathy swallowed, dizzy with the sense of joy his words always provoked—words which pierced her heart with their beauty. Because with Xaviero's declaration of love for her, it seemed that a true poet had been liberated.

Even her projected scenario of the press mocking a chambermaid princess hadn't materialised. It seemed that she had struck some kind of chord and the world was delighted with the marriage. And despite her turning down countless interviews, there were abundant articles on what the magazines were calling 'The Cinderella Syndrome'. Cathy didn't mind a bit. She wanted all women to realise that anything was achievable. That it didn't matter who you were or where you came from— that love truly *could* conquer all.

From his new hotel in the south of France, Rupert had written a sycophantic letter offering them free use of the honeymoon suite—and Xaviero had given a shout of laughter as he'd hurled it straight into the bin.

Even Peter, now married and with his own little parish somewhere along the east coast of Scotland, had written offering his tentative congratulations and had mentioned that his church was badly in need of a replacement roof. And Cathy, feeling expansive, had sent him a cheque to pay for it and wished him every happiness in his new life.

Back on Zaffirinthos Casimiro was fully recovered and back at the helm, though seeing his brother's obvious joy had made him seem a little wistful.

'Perhaps he needs a Queen,' said Cathy hopefully and Xaviero laughed.

'You want the whole world to feel like we do, is that it, *mia tesoro*?'

She rose up on tiptoe and brushed her lips over his. 'Mmm. You think that's possible?'

'No,' he answered thickly, before pulling her closer. 'I don't. I think what we have is unique.'

And of course, it was. No two people were the same as them, nor ever would be. But to Cathy, Xaviero was not a prince or a world-class polo player or next in line to an island kingdom. He never had been. He was simply her man—her gorgeous golden-eyed man—and she loved him with every fibre of her being.

* * * * *

THE BILLIONAIRE'S HOUSEKEEPER MISTRESS

Emma Darcy

Initially a French/English teacher, **Emma Darcy** changed careers to computer programming before the happy demands of marriage and motherhood. Very much a people person, and always interested in relationships, she finds the world of romance fiction a thrilling one, and the challenge of creating her own cast of characters very addictive.

CHAPTER ONE

'DARLING, can you save me?'

Daisy Donohue froze. Lynda Twiggley's distinctive drawl was unmistakeable. It pierced the general buzz of conversation from the celebrity crowd and shot a bolt of alarm down Daisy's spine. If there was any saving to be done, as Lynda's PA, she had to do it, fast and effectively, or be lashed by her employer's sharp tongue for dereliction of duty.

She snapped into action, swinging around to find the source of the problem. The VIP marquee seemed packed with tall people. A bevy of Australia's top models had been flown in to add glamour to the event, which certainly wasn't known as the Magic Millions for nothing. Everyone here was either loaded with or associated with big money and they expected everything to be perfect for them. Especially her employer.

Being only of average height, and wearing sensible low-heeled shoes for all the toing and froing her work demanded today, Daisy stretched up on tiptoe, trying to spot the spray of royal-blue feathers that sprouted from Lynda's much-prized and hideously expensive Neil Grigg hat. A few tell-tale blue arrowheads placed her target near the open bar where there shouldn't be a problem. She had already checked there were ample cases of French champagne and every other choice of drink available. Had there been some spillage on Lynda's blue silk designer outfit?

Bad, bad, bad, Daisy thought in a burst of panic, quickly elbowing her way through the millionaire melee, wondering how she was going to fix some unfixable stain. Her hammering heart was intensely relieved when she arrived on the scene and found her employer working hard at currying the favour of a man. But not just any man. As recognition hit, her heart started hammering all over again for a multitude of reasons.

This was the man reputed to have saved the richest people in Australia from suffering any nasty fall-out from the current global financial crisis—Ethan Cartwright, the whiz-kid financier who had foreseen the crash and diverted all the big cash to enterprises that would always return a profit, even in a recession.

Daisy stopped dead behind Lynda's shoulder and stared at him, a riot of emotions hitting her hard— anger, resentment, a wild hostility at the terrible injustice of the rich getting richer while the poor got poorer, especially her parents who were trapped in a debt they could no longer service. This man, above all others, represented that miserable situation.

She'd read about him, seen photographs of him, but what made her inner turmoil more savage was how stunningly handsome he really was in the flesh. The thick, wavy, black hair, twinkling green eyes, a strong male face that didn't have one unpleasing feature capping a tall, perfectly proportioned physique which

carried the perfectly tailored suit he wore with distinc-
tion…it was so wickedly unfair! The man had absolutely *everything*! She doubly resented the fact that he
had a sexual impact on her. And no doubt on every
woman who was subjected to his power-packed
presence.

It was highly disconcerting when he suddenly shifted
his attention from Lynda Twiggley to shoot a quizzical
look over her shoulder straight at Daisy. Had he *felt* her
hostile stare? The sexy black eyebrows with their late
kick upwards—just like Brad Pitt's—lifted with a kind
of bemused puzzlement, and the startling green eyes
bored into hers, searching for answers that pride forbade
her to ever tell him.

Vexed by his distraction, Lynda swung around to
deal with an unwelcome intrusion. With the recognition
that no finesse was needed on a mere employee, her
steely blue eyes savaged Daisy with displeasure. 'What
do you want, Dee-Dee?' she snapped.

'Nothing, Ms Twiggley,' Daisy replied with as much
aplomb as she could muster, given the squeamish spotlight of two sets of eyes demanding explanations. 'I
thought I heard you calling for assistance.'

Lynda clicked her tongue impatiently. 'Not right
now. And stop hovering. I'm sure you have more useful
things to do.'

'Yes, of course. I'm sorry for interrupting. Please
excuse me.'

Daisy had already begun her retreat when Ethan
Cartwright intervened. 'Wait!' he commanded, stepping
forward, one arm outstretched in appeal. He smiled, his
perfectly sculpted mouth breaking open to show a row
of perfect white teeth, making Daisy instantly deter-

mined that he wouldn't get a bite out of her, regardless of how charming he set out to be. 'We haven't met,' he said in a voice as rich as the rest of him. 'I would have remembered a Dee-Dee. It's such an unusual name. Be so kind as to introduce us, Lynda.'

'They're her initials, not her name,' Lynda said with a tinkling laugh that had Daisy's spine crawling with dislike for her employer and her endlessly patronising manner. If she didn't *need* this job and the pay packet that went with it, she would have walked out on day one when Lynda had stated she couldn't have a PA called Daisy because she associated that name with a lowly cow. Dee-Dee sounded far more upmarket.

'This is my PA, Ethan,' Lynda continued in a dismissive tone. 'No one you need to know.'

The snobbish remark apparently did not sit well with him. 'On the contrary, should I do business with you, your PA may be my first point of contact,' he countered, a hard glint in the green eyes.

'Oh, very well then,' Lynda conceded, realising he was going to persist and if she wanted him to butter her bread she had to toe his line. 'Ethan Cartwright, Daisy Donohue.'

'A pleasure to meet you, Mr Cartwright,' Daisy rattled out, wanting only to escape back into the crowd.

He viewed her curiously, offering his hand as though sensing her desire to bolt and purposely delaying her. 'Probably more of a pleasure for me to meet you, Daisy Donahue,' he said, amusement dancing in his eyes.

Oh, sure! What fun! Big man condescending to the little brown cow, Daisy thought viciously as she took his hand to complete the polite formality. The flesh contact tingled hotly and his grip felt aggressively strong, pressing a dominant will that she fiercely rebelled against when he held onto her hand longer than polite formality required.

'Please excuse me, Mr Cartwright. I don't have time to dally. I'm needed elsewhere,' she said firmly, tearing her gaze from the devilishly attractive green eyes and giving a subservient nod to Lynda Twiggley whose bad temper was probably already simmering at having an important conversation interrupted.

Apparently Ethan Cartwright had enough sensitivity to realise he might be causing her trouble and backed off, releasing her hand, though still smiling at her as though she pleased him, though why she would seemed totally perverse of him when the marquee was full of gorgeous women who would undoubtedly love his attention. She had brown hair, brown eyes and was wearing brown, conscious of keeping herself as insignificant as possible, not blotting one bit of the limelight her boss liked.

'If you have a spare minute, place a bet on Midas Magic,' he said on a parting note.

Put good money on a horse! Not in a million years! Daisy's tongue lost its discipline. 'Is that your best financial advice?' she shot at him in fiery scorn for all he stood for.

He laughed, giving a breathtaking oomph to his sexual magnetism. 'No, but it's a good bet,' he finally answered. 'I bought him at the yearling sales this week, on excellent advice, and he has the bloodline and form to win the big race.'

Daisy recovered enough breath to coolly state, 'I

don't gamble.' She lied through her teeth as she added, 'I wish you luck, Mr Cartwright,' then turned her back on him to effect some fast distance from the troublesome encounter.

'All of life is a gamble, Daisy Donahue,' he floated after her.

Not for her it wasn't, and no way was she going to acknowledge the comment by looking back at him.

They all had money to burn, these people. Having worked the past three months with Lynda Twiggley whose PR agency organised events for A-list socialites, Daisy was constantly amazed and scandalised by how much they spent on having a good time. The pre-Christmas parties had been unreal. The New Year's revels, of course, had to be on a luxurious private yacht for the fireworks around Sydney Harbour to be viewed. Now anyone who was anyone was up on Queensland's Gold Coast for the annual Magic Millions carnival—the first big horse-racing event on the calendar.

It had begun earlier this week with the yearling sales, the largest sale of thoroughbreds in Australia. No doubt Ethan Cartwright had paid an enormously extravagant amount for Midas Magic, and had been celebrating his successful bid ever since. There'd been a ball, a swag of cocktail parties, and today was the day to cap it all off, the third richest race day of the year with almost five million dollars in prize money. Daisy sourly hoped his horse would run last.

All of life should not be a gamble.

Some things should be secure.

Like her parents' home.

If helping to make it secure meant staying in this

rotten job, she would grit her teeth and do it, despite the severe heartburn it gave her.

Ethan had not been having a good time. He'd slipped away from the gaggle of women whose frivolous chatter bored him and then been cornered by Lynda Twiggley who was bent on getting him to handle her investments, which was even more boring and distasteful since this carnival was supposed to be fun, not work. The PR specialist had certainly not been using her expertise on him—far too irritatingly pushy—and her manner towards her assistant had bordered on contemptible.

Daisy Donahue…

Now there was a woman who did interest him—the little brown sparrow amongst all the glitzy parrots, playing the meek servant when there wasn't a meek bone in her body. A pocket dynamo, blasting so much hostile energy at him, it had instantly sparked the urge to engage her in battle. Not that he could, given the unfair circumstances of him being a guest and her being a worker under the eyes of her disapproving employer.

I don't gamble…

Containing herself in such a tight mentality, not running any risks whatsoever, probably had her exploding inside. Ethan found himself thinking he would enjoy liberating her, finding out what she would be like if all that burning passion was released. One thing was certain. Daisy Donahue did not have a frivolous personality. And she wasn't boring, either, he added as he suffered Lynda Twiggley claiming his attention again.

'As I was saying before Dee-Dee interrupted…'

Dee-Dee…what a silly name to give to a person who had so much innate dignity! It also showed a lack of respect for her, which had been obvious in how this unbelievably arrogant woman had dealt with Daisy. Ethan held the firm belief that everyone deserved to be treated with respect, regardless of their position in life. He wondered why Daisy put up with it, then realised that in these tough economic times, she was not about to risk being out of work.

He gave Lynda Twiggley five more minutes so she wouldn't blame her PA for cutting her business short, then excused himself, saying, 'I already have a very full client list, Lynda, but I'll check if I can fit you in when I get back to my office.' He nodded towards his best friend who was chatting up one of the top-line models. 'Mickey Bourke told me we should talk to the jockey before the big race and it's time I went and collected him.'

'Oh!' Her face fell in disappointment before she summoned up a big parting smile. 'I'll go straight away and place a bet on Midas Magic.'

He didn't care if she did or not. He just wanted to get away from her. Mickey had talked him into this horse business, insisting he needed some outside interest to lighten up his life and get him into the social whirl again after his grim disillusionment with his ex-fiancée. A bit of fun, Mickey had argued, especially if Ethan was *off* women.

According to his friend, there was nothing better than the rush of excitement one felt when watching your horse win a big race. Ethan had yet to feel it. Though Mickey should know. His father was one of the most successful thoroughbred trainers in Australia.

Mickey had been born and bred to the horse business. Even at school he would organise sweeps for the

Melbourne Cup—strictly against the rules but he always got away with it. He'd been the livewire in their class—bright, witty, charming—a golden boy with his sun-bleached streaky blond hair and sparkling blue eyes. A natural athlete, too, which was one thing they did have in common, along with their tall, powerful physiques.

Everyone liked Mickey. He was always amusing company. Why he'd chosen to attach himself to Ethan—the quiet, intense student, and his fiercest competitor on the playing fields—had seemed weirdly perverse of him until Mickey had explained.

'No bullshit, okay? I'll give it to you straight. In the quality stakes you're a top-notch contender and I'm naturally drawn to quality. I enjoy the way you think and the way you do things. You could easily cut the rest of us down but you don't. That makes you a great guy in my book.'

The straight face had then broken into a gleeful grin. 'Besides, there are several big advantages in being your friend. First up you're great camouflage. All the schoolmasters think the sun shines out of you, being such a star in class. If I stick with you, the respect they have for you rubs off on me and no one will suspect me of getting up to mischief. Besides which, you're a whiz at numbers and percentages, working out the odds. I like that. I really do respect that. I figure you're going to be a lot of use to me further down the track.'

It was his first demonstration of how smart Mickey was—smart in a way Ethan had not been familiar with, being the only child of dyed-in-the wool academics who did everything by the book, straight down the line. Ethan had instantly decided he could learn a lot from Mickey Bourke who was clearly a very shrewd operator.

'And to me, the writing is already on the wall,' Mickey had continued, adopting a mock-resigned air. 'It's in the way your mind works, Ethan. It homes in on what's absolutely pertinent. You see the play. Your anticipation is incredible. So, regardless of how well I perform on the playing field, I know it will be you the coach will pick to be captain of the cricket team and the rugby. My best choice is to win your friendship, stand at your side and share in your glory.'

Ethan had liked his honesty, his realistic reading of the situation, and his pragmatic judgement of how he could get the most out of his time at school. Other boys might have hated the guy who had the edge on them for the most enviable positions, seen him as the enemy. He and Mickey had ended up the closest of allies in everything, their friendship so solid it had lasted through the years despite their career paths being very different.

They were both still bachelors. 'Too many lovely fish in the sea to settle on one,' was Mickey's attitude. Ethan had long ago reached the cynical conclusion—recently and painfully reinforced by a woman he'd thought was different—that all desirable females had princess personalities, wanting everything their own way and generally bartering sex to get it. Which he'd been reasonably content to go along with. What man didn't want sex?

But every last one of them had been only interested in what he could give them in return for the use of their bodies and the ego trip of being publicly partnered by them. It was an ego trip for the women, too, being seen with him. After all, it was a feather in their cap to have ensnared the interest—however briefly—of one of Sydney's most eligible billionaires.

He would never forget the rotten downer of overhearing Serena preening over her triumphant catch to one of her girlfriends. It would have been a huge mistake to marry her and Ethan hated making mistakes. He still burned over the memory of how deceived he had been in her character.

He wanted honesty in a relationship. He wanted reality. He wanted to be known and appreciated for the person he was. He wanted a woman to give him the kind of understanding companionship that Mickey did. Which was probably impossible because women weren't men. However, if he could just meet one of them who didn't give him the feeling of being buttered up for the kill…

Daisy Donahue slid straight into his mind. It was a pity she wasn't a guest here today. She'd sparked a very lively interest. Not the slightest hint of buttering up from her blunt tongue. The little brown sparrow was full of fireworks which he'd found surprisingly sexy. Nice curvy body, too. He didn't understand Mickey's attraction to models whose stick-like figures had no appeal to him. *They* couldn't swish their non-existent bottoms at him, as Daisy had when she'd made off into the crowd. A very perky bottom.

Booty, the fashionistas called it these days. The word made him smile. He bet Daisy Donohue had *booti-ful* hair, as well, if she ever let it down from the tight knot she'd wound it into at the nape of her neck. Ethan briefly fantasised about letting it down himself, massaging her scalp, getting into her head, watching those blazing dark eyes melt into hot chocolate. He would enjoy that. He really would.

Having reached the edge of the social circle gathered

around Mickey, he caught his friend's eye and nodded towards the exit from the marquee. Not waiting for Mickey to extract himself, Ethan moved on towards it, putting a forbiddingly purposeful expression on his face to discourage anyone from making another unwelcome approach. Mickey caught up with him just as he stepped outside.

'Saw the Twiggley trying to get her claws into you,' he remarked with a sympathetic grin. 'Guess she's one of the wounded, wanting the doctor.'

Ethan grimaced. 'I'm not a doctor.'

'Same thing…fixing up financial fall-out.'

'I prefer the clients who trusted my advice in the first place.'

'Like me.' Mickey clapped him on the shoulder, obviously in high good humour, as they strolled towards the saddling paddock. 'Never doubted your number-crunching for a moment.'

Ethan's mind was still circling around the encounter with Lynda Twiggley. 'She's a revolting woman. Treated her PA like dirt.'

'Hmm…do I detect a note of partiality towards the PA?'

A teasing delight danced in Mickey's blue eyes. He was playing today and he wanted Ethan to play, too. Not that there was any chance of that with Daisy Donahue. Apart from the fact she was unavailable, her hostile glare had hardly been a positive response to him. Though he'd like to tackle the reason for it. Head on. Nothing like a challenge to get the adrenaline running.

'More interesting than your models,' he slung at his friend.

'Ah-ha! This is a good sign that the sly and seductive Serena is no longer casting a pall over your sex drive. So what are you going to do about this new woman of interest?'

'Today she has no time to dally,' he said with a rueful grimace. 'Lynda Twiggley's evil eye is upon her.'

'Easy! Tell the Twiggley you'll take on her financial problems if she releases her PA to you for the rest of the day.'

Giving Daisy no choice? Remembering her stiff-backed pride, Ethan didn't think being traded like a slave would go over too well with her. Besides, he didn't want to work with Lynda Twiggley any more than Daisy did.

'That's not a solution, Mickey. That's a mess,' he mockingly pointed out.

'Well, you figure it out,' he tossed back with a shrug. 'My policy is if you fancy a woman, go after her. Attack the moment. Seize the day. God knows it passes soon enough!'

Ethan rolled his eyes at him. 'Maybe sometimes you should take a longer look before plunging in. As you do with horses.'

Mickey laughed. 'Horses are infinitely more rewarding than women. Forget the PA and concentrate on Midas Magic, Ethan. He'll give you a better run for your money.'

Having moved on to his favourite subject, Mickey regaled Ethan with a potted history of the jockey he was to meet, his many successful rides and his natural empathy with horses—best man for the job today.

Although he listened and made all the expected responses as they strolled on to the saddling paddock, Ethan did not forget Daisy Donahue. She was like a burr in his mind. And his body. He felt a quixotic urge to

rescue her from Lynda Twiggley, make whatever was
wrong for her right.

Absurd, really.

He knew so little about her.

Yet his instincts kept insisting she might be worth
knowing and he could very well regret not pursuing the
interest she stirred.

Seize the day…

The big question was…how to do it?

CHAPTER TWO

THE big race gave Daisy the chance to rest for a few minutes. Quite a few guests had left the marquee to watch the horses being led to the starting gates. The rest of them had their attention glued to the television screens. No one was going to make a fuss about anything while their interest was totally captivated by what was happening on the racetrack.

She found a chair and sat down to give her feet a break. The TV commentator was giving a run-down on each yearling—its bloodline, owner, trainer, the colours the jockey was wearing. Gold and black for Midas Magic. Daisy grimaced as she heard that. Of course, the money man would have chosen gold. And he'd be more in the black if the wretched horse won. No depressing red debts for him.

She thought glumly of her parents' situation—ordinary people who'd worked hard to bring up and educate five children and finally believing they could afford the luxury of renovating their home—a new kitchen, a second bathroom, a playroom for the grandchildren and two extra bedrooms so all the family could come and stay, especially for Easter and Christmas and school holidays. They had mortgaged the house to do it, and the bank which had happily lent the money would just as happily sell the property out from under them if the interest on the loan wasn't paid every month.

And no way would they get the full value of the house in a forced sale, given the current slump in the property market. It wouldn't get her parents out of trouble. Besides, it wasn't fair for them to lose their home at this stage of their lives. They deserved a care-free retirement.

Their investment advisor had got it hopelessly wrong. Last year's share market slide had sliced over thirty percent off their superannuation savings. The resulting loss of income was never going to be recovered. Neither was there any hope of the situation improving during this recession.

The rest of the family wasn't in a position to help. Her three older brothers and one sister were all married with young families, struggling to make ends meet. Two of her brothers, Ken and Kevin, had been laid off by their employers in the workforce squeeze. Keith had gone into business for himself and was feeling the pinch. Violet, her sister, had an autistic son who needed so much care, her marriage was very rocky because of it. They simply couldn't cope with more pressure on their shoulders.

Which meant she was the only one who could carry the load. By far the youngest—the late accidental pregnancy—she had moved back to her parents' suburban home in Ryde to give them the rent money she'd been paying for her share-apartment in the inner city, as well as covering most of the food bills to ensure her parents didn't stint on their diet in their anxiety over the debt.

Her contribution meant the monthly interest bill could be paid, but it was an endless cycle. She didn't make enough money to pay off the loan.

What really irked her was if her parents had sought out Ethan Cartwright to manage their nest-egg… But how were ordinary people supposed to know *he* was the man to go to? There'd been no publicity about him until after the economic crash. Besides, he probably only dealt with multi-millionaires. The big spenders in this marquee only mixed with each other.

The commentator's voice rose several decibels as the race began, calling out a string of names. A hubbub of excitement broke out from the spectators gathered in front of the television screens. Daisy rigidly refused to look, resenting how much money these people were prepared to risk on stupid bets. It was a well-known fact that race-fixing went on all the time. If you weren't *in the know*…although perhaps the Magic Millions was different with all the owners wanting their new purchases to perform well in such a prestige event.

'Midas Magic hits the front at the turn and is starting to leave the field behind. He's two lengths ahead… three…four…no one's going to catch him!'

The screaming from the commentator assaulted her ears. And her heart. The man who had everything was about to get a lot more with his horse winning this race. It wasn't fair. It vexed her even further that he'd put her *in the know* and she had ignored his advice, sticking to her principles of not taking any gambles. Besides, who could believe that any horse was a sure thing?

Lynda Twiggley for one!

Daisy scrambled guiltily to her feet as her employer came bursting out of a group of people, gleefully brandishing a betting ticket and catching her PA sitting down on the job. 'I won! I won!' she cried. 'Isn't it marvellous? Ten thousand lovely dollars!'

'Ten thousand?' Daisy repeated, totally stunned by the amount.

'Yes. I wouldn't have taken such a plunge on a horse if Ethan Cartwright hadn't recommended it,' Lynda archly confided. 'Such a gorgeous, clever man! He's made my day!'

'I'm very pleased for you, Miss Twiggley,' Daisy managed to force out. At least it had put her employer in a good mood, unlikely to snipe at any shortcomings she perceived in her PA.

The glittery blue eyes narrowed in determined calculation. 'Now I must get him to look at my shares portfolio. If I can net him into another tête-á-tête, don't interrupt us for anything, Dee-Dee. Should any problem arise, use your own initiative to solve it. That's what I've trained you for.'

'I won't go near him,' Daisy firmly promised.

She couldn't stand seeing him shine with triumph anyway. It would be sickening. Privately she thought her employer had little chance of *netting* him again. Ethan Cartwright had tried to hang onto the diversion of Daisy's gaffe in interrupting their last encounter, insisting on being properly introduced, continuing to speak to her despite Lynda's obvious impatience for her to be gone.

He wouldn't have bothered trying to connect with her under ordinary circumstances. She was way beneath his notice. He'd simply been using her for his own purpose—breaking up a meeting he didn't like. She wished she could dismiss him from her mind. Everything he stood for stirred her up. Worst of all was the fact that she'd felt an undeniable physical attraction to the man. Which was understandable, given that he was a stand-out male, but she hated him all the more for it, making her want what she knew could never be available to her.

'I'd kill for a cup of coffee right now. I wish they'd get on with serving it.'

The whining complaint from one of the models—very much a VIP, having been chosen to star on the runway for Victoria's Secret—sent Daisy straight to the catering tent to investigate the delay. Lynda Twiggley would have a fit if she heard one of her prized guests being put out by any failure in the arrangements made for their pleasure and comfort. Bad PR. It was up to Daisy to prevent or fix anything bad.

Two of the chefs were having a raging argument and their assistants all looked rigid with tension, doing nothing but watching from the sidelines. This catering outfit was being very highly paid to do a top-class job and they weren't delivering. Daisy steeled herself to walk right into the line of fire between the fighting chefs and remind them of their prime responsibility.

'People are asking for coffee,' she stated briskly, giving both of them a stern look. 'It should be out there being served. VIP guests don't like to be left wanting anything.'

It startled them into turning their attention to her.

'It's also supposed to be accompanied by chocolates and petits-fours. Are they ready to go?' she ran on, re-minding them of what was expected, then adding a sensible warning. 'You don't want to lose your good reputation with these people. They always remember delays like this.'

One of the temperamental chefs threw up his hands

and glared around at the motionless staff. 'Move! Move! Get on with it!'

Satisfied she had made her point, Daisy returned to the VIP marquee, intending to assure the model that coffee was on its way. She stopped in her tracks when she saw Ethan Cartwright chatting to her. Venomous thoughts exploded in her head. Nothing but the best for a man like him! She'd known—of course, she'd known—he wasn't really interested in a little brown cow. This was reality—birds of a feather flocked together.

No doubt the magnificent model had taken his advice to bet on Midas Magic, too. The two high-flyers were both beaming with the pleasure of victory, making Daisy's stomach churn from the terrible injustice of it all.

Ethan felt it again, his whole body tingling from a blast of electric energy. He turned his head, his gaze instinctively homing in on the source—Daisy Donahue, her eyes blazing at him with feral animosity, stirring the urge to do battle with her, catch her, cage her until she was tamed to his satisfaction. The weird, exciting thoughts raced through his mind, swiftly followed by Mickey's catch-cry—seize the day.

He'd looked for her without success when he'd re-entered the marquee after the race. Now here she was a few metres away, within easy reach, the challenge she threw out drawing him like a magnet. He automatically started to move towards her, their eyes locked in a duel of sizzling passion.

'Ethan?'

The full-of-herself model he'd been talking to was

calling him back. He'd forgotten his manners. 'Please excuse me, Talia,' he swiftly tossed back at her. 'Someone I have to see.'

In that brief moment of disengagement with Daisy she'd taken flight, dodging behind groups of people, apparently intent on hiding from him. It spurred Ethan on to catch up with her, force a face-to-face confrontation. He sliced through the throng, his interest aroused to an intensity that surprised him, his heart beating like a battle drum as he intercepted her attempted escape, making it impossible for her not to acknowledge him.

'Hello, again,' he said, revelling in the flush of angry frustration that flooded into her cheeks, giving her pale, flawless skin a peaches-and-cream vivacity, making the eyes that warred with his in flaming fury even brighter.

His abrupt appearance in front of her had shocked her into stillness, but it was the stillness of a tightly coiled spring, nerves twanging at the suppression of movement away from him. Her chin jerked up belligerently. The brown pill-box hat slid slightly from its perch on top of her head. He barely restrained himself from reaching up and straightening it for her. He wanted contact—intimate contact—with this woman.

'Mr Cartwright...' she bit out, obviously hating being trapped into this encounter.

He smiled, intent on pouring soothing balm over whatever was making her bristle in his presence. 'Let's make that Ethan.'

She sucked in a quick breath, her eyes flaring a denial of any familiarity between them. 'Congratulations on your win,' she said tersely. 'I didn't place a bet on your horse.

As I told you before, I don't gamble, so there's nothing more to say, is there? We have nothing in common.'

Ethan was not about to let his feet be cut out from under him before he'd even started to make inroads on getting to know her. He turned his smile into an ironic grimace. 'I need some assistance.'

She raised a disbelieving eyebrow, offering him no encouragement to spell it out.

'That is your job, isn't it? Assisting any of the guests here who have a problem?' he pushed.

'What is your problem, Mr Cartwright?' she demanded, her eyes glinting open scepticism.

'You are, Daisy Donahue.'

She frowned, her certainty that he had no problem shifting into a flicker of fear. 'What do you mean?'

'I have the curious sensation that you're shooting mental bullets at me all the time. I'd like you to tell me why.'

For a moment her face went totally blank, as though a switch had been thrown and defensive shutters had instantly clicked into place. He watched her labouring to construct an apologetic expression—a sheer act of will, against her natural grain. Her eyes took on a pleading look, begging his forgiveness. Her mouth softened into an appealing little smile. She spoke in a tone that mocked herself.

'I've just had to deal with some trouble in the catering tent and it may cause more trouble. I'm sorry if I've channelled my own angst onto you, Mr Cartwright. I didn't mean to attract your attention. In fact, you'll be doing me a great favour if you'll walk away from me right now. My boss won't like it if she sees you talking to me.'

'Surely as a guest I'm entitled to speak to whomever I like,' he argued.

'I'm not a guest and I'm taking up your time—time Miss Twiggley would prefer you to spend with her,' she said pointedly.

'I've said all I intend to say to Lynda Twiggley.'

'That's not my business. If I don't stay clear of you, my job might very well be at risk. So please excuse me, Mr Cartwright.'

'Be damned if I will!' Frustration fumed through him. His hand snaked out and grabbed her arm as she turned away to escape him again. 'This isn't the Dark Ages!' he shot out before she could voice a protest.

'Oh, yes, it is!' she retorted with blistering scorn, the defence system cracking wide open at being forcibly held. Wild hostility poured into wild accusation. 'You're acting like a feudal lord manhandling a servant girl who can't fight back.'

The image was wrong. She could fight back. She was doing it with all her mental might. But for once in his life Ethan wanted to be a feudal lord, having his way with this woman. He knew he should release her yet his mind had lost all sense of civilised behaviour. Imposing this physical link with her was arousing a host of primitive feelings that demanded satisfaction.

'You're denying me the assistance I asked for,' he argued.

'With good reason,' she hotly returned.

'Nonsense! It's totally unreasonable!'

'What is the matter with you?' she cried in exasperation. 'Why bother with me when—?'

'Because you bother me more than anyone here.'

'What? Because I'm not seeking your attention? Are

you so used to women hanging on your every word, your high and mighty ego is pricked by one who doesn't?'

'You did want my attention, Daisy Donahue,' he slung back at her in burning certainty. 'You were looking at me.'

She tried to explain it away, biting out the words with icy precision. 'The model you were talking to had complained about coffee not having been served. I had intended to inform her it was on its way when I saw you with her.' Her teeth were bared in a savagely mocking smile. 'Mindful of my boss's instructions and contrary to your arrogant assumption, I didn't want to draw any more attention from you, Mr Cartwright.'

Ethan was not convinced. It wasn't dismissal he'd felt coming from her. It had been a powerful bolt of passion aimed directly at him. It was still hitting him. His whole body was energised by it. His eyes derided her evasion of the truth as he attacked her reading of his character.

'You can stick me with ego and arrogance as much as you like, but there's more going on in your head than you're telling me, and it has nothing to do with Lynda Twiggley's instructions.'

'What I think is my business,' she whipped back.

'Not when it involves me.'

Impasse.

She glared at him, the wheels of her mind going round and round in a fierce search for an exit line he might accept.

He wanted to drag her into his embrace and kiss her until all her resistance melted. Never had he been so aroused by a woman. For the first time in his life he was in total tune with the cavemen of old who simply hauled off the object of their desire and took their pleasure at will. Was it her hostility that excited him? Had he grown too bored with women who were only too eager in their compliance?

Intensity…the word leapt into his mind. That was what had been lacking in all his other connections with women. Daisy Donahue was transmitting it, hitting the same chord in him. Normally he channelled it into his work. It wasn't a social asset. Intensity disturbed people. Too dark, Mickey said. But there was a dark side to Daisy Donahue, too, setting off a weird wave of exhilaration through his bloodstream. And a compulsion to explore it.

She dragged in a deep breath and tore her gaze from his, dropping it pointedly to the hand still grasping her arm. He softened his grip, rubbing his thumb along the underside of her wrist, finding the beat of her pulse, exulting in its rapid drumming.

She was excited, too.

Or was it fear?

'I'm sorry I bothered you, Mr Cartwright,' she said in a stilted little voice. Her beautifully feminine breasts lifted as she filled her lungs again. Her eyes met his in a plea that held a vulnerability he hadn't seen before in her. 'Please let me go.'

It made him feel like a cad for holding her against her will, yet he couldn't bring himself to let her go. 'You said we have nothing in common. I think we do, Daisy Donahue.'

She shook her head, agitation flickering into definite fear as she was distracted by something behind him.

'Ah, Dee-Dee,' came the smarmy voice of Lynda Twiggley who was obviously about to insinuate herself into the situation.

'Miss Twiggley,' she said in a shaky subservient tone as the woman stepped forward to part them.

It enfuriated Ethan that Daisy should feel it necessary to kowtow to her snaky employer. She was a natural-born fighter. It was wrong for her to be in this position.

'Catering needs a prompt to get the coffee moving.'

It was a dismissive command.

Daisy tried to pull her arm free, anxious to avoid any more displeasure being heaped on her head.

Ethan tightened his grip, determined on keeping her with him.

'Daisy has already done that,' he coldly told the Twiggley who turned an ingratiating smile to him.

'Then she can do it again,' was the unbending reply.

Unreasonable, demanding bitch!

Ethan lost his cool. 'Miss Twiggley…' grated out from between gnashing teeth.

She fluttered her exquisitely painted fingernails and her false eyelashes at him. 'Oh, do make it Lynda, please…'

It revolted him. Words shot out of his mouth in a stream of searing contempt without any thought to their consequences.

'I think it's time you stopped treating your PA like a slave who doesn't warrant any consideration or courtesy.'

Her mouth gaped open in shock.

He felt a shudder run up Daisy's arm.

The ensuing silence was impregnated with the hair-prickling sense that a bomb had just gone off. Ethan revelled in its intensity. He was so off his coolly analytical brain—no number-crunching going on at all—he was actually looking forward to the fall-out.

CHAPTER THREE

DAISY's mind was reeling. Her heart was galloping faster than any racehorse. Any second now her boss was going to throw a major tantrum and she'd bear the brunt of it. Ethan Cartwright was too important a person to cop the whiplash from his strike on her behalf.

Why had he done it?

Why, why, why…?

Even if he'd meant well, he should have known it would rebound on her. He just hadn't cared. It wasn't going to affect his life. He was an untouchable. Anger at not getting his own way with her had spilled over onto Lynda Twiggley. Never mind that Daisy was the one who would pay for it—the selfish, arrogant pig! She'd explained the situation to him, begged him to let her go, and what he'd done was put her job at risk—the job she had to keep or see her parents' home go down the bankruptcy drain.

Panic ripped through her stomach as her boss started puffing herself up to let fly her ferocious temper. Mean blue eyes cut her to ribbons. The attack had the cyclonic force of a fireball.

'How dare you complain about how I treat you, you ungrateful little cow!'

'I didn't! I swear I didn't!' Daisy babbled.

'I speak from my own observation,' Ethan Cartwright sliced in.

It didn't improve the situation. It made it a thousand times worse. Being subjected to such personal criticism from him was so offensive, Lynda turned to him in a towering rage, probably thinking her bid to have him fix her financial affairs had been sabotaged and Daisy knew she was going to be blamed for it, regardless of anything Ethan Cartwright said.

'I pay her very well to do what I tell her. There's nothing slavish about that, I assure you,' she hissed at him, steam pouring from her.

'I take exception to you telling her to stay away from me,' he shot back. 'That's not work. It's—'

Lynda exploded into a tirade at Daisy, cutting Ethan Cartwright off in mid-speech. 'You stupid, stupid girl! Have you no sense of discretion, no brain in your head? Might I remind you that you signed a confidentiality clause in your contract with me. Which you've just broken in the worst possible way with your stupid, wagging tongue.'

She *had* committed the indiscretion.

It was impossible to defend herself.

What could she say…that Ethan Cartwright's persistence had goaded her into it? No way would that be an acceptable excuse. She had not put her boss's interests first. The chaotic effect he had on her had overwhelmed her usual grasp of what was permissible.

Daisy stood in appalled silence, quaking inside as the storm broke over her, her heart sinking as she realised there was no hope of this being forgiven or forgotten.

The inevitable lightning struck.

'You're fired! As of now!'

She felt the blood draining from her face.

The thunder rolled on. 'And don't come back to the office. I'll have your personal things parcelled up and sent home. Untrustworthy blabbermouth!'

Lynda Twiggley's last look of furious disgust barely penetrated the dizziness flooding through Daisy's head. Like some fade-out on a television screen, the back of her ex-employer disintegrated into dots.

Ethan caught her as she started to fall, scooping her into a tight embrace. It was where he'd wanted Daisy Donahue but not limp and unconscious. He had to get her firing on all cylinders again. With a quick stoop to hook an arm under her knees, he lifted her off her feet, cradling her across his chest.

A chair was needed—set her down, lower her head to get some blood back in it, a glass of water…that was what common sense said, yet as he started carrying her towards one, he was riven by the strong temptation to keep right on going, out of the marquee, into a limousine and off to his cave. He'd caught his woman. She felt good in his arms. He wanted her out of this jungle of people and completely to himself.

Problem was she'd probably come to before he got her to the limousine. How long did a faint last? And she'd undoubtedly throw a scene at the hotel before he could take her to his suite.

No, it was a mad idea.

A sheikh might get away with it.

Or a buccaneer of old who was captain of his own ship.

Not Ethan Cartwright in this modern world of political correctness. *He* would have to answer for his actions.

Nevertheless, he was almost at the exit to the marquee when Mickey caught up with him. 'Hey, Ethan. You doing a runner with the girl?'

It stopped him. He turned to his friend whose face was alight with fascinated curiosity. 'She fainted. I have to get her to a chair.'

'You've passed a whole bunch of them.'

'Distracted,' Ethan muttered. He hadn't been aware of anything except the woman in his arms—the feelings she generated in him.

'Over here,' Mickey directed, steering him towards one as Daisy stirred in his arms, her lovely full breasts swelling against the wall of his chest as she gulped in air.

Ethan told himself his brain needed a blast of oxygen, too. As much as he wanted to hang onto Daisy Donahue she was going to rip into him the moment she had regained her wits. He'd be enemy number one for causing her to lose her job, regardless of whether or not it had been a good position for a person like her to have. And freeing her from it so she could be with him was not an argument she was about to appreciate. Somehow he would have to make her see him as her saviour instead of the black dog of disaster.

Daisy struggled to regain her strength and her wits. Never in her whole life had she fainted and to have Ethan Cartwright take advantage of this momentary weakness, manhandling her even more than before, was the absolute pits. At least she wasn't being carried by him any more. He'd put her on a chair and was sitting beside her. Despite the fact that he'd shoved her head down to her knees, it was still swimming, and he had his arm around her in support, which she probably needed, though she hated needing anything from him. He'd just destroyed the lifeline to keeping her parents in their home.

'Fetch her a glass of water, will you, Mickey?'

His voice upset her even further, loaded with concern. *After* the event. No concern when it really mattered.

'Sure. And here's her hat. It dropped off on the way.'

Total indignity on top of everything else!

By the time the glass of water came, she was steady enough to lift her head and sip it. 'Thanks,' she muttered to the man who'd brought it—Mickey Bourke, another A-list bachelor with no worries about where his next dollar was coming from.

'I'll look after her now,' Ethan Cartwright said, dismissing his friend.

'Right!' Mickey Bourke grinned at him. 'Nothing like seizing the day! Go for it, man!'

Seizing the day? The phrase scraped over all the jagged edges in Daisy's mind. Her day, her job, a secure future for her parents had all been wrecked by Ethan Cartwright going for what he wanted. She felt like throwing the glass of water in his face, sober up some of the blind ego that had completely overlooked what he'd been doing to her. But what good would that achieve?

Despair squeezed her heart.

'Are you feeling better, Daisy?' he asked caringly.

Nothing could make her feel better. 'Well enough for you to remove your arm,' she answered tersely, sitting up straight and stiffening her shoulders to show him his support was no longer needed. Or welcome.

'Okay, but you should keep sitting for a while. Maybe you should eat something. Did you have any lunch?'

No, she hadn't, which might have contributed to her fainting, although she was used to running on empty in this job. Except she didn't have a job any more. Which was all *his fault*.

She turned to face him, anger spurting off her tongue. 'It's a bit late to start caring about me, Mr Cartwright. The damage is done.'

He grimaced, but there was no regret in the green eyes boring into hers. 'Lynda Twiggley was doing you a damage, making you bow to her tyranny.'

'I could manage that. If you hadn't interfered, I'd still have my job.'

'You didn't like it,' he said with certainty.

'What's *like* got to do with it?' she cried in exasperation. 'It was the best paid job I've ever had and I need the money. You have no idea how much I need it. You've probably never known a moment's worry over money in your entire life.'

His mouth tilted into an ironic smile. 'Actually I carry the burden of worrying about money all the time.'

'Big money!' she corrected savagely. 'Not life-destroying lack of income.'

He frowned. 'Surely it's not that bad!'

'It most certainly is!' She quickly sipped some more water. The vehement bursts of emotion were making her feel light-headed again. Or maybe it was him sitting so close to her, exerting his mega-male attraction. A woman could drown in those green eyes.

'I'm sorry. I thought you'd be better off in another job,' he said with the first hint of apology.

'You didn't think at all,' she muttered furiously. 'Not on my level.'

'What do you mean…your level?'

She lashed him with grim realities. 'The level where people struggle to make ends meet. Where the job market is getting tighter every day. Where being out of work can bring everything crashing down.'

'Are you in debt?' he asked, his eyes seriously probing hers, making her heart jiggle with the wish he really did care. This was a man who could turn everything around for her parents if he wanted to. And he had a physical magnetism that was getting to her again.

'No. Yes.' She heaved a desolate sigh. 'My parents are. And if I don't pay the interest to the bank, they'll lose their home. They can't do it. It's up to me.'

'Well, there's a twist,' he dryly commented. 'I thought the Y generation lived off their parents, not the other way around.'

He wasn't interested. She'd been stupid to entertain the wild thought, even for a second, that such a high-flyer would come to the rescue of ordinary people.

'You live on a different planet, Ethan Cartwright,' she retorted bitterly.

'I believe in people being responsible for themselves. If your parents incurred a debt, it's up to them to—'

'You don't know anything,' she snapped. 'Sometimes people can't manage for themselves.'

'Okay. Tell me the circumstances,' he invited.

'As if you care!' Her eyes savaged him for his irresponsibility. 'You didn't care about the consequences to me when you ignored my plea to let me go. You didn't care about offending my boss so deeply I didn't have a chance of hanging onto my job. And just how do you think I'm going to get another highly paid position without a glowing reference from Lynda Twiggley? I'm dead in the water.'

She banged her glass down on the floor, stood up, and snatched her hat from his hands. 'Goodbye, Mr Cartwright. I can't say it was pleasure meeting you.'

'Wait!'

He was on his feet so fast and blocking the direct route to the exit of the marquee, Daisy had no choice but to halt and face him again. She lifted a belligerent chin as she demanded, 'What for?'

Ethan didn't have a ready answer. He was acting purely on the need to keep Daisy Donahue in his life. She was magnificent—cheeks flaring with colour again, big brown eyes flashing a fierce challenge at him, her petite figure powering up to fight him. He remembered how her soft, feminine curves had felt when he had been carrying her. Add the vitality of the passion he felt coming from her now…the thought of having all that locked in his arms sent fiery tingles to his groin.

An answer came to him.

He'd created the situation which was driving her away from him.

He had to reverse it.

'I'll give you a job,' he said.

Her eyes widened in astonishment, then narrowed with suspicion. 'What as? Your cleaning lady?'

There was a huge appeal in that image—Daisy on her hands and knees, scrubbing his floors, her perky bottom swaying with the action. But he knew he was

dead if he suggested it. His mind whizzed to other possibilities. He didn't need a PA. His business was fully
staffed. No room for her there. So what could he offer
that she wouldn't turn down flat?

'You need a lifeline, right?' he said, hedging for time
to come up with an acceptable rescue package. 'A
stopgap until you can find a job that suits you?'

'If I have to clean floors, I will, but they won't be
yours,' she vowed rebelliously, one hip jutting out as she
stuck a hand on it, emphasising the fascinating small-
ness of her waist. 'You are the last person I want to do
anything for right now.'

Ethan smothered a sigh. Feudal lord and serving girl
was not an appealing picture to her. Although if he
wrapped it up in gold paper...

'How about executive housekeeper? I've recently
bought a property I've started on renovating. You could
oversee the tradesmen's work, ensure that everything's
kept in order. I'll pay you the same salary you earned
with Lynda Twiggley.'

The fight in her eyes wavered into a sea of vulnerable
uncertainty—the need for no break in her money chain
warring with a mountain of doubts about what she
might be getting into by putting herself in his power.
Her throat moved convulsively. She was swallowing
hard. And blinking hard.

'Are you serious?' she asked huskily.

'Yes. I'm sorry for causing you so much distress,' he
said quietly, realising she was desperately trying to stem
a gush of tears. 'The least I can do is tide you over until
you find better ground for yourself.'

She bit her lips. Her eyelashes swept down. She
lowered her head. Her hand dropped from her hip and

fretted at the pill-box hat she was holding in her other hand. 'It might be months before I can find another job,' she mumbled anxiously.

'I expect the renovations will go on for months. It's a messy business. It will be good to have someone on site, checking up on everything. Even the most reputable builders need a critical eye on them to get it all right and clean up after themselves. In effect, you'd be my PA for a special project. Okay?'

The eyelashes slowly fluttered up again. He had the weird sense of his heart turning over as she looked earnestly at him. 'You're really serious about this? You'll pay me as much as Lynda Twiggley did?'

Down to the bartering line again, he thought with his usual cynicism, but if that's what it took to get this woman he'd do it. He reached for his wallet. 'I'll give you an advance on your salary to seal the deal.'

She stared at his bulging wallet as he opened it—the hook that never failed to work.

'How much were you being paid? A couple of thousand a week?' He riffled through the notes, prepared to give her any sum she nominated. It was irrelevant to him. He'd just won two million dollars in prize money on Midas Magic.

She shook her head.

'More? Less?' he prompted.

Her gaze lifted, meeting his with steely pride. 'I don't take money I haven't earned, Mr Cartwright. My salary was fifteen hundred dollars a week before tax. If you're satisfied with what I can do for you after the first week of being your on-site PA, I'd appreciate it if you'd pay me then.'

'Fine!' he agreed, barely hiding the jolt of surprise at her refusal to grab the money.

Honesty…fair play…Daisy Donahue was exhibiting a fine sense of both, making him feel slightly uncomfortable about having his own secret agenda.

'Where is this property?' she asked.

'Hunters Hill.'

She pressed him for more details, weighing up the information he gave, assuring herself there was a genuine job to be done. Once they'd settled on a meeting at the house at eight o'clock on Monday morning of the next week, she took her leave of him, very firmly, and Ethan let her go, watching the seductive swish of her bottom, content with the thought he'd be seeing a lot more of Daisy Donahue in the very near future.

He was looking forward to it.

In fact, he couldn't remember looking forward to a meeting with a woman quite so much!

CHAPTER FOUR

HUNTERS HILL...*the* wealthiest suburb in Sydney, according to one of the Sunday newspapers. Daisy also recalled reading that a famous Australian actress had a home there, along with other celebrities. It was no surprise that Ethan Cartwright had chosen to buy a property in such a prestigious area. Birds of a feather definitely flocked together.

Why he had chosen to pursue some kind of acquaintance with her at the Magic Millions race-day was odd in the extreme. She could only think his ego had been piqued by her dismissive behaviour. They had nothing in common. Absolutely nothing. Except they were both now paying for the outcome of that encounter—he offering her a job out of guilt, she taking it because there was no other choice immediately available.

It was far from an ideal situation, and as she drove her little car towards the address he had given, she felt increasingly anxious about whether there would be anything of real value she could do for what he would be paying her. Builders were messy and often careless. She knew that from when her parents had renovated their home. Nevertheless, she suspected that for much of the time she'd simply be watching and twiddling her thumbs.

Fortunately Hunters Hill was not a long or difficult trip from her parents' home in Ryde, much less hassle than going across the Harbour Bridge to Lynda Twiggley's office at Woolloomooloo. At least she would save on petrol while she worked for Ethan Cartwright. Her Hyundai Getz was a very economical car, but the price of fuel still hurt.

Anxious not to be late, Daisy had given herself plenty of time to arrive at her destination before eight o'clock. The nearer she got to it, the more impressive the properties became—big old homes set in much larger grounds than any normal suburban block. Some were massive and built of sandstone which would be horrendously expensive these days, but this was an old established area in Sydney, close to the harbour and at the mouth of the Lane Cove River.

She couldn't imagine Ethan Cartwright living in any of them. Why would a bachelor want to rattle around alone in a mansion when a luxurious apartment right in the CBD would provide an easier lifestyle? No doubt he had simply made a shrewd investment. Even the top end of the property market had slumped—dropping millions of dollars in recent months—so it was an opportune time to buy. It was the best time to renovate, too, with so many builders out of work. He'd probably bought an old home in bad repair but on prime real estate, and was anticipating making a huge profit when fortunes changed again.

There were several tradesmen's trucks parked along the designated street when Daisy turned into it, more or less marking the place she had to find. Confirmation of the address brought a flood of amazement. It *was* a mansion and it looked absolutely beautiful the way it was, at least on the outside.

The huge, white, two-storeyed house had been built with perfect symmetry, the windows and doors—all of which had French doors that opened out—matching up on both floors, which also had perfectly matching verandahs with glorious white wrought-iron railings. The roof was dark grey slate and a wide set of bluestone steps led up from a semi-circular driveway to the front door. Within this semi-circle was a large stone fountain.

There were no gardens, just green lawn and trees along the side fence-line, giving the setting a wonderful simplicity that highlighted the splendid grace of the house. The front fence and two side double gates were also of white wrought-iron in the same pattern as the verandah railings. One set of gates was open, obviously for the workmen's use, as there was another driveway down that side of the house to the back.

A black BMW roadster was parked at the foot of the front steps—definitely a billionaire's car, which meant her new employer was already here waiting for her. Daisy decided to drive into the grounds and park behind it. After all, she was supposed to be in charge of this project, right on site.

If Ethan Cartwright hadn't changed his mind in the meantime.

It was a worry.

Her parents had both been very dubious about what they saw as an impulsive and irregular offer of work Daisy wasn't trained for. She'd had to explain the circumstances of losing her job to them and they were only too painfully aware of why she had accepted this one. Her father kept muttering, 'It isn't right,' and they should sell up and move somewhere cheaper—a place in one of the housing estates for senior citizens.

Daisy couldn't bear the thought of that happening. Not only did it deeply wound her sense of justice, but it would also completely change the dynamics of the family. She'd insisted this was only a stopgap solution until she found another proper job and they weren't to worry. She was perfectly capable of managing anything she set her mind to.

Nevertheless, her confidence wasn't so easy to hang onto as she alighted from her car and started up the steps. Her stomach felt downright jittery. She told herself it was caused more by the prospect of having to meet Ethan Cartwright again—being subjected to his powerfully male charisma and those riveting green eyes—than trying to keep a check on the work of a team of tradesmen. Once *he* was gone and out of her hair, she'd be fine.

Not that he'd been in her hair. Neither was she about to let him anywhere near it. The tug of his sheer sexual impact on her female hormones was warning enough that she was dangerously attracted to the man, despite the huge differences between them. She had to maintain a hands-off policy whenever he plagued her with his presence. The way his touch affected her was far too disturbing. It could draw her into very foolish behaviour.

Today she had deliberately chosen a very downmarket appearance—a loose cotton tunic printed with daisies on a blue background, blue jeans, flat sneakers on her feet making her look even smaller in stature, a blue scrunchy holding her long, brown hair back in a ponytail, and no make-up apart from pink-brown lipstick, which was next to nothing.

It had to be patently clear to him that she was not

aiming to be an object of desire in his eyes. Though she couldn't really imagine she ever had been anyway. His pursuit of her on the Magic Millions race-day had definitely been an ego thing, not an attraction thing, and this whole business now was a fix-up thing, which was purely temporary. The X-factor problem was all on her side and it had to be kept hidden.

Having reached the front door, she took a deep, calming breath and pressed the call button. Ethan Cartwright did not give her time to twiddle her thumbs. The door was opened within seconds and the oxygen Daisy had drawn in was instantly trapped in her lungs.

The man was utterly, utterly gorgeous.

He was dressed in a superbly tailored dark grey suit, white shirt and a silk tie striped in red, grey and green. Some nose-prickling exotic cologne had been splashed on his strong, freshly shaven jaw. His thick, black hair flopped onto his forehead in an endearing wave. The green eyes sparkled as though he was delighted to see her and his smile kicked her heart into thumping like a drum.

'Good morning!' he said cheerfully, his rich male voice making her ears tingle.

'Hi!' was all she managed to croak.

'Come on in and I'll show you around,' he invited, stepping back and waving her forward.

He's not for me, he's not for me, he's not for me, her mind wildly recited as she willed her feet to move. The job was obviously still on. All she had to do was be sensible and adopt a strictly practical attitude.

The verandah had been tiled in a grey-and-white diamond pattern. This was repeated in the wide hallway she stepped into, but with an inset border featuring a black-and-white scroll. This border led to and framed a central staircase which curved up to the top floor, the balustrade painted in a shiny black lacquer, the steps carpeted in dark red.

'Wow!' she murmured.

'Do you like the red?' he asked, looking quizzically at her.

'Well, the effect is very dramatic,' she said cautiously, unsure if this was some kind of test.

'I'm thinking of recarpeting in green.'

'Green would look good.'

'You don't have to agree,' he said dryly.

'No, I think green would be easier to live with. The red is a bit in your face. Though it's all a matter of taste, isn't it? I wouldn't bother changing it if you're planning to sell. Let the new owner choose.'

'I'm not planning to sell.'

She looked at him in surprise.

His eyes bored in hers. 'I intend to make this *my* place.'

'It's a big place for one person,' she couldn't help commenting.

'I'm tired of living in an apartment. I want space.'

'Well, you've certainly got it here,' she said, barely stopping herself from rolling her eyes at the sheer extravagance of how much space he'd bought for himself.

His mouth quirked. 'You don't think I'll use it all?'

Caution held her tongue again. 'It's not for me to say.'

Amusement danced in his eyes. He ushered her to double doors to the right of the staircase. 'This was the drawing room. It will become my games room.'

'Games?' she queried, looking at the huge expanse

of dark red carpet and the magnificent white fireplace on the far wall, in her mind's eye seeing it furnished in the kind of graceful antiques people put in grand houses.

'All sorts of board games, card games. I have a group of friends who get together to play on Tuesday nights. I've acquired a large collection of games over the years and I'm having shelves and cupboards built along the internal walls in here to house them.'

She shook her head, amazed that a man like him enjoyed such ordinary pastimes. It was what her family did when they got together, playing games around the kitchen table.

'You don't like the idea?' he probed.

'If no expense is to be spared on these renovations, I'd put in a bar as well,' she suggested, a teasing grin breaking out on her face. 'Gaming is thirsty work.'

It was his turn to look surprised. 'You play, too?'

'I'm the current family champion at Scrabble,' she proudly declared. 'And I've been known to clean them all up at poker.'

He laughed, and suddenly there was a connection sizzling between them that knocked every bit of common sense out of Daisy's head. He didn't seem quite so high and mighty, more human like her, and she wished she could join his gaming group on Tuesday nights.

He cocked his head assessingly. 'I hadn't thought of a bar in here, but it would be handy. And a pantry for nibbles. Speak to Charlie about it.'

'Who's Charlie?'

'Charlie Hollier, my architect. He'll be dropping by some time today. Tell him to add a bar and pantry to the plan for this room. It will save trips to the kitchen.'

Just like that, Daisy thought, remembering how obscenely wealthy he was and telling herself that he and his friends undoubtedly played high-stakes poker which she could never afford. Her family counted their wins in plastic chips, no money involved at all.

'Now across the hall...' he led the way, throwing open another set of double doors '...is what used to be the ballroom.'

Daisy goggled at the incredibly splendid, many-tiered, crystal chandelier centred in the high ceiling above a massive room which obviously ran the whole length of the house.

'That's coming down today,' Ethan informed her.

Daisy goggled at him. 'You're getting rid of it?'

'I'm selling it. It's far too valuable to toss out. I was told it was bought from the Paris Exhibition in 1879. Some specialist lighting people will remove it and I'd appreciate it if you ensure they have adequate covering on the floor when they take it down. I don't want the polished floorboards damaged.'

'No, of course not,' she murmured, staring at the floor which gleamed invitingly for dancing feet. 'You don't intend to hold balls in here?'

He laughed. 'I think that era is well and truly gone, Daisy. I'll be putting a billiard table in this top half of the room with appropriate lighting above it. The bottom half of the room will become a home theatre—television, sound system, comfortable lounges.'

She sighed over the loss of the room's original function. 'It seems a shame. Though you're right about more modern living. I guess the floor will still be used for dancing when you throw parties.'

'Mmmh...you like dancing?'

'I *love* dancing. My favourite show on television is one that features up-and-coming dancers competing against each other. It must have been marvellous, waltzing in here.'

The green eyes twinkled wicked temptation. 'I could waltz you around now before the chandelier goes. You could close your eyes and pretend you're back in Victorian times.'

Her blood instantly heated at the idea of him taking her into his arms, pressing her close to him, their thighs brushing seductively as he twirled her across the floor. This terrible attraction to Ethan Cartwright had to be stamped out, not fed. She'd been running off at the mouth instead of simply taking in instructions. That had to stop. She had to keep in her place and he had to keep in his or this job would go haywire before it had even started.

Ignoring the flush on her cheeks, she gave him a stern look designed to banish any dangerous familiarity springing up between them. 'I don't believe the master of the house ever danced with his staff,' she stated emphatically. 'And I think that's a very good principle in general,' she added for good measure.

Ethan couldn't help grinning. Daisy Donahue was priceless. Here she was drawing battle lines, warning him they weren't to be crossed, establishing herself as forbidden territory, shooting the heady spice of challenge straight into his brain. The anticipation that had been bubbling through him as he'd waited for her to arrive this morning was certainly not fizzling out. His delight in her kept escalating. Winning her over to what he wanted was going to be a glorious game.

'I don't think I'll feel like master of the house until all the reconstruction is done,' he said in mock seriousness, his mouth still twitching with a dancing inner joy as he gestured for her to continue accompanying him on a tour of the property.

He felt no prick of conscience about taking advantage of the fact she was working for him. This was a stopgap position for her, not a serious career where business should not be mixed with pleasure. He dismissed that hurdle as of no account whatsoever, and she would surely come to realise that, too. This was a time-out situation—him from his normal social life, which had been soured by Serena, Daisy from the pressure of keeping a job she must have hated. He saw no reason why they shouldn't enjoy the experience of each other, once he'd opened up the desire for it on her side.

They walked down the ballroom and turned into the area which had been remodelled into a modern kitchen and dining area, facing a lovely view of the harbour. 'I designed the kitchen myself and had it put in first so I could move in here,' he told her.

She gave him a startled look. 'You're living here already?'

'Yes. I can't be here during the day but I wanted to check daily progress.'

She heaved a sigh, her gaze fluttering nervously away from his as she muttered, 'Then I'll be seeing you every morning.'

It was a dead giveaway that his presence disturbed her. Ethan was certain that she was as sexually aware of him as he was of her. Why she felt she had to put barriers between them was a mystery, but he was confident of bringing them down sooner or later.

Either curiosity or unease drove her to check out the design of his kitchen, putting some physical distance between them as she busily opened cupboards and looked at everything. Ethan simply enjoyed watching her. She was not a little brown sparrow this morning, more like a fresh flower with the daisy print tunic and her hair pulled up in a pert ponytail. The tight blue jeans did splendid justice to her very cute and sexy derrière.

He wondered how old she was. Today she could pass as a teenager, but the mature experience in her eyes suggested late twenties. He needed to know more about her life. Clearly she had a close involvement with her family, but what about other relationships? Was there a man causing her hands-off attitude towards him—someone she cared about?

Ethan didn't like that idea. He wanted to know and have this woman. Maybe it was the extreme contrast to Serena that struck deep chords in him, the contrast to all the simpering socialites who sought his attention. He felt newly invigorated with Daisy Donahue and he was in absolutely no doubt he sparked some very lively feelings in her, too.

So if the connection went both ways—which it surely did—she couldn't be strongly attached to someone else. Possibly she was struggling with the newness of the whole situation between them, not wanting to risk losing this job. Whatever…he had to persuade her to stop fighting it, go with it, see how far it went, how good it might be. She was so excitingly different from the women he'd known, he was determined on exploring the difference.

'This kitchen would meet the needs of a master chef,' she remarked in some awe.

He smiled. 'I enjoy cooking.'

Her big brown eyes widened in surprise. 'You do?'

'It's relaxing, as well as being a very sensual plea-sure.'

He deliberately delivered those words in a provoca-tive drawl, revelling in the betraying heat that coloured her cheeks again.

'A man of many talents,' she said ironically, then with a brisk air strode out from behind the island bench and waved him to show her more. 'What else do I need to see before you leave for work?'

She wanted him gone.

But Daisy Donahue would have to face him—deal with him—day after day.

Ethan was content with that situation.

No matter what she did, the attraction would not go away.

It would keep simmering until flashpoint was reached.

He pointed to the room beyond the dining area. 'That will be my home office. I've left a set of Charlie's plans for all the renovations on the desk in there so you can see what is to be done. Also house keys so you can let yourself in and lock up before you leave. The utility room is between the office and the games room. A powder room is located under the staircase. Bedrooms, dressing rooms and bathrooms are upstairs. You can check them out at your leisure. The major work at the moment is being done outside.'

The next half an hour was spent escorting her around the grounds where a swimming pool was replacing the croquet lawn and the old lawn tennis court on the lower terrace was being given an all-weather surface which didn't require constant maintenance. The old carriage house on one side of the pool area was being updated to a double garage with a storeroom at the back of it, and what used to be the staff quarters on the other side was being transformed into a pool cabana/guest apartment with a barbecue area. He introduced Daisy to all the tradesmen as the on-site manager, giving her the authority to make decisions or refer them to him.

'As you can see, there's a lot going on. Should keep you occupied for months,' he remarked with considerable satisfaction as they strolled back to the house. 'It will be good having you here, overseeing the work.'

She frowned. 'Shouldn't your architect be supervising all this?'

'Oh, Charlie pops in when he can. He does have other projects on the go and can't give this place his exclusive attention. But grill him on anything you feel you need to know when he visits this morning. Okay?'

'Okay.' She slanted him a measuring look. 'You're trusting me with a big responsibility and you hardly know me.'

'You're the responsible type. I have no doubt you're up to the job,' he blithely replied.

The look became more probing. 'What makes you think I'm the responsible type?'

'I observed you working for Lynda Twiggley, taking responsibility to a slavish degree.'

She grimaced. 'I shouldn't have been indiscreet.'

'My fault. I drove you to it. Apart from that, you've taken on the responsibility of servicing your parents' debt,' he reminded her admiringly. 'That tells me you can be counted on to rise to any crisis and deal with it as best you can.'

'Oh!'

The enchanting flush rose in her cheeks again. He couldn't resist brushing the soft warm skin with his fingertips, pretending it was a farewell gesture and a salute of respect. 'Got to go. You'll be fine, Daisy. Don't worry. Just do what you think should be done.'

He took his leave before he was tempted into some extreme indiscretion himself. Slowly, slowly, was the best plan of action with Daisy Donahue, he told himself as he climbed into his BMW. But he couldn't stop himself from driving off with an exhilarating burst of speed.

She was in his house.

Within reach.

Whenever he chose to push the connection.

Maybe she would disappoint him in the end, turn into another princess once she gave in to what he wanted, capitalising on the sexual power a woman could always wield. Whether she did or not was irrelevant right now. She was throwing out a challenge which was totally irresistible and Ethan was not about to be deterred from winning it.

CHAPTER FIVE

DAISY watched Ethan Cartwright drive away with very mixed feelings. Not only was he a sexy devil, she was actually beginning to like him, which was even more unsettling. This situation would be much easier if she could hang onto her former judgement that he was a spoilt, self-centred, arrogant egomaniac who had so much obscene wealth he didn't know or care how ordinary people lived.

All of which was probably still true. It shouldn't make any difference that he was into games and liked doing his own cooking and seemed to admire her for coping with her parents' financial difficulties. *Unlike* her ex-boyfriend who'd thought she was completely off her brain for giving up the city lifestyle that matched his and moving out to Ryde which was totally inconvenient for dating.

She'd been a blind fool to think herself in love with Carl Jamieson. When their relationship had involved easily arranged fun times, he'd been an absolute charmer, but he'd had neither any empathy nor patience with her decision to help her parents keep their home. All he'd cared about had been the inconvenience to him and the restrictions it would place on their sex life. He'd only *loved* her because she'd fitted in with *his* needs, and when that wasn't going to happen all the time, it was 'Goodbye, Daisy'.

She could see their relationship more clearly now. At the beginning she'd been enormously flattered by Carl's interest in her—a handsome, *with-it* guy, forging a successful career in computer technology. What did he want with an ordinary girl like her? She was reasonably attractive, reasonably intelligent, a capable kind of person, but nothing special. But that, of course, had made her the perfect choice for Carl—someone eager to fall in with whatever he wanted, someone who didn't outshine or compete with him, who thought he was wonderful...until he showed that he wasn't.

He'd wanted an easy, uncomplicated partner who would always put him first, and she had, oh, so willingly done that until her parents' problems had rearranged her priorities and proved to her beyond any doubt that Carl was not the kind of man to be counted on in a crisis and definitely not someone she would want to marry. Even so, the hurt and disillusionment of the break-up had lingered on, making her disinterested in men in general.

Especially handsome men who always put what they wanted above every other consideration.

It certainly wouldn't be good for her to get interested in Ethan Cartwright, she fiercely told herself. Nevertheless, he had shown enough concern for her crisis to give her this job, which gave some credit to his character. On the other hand, he could well afford it, so maybe not too much credit. Paying her salary was probably only a drop in the bucket to him, totally negligible. However, her own pride insisted she earn it as best she could and it was about time she set about doing something active instead of churning over feelings that had nothing to do with work.

Anxious to be in hearing distance when the chandelier people and the architect called at the house, she remained inside, taking up Ethan Cartwright's invitation to check out the rest of the rooms. He'd set up a computer work station in his office. The utility room was already furnished with a washing machine and clothes dryer, ready for his use. She noticed there was a handy chute in one corner for dirty clothes to be dropped down from upstairs. Very convenient. The powder room under the staircase was positively luxurious—mostly gleaming white with artistic touches of black and silver.

The bedrooms upstairs were huge compared to most modern standards, all of them with built-in cupboards and en suite bathrooms. The master suite, which was the only one furnished and obviously being used, was enormous. Not only did it have its own private bathroom with a jacuzzi and a shower big enough for two, but a large dressing room, as well.

Daisy could hardly believe there was nothing out of place in any of these rooms. No towels left on the floor, no toiletries sprawled over the vanity bench in the bathroom where she could still smell the lingering scent of his aftershave cologne, which undoubtedly occupied a shelf in the mirrored cupboard above the vanity bench. She didn't look for it, uneasy enough about this much intrusion of privacy.

It felt weirdly intimate just staring at the colour co-ordinated rows of clothes in his dressing room, with the matching shoes precisely lined up in specially made racks below them. It had surprised her that his bed had been made, not left in disarray, but all this...was Ethan Cartwright obsessively neat or did he simply like everything in order?

Daisy shook her head in sheer bemusement. She'd never known a man who wasn't messy—her brothers, her father, past boyfriends, Carl in particular, stepping out of their clothes, leaving them on the floor, piling dirty dishes in the sink, shoes being dropped wherever they took them off. They didn't actually expect a woman to clean up after them. Mess didn't seem to bother them. She wondered why Ethan Cartwright was different.

Even the kitchen had been absolutely pristine, though he must have made himself some breakfast since he was living here. All the stainless-steel appliances had been gleaming and there hadn't been so much as a wipe smear on the black granite bench tops. Curiosity drove her downstairs to check his pantry. Sure enough the shelves were packed in precise order, sauces and spices lined up for easy access, other staples grouped together. It was certainly the most efficient way to organise a kitchen. Maybe he was a genius at time and motion.

Daisy couldn't help being impressed by this aspect of his character. She was a bit of a neat freak herself, liking to know where everything was so she didn't get frustrated hunting for mislaid items, wasting time that wouldn't need to be wasted if a bit more care was taken in the first place. But maybe he was a control freak, which wouldn't be easy to live with. She had to stop thinking things that added to an attraction that was already too disturbingly strong.

The doorbell was a welcome distraction.

It was the architect.

'Hi! I'm Charlie Hollier and I presume you're Daisy Donahue,' he rattled out with a broad smile. 'Ethan called me and said you'd be here.'

'Right!' She smiled back. He was short and stocky, not much taller than her, with a rather homely face and friendly blue eyes twinkling at her as though he was happy to make her acquaintance. The fact that he was wearing blue jeans and a blue-and-white checked sports shirt also made Daisy feel immediately relaxed with him.

'He mentioned you suggested a bar in the games room. Good idea! Should have thought of it myself. We won't have to wait until the end of a game to go and get a drink from the kitchen.'

'You're one of his Tuesday group?'

He nodded. 'Always a great night. Let's go and have a look where best to put it.'

They walked inside to survey the situation. Daisy could not contain her curiosity. 'How many of you come to play?'

'Well, there's the old solid core from Riverview. Ethan and Mickey started it amongst the boarders in our class when we were at school together. A bit of competitive fun when we weren't at sport or study. That's three regulars plus Mickey when he's in town, and other friends we've made since then. Usually we have eight people turn up, sometimes more.'

Riverview…it was one of the big private schools at Hunters Hill, sited just across the Lane Cove River from this house. Being a boarder probably meant each student had allotted spaces for his possessions and he would certainly be disciplined into making his bed. If Ethan Cartwright had spent the six years of secondary school there, that could have become habitual, and it would be fairly natural for him to have a place for everything and everything kept in its place—nothing too odd about it.

Daisy was bursting to ask more questions about Ethan Cartwright's personal life, but reined in what could be seen as too much interest from a mere employee.

The architect decided on a corner bar next to the wall that backed onto the utility room—easy to run plumbing for a sink through from there. He would amend the plans and give a new set to Daisy so she could keep an eye on everything and stop mistakes from being made. 'I'm delighted Ethan has found someone to be on the spot all the time,' he added enthusiastically. 'You'd be surprised how often things have to be fixed because they weren't done right in the first place.'

Daisy was relieved to hear this. It made her feel she could be of real value here, earning her salary.

'In fact, I'd appreciate it—Ethan would, too—if you'd ensure that the men laying the slate around the pool today get the mix right,' Charlie ran on as they strolled out to the back of the house where the work was going on. 'Quite a lot of the slate will be charcoal-grey without the blue-green streaks in it. Sometimes they just reach for the next piece of slate in the pile and you end up with a square metre of all grey instead of splashes of colour here and there.'

'Okay. I'll keep an eye on that,' Daisy promised, feeling better and better about the job.

They toured the whole site together with Charlie checking on progress, Daisy listening to how he wanted everything to be. 'It seems a bit weird to me that all this is just for one person,' she couldn't help commenting as they returned to the house.

'Actually Ethan was planning to get married when he bought the place,' Charlie tossed off casually. 'Changed his mind, thank God!'

She shot him a quizzical look. 'You didn't like the woman?'

He grimaced. 'A bit too much into being the lady of the manor for my liking. But I'm glad Ethan decided to keep the manor anyway. It's going to be fantastic when it's all finished.'

'It certainly is,' she agreed, terribly tempted to pump more out of Charlie about *the woman*, but that was none of her business and it should remain none of her business.

Nevertheless, the phrase—lady of the manor— conjured up someone stunningly beautiful with all the airs and graces learnt from an exclusive finishing school where manners were polished and deportment and elocution were perfected. No doubt she had been trained to be the wife of a billionaire, knowing how to hostess every social event and look the part with elegant ease. Ethan Cartwright would naturally choose to marry a woman like that. She wondered what had happened to change his mind about the one he had chosen.

The lighting people arrived soon after the architect had left. As she watched the chandelier being carefully lowered onto the canvas laid out on the floor, it was impossible not to feel a pang of regret at its removal even though it wouldn't suit the lifestyle Ethan planned for himself. Perhaps the lady of the manor had wanted to keep the grandeur of the old house and they'd clashed on that point, realising they'd envisaged different futures together.

Whatever…it was none of her business.

She had a job to do and she would do it to the best of her ability.

Ethan was frustrated. Almost three weeks had passed and he was getting nowhere with Daisy Donahue. What he needed was a good block of time with her—enough time to get past the business of the day and onto more promising ground.

She was gone when he arrived home after work, always leaving him a note on what had been accomplished during the day, informing him of any snags to the flow of progress and how and when they would be corrected. Each morning she arrived all fresh and perky at eight o'clock, provoking an instant rush of sexual excitement, but no matter how long he delayed his departure, she would not be diverted from talk about the job. It was as though she was obsessed with it, not the least bit interested in him as a man, quickly brushing past every attempt he made at a more personal connection.

Nevertheless, the interest was there. He felt it in the tense way she deliberately kept a physical distance between them. He saw it in an occasional flash of her eyes before her gaze quickly slid away from his. He actually sensed her inward battle to suppress it whenever she was in his company.

It was obvious that she needed to feel secure in the position of his on-site project manager, continually affirming that her salary was being earned. Having a regular income was a big issue with her and she was probably determined not to risk losing it by indulging an attraction that could rock her boat.

I don't gamble.

Somehow that steely will had to be broken.

Or at least bent.

His way.

Daisy always rang the doorbell when she arrived at the Hunters Hill mansion each morning. Although she had a set of house keys and could have let herself in, the solid common sense of keeping everything formal between her and Ethan Cartwright stopped her from taking any kind of familiar freedom on his territory when he was at home.

He'd greeted her at the door one morning wearing only a short black silk wrap-around robe. Even though he had been decently covered, the deep V of bared chest with the sprinkle of black, curly hair and the powerful muscularity of his long legs had messed with her head for the rest of the day. No way did she want to catch him by surprise in any state of undress. The man oozed masculine sexuality. The more she saw of him, the more he rattled all her female hormones.

Even when she'd believed herself in love with Carl, he hadn't affected her like this—such a strong physical tug that inspired lustful thoughts. Sex with Carl had been more a natural progression of romance, not some primitive form of sheer wantonness that kept pleading for connection, eroding the common sense she had to hang onto.

She *knew* Ethan Cartwright was too much of a high flyer to ever consider her as a possible wife. She wasn't beautiful. She had no outstanding talent to lift her above her very ordinary background. Her circumstances were such that she was no match for him on any level, and no match meant no serious relationship.

Playing with her…that was something altogether different. She strongly suspected he enjoyed doing that already and wanted to push it further, but since Daisy couldn't see herself becoming *the main event* in his life, pride wouldn't allow her to fall into the role of a bit on the side, not even for the satisfaction of knowing what it would be like to have an intimate connection with him.

Most likely this was a case of her being on the spot and him not having chosen another sexual partner since breaking up with his fiancée. He probably viewed her as a nice little tonic for his hurt pride—a good dose and he'd feel on top of his world again. Which would make Daisy just another feather stuffed in his winner's cap. Her self-esteem insisted she was worth more than that. She'd been used once. She wasn't going to be used again. Despite the fact that Ethan Cartwright left Carl for dead in the attraction stakes.

As she rang the doorbell on Thursday morning of the third week of working for him, Daisy was thinking she had to find a new job. Fast. With a boss who didn't agitate her so *physically* and make her dream impossible dreams.

The door opened and she was confronted by another strong blast of sex appeal, though at least it was encased—enhanced?—by a superbly tailored business suit. 'Ah, Daisy!' Ethan Cartwright rolled out in his rich voice. 'I have a special task for you today.'

The twinkling anticipation in his gorgeous green eyes made her heart flutter. She had difficulty catching enough breath to produce a querying 'Oh?'

He flashed a teasing grin. 'You're so good at leaving me lists of things to note, I thought you'd appreciate getting a list from me. It's in the kitchen. Come on in.'

He set off down the hallway and she followed him at a safe distance, fiercely telling herself not to get besotted by a silly grin. Despite this stern resolve, her stomach was mush and her pulse was pounding at her temples so distractingly her mind barely registered the words he tossed back at her.

'You know the tennis court people and the guys who've done such a great job with the swimming pool…' he cast a sparkling glance back at her '…with your eagle eye upon them will all be finishing up tomorrow.'

She nodded.

'Well, I thought I'd give them a barbecue lunch in appreciation of the fine work they've done,' he continued cheerfully. 'Send them off with good feelings so they'll be happy to return if any problem arises.'

'You want me to do it?' Daisy asked, not expecting him to be on hand during the day.

'No. I want you to shop for it today and help me with the preparation tomorrow morning. I'll do the cooking.'

Surprise tripped her into saying, 'You're going to feed a group of tradesmen yourself?'

He paused at the kitchen doorway, shooting her a quizzical look. 'Why not?'

She almost bumped into him. Heat flooded into her cheeks as she reared back a step, wishing she could evade the riveting intensity of his eyes, but determined not to appear even more disturbed by him than she had already revealed. Since it was impossible to voice her assumption that *he* wouldn't mix socially with ordinary people when he obviously planned to, she had to come up with something else.

'I thought you'd be occupied with your important clients.'

He lifted a hand, featherlight fingertips grazing her hot skin. 'Everyone is important, Daisy,' he said softly, his eyes smiling at her confusion. 'And I believe in rewarding good work.'

Her heart was thundering. She couldn't tear her gaze away from the caring in his, or her face away from his mesmerising touch. She liked him. She really, really liked him. And she wanted...but she couldn't let herself want that.

'Right!' she managed to mutter.

For a long, long, moment he said nothing. Her toes curled with tension. Her mind whirled with dangerous possibilities. What if he stepped forward and kissed her? What would she feel? The terrible part was she didn't want to resist if he did make the move and that could land her in all sorts of trouble.

'Right!' he finally repeated, and with a quickly sucked-in breath added, 'Let's get to the list.'

Daisy sucked in quite a few quick breaths herself as she followed him into the kitchen, sensibly walking around to the other side of the island bench to put it between them. She was still shaking inside from that moment of aching vulnerability and was intensely grateful to have the list to look at as Ethan went through it with her, explaining what he intended to do with everything. The wives of three of the men would also be coming, he informed her, so there would be twelve people to feed, including herself and Ethan.

'Just add anything you think would be good,' he said,

pulling a wad of notes from his wallet. 'This should cover everything.'

She frowned at the amount of money he was trusting her with. 'I'll bring home the dockets and give you the change tomorrow.'

His mouth quirked in amusement. 'I'm sure you'll account for every cent.'

'It's what I'm used to doing,' she shot at him with a touch of belligerence, needing to emphasise the difference between them for her own sake. He could afford to splash money around as much as he liked whereas she…she started to wonder if he would use leftovers or let her take them home at the end of the day.

He immediately changed the subject. 'Do you play tennis, Daisy?'

'Yes,' popped out of her mouth before she thought where that question might be leading.

'Good!' His smile smacked of wicked satisfaction. 'Bring your tennis gear with you. And your swimming costume. I've already spoken to the men about trying out the pool and having a game of tennis. Should be a fun afternoon.'

Fun?

It might be for him, but it wouldn't be for her.

Her mind boggled at the thought of seeing Ethan Cartwright in nothing but a swimming costume. It was bad enough being trapped into spending a whole day in proximity with this treacherously attractive man. She could only hope he wore surfboard shorts.

'Have to leave now,' he ran on, tapping the list. 'Are you okay with this?'

'Yes. Have a good day!' she rattled out, relieved that she was not going to be mentally and physically buffeted by his presence any longer. At least, not today. Tomorrow was looming as an exercise of intense discipline over her mind and body with him around all the time.

Tomorrow…it was like a song of glorious promise in Ethan's mind as he drove towards the city centre. There'd been a moment this morning when he'd almost given in to the temptation to kiss her until she melted against him, the heat in her cheeks coursing through both of them in a firestorm of desire. He'd imagined sweeping her up in his arms, carrying her up the staircase to his bed, ravishing her until she gave up everything she was to him.

Only the constraints of time had stopped him. He had an important business meeting this morning. But tomorrow he'd manipulate a situation where she couldn't deny the strong connection that had unmistakably pulsed between them in the hallway. One way or another he was going to persuade Daisy Donahue to surrender to it with all the intensity of passion he'd felt vibrating from her since the moment they'd met.

CHAPTER SIX

WHEN Ethan opened the door to Daisy on Friday morning, he was wearing black shorts, a black sports shirt with white trim around the collar, black-and-white tennis shoes with black socks. The athletic style of the man in these clothes instantly raised his sex appeal which was already far too high for Daisy's peace of mind.

He gave her appearance a quick cursory glance—a loose blue-and-white striped T-shirt over knee-length white shorts—a sensible, sexless outfit—and his mouth quirked with ironic amusement as though he knew she had deliberately dressed down. For one stomach-churning moment challenge simmered in his green eyes, but he simply greeted her normally, then stood back and waved her inside.

'The men are rigging up the sails which will shade the barbecue dining area,' he informed her as they headed down the hallway. 'The tennis court is getting a last vacuum before the net goes up. Everything should be ready by the time the wives arrive after dropping their children at school. We have about an hour and a half to prepare all the food before taking on the host and hostess roles. Are you okay with that?'

'Yes,' she answered, only too grateful that she could soon busy herself with other people.

It was good to be busy in the kitchen, as well, helping Ethan prepare the salads, cutting up onions to accompany the steak and sausages, spreading garlic butter on the loaves of French bread.

'I see you're used to doing this kind of catering,' he remarked after they'd been working together for a while.

'Family parties. We all get together at Easter and Christmas,' she explained with a shrug.

'You have a big family?'

'Three older brothers and one older sister. All married with children. I was the accident. Mum was forty when she had me.'

'And how old are you?'

'Twenty-seven.'

'No marriage in view as yet?'

'No.'

'Boyfriend?'

She frowned at him. 'That's a very personal question.'

He shrugged. 'You've been working for me for three weeks and I realise I hardly know anything about you, Daisy. Not even where you live.'

'I live at Ryde with my parents.'

'To save money, no doubt.'

She flashed him a grim look at his quick understanding. 'Yes, a fact that my last boyfriend didn't appreciate.'

'Ah!' His mouth twitched into a satisfied little smile.

Daisy was vexed with herself for letting that slip. If Ethan Cartwright was thinking she was free for fun and games, he could think again. She was not about to waste her time and emotion on a man who would dump her when he found another lady for the manor. She chopped up a cucumber with extra vigour.

'How did your parents get into debt?'

The question surprised her, stirring a hope that he might toss out some free financial advice. She arranged her mouth into a rueful smile and looked directly at him as she answered. 'Their superannuation manager directed them into investments which had gone bad. They borrowed money from the bank to renovate their home, believing they would have enough income to service the loan…'

'And then the bottom fell out of the market,' he finished for her. 'Unfortunately a fairly common problem these days.'

It was an offhand dismissal of the subject. Daisy gritted her teeth over the stupid hope, then with a touch of resentment asked, 'How is it that you knew better?'

'My father is an economist,' he answered matter-of-factly. 'He was forecasting this financial blow-up for years. For the most part it didn't suit people to listen to him. Many wrote him off as a crackpot academic.'

'But you didn't.'

He shook his head. 'Numbers don't lie. Numbers made the crash inevitable.'

She wished she could ask him to look at her parents' investment portfolio, tell them where best to put what was left of their money, but such expert advice was his business. It wouldn't come free and even if she could afford his fees, it would still smack of asking him for a favour, taking on an extra client whose nest-egg wouldn't be big enough to earn him much of a commission. Favours put people under obligation to return them and she had nothing to offer Ethan Cartwright.

Except…

No, don't go there, she sternly told herself.

Giving in to sexual chemistry was one thing.

Wanting financial pillow-talk out of it was something else.

But he'd be using her so why shouldn't she use him?

The idea of having sex with him had been squirrel-ling around in her mind for weeks. She *wanted* to know how it would feel. He was, without a doubt, the most attractive man she'd ever met. It was only natural to be tempted to have the experience even though it wouldn't lead to a serious relationship, and if there were side benefits…at least that would make up for being dumped afterwards. She could come out winning.

On the other hand, that was a gamble and she didn't gamble.

The higher probability was she would come out losing…losing this job before she could find another, losing her self-esteem, losing her sense of right and wrong, and it was certainly wrong to barter sex for help. This wasn't exactly a survival situation. She could manage it by herself. But for how long? And at what cost to her own life?

Heaving a despondent sigh, she picked up the punnet of cherry tomatoes and started cutting them in half to add to the green salad. *He* was whipping up a home-made dressing, blending Spanish onion with vinegar, sugar, vegetable oil, water, salt and mustard. The blender was switched off long enough for him to dip a finger into the mixture and lift that finger to his mouth for tasting.

Her heart did a ridiculous flip. It wasn't a deliber-ately erotic action. Although when he saw her looking

at him, those devilish green eyes sparkled wickedly.
The urgent need for some down-to-earth distraction
made her grab at the first non-sexual thought that ran
through her mind.

'How come you're so into cooking?' she blurted out.

'I enjoy eating well. Don't you?'

'Yes. But you could afford to frequent the best restaurants. You don't have to do it yourself.'

'There's more satisfaction in doing it precisely to
one's own taste. My grandmother taught me that.'

'Your grandmother?'

He grinned, delighted to have teased her interest.
'From the time I was a boy hanging out in her kitchen.
I used to go there after school. She loved cooking and
everything I ate with her tasted so much better than the
stuff my parents bought. Neither of them ever cooked.
It was always frozen meals or takeaways, eaten in an
absent-minded fashion whenever they felt the need for
fuel. They're both so wrapped up in their mental world,
the physical world barely impinges on it.'

He must have had a strange upbringing, Daisy
thought, very different from her family life. 'Does that
mean your mother is an academic, too?' she asked,
unable to squash her curiosity about him.

He nodded. 'The law is her life. She lectures on it at
university. Writes books on it.'

'Were you an only child?' He hadn't indicated the
presence of any siblings.

'One was enough for my parents,' he said dryly. 'Not
that they didn't care for me. They did in their own way.
Though I'd have to say the best thing they did for me
was send me to boarding school. I had a great time at
Riverview with Mickey and Charlie and the other guys.'

He poured the dressing into a sauce-boat ready to use later. 'Though the food wasn't up to my grandmother's standard,' he added ruefully. 'When I finally struck out on my own, I wanted to cook for myself.'

Daisy had to agree it was hard to beat a really good home-cooked meal.

'This dressing is one of my grandmother's recipes,' he ran on. 'Have a taste.'

It was impossible to resist dipping a finger in and carrying it to her mouth, though she was conscious of him watching the action, waiting for her response. 'Mmm…yummy.'

He laughed. 'It's always a pleasure to share pleasures.'

His eyes twinkled with a seductive invitation to share many more with him.

Daisy instantly pulled herself back into a defensive shell. Everything about Ethan Cartwright made him too temptingly attractive. It was becoming more and more difficult to hang onto common sense. She couldn't even write him off as a selfish, arrogant pig any more. He didn't act like one.

But there was still the huge barrier of his billionaire status, and she couldn't help resenting how easily he could throw money around, getting absolutely everything he wanted. Somehow that made it all the more imperative that he shouldn't get her, not as anything but an employee who fairly earned her wage.

Ethan observed the shut-down on her face and the belligerent set of her chin as she finished with the tomatoes and moved to the tray where she'd placed the cutlery wrapped in paper serviettes.

'I'll take this down to the barbecue area, save having to bring it later,' she slung at him, avoiding eye contact, and was off, not waiting for him to agree or disagree.

She moved so fast, her pony-tail and her perky bottom twitched from side to side. Ethan grinned to himself, sure that it had become too hot in the kitchen for her and she was taking evasive action. She was so marvellously different from the women who virtually threw themselves at him. With Daisy there was no flirting to encourage his interest, and a swift back-pedalling whenever she felt herself teetering on the brink of responding to him beyond her set limits.

All the no-go signs from her only served to make the challenge of breaking through her barriers more compelling. He had made some headway this morning, moving onto personal ground, drawing out a curiosity about his life which revealed the interest she'd been deliberately repressing.

Maybe her ex-boyfriend had soured her view of men generally and she was wary of letting herself be vulnerable again. Certainly his experience with Serena had reinforced his cynical view of women. But he felt the potential for something very different with Daisy Donahue and nothing was going to stop him from clinching a connection with her. He had the rest of the day to work on cracking her resistance to being with him.

Daisy threw herself into the role of party hostess, determined to avoid being with Ethan Cartwright as much as possible. Luckily, none of the wives played tennis, so she couldn't be drawn into playing a set of mixed doubles. The morning passed agreeably enough. The women expressed interest in a tour of the mansion and with Ethan's permission, she showed them all they wanted to see, then stayed chatting with them at poolside, only moving away to refill drinks and ensure everyone was enjoying themselves.

All the men either played tennis or watched the game, amusing themselves with a lively commentary on the play, then cooling off in the pool before lunch. Daisy was the only one who didn't go into the water, escaping to the kitchen on the pretext of last-minute preparations for the barbecue.

The vision of Ethan Cartwright in a brief black swimming costume had made her so hotly conscious of her own body, no way was she about to don the bikini she had brought with her. It was far more comfortable sticking her head into the refrigerator, staring at the contents which were largely dead meat with no sex appeal whatsoever. She was still blankly looking at the tray loaded with steak and sausages when *his* voice assaulted her ears with a tone of extreme annoyance.

'This is totally absurd! You have no reason whatsoever to act as though I'm Lynda Twiggley, demanding that you toe some tyrannical line of duty every second of the day. I will not have it!'

It jerked her around to face a dripping-wet splendid male physique emanating a savage energy that sent wild quivers through her entire system. He'd slid open one of the glass doors that led onto the back verandah and stood just outside the dining area, glowering at her with fierce green eyes.

'I told you to bring a swimming costume,' he ranted on. 'You know I wanted you to join in the fun. There is no need for you to be up here fussing over food. Since you must be perfectly aware of that I find it distinctly offensive that you choose to turn your back on the rest of us…'

The accusation flustered Daisy into rushing out an apology. 'I'm sorry. I didn't mean to give offence. I was just…'

'Just nothing!' He pointed to her beach bag which she'd dropped at the end of the island bench. 'If that contains what it should contain, get changed and be down at the pool within five minutes. This is play time, Daisy. I expect my staff to follow the agenda I set.'

Having delivered this blistering ultimatum, Ethan strode off to return to his guests. The shock of his anger and the implied threat to her job had Daisy scuttling for her beach bag the moment his back was turned. She raced into the powder room under the staircase, threw off her clothes, dragged on her bikini bottom and fastened the bra top as fast as her fingers could work.

A glimpse in the mirror made her feel dreadfully naked and hopelessly vulnerable. She was too accessible to Ethan's touch and if he did touch her, she was frightened of showing him some uncontrollable response, and he'd know he could get to her physically, know and probably take advantage of it.

Any confidence in maintaining a proper distance between them was shot to pieces. Never had she felt so gut-wrenchingly nervous about wearing a bikini. Never. Ever. She wasn't ashamed of her body. It was slim enough and curvy enough to wear a bikini reasonably well, but how could she hide the effect Ethan had on her with only a few scraps of material for cover? It was no shield at all. It left her terribly, terribly defenceless.

Her frantic mind screamed there was no time to

worry about this. About three minutes had already gone and her job was at stake. Snatching up the towel from her bag, she ran to the door Ethan had left open and kept running, heading straight for the pool, not looking at anything but the water ahead of her, desperately blanking her mind to the fear of revealing far more than her almost-naked body.

A cheer went up from some of the men at the sight of her flying figure stripped of its usual cover-up clothes. Daisy didn't let herself think or care what they thought. She dropped her towel on the slate patio and dived in, staying under the surface of the water until she reached the other side of the pool and had to come up for air. Having taken a few deep breaths to calm her pounding heart, she swam slowly to the steps at the shallow end where the other women were sitting, paddling their feet.

'Love your red bikini,' one of them said, smiling at her.

'Can't wear one any more,' another remarked ruefully. 'Having babies gave me an awful jelly belly.'

'Why not consider cosmetic surgery if you feel bad about it?' the third woman suggested.

This topic was instantly bandied around. Daisy sat on the middle step in waist-deep water, letting the conversation float around her, trying very hard to appear calm and at home with the party scene. It gradually dawned on her that it hadn't worried the women that she'd gone missing. They were older than she was, comfortable in each other's company with the many experiences of motherhood to share. They seemed to view their men as children, too, happy to sit apart and relax on the side-lines while indulgently watching their husbands at play.

Maybe the tradesmen had made some joking remarks to Ethan about her conscientious devotion to duty, suggesting he loosen the work-rein on her today, possibly implying she deserved some time off. The niggling criticism would have irked him, given that she was supposed to be enjoying the party with them. Whatever…she had to be careful not to arouse his displeasure again.

The problem was in not being able to act normally around him. He made her so tense all the time, having to fight the attraction he exerted on her. She should probably check where he was, try to judge from his expression if her swift response to his angry command had mollified the offence she had given. On the other hand, if she just sat here quietly, keeping her attention on the women, she shouldn't get into any more trouble.

'Daisy…'

Her nerves instantly twitched at the sound of Ethan's voice, but at least there was no sharp edge to it this time. The tone held quite a pleasant lilt and she quickly constructed an inquiring smile as she turned in response to the call.

He stood halfway along the side of the pool, beckoning to her, obviously intent on a private tête-à-tête. It meant she had to get out of the water and go to meet him, wearing nothing but a dripping-wet bikini since she'd left her towel on the other side of the pool and she didn't dare keep him waiting while she went and picked it up.

'What's it like working for such a gorgeous hunk?' one of the women slung at her curiously as Daisy rose to her feet and started up the steps.

Difficult almost slipped off her tongue. The spectre

of Lynda Twiggley blasting her for indiscretion rattled her just in time. She flashed a smile at the woman, quickly answering, 'He's actually very kind, very generous.'

'Then you've got a brilliant package there.' An encouraging grin was thrown back at her. 'You should go for him, Daisy.'

She shook her head. 'Not a good idea. But right now I have to go *to* him, so please excuse me.'

The women laughed at her quip and she left them to their own amusement, forcing her legs to walk around the pool to the man who was, indeed, brilliantly packaged, and the *gorgeous hunk* part of the package was very much on display. It didn't matter how sternly she told herself not to find him desirable. She did. Any woman would.

He had the physical perfection of Michelangelo's *David*, every masculine muscle shining under taut, tanned skin, vibrantly alive, not carved in cold white marble. Ethan Cartwright, wearing only a brief scrap of black fabric that seemed like a brazen pouch exhibiting even more sexual power, was hot, hot, hot, and just the sight of him made her own blood race with heat. It was impossible to control the response he drew from her.

Her heart thumped. Her stomach fluttered. She was acutely conscious of her bare thighs rubbing together as she walked towards him. And worst of all, with his gaze directly on her approach, taking in the full vision of *her* body in the red bikini, she felt her nipples tightening into hard bullets with no way of hiding that fact under a wet bra. It was difficult to resist the urge to fold her arms against her chest. Reason insisted that action would only emphasise her self-consciousness and a stiff bolt of pride refused to give into such obvious weakness.

Nevertheless, anxiety rushed her into speech the moment she was close enough to him not to be over-heard. 'Have I done something else wrong?'

His far too sensual mouth moved into an ironic grimace. 'No. I want to apologise for being so curt with you. I didn't mean to frighten you into acting like a scalded cat. Your job here is not at risk, Daisy. I just don't want you to be scarred by your experience with Lynda Twiggley. It won't hurt you to be more relaxed with me.'

'No. Okay,' she agreed, relieved that he was no longer annoyed with her. To be absolutely sure of not making another mistake, she asked, 'What is the agenda now?'

He waved towards the group of men at the other end of the pool. 'The guys and I are about to start the bar-becue and put the meat on. Why not rustle up the ladies to help bring down the salads and generally get ready for lunch? No hurry. Keep it casual and friendly.'

'Will do,' she promised.

'They'll all be gone by three o'clock. Children to be picked up from school and an early start to the weekend for the men. Since you missed out on a game of tennis this morning, I'll play a set with you then.' He gave her a cheerful grin. 'Can't have you bringing a tennis racquet for nothing.'

He tossed these last words at her as he started strol-ling back to the barbecue area, leaving Daisy open-mouthed, struggling for a protest or an excuse to escape playing with him—being alone with him. She had the sinking feeling he would accept neither, anyway.

He wasn't going to let her off.

She would have to play the set of tennis.

Maybe she could surprise him by beating him. He didn't know she was an A-grade player. If his male ego got hurt, that might make him a lot less attractive. And he might not want to play with her any more. In any sense.

It was the only hope she could hold onto for staying on here without this constant feeling of vulnerability where he was concerned. She had to beat him this afternoon. Had to.

CHAPTER SEVEN

EVERYONE had helped clean up after the party before leaving. There was nothing for Daisy to do except play tennis with Ethan. At least both of them had changed back into their morning clothes so she didn't have such an acute physical awareness to distract her. As they strolled down to the court, she tried to keep the conversation between them light and natural, commenting on the guests' enjoyment of the day, pretending to be completely relaxed.

The tennis court was blue with a green surround and a high green wire fence to keep in wayward balls. 'Were you pleased with the surface when you played this morning?' she asked on their way down the flight of steps to it.

'Yes. No bumps anywhere. No odd bounces. They've done a great job with it.'

'I didn't watch the game.' She shot him an arch look. 'Are you terribly good? Will you wipe me off the court?'

He laughed, shaking his head. 'You're quite safe. I'll play to whatever your standard is, Daisy.'

She didn't *feel* safe, not from the attraction that was

so difficult to squash. However, his promise to accommodate her tennis standard did give her the chance to beat him. Hopefully that would be a hit to the ego that had just assumed he was the better player and he'd be so put out he wouldn't want to play other games with her.

'I think you should serve first so I can judge for myself,' she said, anticipating that he would go easy on her to begin with.

'As you like.'

He put down a medium-paced serve which any reasonable player could return and Daisy suspected he deliberately over-hit the ball to let her win the first rally. On the second point she cunningly sidelined him, laughingly declaring it was a lucky shot. The third point was more seriously contested and she was relieved when he netted the ball, giving her three game points. She managed to win one of them with a drop shot he wasn't expecting, which gave her the first game.

'Hmmm...' His green eyes were twinkling suspiciously as they crossed at the net. 'Am I playing with a closet professional?'

'How can you even imagine that?' She grinned at him. 'I never shriek or grunt when I hit the ball.'

She sliced her first serve so wide it was ungettable. She put her second serve down the T, leaving him standing again. He netted her third serve. The fourth he managed to return in court, but his shot was high enough for her to smash a winner from it. Two games to love. It was a great start.

He walked up to the net, no longer under any delusion that she was an easy beat. 'Where do you usually play?'

'At the Chatswood Tennis Club.'

'How often?'

'Most Saturday afternoons.'

Until the annual membership fee became due again. She couldn't risk paying it, not when her job future was still so uncertain and every dollar earned might be important. Her tennis-playing days could soon be over for a long while, but today she was still in good form and very grateful for it.

'A-grade?' Ethan asked.

'Yes.'

He suddenly grinned, which wasn't the reaction Daisy needed to get from him. 'What do they call you? The pocket rocket?'

'No. Just Daisy.'

He shook his head in bemusement. 'I wouldn't call you *just* anything, Daisy Donahue. Compared to all the other women of my acquaintance, you are, without a doubt, the most remarkable.'

The compliment went straight to her head like champagne. The fizz of pleasure completely undermined the wish to bruise his ego. Besides, it didn't seem possible in the light of his amazing admiration. He should be in a snit over being made to look inadequate against her, but he wasn't. His voice held a relish for the competition as he tossed 'Game on!' at her.

She watched him stroll back to the service line, no lack of confidence in his bearing. She couldn't help thinking he was the most remarkable man of her acquaintance and she was riven with the temptation to simply go with the flow of attraction wherever it took her. Which would probably be terribly foolish, given her job situation, not to mention the huge difference in their stations in life.

However, both these factors lost all significance in the intensely fought contest that followed the revelation of her ability to play at a highly challenging standard. Ethan stormed through his next service game. She had to fight hard to keep hers. It felt as though every point was an exhilarating win or an anguished loss. He had the greater strength but Daisy was a well-practised tactician and she refused to let his power dominate.

Ethan applauded every particularly skilful shot she made. There was no acrimony at all coming from him, more a bubbling delight running through the banter he carried on at the change of ends, making the game even more stimulating, mentally and physically. Daisy loved every minute of it, loved playing with him, loved the contest of wits and skill and the sweet thrill of his admiring comments. He was gorgeous, marvellous, and it was like a cocktail of sheer joy to be his match on the tennis court.

He gradually won his way back to six games all, then insisted they play a tie-breaker to decide the victor. Somehow beating him didn't seem important any more, although Daisy still fought hard to take the set. He delivered a fantastic backhand to triumph in the end, and she dropped her racquet to applaud it, wanting to fairly acknowledge the great shot.

In uninhibited joy he leapt over the net, tossed his racquet on top of hers, and before she could even imagine what he intended, he swept her into his embrace, grinning wickedly as he declared, 'Winner takes the prize.'

He kissed her.

Her heart was still banging away from the exertion of their last rally. Her body was hot. So was his. Whether it was the energy drain of the game, being taken by surprise or the sudden wild surge of need to know him like this, resistance was simply beyond Daisy at that moment. Her arms automatically lifted and wound themselves around his neck, and she kissed him back.

Ethan swiftly took advantage of her surrender to his seductive sensuality, changing his kiss to one of driving passion, tightening his embrace, clamping her lower body to his, and Daisy was bombarded by so many exciting sensations, it was totally impossible to extract herself from them. The desire she'd tried so hard to hold in check burst through her in a raging compulsion to experience all of him.

Her fingers spread into his hair, clasping his head as her mouth ravaged his as intensely as his ravaged hers. Her breasts, pressed so hard against the hot heaving wall of his chest, tingled with wild sensitivity. His hands curled around her bottom, lifting her into a more intimate physical connection. She was acutely aware of his erection furrowing her stomach. It didn't set off warning signals in her mind. She revelled in his desire for her, the excitement of it consuming all common sense.

With dizzying speed, he broke off their kiss, scooped her up in his arms and was carrying her, striding off the tennis court, mounting the steps to the pool terrace. Her arms were locked around his neck. She didn't think of questioning his action. She was madly exulting in his strength. Never had a man made her feel so marvellously *taken*, as though she really was a prize. It was incredibly heady stuff and she nestled her face against his throat, breathing in the intoxicating male scent of him.

He charged into the pool cabana. There was a bed in the back room. A last thread of sanity screamed that she should stop him now, but she didn't want to. Her whole being yearned to let this happen, to indulge the desire to have Ethan Cartwright, to feel everything he could make her feel. She was twenty-seven years old and no other man had ever affected her so intensely. Her swirling mind rebelled against sanity, against pride, against everything that should stand in the way of letting herself be swept into bed with him.

He stood her on her feet, whipped off her T-shirt and removed her bra in a few breathless seconds. His shirt was discarded just as fast and she was barely conscious of her own semi-nakedness, being so entranced with his. He was beautiful, magnificent, and what she had thought of as untouchable was suddenly there to be touched and she didn't even have to reach out because Ethan hauled her back into his embrace and was kissing her again, making the excitement of her bared soft flesh pressed against the muscle-toned heat of his even more lusty.

Her hands slid greedily over his powerful shoulders, loving the taut smooth skin, the sense of great strength, of an energy force that was pouring into passion for her. The sheer animal pleasure of feeling him like this completely banished any restraint. She touched everything she could reach—his back, his ears, his thick, silky hair, wildly revelling in the freedom from every inhibition.

He moved her with him to the bed. They tumbled onto it, still kissing each other with a fierce hunger for all they could take from this coming together. He tore his mouth from hers, heaved himself down to kiss her breasts with a hot urgency that drove Daisy to the brink of melting with anticipation for the ultimate intimacy. Her entire body was screaming yes when he lifted himself away to tear off the rest of her clothes and shed his own.

Seeing him so highly charged with desire for her sent a burst of exhilaration through her mind. Her eyes feasted on the glitter of feverish need in his, on the powerful maleness of his perfect physique. Everything female in her quivered with delight at the prospect of possessing some, if not all of this man.

Her legs instinctively spread apart as he came back to her and exultantly wound around his hips as he plunged into where she most wanted him, deep inside, filling her with such sweet satisfaction her throat automatically emitted a soft croon of pleasure. It was so good, and unbelievably better when he began stoking the wonderful sensation with rhythmic thrusts.

She closed her eyes to everything but the inner world she was sharing with him—a world of intense feeling rolling through her in ever stronger waves. She was barely aware of goading him on with her legs, raking his back with her hands, only knowing that she wanted more and more of him, wanted him to take her to a level of ecstasy she had never known and feeling it getting closer and closer, almost unbearably close, her vaginal muscles convulsing out of all control, and she was crying out, begging...

And then it happened.

A glorious burst of release.

The torturous tension disintegrated as a sweet flood of incredible pleasure washed it away, leaving her floating in heavenly happiness with a blissful smile on her face. Ethan brushed his lips gently over hers, sharing her contentment, and she realised he had climaxed with her. Although her arms felt totally limp, she lifted them to hug him, glad that in this moment they were perfectly in tune with each other, and deeply grateful for the amazing experience he had given her. He kissed the tip of her nose, her closed eyelids, her temples, and it was so nice she couldn't stop smiling.

'You can't hide from me any more, Daisy Donahue,' he murmured in a tone of deep satisfaction. 'I was right about you all along.'

Curiosity flicked her eyes open. 'Right about what?'

He was grinning, a devilish delight dancing in his gorgeous green eyes. 'You're a challenging little witch with all the goods.'

Except the worldly goods that could make her a real match for him.

That miserably sobering thought wiped the smile off her face.

Even so she couldn't regret what she had just done with him, though the reality of her situation rushed in on her, loading her heart with a lump of anxiety. Where did *he* see them going from here? She was his employee and a very temporary one. Their positions in life were hopelessly different.

'Okay...' he drawled, placing a finger at the corner of her lips, which had lost their smile, and searching her eyes with determined purpose. 'What did I say wrong?'

'Nothing. I just remembered who you are and who I am,' she answered with black irony.

'A man and a woman who want each other.' He shook his head at her. 'Don't try to deny it, Daisy.'

She didn't. It was impossible to lie in the face of the desire that had brought them both to this bed. 'I'm not sure it's ever that simple,' she said ruefully. 'There are always...other considerations.'

'Neither of us is in a relationship. We're both adults,' he argued with arrogant confidence. 'We don't have to answer to anyone except ourselves for what we do.' He grinned again. 'And don't tell me this wasn't good. It was great! No reason not to go with it and that's what we're going to do.'

In a quick lithe movement he was off the bed and scooping her up in his arms again. 'We need a swim. Refresh ourselves,' he said, dictating action as though everything was settled between them.

She *was* hot and sweaty. A swim would be good. Maybe it would clear her head enough to think straight, which was very difficult when she was so very physically linked to him. 'You don't have to carry me.' It was a weak bid for some independence from his overwhelming attraction.

'I like carrying you.' There was a glitter of gleeful triumph in his eyes. 'I would have carried you right out of the Magic Millions marquee except you probably would have screamed abduction when you recovered from your faint. You didn't like me much then.'

The problem was she liked him too much now. In fact, she was head over heels in love with Ethan Cartwright. Was it possible that a relationship with him could have a future?

Belatedly her mind registered what he'd just told her. 'Why did you want to do that? Carry me out of the marquee, I mean.'

He laughed. 'Because you stirred the caveman in me. Still do.'

He plunged into the pool, still holding her in his arms, only releasing her underwater so she could rise to the surface as she wished. She swam away from him, needing a little time on her own to sort through the situation with Ethan. She'd thought—or had she wanted to think?—he'd given her this job out of guilt. But now it seemed he'd wanted to abduct her, keep her with him until she satisfied his caveman instincts.

He'd called her a challenging little witch.

Said he was taking *his prize*.

Was her sexual surrender simply an ego ride for him?

She swam the length of the pool several times before stopping for a breather at the shallow end. Ethan had swum beside her, apparently content to leave her alone as long as she was within easy reach, and he did instantly reach out and draw her into his embrace again, smiling into her eyes.

'The solar heating for the pool is working well,' he remarked. 'The water is at the perfect temperature for this time of day. Like warm silk. Enjoying it?'

Daisy had never been skinny-dipping before and he was right. The water was like warm silk. So was his naked flesh, seducing her into wanting more of him, despite the questions spinning around her mind.

'Yes,' she said, winding her arms around his neck, wrapping her legs around his hips. He certainly stirred the primitive woman in her—a fierce desire for total possession. Which she knew wouldn't happen, but it was so terribly tempting to have as much of him as she could.

He kissed her and she kissed him back, wishing she could lose the mountain of reservations building in her mind. His mouth broke reluctantly from hers, breathing a sigh over her sensitised lips. He lifted his hands, holding her face between them, his eyes dark green pools of desire demanding a positive response.

'I've not had nearly enough of you, Daisy. Stay the night with me. Stay the weekend.'

An iron fist squeezed her heart. How soon would *enough* come? And how much of herself would she have given him by then? Having any kind of extended affair with him could only bring her heartache and mess up her life. However wonderful this felt with him right now, it was going to be bad for her in the end. Much worse than the break-up with Carl. She shouldn't have let Ethan get to her, shouldn't let it go any further.

'I can't,' she blurted out, adding the first reason that made his invitation unacceptable. 'I live with my parents, Ethan. I'm not as free as you are. They'd worry about me.'

He frowned. 'Call them. Tell them you've been invited to have a weekend away.'

'With whom? My billionaire boss?' she mocked, the reality of the vast social gap between them finally smiting the treacherous desire he aroused in her. 'It would upset them terribly, thinking their financial problem had led me into being seduced by a man who would only be using me for his pleasure.'

He looked affronted, then fiercely belligerent. 'Don't tell me you felt no pleasure with me, Daisy. It was mutual.'

'Yes,' she readily conceded. 'And I thank you for it. But it can't go on, Ethan.'

'It's not right to let your parents rule your life,' he argued. 'You're twenty-seven, not a child.'

'They don't rule *my* life. They'd hate to even think they did. It's my decision. I care about them and I'm not going to upset them. They're going through a bad enough time as it is,' she said vehemently, gathering the strength needed to disconnect from him and make the break that a solid block of down-to-earth sanity insisted she make.

Becoming heavily involved with Ethan Cartwright would not lead anywhere good for her. She didn't believe the Cinderella story worked in today's world. Like married like. He was only serious about getting her back into bed with him until he'd had enough of her.

She managed to summon up a crooked little smile and said, 'You won the prize. Let's leave it at that.'

Then she pushed herself away from him, resolutely determined on leaving the swimming pool, getting dressed and going home.

Tomorrow she would find another job.

Any job.

It was best if she never saw Ethan Cartwright again.

She couldn't trust herself not to give in to him if she stayed working here and putting herself in that kind of constant emotional jeopardy would be hell.

CHAPTER EIGHT

ETHAN couldn't believe it. He'd had Daisy Donahue precisely where he wanted her. She'd responded to him just as he'd imagined she would. The sex had been fantastic. Best ever. For her to reject it, reject him and all they could share together was a development he certainly hadn't anticipated. It was enough to make a man tear his hair out in frustration.

She was up the steps and out of the swimming pool before his fighting spirit erupted through the shock of being told this was all he was going to have with her. No way was he going to accept that. He'd finally found a woman who met all the criteria that satisfied what he'd always been missing and he wasn't about to let her walk away.

Which she was doing, her gorgeously perky bottom bouncing as she strode swiftly towards the cabana, stirring the caveman in him again. But this wasn't the stone age. He couldn't club her over the head and force her to stay with him. Somehow he had to challenge her decision, persuade her to change it. His mind attacked the problem from every angle as he left the pool and followed her to the cabana.

She lived with her parents.

He had to remove her from that situation so she didn't have to consider their feelings about having a connection with him, set her up independently.

But then pride came into the equation.

Her parents were unlikely to accept her rent money if she wasn't living with them and they needed it to keep the mortgage on their home running. Daisy wouldn't leave them in need.

He could pay off the lot with barely a dent in his personal wealth, free them all from the financial bind they were in, but he suspected they would take serious umbrage at such an offer. He very much doubted that Daisy's parents were people who would countenance the idea of him buying their daughter, not even to save themselves from serious debt, and Daisy herself wouldn't accept money she hadn't earned.

Money was at the heart of the barrier she was putting between them.

Because of it she was putting her own life on hold to help her parents.

But she did want him.

Impossible for her to have responded to him as she had with such passionate intensity if the attraction—the desire—didn't run deep.

Money…sex…

His mouth twisted cynically as he picked up a towel from the pile laid out on the bench beside the cabana and tucked it around his waist. He hated choosing the bartering path with Daisy but she was leaving him no other option.

A nasty thought struck.

It was quite possible that her resistance—her rejection—had actually been a ploy to force his hand, induce him to offer his expertise to fix her parents' financial problem. In fact, given the way women generally manipulated their sexual power, it was even probable.

He could do the fixing if her parents were prepared to gamble.

But he sure as hell was going to get his pound of flesh from Daisy for it!

Pumped up with ruthless purpose, Ethan entered the cabana, moved to the opened doorway to the bedroom and propped himself there, blocking the exit. Daisy had dressed so hastily there were wet patches on her T-shirt where she hadn't dried herself properly. Her body was bent over, her fingers working fast on the laces of her shoes.

'It's not so late that your parents would be worrying about you, Daisy,' he drawled. 'There's time for us to talk this situation over.'

She finished tying the laces and straightened up, her cheeks flushed, her hands clenching into determined fists at her sides, her eyes shooting unbreakable resolution at him.

'I'm grateful for the stopgap work you've given me, Ethan, but I have to move on now,' she stated, as though nothing he could say would make any difference. 'I won't come back. I'll find some other way to manage. I'm sure Charlie Hollier would keep a more frequent check on the renovations if you asked him. Please…just let me go.'

'Not until you let me have my say,' he answered, adopting a tone of reason backed by rock-like determination to win what he wanted.

One of her hands uncurled and gestured an impatient dismissal. 'It's pointless. I won't change my mind.'

'Give me the courtesy of hearing me out.'

She grimaced at the criticism of her curtness, then emitted a deep sigh of resignation. 'Say what you want to say then.'

He laid the groundwork for the barter to end up on *his* terms. 'The best estimate at the moment is five years for the market to recover. Five years for the value of your parents' investments to regain enough income for them not to need your financial input any more. Which means you'll be thirty-two before you can lead an independent life again.'

'My parents supported me for many more years than that, Ethan,' she retorted unflinchingly.

'You were a child. That was a natural responsibility. I don't believe your parents want to be dependent on you. I can't imagine they like accepting this sacrifice from you.'

She frowned. 'No, they don't like it, but the other choices...' She shook her head. 'They're not fair. They're not right.'

'I can offer a choice that will resolve the financial worry and minimise the waiting for it to be over,' he stated matter-of-factly.

She stared at him, an anguished hope in her eyes that spoke of immense inner turbulence, and Ethan instantly knew she wasn't immune to the deal he was about to put on the table. Money won. It always won if you tapped into the weakness that would give way to it.

'This will only work if you're prepared to remain on the job here in your supervisory capacity,' he ran on, blocking any escape route via some other job. 'I promise you that will be the only connection between us until after I've delivered the relief your parents need from their current debt.'

No immediate sexual pressure.

This was a waiting game.

He saw that fact register, but the money hook was in far enough for her to ask, 'How do you propose to accomplish that?'

No rush to get away from him now.

'Doing what I do—make money out of money,' he replied with sardonic satisfaction. 'When you go home this evening, tell your father I'm so pleased with how you've managed this renovations project for me, I've agreed to look at his investment portfolio and give him my expert advice on it. I'll put aside a meeting time with him at eleven o'clock on Monday morning. You have to persuade him to come.'

She nodded, looking unsure about where this was leading but willing to do anything to help her parents. 'I think he'd be quite eager to listen to your advice, Ethan.'

'I can't make him take it, Daisy, but if he does and lets me act fast enough for him, there's a very big chance his money worries will be over by the end of next month. Your parents should end up financially secure for the rest of their lives.'

'You can guarantee that?' she asked warily, not completely sold on the plan.

'No. It's a gamble, but one I'd highly recommend, not without good reason. What I can guarantee is they won't be any worse off than they are already. If your father agrees to go with my advice and it does pay off as handsomely as I anticipate, I want a reward in return.'

'You mean…a commission?'

She was shying away from where he was heading.

Maybe she hadn't deliberately set out to ensnare him into doing what she wanted of him. Irrelevant now. He wanted what *he* wanted and nothing was going to stop him from getting it. Not when she had already conceded the strength of the attraction between them by sharing that bed with him.

'No. I'd prefer your parents to think I'm doing this as a favour to you. The outcome will be you'll no longer have to give them rent money, no longer have to live with them. You can resume an independent life, free of any worry about them.' He paused to let that sink in before pointedly adding, 'And that's where my reward comes in, Daisy.'

Hot colour whooshed into her face, but there was no shock in her eyes. She had already grasped the deal he was holding out. Her expression was more a wry acceptance of his reason for making the offer. 'You want an affair with me,' she said flatly.

It vexed him that the idea of an ongoing relationship between them aroused no anticipation of any pleasure for her. Clearly she found the money angle distasteful, too. But she'd left him no other choice. He'd had to force the situation, break all the barriers she'd been putting up, clear the way.

'I'll set you up in an apartment of your own so there's no one else to consider,' he said just as flatly, still determined on the course that would give him the satisfaction she seemed intent on denying him. 'You can find another job at your leisure, carry on whatever career you set your mind to. But your free time for the rest of this year is mine.'

The rest of this year...

The time span jagged around Daisy's mind, hitting

painfully on what she had already known. Ethan Cartwright saw no real future in a relationship with her. He was proposing to keep her as his mistress, undoubtedly thinking his interest in her would lose its current edge over the months he had stipulated for exclusive rights to her free time.

'Nine or ten months on easy street should not be too big a hardship for you,' he said harshly, impatient with her silence. 'Not compared to struggling on to keep your parents out of crippling debt for five years.'

He was angry—angry that she had been bent on walking away from what they had shared in this room. The green eyes were glittering with fierce challenge. He'd probably never had his interest knocked back by a woman in his whole privileged life. And one of the reasons for that was very much on display.

Physically he was the perfect male. The towel tucked around his waist only seemed to emphasise how splendid the rest of his naked physique was, and the power of his sexuality tugged at her even now, when he was pushing a deal that made her feel like a second-class woman, only fit for his bed for as long as his desire for her lasted, tossing money at her to sweeten that humiliating truth.

But if he could do what he believed he could with her father's investments…what a huge difference it would make to the rest of her parents' lives! Instead of fretting over losing their home and moving to a much less welcoming place to the family they loved, they might even have the pleasure of helping her brothers and sister with the windfall Ethan was virtually promising.

And no one need know why it had come about.

Not the real reason.

She had to give Ethan credit for coming up with a plan to save her pride in that sense. Never mind her own personal pride. She might have to lick that wound for the rest of her life. Could she swallow the pain of being only considered mistress material for the rest of this year?

Just keep thinking of the advantages he had laid out, she savagely told herself.

They were very solid advantages. Apart from the lifting of the financial burden, there would be worry-free time for her to find her own feet again career-wise, forge a better future for herself. Besides, it certainly wasn't a hardship to have Ethan Cartwright as her lover. All she had to do was not get too tangled up emotionally with him.

'What haven't I covered?' he demanded, pushing for an answer to break the tense impasse between them, to get his teeth into whatever objection she might have.

Ethan Cartwright was a winner.

Losing was only acceptable if he'd done everything in his power to win.

Daisy couldn't help being impressed by this quality in him even as she bridled against being the target of this particular game...the prize...the reward. Those terms didn't feel special right now.

'I think you've covered everything admirably,' she said, finally making the decision to accept his proposition. 'I'll pass on your offer of advice to my father as soon as I get home.'

He nodded, a look of mocking satisfaction on his face as though he had known all along she would fall in with his plan, but would have preferred a different surrender from her. 'You have my telephone number.

Call me and let me know if he agrees to the meeting so I can rearrange my schedule.'

She nodded, wishing she had refused him, sickened by his view of her—a woman who could be bought. Not in ordinary circumstances, she thought fiercely. This wasn't primarily for herself. Her parents had always been good, hard-working people. They deserved a happy retirement. Ethan was holding out the power to give them that and she couldn't turn away from it. There were worse things than suffering the heartburn of being his mistress for the rest of this year. Much worse.

She swallowed down the surge of bile which had erupted from her churning stomach and took a deep breath. 'I'd like to leave now. If you'll move aside from the doorway...'

His eyes narrowed suspiciously. He folded his arms across his chest in a pose of deliberate rebuttal to her request. 'You haven't given me your word that we have a deal, Daisy.'

The wish to give him a bit of heartburn made her say, 'My father might not want your help. I'll let you know.'

It was a way out, free and clear of Ethan Cartwright.

He stared at her, possibly suffering a moment of uncertainty.

She savagely hoped so.

It wasn't fair that he had all the power and she had none, except for the desire she stirred in him, desire that would be thwarted if she didn't play his game. He didn't like that possibility. She could feel him seething over it and exulted in the little victory over his confidence.

The grim line of his mouth took on a sardonic twist. 'Still the challenging little witch. Well, have it your way, Daisy. The deal is on the table. Take it or leave it. I won't run after you.'

He unhitched himself from the doorway and moved aside, unfolding his arms to extend one in an invitation to take her leave.

The tension inside her was like a compressed spring, needing release. She wanted to bolt from the room. It took considerable willpower to walk at a normal pace, maintaining an air of dignity. His sexual magnetism made her insides quiver as she passed him. Her legs, however, did perform their function of holding her up and she was out of the cabana in just a few nerve-jangling moments and heading up to the house to collect her bag.

He didn't call out to her.

She didn't look back.

But she felt him watching her.

The nape of her neck tingled with heat.

Just as she reached the closest door into the house she heard the distinctive splash of someone diving into the pool. It emphatically reinforced Ethan's statement that he wouldn't run after her. She could leave his property without any fear of pursuit.

It probably should have given her a feeling of relief, but it didn't.

The plain truth was it made her feel easily dispensable from his life.

And the bitter truth was…he wasn't from hers.

CHAPTER NINE

FOR Daisy there was no escaping from the fact that if Ethan Cartwright could deliver his side of the deal, it would make a very positive difference to her entire family. Taking it meant she would have to act quickly on the offer for it to appear all above board. The most natural reaction from her was to look pleased, excited about the wonderful opportunity for her father to benefit from Ethan's financial expertise.

She worked hard at giving precisely that impression when she arrived home, bubbling over with the news that her boss would make time on Monday morning to advise her father on where he might better place his superannuation funds. The look of hope that sprang into her father's eyes relieved the tight band squeezing her heart. It was definitely worth being Ethan's mistress to lift the depression that had sapped the happiness from her parents' lives.

There was no pretence about their pleasure and excitement.

Daisy steeled herself to the sticking point and made the call.

The sound of Ethan's deep, rich voice giving his

name in response sent a shiver down her spine. The memory of how it had been in bed together was suddenly very sharp. She did want it again—wanted him. Too much. Which was where the hurt would come in. But she'd weather it somehow.

She took a deep breath and poured warmth into her voice. 'Ethan, it's Daisy. I want to thank you again for your offer, and Dad wants to thank you, too. I'm passing you over to him.'

Her father took the receiver and expressed his gratitude, as well as confirming he would keep the eleven o'clock meeting on Monday morning. Then apparently Ethan requested to speak to her again.

'Yes?' she asked somewhat breathlessly, her pulse quickening at the thought of him bringing up the relationship he expected to have with her.

'Work on the games room—the shelves and bar—begins on Monday,' he stated matter-of-factly. 'I'll be leaving early for work to make time for your father. I'll need you here to let the tradesmen in. And supervise as usual. Can I count on you?'

'Yes. No problem,' she assured him. 'I'll keep checking what they're doing against the plans Charlie Hollier drew up.'

'Fine! I'd appreciate it if you also keep leaving me your little notes at the end of each day. Progress and problems.'

'I will,' she promised.

'I'm glad you'll still be around, Daisy. I would have missed you if you weren't.'

'Well, I'm glad I rate that much,' she said dryly. 'Have a good weekend, Ethan. I guess I'll see you when I see you.'

She put the telephone down before he could say anything more personal, making it difficult to transmit to her parents that nothing out of the ordinary was going on. She knew *they* wouldn't accept the deal if they knew about it. Now that it was already in train, she had to make it work right so they would never suspect what Ethan was extracting from her as his reward.

Monday was not an easy day for Daisy at Hunters Hill. While she assiduously supervised the work being done, her mind kept fretting over what was going on between Ethan and her father at their meeting. It wasn't certain that anything would be agreed upon. Her father had always been a cautious man with money—budgeting, saving. He might find Ethan's advice too much of a gamble to take. In which case, she wouldn't have to be Ethan's mistress and there'd still be the financial problem at home.

Weirdly enough, she found herself willing the deal to go through.

And she honestly didn't know if this was because she wanted her parents to feel secure for the rest of their lives, or because she actually did want an affair with Ethan, regardless of its being a primrose path that would inevitably dwindle out. He was, without a doubt, the sexiest man she had ever met. If she could just let herself enjoy having him for the rest of this year or until he lost interest in her…surely she could manage that if she kept her head on straight about it ending sooner or later.

Her nerves were totally strung out by the time she arrived home and her mental ambivalence was finally settled by her father's announcement that he had placed his financial affairs in Ethan's hands and was convinced there would soon be an upturn in their fortunes. He wouldn't go into detail about the decisions made. Ethan had insisted on absolute confidentiality regarding the advice given. However, her father's happy demeanour clearly demonstrated he believed in it and trusted it.

The die was cast.

Now came the waiting to see if the advice proved good.

It was a strange kind of hiatus, being at Ethan's house each workday, watching it evolve into his personal home, yet not ever seeing him. He was gone before she arrived and she was gone before he returned. The only connection they had were notes they left for each other—all of them relating to the renovations.

Time rolled on. The games room with its bar was completed and the shelves were filled with an incredible array of board games, which Ethan must have had in storage somewhere. One morning she found a selection of carpet samples in various shades of green laid out in front of the staircase with a note attached—'Which one would you choose to live with?'

Why would he want her opinion?

It wasn't as if he'd invited her to live with him.

She was to be set up in an apartment, completely separate from his residence.

At first Daisy was inclined to dismiss the question, leaving a reply that read, 'It's up to you to choose.'

However, as the day wore on, she kept looking at the carpet samples, imagining how each one would look on the staircase. The moss green seemed more right than the others. Possibly she was drawn to it because it was the colour of Ethan's eyes. In the end she left a note pinned to it, saying, 'This one,' even though it was irrelevant to her what went down in his home.

At the end of the week, the carpet-layers came in, took up the red carpet and replaced it with the moss green. It was absurd how much pleasure it gave her. Most probably her choice had coincided with his, simply reinforcing it, but she still wore a smile all day, happy that he liked what she liked. Which was true about a lot of things. And in her heart of hearts, Daisy couldn't help wishing that Ethan might come to appreciate how compatible they were and not ever lose interest in her.

Which was dangerous thinking, she sternly told herself.

Sex with her whenever he liked was Ethan's aim. It had been from the day they'd met. In one sense it was flattering that he should go to such extraordinary lengths to acquire her acquiescence to it. On the other hand, Daisy suspected it was in the nature of the man— a ruthless drive to manipulate circumstances so he would get what he wanted.

She shouldn't forget that.

The friendly little notes, the carpet question, the laying off of any physical pressure could all be a softening-up process so she would be a more amenable mistress, not a grudging one who had been pushed into the position.

The whole house gradually turned into what Ethan had envisaged. Furniture arrived—the billiard table, wonderfully comfortable sofas in moss-green velvet for the home theatre section, bedroom suites for the guest rooms. Different lighting fixtures were put in to suit the new decor, plus all the electrical apparatus for the sound system and the massive television screen.

Daisy had little left to supervise. Once the renovation of the old carriage house was done she wouldn't be needed here and still she hadn't been able to land a job elsewhere. She began to feel anxious about everything—her lack of work to justify the salary Ethan paid her, the whole money problem, whether his side of the deal would, indeed, pay off, and how soon.

Each night her father was glued to the financial report on television news programmes. Almost six weeks went by before the item he was waiting for hit the headlines. The government had approved a Chinese corporation's bid to invest in the Redback Mining Company, which was rich in iron ore deposits but too deeply in debt to exploit their holdings. The share price, which had bottomed out at five cents months ago, had already exploded up to a dollar.

Her father whooped with glee, leapt up from his armchair, pulled her mother out of hers and danced her around the lounge room in a joyful polka, yelling out, 'He did it! He did it!' in a wild version of a song from *My Fair Lady*.

He eventually calmed down enough to confide that, on Ethan's advice, he had plunged everything on the Redback Mining Company. He would sell the bulk of his shares tomorrow and make a massive profit, pay off the bank, help the family out with whatever they needed, live sweetly for ever after.

So this was it, Daisy thought, dizzied by the spectacular nature of her parents' sudden rise in fortune. Ethan had delivered. And watching her father brimming over with ebullience, her mother beside herself with happy relief and excitement, she felt a fierce gladness in the outcome of the deal, regardless of any cost to herself down the track.

Ethan was not slow in claiming his reward. The next morning a note from him spelled it out—'Make some excuse to your parents for being away this weekend and spend it here with me. I want you waiting for me when I come home after work on Friday.'

It was a straight-out demand. The first of many, Daisy realised, feeling a jolt of stark truth. Her mind had instinctively softened the situation, shaping the relationship she would have with Ethan into an affair, colouring it with hopes and wishes and desires. It struck home now that an affair was a two-way street and Ethan's mind was set on having their connection only one way—his way. That was the deal she had accepted.

The idea of being so very deeply in his power shot a shiver of fear down her spine. She was used to being her own person, making her own choices. What if Ethan's demands became intolerable? She couldn't let him completely dominate her. The line had to be drawn somewhere.

Daisy fought a sense of panic for the rest of the day, telling herself Ethan was a reasonable man. He had shown anger at what he'd considered Lynda Twiggley's tyranny. He'd treated all the tradesmen with respect. He was not about to use her badly. It wasn't in his character.

Besides, pride wouldn't allow her to show him any fear.

In fact, pride insisted she accept his demand gracefully.

In the end, she wrote him a simple little note in reply—'Thank you. I'll be here.'

Her parents were in such a euphoric state with future plans of their own, they didn't question her announcement that she would be away for the weekend, having been invited to spend it with a friend. They were eager for her to have a good time, delighted that she was free to do it and not be tight about money any more.

Daisy packed everything she thought she might need—her tennis gear, bikini, a couple of sets of casual clothes, two dressy outfits, and the gorgeous silk kimono she had bought at a second-hand designer shop, having fallen in love with the wild floral pattern that swirled with red and yellow and orange, chartreuse and olive-green.

Her mouth curled with irony as she folded this garment into her bag. It was a very apt casual robe for this weekend, since she was about to become Ethan's geisha girl. Certainly there wasn't any point in taking her pyjamas. She was careful, however, to include the contraceptive pills she'd been taking amongst the toiletries she was packing.

No way was falling pregnant part of the deal. She had her own life to live after these nine months with Ethan, establishing a new career, possibly meeting a man who would want marriage and children with her. She would only be twenty-eight when this was over.

She left home early enough on Friday morning to make a quick shopping foray at the local supermarket before continuing on to Hunters Hill. In keeping with accepting her fate gracefully and also showing gratitude for what he'd done for her parents, she'd decided to welcome Ethan home with the tastiest meal she could cook, as well as wearing her prettiest dress and looking her absolute best. Pretending it was a dinner date would surely help her feel less nervous, and hopefully stop Ethan from jumping on her bones the minute he was through the door.

· It had been well over a month—almost two—since their deal had been struck, with no physical contact since then, and he wouldn't be feeling any need to carry through any seductive routine. The prize was his to take whenever he wanted. She just hoped he'd let her feel… not like a sexual commodity to be used at his convenience.

The renovations to the house had been completed so she had it to herself to do what she wanted without raising any curiosity in the tradesmen who were still fixing up the garage and the storeroom at the back of it. In between dutifully checking their progress, she cooked a lamb ragout, made the sweet corn and sour cream dip her family always devoured first at parties, wrapped slices of prosciutto ham around melon balls, opened a packet of Brie cheese and laid pitted dates beside it, prepared the snow peas and florets of broccoli for last minute microwaving.

Keeping busy helped hold the build-up of tension at bay until after the men had left for the day. Daisy then went into a frantic whirl of getting herself ready for Ethan, using one of the guest bathrooms to take a shower, wash her hair, blow-dry the long brown tresses into curling softly around her shoulders.

Her make-up took longer than usual. It was difficult to stop her trembling hands from smudging the eyeliner and making a mess with the mascara, but the end result was worth the trouble. Her eyes were her best feature and with her hair making a dark, shiny frame for her face, she looked better than Ethan had ever seen her before. Her heart was thumping with the need for him to be surprised at how attractive she could look. The hope that he might see the possibility that she could be a partner for him beyond the bedroom kept sliding through her mind, regardless of how unlikely it was.

Her dress was a lovely, feminine design, made of silk patterned in red and white swirls. It had little cap sleeves, balancing a low, sweetheart neckline which left a hint of cleavage on display. The tightly fitting bodice was styled in a crossover ruche and the swingy skirt fell in graceful folds to knee length. Her bare legs and high-heeled strappy white sandals definitely made it a sexy dress, but not overtly so. She felt good in it, and Daisy needed to feel good about herself. Especially tonight.

Nevertheless, she was hit with a painful pang of total inadequacy when she paused to examine the overall result of her efforts in the mirror. She didn't match the rich socialites Ethan was accustomed to mixing with, didn't have their sophisticated polish or their perfect styling. The woman in the mirror might have been good enough for Carl Jamieson but Ethan Cartwright was light years ahead of Carl in the eligibility stakes.

It had been stupid of her to even try to pretend this was a date. She should be wearing her usual jeans, not caring how she looked because it wouldn't change anything. For whatever reason, Ethan wanted her in his bed. She should probably greet him stark naked, save the bother of taking off her clothes, but everything within her recoiled from taking that line of brutal reality. At least making the most of herself was like putting on a brave face and she needed a brave face to cover up the nervous mess she was fast becoming.

With nothing left to do and not knowing when Ethan would arrive home, she sat in his home theatre and watched quiz shows on television, trying to keep her mind occupied by answering the questions put to the contestants.

She was ready for him.

As ready as she was ever going to be.

CHAPTER TEN

For Ethan, it had been a hectic end to the week with clients rearranging their investment portfolios after the share price for the Redback Mining Company had sky-rocketed. He was mentally fatigued by the time he finished up on Friday evening—later than he'd wanted to be with Daisy waiting for him at home. He settled into the driver's seat of his BMW and closed his eyes for a few moments, trying to re-energise himself for the night ahead—a night he'd been looking forward to, impatient for—ever since Daisy had walked away from him.

No more walking away, he thought with grim satisfaction. He didn't understand why she'd been so damned perverse about denying the natural progression of a relationship between them, but it didn't matter now. He'd won the time he wanted with her, and from her brief note, it seemed she was not about to baulk at fulfilling her end of the deal.

The power of money.

In this instance he hated it.

But he was going to take what it had bought him—take everything that Daisy Donahue could give him.

Starting tonight.

He sucked in a deep breath, rolled his shoulders, opened his eyes and began the drive home.

Over the past few weeks he'd kept up his usual social life, attending a few A-list parties, going to a couple of race meetings with Mickey, the regular games nights with the guys, holding Sunday afternoon tennis parties now that his court was ready for action. He'd actually been curious to see if any of the women he met raised a spark of interest in him—anything that might divert or supplant this obsession he had with Daisy Donahue. As absurd as it was, a businesslike little note from her gave him more of a buzz than anything else.

And despite his fatigue, he felt a buzz of anticipation growing as he drove out of the city centre, heading towards Hunters Hill. The peak-hour traffic had already thinned so the journey was not frustratingly long. It was just on six-thirty when he turned the BMW into his driveway and it gave him a sweet sense of pleasure to see Daisy's car was parked at the front steps.

She was here…waiting for him.

He drove down the side of the house to the garage, which was now in a usable state. Was Daisy listening for him to arrive? How was she feeling about losing her freedom to him? Ethan couldn't imagine her totally giving up the challenging attitude which had made winning her so compelling. The little brown sparrow had the heart of a lion.

Excitement zinged through him as he alighted from his car and strode towards the back entrance to the house. The wall of glass which gave a wide view of the harbour from the dining area and kitchen also gave a direct view inside. He halted in surprise when he caught sight of Daisy standing by the opened oven door, checking the steaming contents of a casserole dish, giving them a stir with a wooden spoon.

She was cooking him a meal?

His gaze swept the island bench. She'd laid out pre-dinner nibbles, as well. And her hair was down, falling around her shoulders in a shiny, touch-inviting curtain instead of scrunched up in a ponytail. Pleasure welled up in Ethan. He hadn't expected to be welcomed like this.

It flitted through his mind that Serena had never once cooked for him, always expecting to be taken out to restaurants or getting professional caterers in if she threw a party. Daisy wasn't in the princess mould. She hadn't put any of the tradesmen off-side with her. No getting up their noses with uppity airs and graces. She'd carried out her job here in a very diplomatic fashion.

Quite possibly cooking him dinner was a diplomatic action, as well, nothing to do with welcoming him home. Don't assume anything, Ethan cautioned himself, a wave of cynicism overriding the pleasure. She could be buttering him up to get something else from him—the good, old bartering trick. He wasn't going to fall for it. This time everything would be on his terms, exactly how he wanted it.

He resumed his approach to the back door, watching Daisy through the glass, his heart jolting again when she turned around after closing the oven door again. She looked lovely. No trace of the teenage appearance tonight. She was all woman. Some smoky make-up accentuated the bright chocolate of her beautiful eyes. Her lips were a stunning, glossy red. The upper swell of her breasts gleamed above the low neckline of her dress—a red-and-white dress—its saucy skirt swirling around her legs as she stepped quickly out from behind the island bench, her feet strapped into sexy high-heeled sandals.

She had shed the little brown sparrow image.

It had always been a deceptive image. He'd known it all along.

The lioness was out and prowling.

Desire kicked so fast into Ethan's groin, his whole body was instantly invigorated—the earlier fatigue gone and forgotten. A few quick strides and he was sliding open the glass door, enjoying the slight shock on Daisy's face as she stopped and stared at him. *Caught*, he thought, grinning with exhilarating triumph as he closed the door behind him and tossed his car keys on the dining table in passing, moving straight to the woman who could no longer escape him.

Daisy was stunned anew by Ethan's physical impact on her. Her heart started galloping. An electric tingle raced around her veins. Her stomach contracted. Weird little quivers ran down her thighs. She forgot to breathe. The welcome home speech she'd rehearsed flew right out of her mind.

He didn't give her any time to remember it. He picked her up, hoisted her over his shoulder, and was out of the kitchen and heading for the staircase before she found breath enough to speak. 'What are you doing?' she squeaked, coming out of shock enough for her dangling hands to find some purchase on his trouser belt and try pushing herself up.

'Taking you to my cave,' he replied with relish, keeping her thighs pinned to his chest with one arm and patting her bobbing derrière with his free hand. 'Did I ever tell you I loved this bottom? Sexiest bottom I've ever seen on a woman. It's been taunting me ever since we met. I think I'll eat it.'

Eat it?

'Dinner!' Daisy squawked, realising the balance of her weight made it impossible to change his hold on her. She batted *his* bottom with more vigour than he'd used on hers. 'I cooked dinner for you. It's going to spoil.'

'No. I switched off the oven. We can eat later. This hunger demands satisfaction first. Hit me some more. I like you being feisty. It's very exciting.'

She did out of sheer exasperation. 'I wanted you to appreciate my efforts.'

'I do. Red suits you. It's your true colour. Full of fire.'

'I meant the food I prepared!'

'Won't be wasted. We'll work up an appetite for it. Sex, food, wine…'

He was charging up the stairs, completely undeterred by anything she said. Part of Daisy was enraged by the indignity of being carried like a sack of grain, yet another part was excited by the rush of primitive physicality. Ethan was having his way with her and there was a kind of relief in having him act so fast. Though what was the act going to entail?

Eat her bottom?

She squirmed and thumped his some more. 'Don't think you can do anything with me, Ethan Cartwright. I won't be your sex slave.'

'You could try it,' he blithely suggested. 'You might like it.'

'I won't let you tie me up or do weird stuff like that.'

'Frightened of losing control, Daisy?'

Fear welled up in her as she recalled wondering if he was a control freak. 'You'd hate it, too,' she cried.

'Don't worry. I'm not into bondage. I want to feel your hands on me. Your hands tell me what you're feeling more eloquently than any words.'

She smacked his taut buttocks again. With relish. 'Then that should tell you I'm feeling mad at you for treating me without any respect.'

'I'm beginning to understand why men—I think it's in Finland—like having their bodies birched before sex. It sensitises the skin. Gets the blood flowing hotly.'

'Oh, you…you…'

He laughed. 'Lost for words, my sweet?'

'I'm not your sweet.'

'Oh, yes, you are! Like a very tasty lollipop. I'm going to lick you all over and make it last as long as I can. I think I'll start with your toes. They look good enough to eat. Sexy red toenails inviting me to taste them.'

Her toes curled in instinctive defence. Or was it excitement? She had terribly sensitive toes. If he started on them…

'On the other hand, maybe I want your mouth to surrender to me first,' he ran on. 'Or should I work my way up to it? Take every other bit of ground before claiming the citadel.'

'This isn't a battle,' she cried, beginning to feel frantic inside at the thought of losing all control to him and what it might mean to her. 'You've already won me, remember?'

'No. I've only won time with you. Not the same thing at all. In fact, you made me *buy* time with you. That's not a good feeling for me. I want to blot it out.'

'Being bought doesn't make me feel good either' shot straight out of her mouth.

'Got to put all that aside. Make this the real deal.'

'What deal?'

'You and me together. As we should have been.'

Her head was too dizzy to find a reply to smack his arrogant claim down, although it pounded around her mind that what was right for him wasn't right for her. They were already up the stairs and he was carrying her into the master suite and being *intimately* together was so imminent, her nervous system was going haywire and it was probably better not to think any more, to let whatever happened happen because it was unavoidable anyway.

He dumped her on the bed and followed her down, covering her body with his, lifting her hands up above her head and pinning them there as he loomed over her, a wide, wicked grin on his face. 'Forget about seizing the day,' he said. 'I'm seizing the night. You're finally mine, Daisy Donahue.'

Not *finally*.

Only for a while within the time he'd stipulated.

Until he'd had enough of her.

Unless it could somehow turn out differently.

The wish…the hope…thundered through her heart.

He lowered his head and slowly ran his tongue over her lips, making them tingle with sensitivity. 'Mmm… yummy lipstick. What's it called?'

A hysterical little laugh gurgled up from her throat. 'Passion Red.'

He grinned in devilish delight. 'Reminds me of a song in the musical *Les Misérables*. There's a line in it that goes—*"Red…the colour of desire"*. Whoever wrote it got it right.'

He kissed her with full-blooded desire, inciting Daisy to respond just as hotly. She couldn't help herself.

No matter what her head told her, her body was tuned to this man, madly eager to experience all of him again. She wanted a new deal with him, wanted the old one blotted out, wanted much more than she could ever tell him. Except with her hands.

Which he suddenly freed.

Though in a seemingly perverse action, he moved himself out of touch. His mouth broke from hers and he rolled away from her to sit on the side of the bed and lift her legs onto his lap. 'Feet first,' he muttered, working on unbuckling her sandals.

Daisy sucked in a quick breath. Her pulse was pounding through her temples. Her thighs were quivering. Her toes scrunched up in tense anticipation as he removed her sandals, stroking her ankles and the soles of her feet with tantalising gentleness. He started lifting one foot towards his mouth and Daisy tore it out of his hold and jackknifed forward, reaching out, seizing handfuls of his shirt.

'Off,' she cried in a wild frenzy—anything to avoid the toe-licking which would shoot her into uncontrollable spasms. 'Take it off so I can touch you. You said you wanted that. You said…'

'I wanted all of you,' he reminded her. 'And I do.'

It was almost a relief when he reached around her and unzipped her dress, smiling into her frantic eyes as he peeled it off her shoulders, drawing the sleeves down her arms. She hadn't worn a bra. The tightly moulded bodice hadn't required one. She felt her nipples stiffening into hard bullets as the silk fabric slid over them and fell to her waist.

'You take my shirt off, Daisy,' he commanded. 'Go ahead. Unbutton it.'

He was filling his hands with her breasts, revelling in their softness. And their hardness, his thumbs fanning the taut peaks in a slow teasing motion. Her fingers scrabbled over his shirt buttons, working as fast as they could at releasing them. She didn't linger over dragging the garment from his shoulders, wrenching it down, baring his chest, wanting them to be on equal terms, wanting it with a fierce intensity that poured from the depths of her soul.

He released her long enough to rip it off entirely and free her arms of her sleeves, as well. In a flurry of action, he scooped her into his embrace, crushing her bared breasts against the hot hard wall of his chest, pinning her there as he stood and pushed her dress and panties down over her hips and bottom.

She dug her hands between them and unzipped his trousers, hooked her thumbs on the waistband and made him as naked as she was. He lifted her chin and kissed her. She wound her arms around his neck and kissed him back, needing to lose herself in all-devouring passion. She was barely conscious of him working off his trousers, kicking off his shoes, freeing her completely of her clothes. His mouth was everywhere, her neck, her breasts, her stomach, burning trails that incited her to kiss and touch him wherever she could.

There was no more talking, only huge wells of feeling. They were back on the bed and Ethan was driving into her and her body was exploding with the sensation of having him deep inside her. They rocked together—a wild, powerful rhythm, their bodies locked in the feverish urgency to reach the ultimate peak of pleasure. Her mind swirled with the primitive triumph of possessing him as completely as he was possessing her. Her hands and legs urged him on...more, more, more...

Her inner muscles convulsed around him. He bent his head, his mouth invading hers, his tongue thrusting, reinforcing each plunge to the melting heart of her, taking an ownership that she was beyond matching, her entire body fusing as ecstatic waves washed through her, wiping out all the frenzied tension, sweeping her into a sweet nirvana made even sweeter as he climaxed and relaxed in her embrace.

It was done, she thought hazily, and there'd been no humiliation in it.

None at all.

Which made her feel a lot better about being his mistress.

Ethan hauled Daisy with him as he moved onto his side, keeping the intimate connection intact for as long as it would last. He revelled in the feeling of deep physical union with this woman, smiled ironically over the fact that she'd blown his mind again. His plan to have sex with her on his terms had been totally sabotaged. Not that he would change one bit of what they had just shared. Were still sharing, although the intensity level had eased—the lull of peace after the storm.

One thing was definitely settled. It had been well worth while helping her parents with their financial affairs. Having this with Daisy Donahue was a new benchmark in his sex life, one he couldn't imagine ever being surpassed. Of course, it could go down from here. In his experience, the highs were always at the beginning of a relationship. The best part was he'd have them all, since he had the guarantee of lots of time with her, as much time as he wanted.

He stroked her hair, content to lie quietly for a while, soak up the satisfying fact that their desire for each other *was* mutual. Not that he'd ever doubted it. Neither did he care any more why she had turned away from it before. They were together now.

A nasty little thought wormed its way into the bliss of the moment. Once the money came through for her parents and they actually had their hands on it, would Daisy still comply with the deal? What if she kissed him off and walked away, wagging her sexy bottom at him in scornful contempt for his belief in her word?

He hated being played.

And he'd hate her if she did it.

So that would be the end of any desire for her.

In the meantime, he was assured of this weekend of compliant togetherness and he'd enjoy it more if he put the trust issue out of his mind. It might not ever raise its ugly head. Daisy had a strong streak of integrity. And many other qualities he liked. He wanted to enjoy her. He *would* enjoy her.

Besides, if she did renege on the deal once his side of it had been finalised, he still came out the winner. She would have spent more time on his terms than he'd spent on her parents' financial problem.

He grinned to himself.

Before this night was out, he would definitely do everything he wanted to do with Daisy Donahue.

CHAPTER ELEVEN

THE morning after…

Daisy lay absolutely still, acutely conscious of the naked body her own naked body was intimately spooned against and the strong, masculine arm holding her there with its weight. Even asleep, Ethan was making his dominant presence felt, ensuring she remained with him in his bed.

What next? she wondered. How did he intend to fill in two whole days with her? Non-stop sex wasn't really possible, was it? Not that she had anything to complain about in that department. He had pleasured her so much and in so many different ways last night, he could go on doing it as long as he liked. Being his mistress in that sense was certainly no hardship. In fact, he was such a fantastic lover she could very well get addicted to having sex with him. Just go with the flow, and try not to get too carried away by it, she told herself. She was his toy until he got tired of her. That was the inevitable bottom line.

Probably the best attitude to adopt was to think of him as her toy, as well, not let herself take anything too seriously, enjoy everything she could while somehow building and maintaining a shield around her heart. She should try to gain some control of their relationship, at least not leave all the decisions to him.

Lying here, waiting for him to wake up and direct the play was too submissive. Surely her time was her own when he was out of action. There was no reason not to take some initiative herself, like getting out of bed and making herself coffee as she did every morning.

Very slowly and carefully she lifted Ethan's arm enough to slide out from under it. Having eased herself off the bed, she quickly headed for the guest suite where she had unpacked her bag. One look at her reflection in the mirrored doors of the built-in cupboards made an immediate visit to the bathroom mandatory. She hadn't cleaned her face of make-up last night, resulting in clownish eyes from smudged mascara, and her hair was a mess.

Daisy brushed her hair, fastened it in a top-knot, took a long, hot shower, tried not to think of Ethan's hands caressing her body as she soaped herself clean—half wondering if he would start that all over again when he did wake up—then gave herself a brisk towelling to erase the wickedly wanton tingling in her skin.

She was in the act of donning her silk kimono when the call of her name made her heart jump. Ethan's tone was not the rich, seductive purr of last night's satisfied lover. It was sharp, harsh, demanding. An apprehensive shiver ran down her spine. Was he angry at finding her gone from his bed?

Daisy's spirit of independence fiercely reasserted itself. He had not bought a slave and she wasn't going to be turned into one. She took a deep breath and stood her ground, calling back, 'I'm over here in the guest suite.'

She was tying the belt of her kimono when he barged into the bedroom, coming to an abrupt halt when he saw her. He was still stark naked and every taut muscle of his magnificent physique seemed pumped up with intimidating aggression. It was an act of will for Daisy not to freeze with fear on the spot.

The grim, fighting expression on his face slowly relaxed and the blaze of battle in his eyes dimmed as he took in the long, vivid gown she was wearing. 'The colours of Africa,' he said with a musing little smile. 'It suits you.'

Enormously relieved that the blast of tension had eased, Daisy held out her arms to show him the long drops of the sleeves. 'It's a kimono. I thought I'd be your geisha girl and make you tea.'

He threw back his head and laughed, a great peel of joyous laughter that rippled right through her heart, which should have been shielded but quite hopelessly wasn't. He strolled towards her, a huge grin on his face. 'Dinner, morning tea…you're full of surprises, Daisy. What next?'

He picked her up and twirled her around in sheer exuberance. Daisy felt like an aeroplane with her long sleeves flapping, her own spirits lifting sky-high. He was still grinning when he set her on her feet again. 'Make it coffee, not tea,' he happily instructed. 'Give me ten minutes to shower, shave and clean my teeth and I'll be down to cook you breakfast. Let me surprise you.'

He left a smile on her face—a ridiculously happy smile. She told herself it wasn't because she was stupidly in love with him. It was simply great to know he didn't expect her to be his slave. He was going to cook for her. Which probably wasn't so wonderful since he liked cooking. Nevertheless, Daisy felt much better about the situation.

Ethan was still in an ebullient mood when he breezed into the kitchen, carrying the Saturday *Morning Herald* which must have been delivered to the door. He couldn't have gone far to get it. He was only wearing the short black silk robe, which she'd found so disturbing before becoming intimately involved with the body beneath it. Daisy had no problem with looking *him* over now. It gave her a pleasurable sense of possession.

She had to remind herself he was not her man.

Ethan Cartwright was his own man.

But she didn't mind at all being his mistress when he dumped the newspaper on the kitchen bench, drew her into his embrace, cheerfully declared it was a beautiful morning and kissed her in a lovely, lingering sensual way that made her feel beautiful, even though she knew she wasn't.

'Now for breakfast!' he said, setting her aside to take command of the kitchen. 'You can sit on one of the stools on this side of the bench, drink your coffee and watch me work.'

'Okay. What are you going to surprise me with?'

The green eyes danced teasingly. 'The challenge is to serve you something that meets your *yummy* mark.'

He was yummy. As Daisy made herself comfortable on a stool, she decided to consider herself lucky to have this experience with him. The trick was in not hankering for the whole moon and stars package.

He raided the refrigerator for eggs, butter, tomatoes, bread, Spanish onions. Daisy admired his deft movements as he lined up more ingredients from the pantry…

Ethan Cartwright, very much in control of what he was doing.

Though there had been that frightening loss of cool when he'd woken up and found her gone from his bed. Had he thought she'd skipped out on the deal? He should have known she'd keep her word. Perhaps he had been scarred by other women who had taken him for a ride, using him for what he could give and not giving what he wanted back. Had something like that happened with his *ex*-fiancée—a recent serious relationship gone sour because of a lack of integrity?

He started cutting up the tomatoes and onions, shooting an oddly weighing glance at her. 'I've lined up a job interview for you if you want it, Daisy.'

A job? A real job? She hadn't managed to snag one interview for any of the positions she had applied for in the past two months. Either there were too many applications to wade through and hers was missed or her work résumé—minus her stint with Lynda Twiggley, which should have been the jewel in her crown but couldn't be mentioned due to the circumstances of her sacking—had not impressed enough.

'I'm desperate for one,' she cried. 'Please tell me about it.'

'I was chatting to one of my clients yesterday—he runs a publishing house—and he mentioned needing a good PR person for marketing, but he was dreading dealing with the response to advertising the position. Said it was a nightmare wading through the mountain of applications these days, trying to find the gold amongst the dross.'

Daisy grimaced at hearing the other side of the coin. Everything to do with the job market these days was difficult.

'So I told him about you,' Ethan ran on. 'Said you'd been behind the organisation of the Magic Millions Carnival earlier in the year. Told him I'd snaffled you to run a special project for me, coordinating and dealing with a diverse workforce, which you'd done without a hitch, and was about to move on. He more or less decided on the spot to interview you before advertising the job. You're to call him on Monday morning if you're interested.'

Just like that…on Ethan's personal recommendation, she'd zoomed straight to the top of the list. Daisy was too stunned to speak. Ethan looked enquiringly at her and she shook her head at the injustice of it all. 'It's not what you are. It's who you know,' slipped out of her mouth.

'Connections do cut through a lot of time-wasting,' he remarked. 'But this isn't a case of jobs for the boys. I'm not passing my client a lemon. I wouldn't do that. I'm confident you're capable of pulling off anything you set your mind to.'

She flushed with pleasure in his high opinion of her. 'Thank you, Ethan. And thank you for recommending me. I won't let you down.'

His mouth tilted in an ironic little smile. 'No. You're not into letting people down, are you, Daisy? Forgive me for doubting you, even for a moment.'

The moment when he'd thought she'd gone. 'You can count on me to keep my word, Ethan,' she quietly assured him.

'Yes. I believe I can,' he said, and this time his eyes twinkled with his smile. 'I'll give you all the job details after breakfast. I've written them down.'

She smiled back. 'Great! Thank you again.'

His smile stretched into a grin. 'And may I suggest

you don't wear brown to the interview. This is a guy, not a Lynda Twiggley. You'll be fronting for his publishing house. He'll want you to power-dress. Red is good. You look great in red.' His gaze dropped to her kimono. 'And orange and yellow and green.'

She laughed, a lovely bubble of joy dancing inside her. 'Okay. Not brown.' The future was definitely looking up for her, regardless of how and when this time with Ethan ended.

Breakfast was, indeed, yummy. Ethan cooked a tomato salsa with a spicy touch of Tabasco sauce, placed a poached egg in the middle of each serving and accompanied it with fingers of French toast. They shared the newspaper while they ate, which put Daisy in a very relaxed mood, no longer worrying about what they'd do for the rest of the weekend.

They played tennis. They swam and lazed around the pool. He beat her at Scrabble, right at the death, scoring eighty points with a seven-letter word which Daisy declared was grossly unfair since she'd led all the way. She asked him to teach her some of the board games he played with his friends, which he willingly did. It was fun. There was not one boring or unpleasant moment, probably because underlying everything was a highly acute sexual awareness of each other, a constantly buzzing excitement that was ready and eager to burst into arousal with a touch or a kiss.

After their swim.

After Scrabble.

During the movie they semi-watched after dinner.

When they retired for the night.

Daisy did not leave Ethan's bed on Sunday morning until they left it together, satisfied that the harmony they'd reached on Saturday was still a beautiful thing between them. It continued without a hitch until after lunch, when Ethan announced he would show her the apartment she was to move into for his convenience.

He didn't use those exact words, but the illusion of mutual lovers enjoying each other was jolted straight out of Daisy's mind by the reminder of the mistress deal. The apartment *was* for his convenience—no parents to consider, no one else sharing it with her except him when he wanted to.

'Where is it?' she asked, trying to sound interested instead of totally flattened by the reality of their relationship.

'At Pyrmont. It will be handy to your work if you get the job, with the publishing house situated in Market Street—just a walk across Pyrmont Bridge to the city centre.'

Handy for him, too, dropping in after his work in the city.

She forced a smile. 'Sounds good. Let's go and see it.'

He took her to an apartment complex which had direct harbour frontage at Pyrmont. It had a community gym and indoor swimming pool for the use of all residents. They rode an elevator up to the penthouse floor and he ushered her into an apartment, which had to be worth millions of dollars with its commanding view of the harbour and the great arched bridge that crossed it.

The living area—kitchen, dining and lounge—was incredibly spacious, all making the most of the view, as did the master suite. There were two other bedrooms, a second bathroom and a study. Every room was furnished and the decor was mostly black and cream which felt very masculine. Daisy didn't see any feminine touches anywhere. Even the kitchen seemed male with its black granite benches and stainless-steel fittings.

A billionaire bachelor pad, she thought, and asked, 'Is this where you lived before moving to Hunters Hill?'

'Yes. I haven't yet decided on whether to keep it or put it on the market' was his carefree reply.

Obviously he felt no urgent need to capitalise on what had to be a huge investment.

This was how the very wealthy lived, Daisy thought as she wandered over to the wall of glass in the living room and gazed down at the white wakes of the water traffic on the bright blue harbour. She would be sharing these heights with Ethan for a while, but she had to keep remembering she was an ordinary person who would have to return to an ordinary life when his interest shifted to someone else.

This apartment probably should be delighting her. She had never had such glamorous living quarters and she would have them all to herself except when Ethan visited. Yet she could not stop a black wave of depression from rolling through her soul. Her arms instinctively folded themselves across her chest, hugging in the dark sense of misery.

Her mind insisted she should be feeling good.

Ethan had given her parents what she had wanted for them.

He was giving her a new start with the top running for a good job and a lovely place to live until she became independent again.

He was a generous man, a fantastic lover.

It was stupid, stupid, stupid, for her heart to yearn for a different situation with him. This was what she had agreed to. This was where she was, and next year she would be down there with the ordinary people. Nothing was going to change that.

Ethan had strolled on to the kitchen. He'd placed a bottle of champagne and a dish of strawberries in the refrigerator on Thursday night, planning ahead to this move with Daisy, intending to take her to bed with him after she'd looked through the apartment. As he placed two flute glasses on the bench which separated the kitchen from the dining area, he checked that she was still engaged with the view.

She'd dressed in jeans for this trip out and he smiled at the sexy way they hugged her cute derrière. This weekend with Daisy had been better than he could ever have imagined. Not only was she great in bed, she was great company, as well. He had enjoyed every minute of being with her.

He wished she was staying on at Hunters Hill. He would miss not having her there. The idea of asking her to live with him flitted through his mind, but he instantly shied away from it. Involving himself in a de facto relationship left him vulnerable to being stripped of a lot of money, possibly even losing the house he now considered his home. No way was he about to leave himself open to massive plunder.

As it was, Daisy could possibly take this apartment from him if he let her live here without paying any rent, but he'd already decided to risk that outcome. She hadn't shown any bent for filching anything that didn't belong to her and had been absolutely meticulous about not taking money she hadn't earned. Given her willingness to stick to the deal this weekend, he believed she would keep to the letter of their agreement.

Integrity was a marvellous thing.

Especially in a woman.

Of course, he could be proved wrong, but right now he had Daisy Donahue locked into a relationship with him for the foreseeable future and he saw no darkness in that future with her.

Still smiling, he loaded the bottle of champagne and glasses into an ice bucket, grabbed the dish of strawberries, and carried the lot into the master suite. He had a few more hours with her before she'd have to go home to get ready for tomorrow's interview. Ethan intended to make the most of them.

Daisy's heart jumped at Ethan's touch as he slid his arms around her waist. She hadn't heard him come up behind her, the thick cream carpet muffling any sound of footsteps. He gently pulled her back against him, bending his head to brush her hair away from her ear with his cheek. 'Happy with the view?' he murmured, his warm breath tingling over her skin.

'Yes. Who wouldn't be?' she answered, making a conscious effort to relax and be happy with what she did have of him.

'You could move in tomorrow afternoon.'

So as to be ready for him tomorrow night…his convenient mistress.

Daisy clamped down on the bitter thought. She had nothing to be bitter about. Nothing!

'I should be able to do that,' she agreed. 'I'll have to square it with my parents first.'

'Say the friend you spent the weekend with has asked you to share an apartment in the city. It's the truth.'

True enough, she thought, and the move made sense

if she was offered the job at the publishing house. Her parents wouldn't quibble over it. They were happy, making plans for their future, and would be happy for her to do whatever she wanted.

And she wanted him.

There was no denying that truth.

She wanted him for as long as she could have him.

On a fierce wave of determination and desire, Daisy wheeled around in his embrace, flung her arms around his neck, and kissed him in a savage need to put everything else aside, to generate once again the intense, all-consuming passion where nothing else mattered.

Seize the day...

She would face whatever tomorrow brought when tomorrow came.

CHAPTER TWELVE

To Daisy's astonishment, delight and immense relief, she was given the PR job at the end of the interview—no waiting to hear and no waiting to start work, either. Her new boss remarked that since Ethan Cartwright was prepared to release her from his project and he, himself, needed her services immediately to set up a publicity tour for a new author, he'd like her to begin tomorrow. Even better, the salary being offered was more than she had ever earned before.

It made her wonder if Ethan had exaggerated her worth. Certainly his personal recommendation had worked wonders. Of course, it all fitted nicely into his plan for her to move into his apartment today, but it would suit her, too, which was readily understandable to her parents—a simple case of picking up her independent life again since their financial problems had been resolved. She had already told them she'd seen an affordable place at Pyrmont at the weekend and intended to take it.

It was up to her now to make a success of this new career, get it solidly established so there wouldn't be too big a hole in her world when her time with Ethan was over. Ever since she had lost her job with Lynda Twiggley, she had been inescapably dependent on him. The apartment was part of the deal, but at least he was no longer the only source of income for her. She would be able to strike out on her own whenever she had to. That was a good feeling.

There was more champagne that night to celebrate the beginning of her new career. Ethan was happy for her to be happy about it. Certainly he saw it as no threat to what he wanted with her. Even when she explained that a publicity tour would involve overnight trips to Melbourne and possibly other capital cities, he made no objection, seemingly taking it for granted she would not always be free when he was free.

He was definitely not a control freak.

And Daisy was hopelessly in love with him.

She looked forward to the evenings he spent with her during the week. Never on a Tuesday night because that was games night with his old friends, but most other days he dropped in at the apartment after work. They chatted over a relaxing drink, cooked dinner together, watched television, made love, after which he would always go home.

It made her wonder if that was some legal point with him—protection against any claim she might make on him in court when he wanted out of their relationship. She was living in his apartment, but they were not live-in lovers. They weren't a couple in public, either. Although he invited her to Hunters Hill on weekends, it was only ever the two of them there—no parties. He didn't take her out nor ask her to accompany him to any social events. Which all hammered home to Daisy that she was his private mistress and for anything more to develop between them was sheer pie in the sky.

Having resigned herself to taking each day as it came, she could hardly believe it when Ethan suddenly changed the parameters of their relationship. They were lying in bed one Sunday morning, languorously content not to move for a while.

'It's the Golden Slipper next Saturday,' he remarked, running gentle knuckles up and down the curve of her spine.

'What's the Golden Slipper?' she mumbled, nestling her head under his chin.

'Only the richest horse-race for two-year-olds in the world,' he answered dryly. 'The prize money is two million dollars and Mickey has Midas Magic lined up to win it.'

Ethan's horse—the one that had won the Magic Millions just before the terrible debacle with Lynda Twiggley, which had been immediately followed by Ethan's determined drive to have her in his life. 'I guess you want to go and see him race,' she said, thinking of spending the day shopping since he wouldn't want her with him in some celebrity marquee where his high-society friends would be gathered.

'I know you're not into gambling, Daisy, but I think you'd find it a fun day anyway. Fashions in the Field can be eye-popping stuff. There's the whole glamorous spectacle of the Golden Slipper ceremony, plus live entertainment—a guest star singing. Mickey has booked a table for ten in the Winning Post restaurant which has the best view of all the action. We can sit there, eating a gourmet lunch, drinking fine wines and watching it all unfold below us.'

Daisy could hardly believe her ears. She jerked up to look him in the eye. 'You want me to go with you? Be introduced to your friends?'

He frowned at her incredulous tone. 'They won't be all strangers to you. You saw Mickey at the Magic Millions and you know Charlie.'

'Yes, but I thought…' She struggled to find the right words. 'I thought you were keeping me in the background of your life. Not upfront.'

His frown deepened. 'You were worried about what your parents might think of our connection. I was waiting for a reasonable amount of time to pass in your current career for them to accept it was okay for me to pursue my personal interest in you.' He grimaced. 'There's bound to be publicity about us once we're seen together.'

Daisy was stunned again. She'd had it all wrong. Totally wrong! He'd been considering her, caring about her. In one huge galloping leap, the hope she had so sternly repressed emerged from its dark dungeon and bloomed in bright sunshine. She had just been elevated from secret mistress to public partner. Her heart skipped and jumped in wild joy. There was a chance this relationship could become a serious one if Ethan was happy for them to be seen as a couple.

'I have to go shopping. Today,' she announced, giving him a look of determined purpose. 'I won't have enough free time during the week to find something suitable, Ethan.'

'You could wear your red-and-white dress,' he suggested. 'You look great in that.'

'No, it won't do.' She shook her head emphatically. 'I saw what your crowd wore at the Magic Millions, remember? I need a fantastic outfit with a matching hat.' She grinned at him. 'Not brown.'

He laughed. 'Okay. I'll take you shopping, buy you whatever you want.'

'No, you won't!' she cried indignantly, bridling against being put in the bought mistress bracket again. 'I have to accept the free accommodation you give me because of the deal I agreed to, but I'm making good money now and I can afford to buy some fine feathers of my own, thank you.'

She flounced off the bed and stood up in a challenging stance, hands on hips. 'Those are *my* terms, Ethan.'

He rolled onto his side, propping himself up on his elbow, the green eyes regarding her with a glint of triumph, as though he had just won something. 'Then I'll just tag along, be your chauffeur, take you to lunch somewhere along the way.'

She couldn't argue with that. Her free time was exclusively his. Besides, having lunch with her out in public was more delightful proof that he didn't want her kept hidden away. Nevertheless… 'I'd prefer you not to be with me in the boutiques. It's much more fun for me to surprise you on the day.'

He smiled. 'I'll park myself in a coffee shop with the Sunday newspapers.'

Daisy smiled back, bubbling with joy inside. 'You'd better come and shower with me. We have to get moving. And I warn you this might be a marathon shopping trip. I'm not going to settle for anything less than spectacular.'

Pride insisted she look at least as good as anyone in his party—good enough to be accepted as Ethan's partner in everyone else's eyes. She wanted to make him feel proud to have her on his arm, make him feel she could be his partner in every sense. For the first time she thought it could be a real possibility. It wasn't about just having her in his bed. It was about pursuing his interest in her.

Ethan felt an exhilarating sense of triumphant satisfaction all week, leading up to the Golden Slipper Saturday. Daisy's response to being with him for the big horse-race proved beyond a doubt that his judgement of her character had not been astray. If she'd been into bartering sex for gain, she would have pounced on his offer to buy her clothes. And he was quite sure now she would walk out of his apartment at the end of the year—the deal done—without any thought of making a claim on it.

His cynical view of her resistance to having an affair with him—a form of manipulation to get him to solve her problems—no longer seemed feasible. There was nothing underhand about Daisy. She played everything straight down the line. Best of all, since the way had been cleared for her to have an open relationship with him, she seemed happy about it. Genuinely happy. Which meant he wasn't buying her submission to what he wanted of her any more.

He was tempted to remove all force from the situation, free her from the deal, but he liked having her in his apartment, liked having the security of knowing she was his to have. As it stood, she couldn't walk away from him, not without breaking her word, and Daisy wouldn't do that. He wanted more time with her. It was stupid to risk not having it.

Mickey called him at work on Friday. 'Just letting

you know Midas Magic had a great trial run on the track this morning,' he said, his voice brimming with cheerful confidence. 'And in case you're not already aware, Serena has attached herself to James Ellicott.'

James Ellicott… Ethan winced at one of his clients being sucked in by Serena. The man had made a fortune in advertising and had already been divorced twice, costing him a lot of money in settlements. He liked beautiful women and was apparently prepared to pay for them.

'They were both here at dawn watching his horse trial,' Mickey ran on. 'No doubt she'll be included in his party dining in the Winning Post restaurant tomorrow. Thought I'd better warn you.'

'Thanks, Mickey. No problem. I'm not the least bit troubled about Serena being with someone else.'

It was true. Though Mickey's news report had instantly incited the cynical thought that Serena was buttering up another billionaire for the kill. She was not a morning person. If James Ellicott married her, she wouldn't be accompanying him to dawn trials again. He would have to be satisfied with her gracing his arm in the winners' circle, which Serena would do beautifully.

Ethan suddenly realised that should Midas Magic win tomorrow, he and Daisy would be in the spotlight for the presentation of the Golden Slipper. She'd been delighted with her shopping trip. He hoped her outfit was spectacular enough to shut Serena's mouth because his ex-fiancée had no grace at all when it came to losing.

When he walked into the apartment the next morning, any worry that Daisy might be put down by *anyone* disappeared in a flash. She looked absolutely gorgeous. And elegant. And so sexy, desire instantly sizzled through him, making his tailor-made suit feel more snug than it should around the groin area.

Impossible to race her off to bed. It would mess up the image she had created and it was too marvellous to spoil. She twirled around in front of him, the calf-length skirt swirling in a froth of vivid colour. 'Like it?' she asked, her big chocolate-brown eyes sparkling with confidence in her fine feathers. 'It's called *neon butterfly*.'

The dress was a brilliant pink, the shiny silk patterned with white and purple and orange and bright green butterflies. Its low V neckline and the wide band from under her breasts to her waist emphasised her beautiful, womanly curves. Her long, dark brown hair was piled on top of her head, and curling from one ear over her crown was a stunning concoction of bright pink flowers and feathers.

'I'm dazzled,' he said, shaking his head in bemused appreciation. Gone was the brown sparrow. This butterfly would outshine every other woman at the Rosehill Gardens racetrack.

Her smile wavered. A flash of wary vulnerability took the sparkle from her eyes. 'Is that good or bad?'

He grinned, warmly assuring her, 'It's amazingly good,' as he walked forward to draw her into his embrace. 'I'll have to beat off Mickey from trying to steal you from me, because he'll definitely see you as the most beautiful fish in the sea today.'

She laughed, relief melting into pleasure. 'I just didn't want to let you down, Ethan.'

'You never let me down.' He kissed her forehead and smiled into her eyes. 'And that's something I really value, Daisy.'

'You haven't let me down, either,' she rushed out somewhat breathlessly, and there was a yearning look in her eyes—a look that did something weird to Ethan's heart. It was as if a hammer had smashed into the hard shell he'd kept around it since his disillusionment with Serena, and a gush of warmth made his chest swell with waves of emotion.

He wanted to look after this woman.

Protect her.

Give her everything she needed.

The instincts that had driven him to act as he had when he had first met her suddenly made perfect sense. The need to have her, to nail her into a relationship with him…it was because she was uniquely special in his experience…a woman he could trust, a woman he could love, a woman he could share his life with.

The look in her eyes told him she wanted to be convinced that could happen and the realisation hit him that all along she hadn't believed it was a possibility. Her determined avoidance, her resistance to an affair with him, her stunned surprise that he wanted her to appear in public with him…she simply hadn't believed a relationship with him would work, that it would always be limited to sex on his terms.

And that wasn't good enough for Daisy Donahue.

Nor should it be.

Today was a testing ground.

He must not let her down.

CHAPTER THIRTEEN

DAISY and Ethan arrived at Rosehill Gardens in a chauf-
feured limousine—no parking problem, no drunk-
driving problem. A crowd of people were milling
around the entrance gates, waiting to get in, although
showing no impatience about it. It was a bright sunny
day and everyone seemed to be in a festive mood—the
men mostly dressed in suits, the women favouring
cocktail dresses, with more of them wearing fascinators
than hats, which gave Daisy extra assurance that her
outfit had been a really good choice.

As Ethan escorted her towards a side gate with his
member's pass in hand—no queuing for him—quite a
few people turned to look at them. Ethan, of course,
was a strikingly handsome man, superbly attired in his
grey pin-stripe suit, white shirt and gold and grey silk
tie, but Daisy felt she really matched him today, as
well as she could.

'Hey, Daisy!'

The call of her name startled her and she stopped
dead as she spotted Carl Jamieson striding out from a
group of people, grinning at her as though he was delighted to claim acquaintance with her again. With un-

believably crass arrogance he ignored the fact she was with another man and focussed entirely on her.

Still grinning, he said, 'You look fabulous, Daisy. No more penny-pinching, huh?'

Daisy instantly stiffened with resentment. Her ex-boyfriend was proving once again he was a fine weather friend. 'I didn't know you were into horse-racing, Carl,' she said coldly.

'It's not usually my bag. I'm here with a bachelor party. One of the guys is getting married tomorrow.'

'Then I suggest you rejoin your party.'

His ego took umbrage at her blanket rejection and he shot a sneering look at Ethan. 'Got better fish to fry, have you?'

'Yes, she has,' Ethan replied with unruffled aplomb. 'And I suggest you take Daisy's advice and return to your party.'

Carl's chin jutted up belligerently, but something in Ethan's expression quickly changed his mind about challenging anything. 'Fine!' he snapped. 'Have fun!'

Ethan's arm tightened around hers as Carl turned his back on them. 'Let's move on,' he murmured.

Daisy forced her feet to fall into step with him. 'Sorry about that,' she mumbled. 'I didn't expect to run into him here.'

'Your ex-boyfriend?'

She winced. 'Yes.'

'I'm glad you didn't give him any encouragement,' he said dryly.

She lifted her gaze to his and found amusement twinkling in his green eyes. Her vexation with Carl broke into a giggle. 'Well, he was very rude, Ethan, breaking in on us like that.'

He smiled with devilish humour. 'And got his just deserts.'

Having regained her pleasure in the day, Daisy hugged his arm as they moved past the gate and strolled up the rose-bordered path to the pavilions overlooking the racetrack. She sniffed the scented air and felt a blissful joy in Ethan's company. He was so different from Carl—caring, considerate and best of all, a giving person. Although he did want what he wanted in return. Which was fair enough, Daisy decided.

He had also stood up to Lynda Twiggley on her behalf—not that she had appreciated it at the time—and she had no doubt he would have dealt comprehensively with Carl's rudeness if her ex-boyfriend had pushed it any further. He was definitely the kind of man she wanted at her side. If only it could last...

'I should probably mention that my ex-fiancée will be here today, too,' he suddenly drawled.

All the lovely warmth she had been feeling was plunged into ice.

He had never spoken of his ex-fiancée.

Daisy only knew of her through Charlie Hollier.

Was this why Ethan had invited her to the Golden Slipper, to show his former love he was happily involved with another woman? Off with the old, on with the new?

'I broke up with her last year,' he said matter-of-factly. 'I wouldn't put it past her to be rude to you on the sly. If that happens, Daisy, it's because she didn't get what she wanted. Okay?'

She glanced up at him, needing more information than that to ease her inner tension. 'Why did you break up with her?'

His mouth took on a cynical twist. 'I found out the money was more important than the man to her. She's with James Ellicott now. I don't think he cares why as long as he has her.'

She knew of James Ellicott. The flamboyant billionaire was quite ugly compared to Ethan, his big physique made bigger by a beer belly, his sandy hair thinning on top and a large nose dominating his face. Regardless of his looks, he had acquired a beauty queen and a famous model as wives in the past.

'Is your ex-fiancée very beautiful?' she asked.

'On the outside, yes. And she knows how to trade it. I was completely fooled for a while. I'm glad the wool was pulled off my eyes before I married her. Believe me, that relationship is stone-cold as far as I'm concerned.'

What she had with Ethan was still running hot, but… 'I traded myself for money, too,' she blurted out, all her insides squirming horribly at that undeniable truth. She had no chance of a really solid relationship with Ethan. None at all.

He halted, turning to her, gently cupping her cheek and chin with his free hand, his gaze burning into hers with absolute conviction. 'Not for yourself, Daisy,' he said quietly. 'Your character is so far removed from Serena's, it's like night and day.' He lightly pinched her cheek and smiled. 'Now smile back at me because we're going to have a happy day together.'

She did smile back, intensely relieved that he didn't see her as similar to Serena, despite their deal, which was still in force. It actually seemed he was dismissing it as of no account at all.

'That's my girl,' he said warmly, and the possessive note in his voice sent hope soaring through her heart again, making Daisy determined to be happy, no matter what happened throughout the course of the day.

Ethan gave her a tour of the amenities provided for race-goers at Rosehill Gardens—every taste and class-level catered for. There was a buzz of excitement every-where, people partying, having fun. Some groups were wearing mad clothes and hats, adding to the colour of the scene. Many of the young women were wearing in-credibly high-heeled shoes and Daisy wondered how their feet would fare by the end of the day. She was glad that her strappy gold sandals were not so high and easily walkable in because they were doing a lot of walking.

Eventually they met up with Ethan's friends in the Champagne Bar. Charlie Hollier did a double-take when he saw her. 'Wow, Daisy! That's some transformation!'

She laughed. 'Well, I couldn't come to the Golden Slipper in jeans, Charlie.'

'Oh, I don't know,' Ethan drawled. 'You always looked sensational in jeans, too.'

'Okay, you guys,' one of the women chided good-humouredly. 'You can stop drooling and start introduc-tions.'

Daisy, glowing from the compliments from both men, did her best to memorise the new names. Mickey Bourke fetched glasses of champagne for them and it was his girlfriend, Olivia, who raised the background question, her curiosity piqued by the men's comments.

'So where are you from, Daisy, and how did you and Ethan meet?'

'I can tell you that,' Mickey cut in archly. 'Daisy was doing PR at the Magic Millions back in January and Ethan was so taken by her he almost carried her off. Had to stop him from making a fool of himself.'

'January!' one of the other women, Allyson, exclaimed. 'But we haven't seen Ethan with Daisy until now!'

'Most difficult woman I've ever met,' Ethan rolled out in a tone of mock exasperation. 'First up she didn't like me. Didn't want anything to do with me. On top of that, I interfered between her and her boss and caused her to lose her job, which made me not only unlikeable but a total villain, as well.'

He threw up his hands and they all laughed at Ethan Cartwright in such a dilemma.

'So then I had to turn myself into a hero and give her a job until she found another suitable PR position,' he continued.

'Supervising the renovations of his house,' Charlie chimed in. 'And let me tell you she was a stickler for detail. Didn't let the tradesmen slip up on anything. They didn't need any supervision from me until after Daisy left.'

'But did she look kindly on me for this rescue act?' Ethan queried theatrically. 'As far as Daisy was concerned I was just another boss. I remember very clearly her first day at the house when I was doing my best to charm her. She looked sternly at me and laid down the law—*the master of the house does not dance with the staff.*' He rolled his eyes and pulled a sad grimace. 'No dancing with Daisy.'

Everyone was vastly amused by his show of frustration.

'This has to be a first for you, Ethan, having your interest in a woman turned down,' one of his old friends from Riverview, Dave Marriot, commented, grinning widely. 'Now you know what it's like not to be an instant winner.'

'And good for you, Daisy, keeping him on toast,' his wife, Shannon, said approvingly. 'Guys like Ethan get used to women falling in their laps.'

'I didn't deliberately keep him on toast,' Daisy quickly slid in. 'It just took me a while to realise he wasn't so insufferably arrogant, not caring about anything but what he wanted.' She smiled up at him. 'I found myself liking him for lots of reasons. He didn't even mind when I was beating him at tennis.'

'You beat Ethan at tennis?' Mickey crowed.

She laughed. 'No, he won in the end. He made the mistake of going easy on me early on and the set went to a tie-breaker.'

'I give you all fair warning,' Ethan said. 'The next tennis party I hold, Daisy and I are going to wipe everyone else off the court.'

'Was that how you finally won her over, being a good sport?' Olivia asked, looking thoroughly entertained by the story.

'No. I was still the boss and Daisy has principles with a capital *P*.' He sighed over her recalcitrant attitude, making everyone laugh again before he delivered the punchline. 'I had to wait until she moved on to a new PR position at a publishing house. Only then did she consider it appropriate to let me into her personal life. Which is why you haven't seen her with me before today.' He tossed off a helpless gesture. 'All her doing, not mine. As I said, a terribly difficult woman.'

It was a very clever spin on the real story and Daisy was deeply grateful that it made their relationship so readily acceptable by his friends. Who she was didn't matter. They simply loved the idea of Ethan having to chase her for months to win what he wanted, which clearly made her quite marvellous in their eyes.

And made Ethan even more marvellous in hers.

There'd been no ego in that story. He had deliberately played her up and played himself down and she loved him all the more for it. The tension she'd been feeling about meeting his friends had been completely dissipated, and the foundation set for a delightfully happy day together.

They moved on to the Winning Post restaurant, the starched white linen tablecloths and classy settings adding their special touches to it. The floor was constructed in tiers, giving all the diners, wherever they sat, a clear view of the action out at the racetrack. For an even closer look at every entire race, a television set was attached to each table.

Directly below them was the parade ring where the horses circled around before moving out to the starting gates. At one end of that was the stage where presentations of prizes were made and other entertainment took place. Just beyond this area was the finishing line for each race. All the fences were lined with roses in full bloom. It was a great view with much to see and enjoy.

They had just sat down when they saw a helicopter coming in to land in the middle of the field. 'James Ellicott making his usual entrance,' Mickey remarked, shooting a quizzical look at Ethan who shrugged and openly said, 'No problem. Daisy knows about Serena.'

'And may I say I much prefer your current partner,' Charlie said, grinning at Daisy. 'I'm far more comfortable with down-to-earth than airs and graces any day.'

'Yes, Serena does tend to put it on,' Allyson commented with a warning look. 'Don't let her patronise you if she stops at this table to say hello.'

'Just remember, you've got Ethan. She hasn't,' David pointed out.

'And I bet James Ellicott is second prize in her book, so watch out, Daisy. Serena can be a bitch when she doesn't get her own way,' Shannon put in.

It amazed and warmed her that they were all on her side. While it might be out of loyalty to and support for Ethan, they did seem to genuinely like her.

The first course of their gourmet lunch was served, a delicious chicken and pistachio nut terrine, accompanied by a glass of a very good Chardonnay. Daisy relaxed and enjoyed herself. The mood of the party was highly convivial and Ethan was looking after her as though she really was a prize he'd won.

They had just started their entrée—a smoked salmon parcel containing crab and avocado and tomato—when James Ellicott led his party into the restaurant, making a somewhat boisterous entrance. He descended on their table, loudly but good-humouredly declaring, 'I see the opposition is here already. Got to say Mickey's got Midas Magic running well, Ethan, but I'm betting on my horse for The Slipper.'

'Each to their own, James,' Ethan answered equably, standing up to shake hands with the man, who had a stunningly beautiful blonde in tow—skin like porcelain, cornflower blue eyes, an hour-glass figure poured into a high-fashion black-and-white suit with a matching hat that only an amazingly creative milliner could have made.

'Who's your little filly?' the big man demanded, eyeing Daisy with interest. 'Haven't seen her around before.'

'Daisy, may I introduce James Ellicott and Serena Gordon. Daisy Donahue.'

'What a quaint name!' Serena drawled, icy blue eyes sizing Daisy up as she stood to acknowledge the introductions.

'I think it's a great name, full of sparkly sunshine,' Ethan quickly slid in, smiling his approval of it.

It probably stopped his ex-fiancée from saying it was usually attached to a cow.

'Hello to both of you,' Daisy said brightly, shaking James's offered hand.

'A pleasure to meet you, Daisy Donahue,' he replied, as though relishing the roll of her name off his tongue, twinkling hazel eyes flirting with her. The man was definitely a womaniser with a big personality to go with his even bigger pockets.

'I see you're wearing Liz Davenport,' Serena remarked, naming the designer who'd created *neon butterfly*.

'Yes,' Daisy answered in surprise, not being so familiar with the fashion scene that she could actually recognise individual styles.

'She seems to have gone all gaudy this year.'

Daisy smiled to take the sting out of the snipe. 'I guess, with your colouring, you don't wear bright colours well.'

'Each to their own,' she said, giving Ethan a mocking look as she parroted his words. 'I much prefer European designers. James bought this Christian Dior suit for me in Paris.'

'How lovely for you!' Daisy said sweetly. 'I hope your outfit gives you as much pleasure wearing it as I'm having wearing mine.'

She sniffed haughtily and patted James's arm. 'Let's move on to our table, darling. I'm dying of hunger.'

'Got to feed the beauty and the beast,' he said jokingly, grinning at Ethan. 'Good luck with Midas Magic!'

'Good luck with your choice, too,' Ethan replied.

They moved on.

As she and Ethan resumed their seats at the table, Shannon raised a hand and said admiringly, 'Daisy, I salute you. That was a brilliant piece of sticking it right back at Serena.'

'Believe me, give Daisy a challenge and she rises to it every time,' Ethan declared, making them all laugh again at how challenging she had been to him.

Daisy was awash with pleasure. Ethan was proud of her. And he'd said so many complimentary things about her, leaving his friends in no doubt he held her in high regard, she was beginning to believe anything was possible between them, no limits at all on their relationship.

The races were watched and commented upon between the many courses of their lunch. Mickey had to leave the party when two other horses he'd trained were running. He returned each time in a celebratory mood after the horses had performed well, one coming second, the other third.

'Waiting for the big one,' he told Ethan with ebullient confidence.

The big one was preceded by an amazing ceremony. A helicopter hovered over the field beyond the finishing line as a man carrying a box descended on a rope to a podium which had been set up over there. A string of models wearing gold catsuits moved out across the racetrack, forming a line between the podium and the stage in the parade ring. The man unlocked the box to reveal what actually was a golden slipper. He presented it to the model closest to him, who passed it to the next, and so on down the line to the stage while an operatic tenor sang 'Nessun dorma'.

'Time for us to go,' Ethan said, taking Daisy's hand as he rose from his chair.

'Go where?' she asked. Mickey had already left the table to ensure everything was right for Midas Magic.

'To one of the owner's boxes beside the stage. We have to be on hand for the presentation if Midas Magic wins.'

As she leapt up to accompany him she saw that James Ellicott and Serena Gordon had already vacated their table. It only took a few minutes via a long elevator to arrive at the parade ring. The master of ceremonies was still introducing the jockeys who were to ride and photographers were everywhere, taking shots of the scene. A formal usher opened the gate for Ethan and Daisy to enter the fenced-off area and Ethan escorted her to the only empty box left—the rest of them already occupied by groups of people.

'Most of the horses are owned by syndicates,' Ethan explained. 'Mickey talked me into buying Midas Magic outright so we're on our own here, Daisy.'

Together, she thought happily.

They didn't have long to wait for the big race. They watched it on the huge television screen set up for the crowd and Daisy found herself sharing Ethan's excitement as Midas Magic shot to the front at the turn and sped away from the rest of the field, winning by seven lengths as though he was in a league of his own.

'What did you feed that horse, Ethan?' James Ellicott yelled out from his box.

'It's all in his genes,' he yelled back. 'You should listen to Mickey about bloodlines, James.'

Daisy couldn't help grinning at the vexed look on Serena Gordon's face. She felt like a huge winner today.

Ethan took her up on the stage with him for the presentation. He made a charming speech, giving all credit to his friend for the win, calling Mickey a brilliant trainer, then smiling at Daisy while saying Midas Magic had brought some magic into his life and he hoped it would last for a long, long time.

Some magic…her?

Daisy tried to caution herself not to read too much into everything Ethan said today. She was riding such a dizzying high, it was difficult to grasp any down-to-earth common sense. Nevertheless, she did manage to remind herself that when Ethan set out to do something, he carried it through, covering every detail. He was determined on having a happy day which meant giving her one, too. Midas Magic winning was icing on the cake—two million dollars' worth of icing! He was probably so happy, wonderful words were simply spilling off his tongue.

And continued to do so.

On their way back to their party in the Winning Post, they were accosted by Lynda Twiggley. 'Ethan!' she cried, pouncing on his arm, her eyes glittering with gambling triumph. 'What a fabulous win! Congratulations! I bet on Midas Magic again.'

'Splendid!' he tossed at her.

She gave Daisy a saccharine smile. 'And *you've* certainly come up in the world, Dee-Dee.'

Ethan pointedly picked her hand off his arm, saying in a cutting tone, 'Ms Twiggley, my partner's name is Daisy Donahue, who, I might add, is well worth knowing. A loss to you. A win to me. Have a good day!'

He swept Daisy off, leaving Lynda Twiggley's mouth agape. It was marvellous! Bubbles of joy inside Daisy burst into giggles as they rode the elevator up to the restaurant.

'What?' Ethan asked.

She sucked in a sobering breath, but her eyes were still dancing with laughter as she looked up at him. 'I did hate being called Dee-Dee.'

'Insufferable woman! I hated how she treated you. I was right to rescue you from her, Daisy.'

'Yes, you were,' she had to agree. Despite all her heartache over the past few months, she was in a far better position at the publishing house and whatever happened with Ethan, she was happy to have had him in her life.

Ethan felt intensely gratified by this admission from Daisy. She had been at war with him for so long, holding out against his siege, only giving in under force. To have her freely concede that he had been right to push for where they were now really did make him a winner.

There was not the slightest bit of tension coming from her for the rest of the day. She was completely relaxed with his friends, showed open affection towards him, delighted him with her attitude towards everything, and incited a burning build-up of desire which took all his willpower to keep under restraint until he had her to himself again.

The moment the door of the apartment was closed behind them, she was in his embrace and kissing him back as feverishly as he kissed her. They were on fire together, couldn't have enough of each other, and she discarded her clothes as urgently as he discarded his, leaping onto the bed, welcoming him with open arms, her legs winding around him in fierce possession. The sex was fast and incredibly intense, mounting swiftly to an explosive climax that was totally out of his control but he didn't care. She shared it with him and she was all his…all his…

Until the telephone rang.

CHAPTER FOURTEEN

DAISY automatically reached out and picked up the telephone receiver from the bedside table, not even wondering who was calling, her mind still floating from the pleasure of the deeply intimate connection with Ethan. It was a jolt to hear her mother's voice.

'Oh, good! You're home! I thought you might still be out partying.'

'Partying?' Daisy repeated, trying to get her wits together. She sat bolt upright and shot Ethan a warning look, putting a silencing finger on her lips.

'We saw you on television, standing right next to Ethan Cartwright when he was presented with the Golden Slipper. It was such a surprise. We couldn't believe our eyes. You didn't tell us you were going out with him.'

The chiding tone caused Daisy's heart to skitter all around her chest. She took a deep breath to shoot some oxygen into her brain, knowing she needed an explanation that sounded reasonable. 'Well, Mum, it was our first date and I didn't know what to expect. I wasn't sure. I mean he's such a high-powered person, I felt nervous about going out with him, fitting in with his friends. It might have ended up awful, so I didn't want to tell you about it. But I actually had a wonderful time. It was a marvellous day.'

'Your first date.' Her mother sounded pleased. 'You looked beautiful, dear. Such a gorgeous dress and head-piece. Did you buy it especially?'

'Yes. I splurged, but the outfit made me feel good so it was well worth the money. Lucky I have such a highly paid job now.'

'And it's lovely that you're spending your money on yourself instead of on us.'

'I didn't mind that, Mum.'

'Well, thank heaven it's behind us. Or I should say thank Ethan Cartwright for his good advice. When we saw you together on the television, your father wasn't as surprised as I was. He thought the man must have been sweet on you all along to have offered his help with our financial problems. Will you be seeing him again, dear?'

'Yes. He's invited me to a tennis party at his house.'

'No need for you to be nervous about that,' her mother said confidently. 'You're a better player than most people.'

'I'm over my nerves now, Mum. I'll be fine.'

'I was thinking… Easter is coming up next week. The whole family will be here as usual. Why not invite Ethan to come to Sunday lunch?'

A vision of her family swarming around him, prob-ably assuming things about their relationship they shouldn't assume and making stomach-squirming com-ments, played havoc with the nerves she had just de-clared in fine condition.

'I think it's too soon for that,' she said, inwardly recoiling from any move that might bring rejection and the crushing of a dream that she hoped might come true, given enough solid time together.

'It would be a nice way of showing our appreciation for what he's done for us,' her mother pressed.

'Mum, it was business,' Daisy said emphatically. 'Ethan would have been rewarded for it, taking a commission on the deal.' Her cheeks burned. She couldn't look at him.

'But that's so impersonal, Daisy,' her mother argued. 'And what he did was personal. It was because he was pleased with you. You told us so yourself. And it's obvious he's still pleased with you. Ask him if he'd like to come.'

Daisy gritted her teeth and thought hard. 'He probably has family of his own to go to at Easter.'

'Well, if he has, he has. There's no harm in extending an invitation.'

'Okay. I'll let you know.' Please, God, let her stop now, Daisy prayed.

She didn't.

'You'll be coming home anyway, won't you, dear? We haven't seen you since you took up your new job.'

Her free time was exclusively Ethan's. That was the deal. But surely he'd understand she had to attend the family get-together at Easter. 'Yes, I'll be there,' she answered unequivocally, not wanting to make some excuse unless she was forced to.

'It will be such a happy day,' her mother rattled on. 'Ken and Kevin are both employed again. Your father has paid off Keith's business debts, and we can now afford to send Violet's boy to a special school for autistic children.'

'That's great!'

It really was—alleviating a lot of stress in her sister's

life. Money was not the root of all evil, Daisy thought. It could be a huge blessing.

'Well, I'll let you go, dear, but do ask Ethan if he'd like to join us for Easter Sunday. He'll be most welcome. Such a handsome man, too,' she added in a tone overflowing with benevolence, causing Daisy to fly into a panic.

'Mum, don't get ideas. This was a first date, remember. It doesn't *mean* anything.'

'Of course it does, Daisy. It means that he likes you and you like him. Now don't do anything to spoil it, dear. I thought you looked perfect together. Bye now.'

Daisy fumbled the receiver's return to its cradle, dropped back down on the pillow and closed her eyes. Tight. To shut out the dreadful embarrassment of knowing Ethan had overheard that conversation and had undoubtedly pieced together her mother's side of it.

She felt him shift onto his side, prop himself up to examine the expression on her face, felt his eyes probing under her skin. A featherlight finger teased one corner of her mouth. 'It doesn't *mean* anything?'

For some reason his repetition of those words hurt unbearably. She opened her eyes and attacked with defensive ferocity. 'You know perfectly well why I'm here with you, Ethan. Just because you've taken me out of your closet hasn't changed the deal, has it?'

He frowned. 'Weren't you happy with me today?'

'That's not the point! My parents saw the presentation of The Golden Slipper on TV, saw us together, and my mother has leapt to the rosy conclusion that we're a match made in heaven.'

His mouth quirked in amusement. 'Maybe we are.'

'Don't make fun of it!' she cried, hope giving her

heart a painful kick. 'I have to deal with this now. My family always get together at my parents' home at Easter. They'll be full of questions about you and…' Her eyes pleaded to be let off his hook. 'I know you demanded all my free time, but I'll be breaking our family tradition if I'm not there with them.'

'No problem.' His eyes glinted with determined purpose. 'I'll go with you.'

She stared at him, her stomach curdling at the thought of what he'd be walking into. 'I'm only asking for one day with my family, Ethan. Not even one full day. Lunch on Easter Sunday will be enough.'

'Fine!' he said. 'We'll roll up for lunch on Easter Sunday.'

Daisy closed her eyes again as she tried to swallow the sickening surge of panic. There was no moving him. He was bent on having his own way, relentlessly ruthless about getting it.

'Your mother did invite me, didn't she?' he said without any doubt in his voice.

'Yes,' she bit out between gritted teeth.

'Then tell her I accept.'

Daisy summoned up one last effort to change his mind, shooting him a begging look. 'We're a big family, Ethan. And because I've never brought anyone into it, they'll pepper you with questions and size you up like you wouldn't believe.'

She had invited Carl when she'd believed in their love for each other, but he had always found some pressing reason not to be available when she'd wanted him to accompany her. From the arguments preceding their break-up, she'd realised he resented her family and the hold it had on her, taking her away from what he wanted to do. If Ethan also resented their claim on her...

'It won't worry me, Daisy,' he said, obviously not caring about being put in a hot seat. 'I'm curious about them, too. I'll enjoy meeting such a close-knit family. I haven't had one myself.'

She heaved a resigned sigh. He was resolved on accompanying her, no matter what. She could only hope he did enjoy himself and somehow, miraculously, feel he could become a part of her family because there was no long-term future with him if he couldn't.

The week slipped by all too quickly.

Daisy's emotions were worn ragged, fretting over how her family would receive Ethan and vice versa.

He peppered her with questions about them, memorising all the names and connecting the children to the right parents, doing his homework before making an entrance. Applying good business practice, Daisy thought, but meeting a diverse group of people whose life experiences were nothing like his was much more complex than sitting down with a bunch of clients with similar interests—namely big money and what to do with it. She remembered how she'd hated him for being what he was—obscenely rich, stunningly handsome and sinfully sexy. Her brothers and sister could feel the same way.

It did alleviate a little of her inner stress when he showed a particular interest in Joshua, Violet's autistic son. She explained that he didn't seem to relate to people at all. It was as though he was locked into a world of his own and he was obsessed with numbers, always counting everything. It was important to simply accept this, not treat him as odd, and Ethan assured her he understood.

But he didn't understand what he was walking into. She had to stop him from buying a huge basket of chocolate Easter bunnies and eggs for the children. Their parents, who couldn't afford such expensive luxuries, might resent such largesse, although she couldn't bring herself to tell him so, saying only she'd be taking a bag of little Easter eggs to be hidden in the garden for the treasure hunt, and too much was too much. It would be enough if he gave her mother a box of chocolates as a thank-you gift.

The family day loomed as a nightmare.

She had no happy dreams about it at all.

In fact, she was fairly certain it would end the dream she had been nursing.

She and Ethan came from different worlds which were too far apart to bridge the gap. Common sense had told her that this was an ill-fated attraction, leading only to bed while lust was running hot. She should have stayed in the closet for the rest of this year—deal done and free to run. That wouldn't have raised any family problems and she wouldn't be feeling so horribly torn, wanting the impossible.

Ethan was acutely aware of Daisy's tension over this coming visit with her family. He gradually came to realise she didn't believe he could fit into her world. Proving to her that she could fit into his only resolved half the problem that had made her keep him at a distance until he'd forced her into a relationship with him.

She hadn't come into it feeling it was right for her. She'd done it for her family. That close-knit unit meant more to her than anything else and Ethan was beginning to sense he had to win acceptance and liking from every one of them to free Daisy of her misgivings about their connection.

This was a completely foreign situation to him. He'd been more or less detached from his parents since boyhood. While he was quite fond of both of them, they played absolutely no part in his relationships with other people. That was his personal business, nothing to do with them. He didn't seek their approval. They never showed disapproval. The decisions were his. He was the one who had to live with them. That had been drummed into him for as long as he could remember.

This definitely was not the case with Daisy. How he reacted to her family and how they responded to him was obviously a huge issue in her mind. He'd met her father and liked him, but money had been the only agenda at those meetings, not his daughter.

All he knew for certain was he had another battle on his hands.

And Daisy was worth fighting for.

CHAPTER FIFTEEN

'MY BROTHERS always wear jeans,' Daisy told Ethan before he dressed on Sunday morning.

He obligingly took the hint and dressed in jeans.

'It's better if we go in my car,' she said as they were about to leave.

The green eyes turned hard and resolute. 'There's no hiding who I am, Daisy.'

True, but he didn't have to rub their noses in his wealth with a flash BMW. She returned a challenging look. 'This is a first meeting. Do you want my family to see you or your car?'

It was a major test, and to Daisy's intense relief, Ethan acknowledged her point. 'Okay, we'll go in yours.' His mouth quirked in wry appeal. 'Will that help you relax?'

She heaved a sigh to loosen up the tightness in her chest and managed a wobbly smile. 'I can't help feeling a bit anxious. I want them to like you.'

He smiled back, taking her hand and squeezing it. 'I want that, too.'

It lifted some of the burden from her heart. As she drove them both to Ryde, she kept telling herself Ethan had shown himself master of any situation and he would handle this one as well as he'd handled the barbecue with the tradesmen. However, that wasn't really the problem. If their relationship was to have any chance of a long future, this visit would be the first of many, not a single occasion that could be easily negotiated. The big question was whether he would want to repeat the experience or prefer to back off from it.

She parked her car in the street adjacent to the one where her parents lived. 'Which house?' Ethan asked, eyeing the nearby residences.

They were all ordinary brick houses, as was her parents', their architecture very basic. Nevertheless, it was a good, friendly neighbourhood, neat, tidy, gardens well tended, and Daisy was not about to apologise for its lack of class. This was where she came from and where she would come back to if Ethan couldn't accept it.

'Not here,' she answered. 'Around the corner. Our house is in a cul-de-sac and all the children will be out playing street cricket. I don't want the car to be in their way. It's not far to walk.'

'Street cricket?' Ethan looked bemused.

'It's a family tradition. Every Easter Sunday morning.' She nodded to her brothers who'd spotted her car and were waving at them. 'That's Ken and Kevin standing on the corner, watching out for any incoming traffic and fielding any long balls anyone hits.'

'Sounds like fun. Can I join in?'

'If you want to. Though you'll need to meet everyone first. Mum and Violet and my sisters-in-law will be in the kitchen preparing lunch.'

They alighted from the car and Daisy watched her

brothers eyeing Ethan over as they walked up to meet them. They were older than him, in their forties, and they were both grinning as though they were happy to see their baby sister with a man in tow. They made the introductions easy, warmly welcoming Ethan and calling out to the children to say 'Hi!' to their aunt Daisy and her friend. The game was briefly interrupted for yelled greetings and clamours for Ethan to play with them after he'd said hello to Nan and Pop.

There was no awkward hitch in any of the introductions. Ethan impressed everyone with already knowing their names and enough about them to strike up a friendly conversation. When her father led him out of the kitchen to join the street game, her mother gave Daisy a big hug, declaring him a lovely man.

'He is a bit much, though,' Violet commented with a worried look. 'What I mean is…he must be used to women falling all over him and getting his own way. Be careful about giving him your heart, Daisy. He might not be good husband material.'

'That was part of why I was reluctant to become involved with him,' she confided, understanding precisely what her sister meant. 'But the more I've come to know him, the more I like him, Violet. Not for his wealth or his good looks. They were stumbling blocks to me, too. I don't know where this relationship is going. I just like being with him. Okay?'

'Okay.' She smiled and raised her hand. 'Fingers crossed that it works out fine for you. Now tell us more about him.'

Daisy carefully chose to give what she thought was sympathetic information, concentrating on Ethan's family background—parents wrapped up in their academic careers, how he learned to love cooking from his grandmother, being sent to boarding school, his pleasure in games. It seemed to satisfy the general curiosity and gave a more rounded view of the person he was.

Her mother was roasting the traditional leg of pork with all the trimmings. The men had already set up a long trestle table in the family room with the twenty-four chairs needed to seat everyone, and as the women chatted, they did all the settings with colourful Easter motif serviettes and bon-bons. The centrepiece was a large round white chocolate mud-cake with a hole in the middle which was filled in and piled high with brightly wrapped miniature Easter eggs. They mixed a fruit punch for the children and put out wineglasses for the adults. It all looked wonderfully festive and Daisy hoped Ethan would enjoy what was always a rowdy luncheon with her family.

She slipped out to the back garden and hid her Easter eggs for the treasure hunt before the children trooped inside from the street. When everything was done and ready they called everyone in to clean up and sit down, which they did in high good humour. From comments flying around, Ethan had endeared himself to the children by hitting lollipop catches when he was batting, and the easiest to hit balls when he was bowling. Masterly control, Daisy thought, and was pleased he'd applied it to make the game more fun.

She actually started to relax over lunch. Ethan happily joined in the many topics of conversation raised, though he listened more than he talked. He complimented her mother on the pork crackling—the best he'd ever eaten. He laughed at her brothers' jokes. He really seemed to be having a good time.

After the cake had been served and eaten, the children were allowed to leave the table and go on the treasure hunt. They leapt from their chairs excitedly, eager to add to their hoard of chocolate—all except Joshua, who remained seated, counting and recounting his share of eggs from the cake. Violet left her seat to coax him into joining the others. He ignored her efforts and when she took him by the hand, he lashed out, hitting her arm to leave him alone, then flying into a major tantrum, screaming and throwing a flurry of punches at her.

They were all used to this kind of sudden eruption from him, but Violet was upset and embarrassed that it was happening in front of Ethan, breaking into tears and throwing them a helpless look of despair at her inability to control her autistic son. Her husband, Barry, rushed to her side, swooped on Joshua, lifted him up to his shoulder and carried him out of the room.

'I'm sorry…sorry,' Violet cried, covering her face with her hands.

Her mother enveloped her in a hug, patting her back and speaking soothingly, 'Don't take on so, dear. We all understand.'

'It's spoiled the day for Daisy,' she wailed.

'No, it hasn't,' Daisy insisted, going to her sister to add her comfort. If Ethan was put off by a child with a condition that sometimes defied control, then so be it. No family was perfect, but it was a poor family that didn't give each other support when it was needed.

To her astonishment, Ethan joined her, appealing to her sister in a gentle voice. 'Would you mind if I tried something that might interest Joshua, Violet, calm him down?'

'Oh, dear God, what?' she cried.

He whipped what looked like a slim black notebook from his shirt pocket. 'Look! It's a Nintendo brain-trainer. Daisy told me Joshua was fascinated by numbers. I can bring up a program that might catch his attention. How about you take me to him and we can give it a go?'

Violet shook her head at him in wonderment. Daisy, too, was amazed at his initiative. Her mother took charge. 'Go on, Violet. Give Ethan a chance of focussing Joshua's interest on something.'

'All right,' she answered dazedly, and led him off to the bedroom wing.

Daisy and her mother started clearing the table, needing to do something. The rest of the adults left their chairs to help.

'You've got a good guy there, Daisy,' Ken commented approvingly.

'He was great with the other kids, too,' Kevin remarked.

She flushed with pleasure in their liking of Ethan, though she felt constrained to warn them it might not be a serious relationship. 'We haven't been together long,' she started.

'You don't have to be to know you've found someone special,' her mother slid in with an arch look.

'Yes, I wouldn't be letting him go in a hurry, Daisy,' Keith's wife tagged on.

'Rope him in and nail him down,' Keith advised with a grin.

They all laughed, though Daisy couldn't help thinking they were missing the point. There was no question that Ethan was special. The problem was whether she was special enough for him. He was certainly making an extraordinary effort to draw her family onside with him. If he managed to pull Joshua into a state of contentment again, he'd be the hero of the day.

Her mother had opened Ethan's gift box of chocolates and put it on the table for everyone to help themselves and they were just sitting down again to relax over cups of coffee when the three missing adults returned with smiles on their faces.

'I can't believe it!' Violet crowed happily. 'Ethan showed Joshua how to do Sudoku puzzles on that Nintendo gadget and he's enthralled with it.'

'Problem is, he won't want to give it back, Ethan,' Barry said ruefully. 'If you tell me how much it cost, I'll pay you for it.'

'No, please…I'm happy for him to keep it.'

Barry shook his head. 'Can't let you do that.'

'To tell you the truth, I didn't buy it for me. I bought it for him, Barry.'

There was a moment of stunned silence.

Ethan shot Daisy an ironic grimace, then explained how he'd come to do it. 'I'd already made the purchase before Daisy said I wasn't to bring gifts for the children. She'd told me about Joshua's fascination with numbers and it struck a chord with me because numbers have always played a big part in my life. Anyhow, I slipped it into my pocket, just in case the opportunity came up to share a game with him. I honestly have no use for it, myself.'

More silence that sent prickles all the way down Daisy's spine.

This was the kind of buying-power thing she'd wanted to avoid—obvious evidence of how easily Ethan could acquire anything, cost no object.

The expensive gift could hurt Barry's paternal pride.

It could instantly undermine the liking Ethan had earned earlier, making her family see him as the big-shot financier, intent on buying himself into their midst, so wealthy himself he was beyond empathising with the difficulties they'd faced and were still facing though their situations had improved. Partly because of him.

Although a gift could be welcomed out of sheer need, the giver could be deeply resented. Daisy was painfully aware of how negatively she had reacted to Ethan until she'd come to know him.

Violet broke the uncomfortable impasse. 'That's very thoughtful of you, Ethan. Very kind,' she said appreciatively.

'Yes,' Barry backed her up, grimacing over his own lack of understanding of his son as he added, 'I've always found Joshua's fixation on numbers weird. I would never have connected it to a game he could play.' He clapped Ethan on the shoulder. 'I'm glad you did. It might be a step forward for him.'

They were smoothing over his gaffe in not accepting Barry's offer to pay.

The iron fist squeezing Daisy's heart eased its grip.

Ethan gestured an apologetic appeal to the rest of the family. 'I hope the other children won't mind him having it.'

'Not at all,' Ken replied cheerfully. 'They'll be too busy feeding their faces with chocolate. Like us. The three of you had better sit down and indulge yourselves before we polish off this whole decadent box you brought for Mum.'

'If you've scoffed all the ones with caramel fillings, Ken, I'll scalp you,' Violet threatened, quickly coming to look.

'Haven't got enough hair left to worry about,' he retorted, grinning evilly at her.

Everyone laughed and Daisy's pent-up tension was finally expelled. Ethan resumed his seat beside her and she gave his hand a quick squeeze, grateful for what he'd done for Joshua and relieved that no one seemed to be holding his generosity against him, not on the surface anyway. What they thought privately would probably never be discussed in her hearing. She could only hope that his kindness overrode any niggles about the gift.

The party mood was quickly re-established.

Daisy relaxed again.

Keith opened a bottle of champagne and insisted they all have a glass of it because he had things to say and people to toast. Her oldest brother enjoyed making speeches, which were always amusing, so as Keith took his stand, glass in hand, Daisy was smiling in anticipation, not expecting the tenor of this speech to be different today.

'This past year has been a difficult one for all of us. It's great to have it behind us with better times to look forward to,' he started seriously, drawing murmurs of agreement from around the table.

'The first toast I want to make is to our baby sister. The rest of us were not in a position to help Mum and Dad when they needed it, and Daisy took up the slack like the little champion she is. We all think the world of you for contributing all you did, Daisy, and if there's anything we can ever do for you, you have only to ask.'

More murmurs of agreement.

Daisy flushed with embarrassed pleasure. While it was lovely to have her resolute support of their parents appreciated, she couldn't help wondering if her family had gone out of their way to welcome Ethan just to make her happy. It fitted with Violet's distressed cry about spoiling her day. Was there genuine liking for him or an act put on for her sake?

'To Daisy,' Keith went on.

They all toasted her.

'Next, I want to thank Ethan for taking on Dad's investments and giving him his expert advice, turning what looked like a black hole into a gold mine.' He grinned at Ethan. 'That was a real bonanza, and for us to see the worry lifted from Mum's and Dad's faces, to see them enjoying life again…you've done us all a power of good, Ethan. We salute you.'

They all raised their glasses again to toast him.

Ethan frowned, shifting uncomfortably, then lifted a hand in protest at the toast. 'No, I can't accept that, Keith. What I did… I wasn't thinking of your parents or this family. I didn't know you.' He shot a wry smile at Daisy. 'It was to hold onto this woman, to win more time with her, because I wanted her in my life and she was walking out of it.'

'Well, we did think there was a bit of self-interest involved,' Keith said dryly. 'But that doesn't alter the fact that you changed everything around for Mum and Dad and you deserve some acknowledgement for it.'

'Then let me acknowledge something, too,' Ethan swiftly put in. 'Now that I've been amongst you, I see more clearly why Daisy is the very special person she is. Being an only child myself, I haven't had your experience of family, but today I've learnt why it means so much to her. You all share something very special. It's what I'd love to have in my own life, and I'm hoping

Daisy…' he turned to her, his green eyes glittering with determination '…will want to make it happen with me.'

Daisy was totally stunned.

Was he saying what she thought he was saying?

Making a family of their own?

Marriage…children?

Her heart broke out of its suspended state of shock and started to gallop.

''Right!' she heard Keith say. 'Got to agree our little sister is special and we're glad you recognise it, Ethan. Makes you special, too. Seems like a good idea if you two wander off to the front porch or behind a bush along the side fence and talk about what you want together while we clear this table for some serious poker.'

Seize the day…the thought had instantly leapt into Ethan's mind.

Keith had just given him the family's stamp of approval. That barrier in Daisy's mind had to be down. If he acted now, before she could get herself in a twist about something else, he should be able to clinch the real deal.

'Yes. Good idea!' he shot at Keith with a huge man-to-man grin.

He grabbed Daisy's hand, pulled her up from her chair, and swept her out to the front porch, his heart drumming him into the battle he was intent on winning. The moment the door was closed behind them, ensuring privacy, he scooped her hard against him, one arm curling possessively around her waist, his free hand cupping her chin so she couldn't look away from the intensity of purpose shooting from his eyes to hers.

'There's no more to prove, is there?' he fiercely challenged. Without waiting for a reply he plunged on with vehement conviction. 'We're fine together, Daisy. Doesn't matter who we're with or where we are. The world is our oyster if you'll just open up to me and admit that I'm the right man for you. The right man in every respect. Because I am. I know it. And you're the right woman for me. No question. We could build a great future together. Have a family like yours. Nothing should stop us. Nothing!'

The right woman for him…

He meant it.

It was in his voice, in his eyes, and at last Daisy could let herself believe it. All the doubts that had plagued her disintegrated under the forcefulness of Ethan's insistent claims. A huge welling of emotion brought tears to her eyes. She couldn't speak. She flung her arms around his neck and kissed him, pouring into passion the hopes and dreams he had just turned into incredibly ecstatic reality.

He *was* the right man for her. In every respect. Her heart and soul told her so, and her body exulted in the passion he returned with its promise of always being there for her—no time limit—for the rest of their lives, not the rest of this year.

'Now that *meant* something,' he muttered with certainty as his mouth broke from hers.

A sublime joy bubbled into laughter. Her eyes danced total agreement with him as she sobered up enough to say, 'I love you, Ethan Cartwright. I just didn't know if *you'd* ever think we'd be fine together.'

'Thought it from the first day we met,' he answered, his eyes sparkling with delight in her open admission.

'You didn't even know me,' she protested.

'Knew it instinctively. Convincing *you* of it was the problem.'

She shook her head at him. 'You only wanted me.'

'Very badly. And once I had you, Daisy Donahue, I very quickly knew I never wanted to let you go. I love everything about you. Absolutely everything.'

It was what she had secretly yearned to hear and it was happening.

It truly was.

Ethan cocked an eyebrow enquiringly. 'Does your father expect me to ask him for your hand in marriage?'

'You haven't asked *me* yet,' she reminded him.

He laughed. 'Shall I go down on bended knee?'

'No, I like you better up here,' she said, swaying her body provocatively against his, revelling in the freedom of being able to express her love for him without any inhibitions at all.

'Will you…' he kissed her forehead '…be…' he kissed the tip of her nose '…my wife?' He brushed his lips over hers.

'Yes,' she breathed against his mouth and they kissed again, celebrating the soul-deep satisfaction of knowing they were, indeed, right for each other.

They stayed out on the front porch for quite a while, not wanting to break the marvellous sense of solid to-getherness. It seemed to Daisy they had come on a long, long journey to this point, and there was much to talk about—the inner turmoil that had constantly infiltrated her part in their relationship, the moves Ethan had made to give himself the best chance of winning her over to what he wanted, the reasons why he'd decided she was the right woman for him, his realisation that her integrity was rock-solid, that there was no intention of *taking* him for anything beyond what had been agreed—so many feelings to be expressed, explained, understood.

And a future to be planned.

Ethan wanted to fill the house at Hunters Hill with children, to play games with them, to sit down to family meals, which matched Daisy's dreams perfectly. They would make it happen together. They were one in mind, one in heart—soul mates for ever.

It was the most blissful day in Daisy's life and, wonderfully imbued with the absolute confidence he gave her, she knew with Ethan there would be many more to come.

He did ask her father for her hand in marriage.

In front of the whole family.

And their response made the day even better—nothing but genuine, heart-warming pleasure for both of them all around.

Easter Sunday...

Not a nightmare.

A dream come true.

THE TUSCAN
TYCOON'S PREGNANT
HOUSEKEEPER

Christina Hollis

Christina Hollis was born in Somerset and now lives in the idyllic Wye Valley. She was born reading and her childhood dream was to become a writer. This was realised when she became a successful journalist and lecturer in organic horticulture. Then she gave it all up to become a full-time mother of two and to run half an acre of productive country garden. Writing Mills & Boon® romances is another ambition realised. It fills most of her time, between complicated rural school runs. The rest of her life is divided between garden and kitchen, either growing fruit and vegetables or cooking with them. Her daughter's cat always closely supervises everything she does around the home, from typing to picking strawberries!

To all carers, everywhere

CHAPTER ONE

ANY MINUTE now! Michelle thought as the prow of the *Arcadia* nosed around the headland of St Valere. She had been waiting for this. Even so, she took a moment to admire her employer's vast yacht as it cut a white slit through the bright blue Mediterranean.

It would be a terrible wrench when this temporary job came to an end—if anyone could call being house-keeper at the villa Jolie Fleur 'work'. This position was a godsend, although the thought of her contract coming to an end lurked on her horizon like a big black cloud. And right now she was watching a thunderhead arrive to join it.

The previous day, her employer's domestic manager had rung Michelle from the yacht. Sounding tense and exasperated, the woman had warned her that an unex-pected guest was going to be staying at the villa. Michelle had soon found out why. One of her employer's grandest guests was not fitting in to life on board ship. Michelle had laughed at this, thinking it was because of seasickness. But the truth was more than that.

Billionaire art dealer Alessandro Castiglione couldn't

be confined to the ocean. He was *supposed* to be taking a few weeks' complete break from work, the house-keeper had said, but her tone had told Michelle more than her words. She had known then what was in store for her, because she had seen plenty of men like him. Alessandro Castiglione would be a driven man, who drove his staff mad at the same time. He might be, as the woman had told her, 'The best-looking thing in every magazine!', but Michelle knew it took more than good looks to keep a tycoon at the top of his game.

Cleaning offices in central London had given her a glimpse of the brutal side of business life. So when the domestic manager had added a bit of gossip, Michelle had taken it with a pinch of salt. This man, she'd said, had recently taken over his father's firm and sacked nearly all its employees. If that wasn't bad enough, the woman had added in a low voice, they were all his aunts, uncles and cousins!

What sort of man would sack his relatives? Even Michelle's mother had never done that! She thought back to the life she had been so glad to abandon a few months earlier. Working for her mother had been hell. Mrs Spicer was an absolute perfectionist. The two of them, as Spicer and Co, had built up a reputation for fast, discreet domestic service anywhere in central London. Mrs Spicer had given the orders. Michelle had been the 'and Co' part of their business. She did all the dirty work.

But I'm in sole charge now! Michelle thought. Despite her nervousness, she allowed herself a small smile as she waited to greet her famous house guest. However bad he was, Alessandro Castiglione couldn't possibly be a worse task-master than her mother.

Michelle always kept Jolie Fleur spotless, so this unexpected arrival hadn't made too much extra work for her. And what was the worst this man could do? Sack her? She only had a few weeks left in this position anyway. He might be an unexploded bomb, but Michelle had total confidence in her skills. She knew that if she worked hard and kept out of his way there would be no reason for him to lose his temper—at least not with her.

A man who dumps his own relatives will think nothing of throwing me out on my ear, and I'm not ready to leave! She thought. A keen sense of self-preservation had got her this far in life. Now she had escaped from England, she was curious to see how much further she might go.

As she watched from the clifftop overlooking the bay, a shape detached itself from the yacht's flight deck. It was a helicopter. Michelle shaded her eyes with her hand. It was always exciting to watch it swing into the hard blue sky with the grace of a wheeling seagull. She spent so long gazing up, the helicopter was almost overhead before she remembered she ought to be in position to welcome her unwelcome guest. She walked around to the front doors of the villa, making one last check of the exterior as she did so. The windows and white paintwork gleamed in the blinding sunlight. Inside the house, everything was ready. The caretaker and the gardener were the only permanent members of staff during the holiday season, but they weren't anywhere to be seen.

Nervously, she checked her fingernails and her uniform. Everything was clean and neat, as usual. Keeping busy was Michelle's way of coping with the world. With nothing left to panic about, she ran through what she would do when the unexpected house guest landed.

I'll give him a smile and a slight bow of my head, she thought. *Then I'll extend my hand for a handshake, tell him to ring me if he needs anything, and vanish.*

That didn't sound too difficult. The tricky part was actually managing it. Michelle loved this job because it gave her the chance to spend a lot of time on her own. People always made her nervous. The prospect of meeting a man who was apparently never photographed with the same model twice—woman or car—terrified her.

The incoming helicopter's rumble increased, until it vibrated right through her body. She looked down at the palms of her hands. Tiny beads of perspiration sparkled in their shallow creases. Absent-mindedly she ran them over the severe black skirt of her uniform and then stopped. A proper French chatelaine would never do such a thing!

I might be lucky and find he spends all his time out on the town, she thought, desperately trying to buoy up her spirits. *In that case he'll be nocturnal, so I'll hardly see him. Making his stay run smoothly will be enough for me.*

She walked quickly round to the front of the villa, the stiff sea breeze at her back. All the windows and doors were wide open, letting a cooling draught rush right through the house. Michelle thought the rich smell of the maquis was much nicer than the soulless scents pumped out by the air-conditioning system. Once she was in place, she could watch the helicopter land with a clear conscience. As it drew closer to the helipad, the racket of its rotors was almost too much to bear. Michelle turned away from the sound and moved closer to the door for protection.

Turning around again, she expected to see the helicopter on the lawn. She got a surprise. It was still hanging in the air. Something must be wrong. Gaston, the pilot, was usually in such a tearing hurry to get back to his poker game on the yacht that he plonked the machine down anywhere. Smashed shrubs and crushed flowers were painful reminders of Gaston's previous overshoots and under-steering. Jolie Fleur's carefully tended mixed borders weren't so much a reminder of their English owner's homeland, they were more of a war zone.

This time was clearly going to be different. Michelle assumed there was a new pilot at the controls. Gaston would never take so long lining up his approach. But when the helicopter suddenly swung away and made a circuit of the house to try another approach, she caught sight of the pilot's face. It was the same old Gaston—but, from the furious look on his face, a perfectionist was schooling him in the art of landing.

By the time the helicopter finally came to rest, its skids were lined up exactly with the white letter 'H' stencilled in the centre of Jolie Fleur's main lawn. The racket had been deafening. Michelle's carefully brushed hair was blown to a thatch. As she tried to tame her mousy brown tangle, disaster struck. The helicopter's rotors slowed and its downdraught eased. The drop in pressure meant a gust of wind off the sea got behind the villa's door and slammed it shut behind her with a thunderous bang. Michelle jumped—or would have done, if her uniform hadn't held her back. Its skirt had been sucked in between the heavy door and its jamb. She was trapped and could hardly move.

Tugging at it with growing horror, she realised this was the first and only low point since she'd left England—but it was bottomless. She knew the door would have locked.

Desperately hoping for a miracle, she tried the handle anyway. The door didn't move. Her guardian angel must be on holiday.

Michelle's pulse had been galloping with nerves all morning. Now it went into overdrive. What could she do? Wave hopefully at the tall, rangy figure unfolding itself from the helicopter? Appealing for help to a guest when she was supposed to be so efficient wouldn't be the best start to their working relationship. Someone who could teach precision to a slap-dash pilot in one lesson was unlikely to have any time for accidents or mishaps.

Desperately, she tried working her skirt out through the crack, pulling it up and down, backwards and forwards. Nothing worked. The alternative was to tear herself free, leaving her skirt behind. That wasn't an option. A careless housekeeper was one thing. A half-dressed one was unforgivable—and totally unforgettable. Trussed up like a chicken, she resigned herself to a roasting.

Signor Alessandro Castiglione stood on the parched lawn, his back to her, as he waited for his designer luggage to be unloaded. Michelle watched, getting hotter and hotter. Long, agonising seconds dripped away. She tensed, ready with a million explanations. Taking possession of a briefcase and laptop, her guest left Gaston to deal with everything else. Marching towards the house, he covered the distance in a terrifyingly short time.

He was nothing like as old as she'd expected, but to think such a young man was already notorious in the newspapers somehow made her situation much worse. Michelle's spirits skidded along rock-bottom. Despite his hunched shoulders and considered pace, he was moving quickly. Instead of taking the track of scuffed, dead grass leading directly from the helipad to the house, he took a much longer route. This went by way of paved paths through banks of thyme and sage, and stretched out her agony still further. Watching bees working among the herb flowers always persuaded Michelle to relax and linger. They had absolutely no effect on this man. He was totally single-minded. Looking neither to left nor right, he homed straight in on the front door of the villa.

If Michelle hadn't been so frantic she would have appreciated his fine features. The natural curl in his thick, dark hair, his quick brown eyes, frowning brow and heavy tread would normally have made such an impression on her she would have been struck dumb. Instead she was speechless with embarrassment. Hands behind her back, she went on easing, tugging and wheedling at her skirt to try and free it. It was no use.

The closer the newcomer got, the more frantic she felt. Her fingers throbbed from trying to break free. So did her pulse. It was so hot. She might as well have been a butterfly beating its wings against a closed window. She was well and truly stuck. If that wasn't bad enough, she was beginning to see why this guest hadn't fitted in on Mr Bartlett's yacht. It was designed for holidays and having a good time. Alessandro Castiglione looked as though he didn't know the meaning of the words. Despite the heat, he was wearing a top-quality suit and a hand-finished shirt. His only concessions to the Mediterranean were the ivory colour of his linen trousers and jacket, the open buttons at his neck, and the mulberry-coloured tie peeking from his pocket.

Michelle swallowed hard. The time for practising her welcome was over. Now for it…

'*Buongiorno*, Signor Castiglione. My name is Michelle Spicer, and I'll be looking after you during your stay here at Jolie Fleur.'

His pale, aristocratic face was compressed. 'I don't need looking after. That's why I jumped ship. There were too many people running round after me. All they do is get in my way,' he growled in faultless English, speaking with the accent of a Caesar. It drove everything from Michelle's mind except her fear of explaining exactly how much of a fool she was.

And then, ten feet away from her, his expression changed from distracted to thoughtful. He stopped. Michelle tried to take a step backwards away from him, but her heels rattled against the firmly closed door. There was no escape. She stood and quailed, while he stood and watched her. He pressed his lips together in a tight line, matching the deep furrows on his brow. Michelle couldn't think of a single thing to say. This was worse than she had ever imagined it would be. She was pinned to the door by his unblinking stare. Michelle tried to tell herself this was just another job and she really shouldn't care what impression he was getting of her. The truth was, she cared very much. Staff should be invisible and silent. Here she was, pegged out with no hope of release. You couldn't get much more visible than that.

Why does he have to be so good-looking? she thought. *It wouldn't be half so bad if he was old, or ugly, or ranted and raved at me—anything would be easier to bear than this slow, silent interrogation…*

'Well! What have we got here?' he drawled eventually. 'You're trapped.'

So tell me something I don't know! she thought, but the relish in his eyes was too obvious. Instead, she nodded and tried to smile.

'I—I'm the housekeeper here at Jolie Fleur and I shall be doing everything I can to make your stay as pleasant as possible...' *Though how I'm going to manage it from here...* she added silently.

It didn't seem much of an obstacle to Alessandro Castiglione. He pinned her to the door with a knowing look.

'Everything?' he questioned with a mischievous twinkle. 'You mean my wish is your command? That's dangerous talk, *signorina*, when you look to be stuck fast!'

Michelle burbled something wordless, her mind melted by flames of embarrassment. She needn't have bothered. He was far too interested in her problem.

'I was trapped too—on that damned boat,' he added, almost sympathetically.

After a moment's hesitation, Michelle screwed up all her courage and tried an explanation.

'The door slammed shut in the helicopter's down-draught. The key is in my pocket, but I can't reach it,' she said, in a voice so small she hardly recognised it.

To her surprise he gave a quick nod of understanding. 'You must be more careful. This is a very heavy door, Michelle. You're lucky it's only your dress. You might have lost your fingers.'

Her heart slowed to about five hundred beats a minute. Looking into those *nocciola*-brown eyes was having a very strange effect on her. None of the bad things she had been told about him mattered any more. This was a man who had been through a lot. She could see that from his face. He must be in his late thirties, and creases etched between his brows added to the character of his otherwise fine features, but to Michelle he was at his loveliest when he smiled.

'My keys—' she tried to say, but no sound came out. Clearing her throat as delicately as she could, she tried again. 'My keys are in my pocket, but I can't reach them.'

'Then it's easily fixed,' he said as he moved towards her.

The villa's overhanging eaves meant she was imprisoned in the shade, but her temperature began to rise. The closer Alessandro got, the better-looking he became. Any lines on his face now were drawn by concentration. His aura of confidence should have put her at her ease, but it had exactly the opposite effect. There was nowhere for Michelle to look except straight at him. She was swept into the steady depths of his eyes and could study them all she liked. Alessandro Castiglione was far too busy to notice. He was concentrating on her waist.

'Surely if you were to turn around—?'

'How? I'm stuck!'

'I'll show you.'

He closed in on her until they were almost touching. She gazed up at him, her hazel eyes wide with anxiety. He placed his hands on her shoulders, and she flinched.

'Michelle! Anyone would think I was a monster.' He laughed.

'I'm sorry,' she muttered.

'Don't worry. I've had my quota of virgins for the day.' With that, he turned her—not to the left, as she'd imagined, but to the right. Now she was facing the door. She couldn't see him any more, but hardly needed to. The mere presence of him was sending out enough vibrations to tell her he meant business.

'That's given you more room to play with, hasn't it?' he asked in his deep brown voice.

Michelle tried, struggled and failed.

'Yes, but it's not enough. I still can't get my hand around into my pocket.'

The fragrance of his new clothes and expensive cologne retreated a little, but then returned with full force.

'How about if I try?'

Michelle nodded. His hand slid over her, and she was spellbound. His touch was slow and measured. Michelle felt it like a caress. She tried to steady her breathing. It was impossible. The air filling her lungs was superheated with his clean, understated fragrance.

'No—please—don't do that...' Michelle's protest sounded feeble and fake, even to her.

Alessandro's hand stopped moving, but he didn't take it away. She felt the warmth of it burning through the thin fabric of her uniform like a brand.

'What is it, Michelle?'

His rich accent made even those few simple words sound beautiful.

Michelle pressed her cheek hard against the impassive face of the front door and tried to keep cool. It wasn't easy when she could feel every one of his fingers.

'Nothing.' She shook her head.

Only, it's the first real time I've been touched by a man, she thought to herself.

The tips of his fingers slid lazily over her, searching. When he found what he was looking for, she gasped. His hand slid into her pocket and closed over her key fold.

'Now...I'm afraid I shall have to move in a lot closer to reach the keyhole...'

Michelle couldn't speak. He was leaning against her

as he searched for the lock. The feel of his breath on her hair was intoxicating enough. When his right hand slid around her waist the breath caught in her throat. There was a click, and the door swung open. His supporting hand fell away from her and he stood back.

'You're free,' he said, nodding towards the entrance hall, smiling. It lit up his face, and she couldn't help pausing in wonder. Then a breeze rippled around them, bringing her situation right back to life again. She flung out her hand to stop the door slamming a second time. Alessandro's hand was already there. Electricity crackled right through her body. She felt his firm, warm fingers again—then snatched hers away.

'Thank you, Signor Castiglione. I'll show you to your suite. Then I'll take you on a tour of Jolie Fleur—' she gabbled, desperate to prove how capable she was.

'No—I'll be fine.' Alessandro cut her off. 'There's no reason why you should worry about me. Go and do whatever you have to. I'm more than capable of finding my way around a house alone.'

'Of course, Signor Castiglione.'

Michelle dipped her head politely and reversed away from him.

'Where are you going?'

'I'm going to change—this dress is all creased now. I live in the studio house. It's in the grounds, just over there.'

He frowned. 'Why don't you live in the main house?'

'I'm only temporary staff, *signor*. Given my position, I don't really fit in anywhere up at the house.'

'But Terence Bartlett told me his house was deserted—there must be plenty of spare rooms. All his staff are with him on the yacht. That's the only reason I got him to drop me off here, rather than heading for home. I employ even more people than he does,' he said, with a voice full of feeling.

Michelle wondered if this was before or after the redundancies, and shivered.

'To be honest, I prefer living away from the main house, *signor*. I like my own company, so the studio is ideal for me.'

'Do you mean the artist's studio?' he said slowly.

She nodded. 'There's a lot of equipment and things stored in there, *signor*, but none of it has been used or even opened.'

'Terence had it built so he could dabble, but he's never had the time to use it. Or the talent,' he added regretfully. 'Is it a good building?'

'It's wonderful, *signor*.' Michelle smiled.

Living in a place where works of art might one day be made was another reason why she loved Jolie Fleur. The place was so beautiful it cried out to be drawn or painted. She wished she had one percent of the equipment that was lying abandoned in the apartment she was using. Then she reminded herself none of it was any use to her, as she lacked the nerve to try.

'May I take a look inside this studio of yours?'

How could she refuse? Alessandro was the boss, after all. She nodded. The idea of a man intruding into her personal space would normally set her teeth on edge. And yet something about *this* man made agreeing to his request the most natural thing in the world. She didn't want to cross him, but that wasn't the only reason. In the few minutes since he'd landed Michelle had realised something. He might be used to the company of stars and billionaires, but Alessandro Castiglione was the most natural, unaffected person she had ever met. He didn't waste words, either. That was something else in his favour. She much preferred an employer who kept quiet and let her get on with things, although the magnetic Signor Castiglione was bound to be quite a challenge. But Michelle knew her place. It was his holiday: her job was to keep him happy while keeping out of his way.

She found herself wondering whether he would be spending much time at the villa, or whether he would be travelling farther afield. And, whatever he did, would he have company? She began to think that keeping an invisible watch on this gorgeous man might be a lot more fun than hiding away from him completely…

CHAPTER TWO

MICHELLE'S heart leapt each time she saw her temporary home. It nestled in a sheltered part of the garden, and was designed so that the banks of flowers billowing on every side could be enjoyed whatever the weather. Glass made up most of the front of the building, while deep eaves shaded a swing-seat. Michelle unlocked the sliding French doors and stood aside for him to go in.

'This is impressive.' Alessandro Castiglione looked around the living room, with its stacks of art boxes and storage bins. Wandering into the kitchen, he nodded appreciatively at the big stainless steel sink and double drainers that took up most of the room. 'It wouldn't take long to remove this partition wall to make better use of the space,' he murmured to himself.

Michelle stood silently in a corner while he roamed around, occasionally taking something from the huge collection of equipment and supplies she had to squeeze around. Once he had studied a packet of paper, a box of pencils, an easel or some brushes, he put them back carefully in their place. Michelle was glad to see that. Most employers would have put them anywhere. *They pay you to be tidy for them*, her mother had always said.

She found it fascinating to watch him when she could. Each time he caught her doing it, he smiled. Michelle found herself blushing madly, and had to look away. Her guest knew exactly the effect he was having.

'I never knew Terence had so many art books!' He ran his finger along the spines lining the shelves, but it was a volume open on the coffee table that really caught his eye. 'Raphael. He's one of my favourites. Do you mind if I borrow this one and take it back to the villa with me?'

He picked it up and began flicking through the pages, from the back to front of the book. Of all the ones to choose… Michelle felt as though he had reached inside her ribcage and pulled out her heart. She knew exactly what he was thinking, because she had experienced it so often herself. As he revelled in the beautiful pictures and glowing colours, it showed clearly in his face. It was only when he reached the flyleaf that he stopped smiling.

'"Presented to Michelle Spicer as part of the Lawrence Prize for the year's outstanding portfolio,"' he read aloud, and then looked at her directly. His eyes were smiling, 'So this is yours?'

Michelle nodded, too struck by the sparkle in his eyes to speak.

'A little light bedtime reading?'

'It's a bit too heavy for that, *signor*.'

'For one person, maybe…although two might manage, I suppose. One could read while the other looks on?'

A vision of Alessandro Castiglione in bed came to Michelle, and it didn't involve any art books. She managed not to gasp aloud, but couldn't help taking a step backwards, away from him.

When he put her presentation book down on the table again Michelle was puzzled.

'Aren't you going to take it after all, *signor*?'

He shook his head. 'I couldn't possibly. It's yours and must mean so much to you.'

'It does—but if you want it…'

'Thank you. I'll let you have it back as soon as possible.' Taking possession of it again with relish, he patted the cover. 'This must be an inspiring place to work for you, as an artist. How many pictures have you done while you've been here?'

'None, *signor*. There's always too much work to do.'

He laughed politely, and brandished her book. 'Where's your portfolio now? You haven't got it here by any chance?'

Michelle clenched her teeth at the memory. The words had to struggle out.

'It got burned, *signor*.'

'I'm sorry.'

He sounded genuinely touched. 'I would have liked to have seen it. Never mind. I won't be a demanding guest. You'll have plenty of time for your art while I'm in residence here.'

He was right. Over the next few days Michelle found she actually had some spare time. It was unheard of. The Bartlett family were always thinking of bits and pieces that they'd forgotten to get delivered for their stay. Without having to drive into town several times a day, Michelle could open her own art box for the first time since arriving in France.

Her efforts at sketching around the estate weren't very successful. Each time she caught sight of Alessandro she hid her sketchbook in case he wanted to look at her work. She couldn't bear showing her pictures to anyone. The only reason she had won the Lawrence Prize was because a tutor had entered Michelle's portfolio without her knowledge.

She was surprised at how often she bumped into Alessandro around the estate. He always smiled at her, and they often swapped a few words of polite, meaningless conversation. Michelle was intrigued. The Bartlett family and their other guests spent all their time indoors, bent over computer screens or mobile phones. Alessandro seemed to like fresh air as much as she did.

Once the ringing of his mobile phone joined the rustle of grasshoppers and the chirrup of birds echoing through the dusty landscape. Then it fell silent. It was only when Michelle went to fetch some water for the houseplants that she found out why. A state of the art PDA was lying in the bottom of the soft water tank. Pulling it out, she dried it off as best she could and rushed to find him. The red 'do not disturb' light was showing on the console beside the door of his suite, so she left the soggy device there without knocking. An hour later, Alessandro sought her out as she arranged flowers for the music room.

'I have something for the trash.' Taking her hand, he put the PDA in her palm and carefully closed her fingers around it. 'They say I need a break. Now I've had a few days' rest, I'm inclined to agree with them.'

All the time he was pressing her hand between both of his. It brought back memories of his touch gliding over her body as he'd searched for her keys. His grip was warm and reassuringly firm. In contrast to the grating tension in his voice when he'd arrived, his speech was now softer and lilting. He was so different from the hard-bitten workaholic she had been expecting that Michelle laughed out loud.

'You can't throw this away! It must have cost a fortune!'

'Michelle, it will not work now it has got wet. It's been nothing but a curse to me.'

Looking into the turbulence of his eyes, she could believe it. In that moment her heart went out to him. 'Don't worry, *signor*. I'll take care of it.' She smiled.

When he smiled back, it illuminated his face in a way that stopped Michelle's heart. Alessandro Castiglione was gorgeous, and he was smiling at her...

Alessandro wasn't someone to be tiptoed around, like her usual boss. He was much more approachable, but his reputation still haunted her, so she kept out of his way. All the same, every tiny sound made her glance up in case it was him. She found herself looking out for him all the time. When they passed in a corridor he'd smile at her. That simple gesture made up for the hours of worry she had endured before he arrived.

Michelle kept herself busy around the villa, which helped stop her daydreaming. But after work, when she got back to her silent apartment, her mind always went into overdrive. She'd relive every single moment of his arrival. The touch of his hands on her as he searched for her pocket. His firm grasp when he supported her as he opened the door... And, more than anything else, his beautiful dark eyes with their long, dense lashes. She tried to distract herself by getting out paper and pencils and sketching. But although she sat outside, intending to draw the garden, her pencil kept trying to catch Alessandro's likeness instead.

One evening, strangely dissatisfied, she decided on an early night. Sleep was impossible. The memory of him filled her off-duty hours as easily as he touched every moment of her working day.

It was long after midnight before she gave up trying to get to sleep. Staggering blearily into the studio house's kitchen, she made herself a cup of tea. Comfort eating was the only way to distract herself from thoughts of her delicious employer—or at least push him to the back of her mind—so, grabbing a packet of biscuits, she headed back to her bedroom. One look at the tangled bedclothes was enough to put her off. She decided to take her guilty pleasure out onto the veranda.

Unlocking the studio's French doors, she opened them wide. The night air was still, and fragrant with flowers. Stepping out into the dusky garden was like the first welcome of a deliciously cool swimming pool. She shivered at the thrill. It was a perfect night with no moon; every star was visible above the darkness of the estate.

'*Buona sera,* Michelle.' Alessandro's voice came to her, soft and low through the dusk.

She whirled around. He was leaning back lazily on the swing-seat outside her apartment, a glass in his hand. Immediately she tried to cover herself with her hands, conscious that the sliver of satin and lace she was wearing was hardly decent enough to wear in front of a guest—especially *this* guest!

'Would you like to join me for a drink, Michelle?' He picked up a bottle of wine from the table beside him and filled his glass. Holding it out to her, he watched her hesitant approach with a smile.

'Me?' she breathed.

'I don't see anyone else around.'

'But—but I can't! I'm not dressed…'

'You look fine to me.' His smile flashed very white in the soft glow filtering through the studio's curtains. 'I couldn't sleep, and came out looking for some fresh air. Was there ever a country estate with fewer places to sit? Don't the Bartletts *use* this place?'

Michelle shook her head. 'They prefer their computers. Guests are sometimes shown around before dinner, but apart from that I've usually got the gardens to myself.'

He chuckled. It was a soft, intimate sound, perfectly in tune with the warm dusk. 'I never expected *you* to venture out here after dark. You seem so quiet and reserved.'

'I love it out here, and it's perfectly safe.'

'That's not surprising. The security lights around the villa are triggered by every step. When I was walking on the terrace I felt as though I was in a Broadway production. I wanted somewhere relaxing.'

He was wearing an open-necked shirt, as perfectly white as the one he had arrived in. It shone like nicotiana flowers against the gloom, but the fragrance of him was altogether more sexy. It combined male musk with an elusive cologne that was expensively discreet. Michelle's fingers clenched on the condensation-frosted glass in her hand. It wasn't enough to cool her thoughts.

She took a sip of her drink and coughed, not accustomed to the champagne bubbles.

'Champagne is my secret vice.' He chuckled, and as they sat back the atmosphere relaxed. 'I met the gardener this afternoon. He's very proud of the estate's strawberries. When they didn't appear on the menu this evening, I engaged in a little private enterprise and picked some for myself. Can you think of any better way to make the best of a sleepless night?'

Michelle shook her head. Her eyes were becoming more accustomed to the dark. Now she could see there was a dish on the table, too. He took a few berries from it and dropped them into her glass of champagne. Each one made a loud plop and an indulgent fizz in the stillness.

'The perfect finishing touch,' he murmured, watching her.

As she raised the slender glass to her lips she wrinkled her nose with pleasure at the rich aroma of ripe fruit and vintage wine. He smiled. Women were one of his greatest pleasures, but Miss Michelle Spicer was unlike any girl he had met before. She was as refreshing as a glass of ice-cold Vernaccia. He watched her, and knew that drinking champagne must be a rarity for her, from the way that half-smile danced across her face each time she took a sip.

She had completely forgotten the low cut of her nightdress, and the way its bias-cut satin clung to the rise of her breasts. Only a woman who spent too much time studying the form of other things could be so unaware of her own beauty. Alessandro knew a lot of women. They all played on the effect they could have on a man. By contrast, Michelle seemed totally innocent.

'You eat the strawberries when they've had time to marinate in the champagne.'

Michelle smiled and popped one of the ripe berries into her mouth. The strawberries were like no others she had ever tasted. There were as soft and sweet as an angel's kiss. The thought made a connection in her mind.

As they sat together in the warm night, she looked across at Alessandro shyly. His profile was stunning as he looked up at the wide sky full of stars. In her mind, his lips promised beautiful words, spoken just for her. More than that, she fantasised about the touch of them against her skin. Sitting next to him like this was a fragile bubble of happiness. The gentle chorus of insects, the cool breeze on her skin, and the perfume of ripening fruit and flowers all added to the magic. Not even a bat, arriving to flicker around the heliotropes, could destroy this moment.

Alessandro looked to see if she was affected by it, and chuckled. 'Strawberries, champagne and a stranger after midnight—you're taking it all in your stride, Michelle,' he teased her gently.

There was a bitter-chocolate quality about his voice that sent a tremor right through Michelle's body. He noticed.

'You're cold—*dannazione*! If I'd brought my jacket I'd offer it to you. Why don't you go inside and fetch something?'

'I don't have anything,' she replied, hoping he would believe her. This was all too precious to spoil.

'Then sit closer to me. I can shield you from any chill.'

'I'm not cold.' *Not any more*, she thought, taking in a long, slow breath.

She wondered what to do if he insisted she moved nearer to him. Torn between doing the right thing and imagining how wonderful the wrong thing would be, she was tense with indecision. Then the fragrance of night stole over her. Sultry top notes of lavender and jasmine were lightened by the sweet, more elusive scent of roses. For Michelle, this was a dream come true. With nothing to do but enjoy her surroundings, she began to lose herself in fantasy.

'This is what I imagine a real English country garden would be like,' she said eventually.

'Then you are homesick, Michelle?'

'Oh, I'm so sorry, *signor*! I didn't mean to say that out loud.'

'Don't worry about it.' His voice was a low, seductive sound, steady against the background crackle of insects. 'And, as I shall be calling you Michelle, you should call me Alessandro.'

When he said that, she tensed, concentrating on the strawberries clustered at the bottom of her glass. He handed her a solid silver teaspoon. One by one she spooned them out, savouring every mouthful and every moment.

'You didn't answer my question, Michelle. *Are* you homesick?'

'No, not at all—unless you count being sick of home.' She stopped, remembered that part of her life was over, and smiled. 'Although I've put all that behind me now. I'm a free agent.'

She saw him raise his eyebrows and rushed to explain.

'That is—I mean—I don't have a home in England any more. And I never did manage to get my wish of a lovely little house like this, with roses around the door.'

'This isn't a house, it's a studio—and one I was hoping to use,' he said softly.

Michelle was quick to pick up on the tinge of regret in his voice. 'You can work from the house, *signor*—'

He shot her a warning look and she corrected herself, 'I mean, *Alessandro*. You should have let me show you around. The whole house is set up as a satellite office. It's got everything—'

He silenced her with a raised hand. 'This is all I need at the moment—some peace and quiet. Tonight I want to drink in this atmosphere and the starlight.'

He gestured towards the sky. Michelle lifted her eyes, following his finger as it pointed upwards. With the coast behind them, they were looking out over the velvety blackness of the villa's estate. Beyond its boundary walls lay miles of lavender fields and patches of undeveloped maquis. There were no disco lights to outshine the stars as they twinkled like pinpricks across the deep indigo of the night.

'Have you ever seen anything so beautiful, Michelle?' he asked.

She shook her head, although she thought *he* was more wonderful than anything else on show that night. Her emotions were in meltdown. Part of her wanted him to say more. Seduction would have been extra-sweet in this heavenly setting under the stars. Yet a spider's web of warnings tugged at her, holding her back.

Her mother had always told her how untrustworthy men could be. None had stuck around for long after they'd met the fearsome Mrs Spicer, that was for sure. The result was that Michelle couldn't fully enjoy the experience of being alone with such a wonderful man in this tempting situation. She was too busy watching for warning signs.

But if Alessandro realised how tense she was, he made no allowance for it.

'I think this has been the most miraculous evening I've ever experienced.' He took the champagne glass and spoon from her hands. Smiling, he saluted her with it. 'Thank you for sharing it with me.'

Michelle was stunned. No one had ever said anything like that to her before. 'If there's ever anything you want, Alessandro, you only have to ask,' she whispered.

He put the glass down on the table behind him.

'That's dangerous talk, Michelle.' There was a provocative look in his eyes that almost stopped her heart. 'But...if you're sure you don't mind...perhaps you could do me a favour?'

'What is it?' she asked—much too quickly.

His expression moved slowly but surely into a wide, tempting smile.

'How would you feel about moving into the villa while I'm staying here?'

CHAPTER THREE

MICHELLE gazed at him, totally unable to form any words. Alessandro leaned forward a little, adding mischeviously, 'I can guess how wicked it will make you feel, but don't worry. We'll keep it our secret. No one need know.'

That forced Michelle to find her voice. 'What are you saying?' Blushing, she lowered her head. Silence closed in around her. When she looked up again, his understanding smile set her tingling from head to foot.

'I want to use your studio for my art. I know you like to keep your distance from the rest of the indoor staff, but there's no one here right now. You could move in for a while and give me free rein.' She was caught in his piercing gaze. 'Trust me. There's nothing more intimate on offer than that.'

Everything went very still. In the silence, Michelle became painfully aware of a sound inside her head. It was all her dreams crumbling into dust.

'Unless,' he said as an afterthought, 'you have something more intimate in mind…?'

His voice lilted with danger. Michelle sensed it. Her mother might have seen off all her boyfriends in the past, but when it came to Alessandro Castiglione no previous experience was necessary. This man was seduction in the flesh.

Pressing his foot into the carpet of tiny sweet herbs beneath the swing-seat, he set it moving. It rocked gently in the warm breeze, scented by low-growing thyme. Michelle hoped it would cool her flaming cheeks. Instead, she felt hotter than ever. She began moving uneasily. Strange feelings flowed through her body every time she looked at him. She had never experienced anything like this before. At home, eye contact had been something to be avoided. Here, held by his steady gaze, it was to be enjoyed.

His arm dropped lazily along the back of the bench. Michelle had an overwhelming urge to lean against it. She had felt the strong security of his hands once already. To feel them a second time, in a caress rather than as a support, would be heavenly. It took a real effort to shake free from the power of his eyes.

'What's the matter, *cara*?'

She stood up quickly. 'I don't like this.'

He laughed. It was a low, provocative sound.

'No…? I think you like it very much.'

Michelle couldn't answer. Telling the truth at a time like this would only catapult her straight into trouble.

'Tonight belongs to you and me, Michelle. There are no spectators, no listeners behind doors. We are free to be ourselves for once.'

He looked her up and down with a practised eye. She felt like a rabbit, cornered by a very attractive fox. She sat down again, faintly surprised by her new courage. A slow smile warmed his eyes. He stretched out his limbs, extending his legs across the gravel in front of the studio house. His body language and his expression were so open and inviting. He looked a completely different man from the world-weary professional who had stamped up to the villa a few days earlier.

Michelle caught her breath. He was wonderful. *Wonderfully dangerous*, she reminded herself. Something about that look in his eyes warned her to take care. She was only the hired help, after all. She would be mad to encourage him. He had burst into her life from nowhere, and he would vanish with the same speed.

A mischevious breeze ruffled his night-dark hair.

'Would you like some more champagne, *signor*?' she said, before he could draw her further into his orbit.

He shook his head, and she pursed her lips. He must think she was a complete innocent, talking about wine when there might be so much more on offer. It was a short step from that to imagining she was stupid. Michelle knew that wasn't true—despite the number of times her mother had said it.

'So—what's your answer?' he went on. 'Will you move out of here so I can indulge myself in Terence's purpose built art studio? The change would do us both a lot of good. Trust me,' he repeated.

Michelle sensed it was the last thing she should do. On the other hand…she needed to prove she wasn't a naïve fool. Alessandro had looked so careworn when he'd arrived. He already looked a lot better. How much more improvement might there be if she gave in to him over this little matter? Music was supposed to work wonders as a form of therapy. Art might do the same for him.

'All right,' she agreed, before she could change her mind. But she knew his reputation couldn't be allowed to frighten her into falling in with all his plans. She was determined to have boundaries.

'Good…you're making a work-worn billionaire very happy.' He laughed softly.

Michelle could tell he hadn't said it to pull rank. His words had been hollow, and his gaze told of something deeper behind his words. Michelle shivered, and he snapped out of his reverie.

'You *are* cold. I can't keep you from your bed any longer, Michelle. I must go.' He stood up and, bending forward until his head was almost touching hers, took her hand and raised it to his lips. His parting kiss was the light touch of a butterfly dancing on her skin, but it burned like the passion that fuelled his life.

'*Buona notte*, Michelle. Sweet dreams,' he added with a flash of mischief as he swung away into the night.

Michelle watched him move away through the shadowy garden. His white shirt was visible for a long way, despite the gloom. It only disappeared when he closed the villa door behind him. It extinguished the last hold he had over her. Standing up, she went slowly into the studio house. How could she have been so wrong about him? Although there was no doubt that beneath his handsome exterior Signor Alessandro Castiglione was ruthless, tonight he had been devastatingly charming. She drifted back into the studio house in a daze.

Michelle set her alarm clock for 4:00 a.m., but was awake in time to switch it off. It would have echoed through the peace and quiet of the Jolie Fleur estate. The memory of Alessandro's midnight visit was still hot in her mind.

It took her no time at all to pack. When she had stacked her few possessions on the doorstep of the studio house, she showered and then dressed in her bikini. It had been a long night, with not enough sleep. A swim before breakfast would perk her up. Dawn in the garden was as magical as dusk, and she could hardly wait to experience it again. She pulled on her dressing gown for the short walk to the villa's outdoor pool. The sun was still low, and filtered by a slight sea mist.

Leaving her studio apartment for the last time, she immersed herself in the chilly dawn. Rounding the hedge sheltering the pool she stopped and stared. Alessandro was already in the water, moving through it as though he owned the element.

'*Buongiorno*, Michelle.' He raised a hand to her. Water cascaded from his long, muscular limbs. He swam to the side of the pool in a few strokes. Folding his arms on the edge, he looked up at her appreciatively.

'The water is cold, but this is a great way to kick-start your system first thing in the morning. Come on in.'

'Er…no, thanks. I'm not here to swim. I—I only came for a walk around the grounds.'

Alessandro threw himself backwards in a creamy foam of water. Michelle knew only too well where to look, but didn't. The temptation was unbearable, but she tried to act as though muscular men stripped down to their Speedos were an everyday part of her life.

'If you didn't come to swim, why are you wearing that bikini?'

Michelle dropped her attention to the tiles at her feet. As she did so, she saw that the ties of her dressing gown had worked loose during her headlong dash to the pool. Wrapping it tightly around herself, she secured it with a firm knot.

Alessandro slid through the water like a seal to take up

a position at the side of the pool again. Heat flared in Michelle's cheeks. She went over in her mind everything that had gone on between them the night before. The embarrassment had all been on her side, the easy charm on his. As she burned, she wished with all her heart she could come up with some wonderful remark. Anything— *anything*—to recapture the magic of last night...

'So? What are you waiting for? Join me.'

She twiddled the tie of her dressing gown. 'I couldn't possibly...I only work here. You're a guest.'

'And I'm only inviting you into the water. There's no rule that says staff can't come in with me, is there?' He shrugged.

With her body reacting to everything Alessandro had on show, Michelle didn't know what to do. Instinct told her to take a chance, but her sense of decency said *run*. She stared down at a ladybird creeping across the tiled surround of the pool. It was heading for her toes with the sort of determination she desperately needed.

'I'm sorry, Alessandro,' she said, with more truth that he could ever have imagined. 'It's not my place.'

He was floating on his back, watching her. When she said that, he stood up in a shower of droplets. Michelle's eyes were instantly riveted on him. She couldn't tear them away. He looked magnificent. Two metres of tightly packed muscles and smooth, flawless skin. He had the pale colouring of someone who spent all day behind a desk, but who would toast to a golden tan in no time at all. Michelle was imagining the effect already. Tiny trickles of water led her gaze down over his bunched pectorals and his flat, muscular belly.

Laughing at her expression, when he said his next words he gave her exactly the push she needed.

'If you're determined to be a member of staff, then I'll stick to the rules too. I'm going to give you a direct order. It's OK to enjoy life—so get into this pool and start,' he called to her.

Every second of Michelle's upbringing had been geared towards following orders. But this one sent a thrill through her.

Throwing off her dressing gown, she dived straight into the water. Once beneath its surface, the simple feeling of freedom relaxed her in a rush. The chill shock invigorated her, as Alessandro had promised. She surfaced, laughing and splashing. Looking around to orientate herself, she saw his dark head dip beneath the water again. Suddenly she felt his hands on her legs. Frictionless, they glided upwards over her body. Flipping onto her back, Michelle kicked away towards the side of the pool with frantic strokes. When she reached it, gasping, he was right beside her.

'No—please don't fool about, Alessandro. I'm not a very good swimmer!'

He smiled, his white teeth as perfect as his reply. 'That dive looked pretty impressive to me.'

Michelle giggled. 'It gets the shock over quickly. I'd rather do that than suffer inch by inch, edging down the steps.'

As she spoke, he looked down at her legs through the shimmering water. She blushed.

'You're an athlete.' He nodded at the pale marks exposed by her bikini. 'I can tell from your *bronzage*.'

During her few precious weeks of freedom Michelle had heard plenty of French spoken with a local accent. She had heard it spoken with an English accent, too. But this was the first time she had heard it given an Italian glow. She couldn't help laughing at the sound.

'No, I'm not! I just run whenever I get the time. It helps me think through my problems.'

'I'm amazed a pretty young woman like you has any problems. The immaculate state of the villa shows how good you are at your job. What else is there to worry about?'

'My mother died in April.'

His expression softened. 'I'm sorry.'

Michelle mentally kicked herself for troubling a guest with her affairs, and spoke quickly to defuse the situation. 'There's no need to apologise. We were never exactly close.'

'Close?' Alessandro's face compressed. He looked down at the fingers of his left hand as they spread out beneath the water. 'Some relationships are a waste of good working time. My own mother couldn't have picked me out of a police line-up.'

Michelle was so stunned she forgot to be polite. 'You can't mean that?'

He gazed across the water to the villa's herb garden. She guessed it wasn't because he was admiring the ornamental thyme.

'Everything I've achieved in my life has been in spite of my family, not because of them.'

Michelle wondered if his remark had anything to do with those sacked relatives. She decided it was better not to ask.

'Then I'm sorry for you. Even *my* mother wasn't as bad as that.'

His attention snapped straight back to her. 'Don't waste your sympathy on me. It will only lead to trouble.'

Curious, she put her head on one side. 'What do you mean?'

His eyes were twin pools of mystery. 'If you keep looking at me like that, Michelle, you'll soon find out.'

Chilly rivulets of water trickled from her hair and she shivered. The points of her nipples were rising—and not only from the cold. It was the way Alessandro's gaze was totally focussed on her eyes. She could almost feel him searching her soul. No one had ever studied her so intently—not in her whole life. If she was honest, no one had paid any attention to her at all. They only noticed when she *hadn't* done something. The interview she'd missed because her mother had destroyed her portfolio, the single occasion she had been too sick to turn out for Spicer and Co…

'You have a fascinating face, Michelle. Let me draw you,' he said abruptly.

In all her years of sketching Michelle had never had the nerve to ask a stranger to pose for her. She thought of all those lost opportunities and wished she could be spontaneous, like Alessandro. He had come straight out with a suggestion she would never have been brave enough to make in a million years. So many times she had felt the urge to sketch or paint a person, but had been too shy to do anything about it. Now he was showing her how it should be done.

'I—I don't know.' She scraped her wet hair back from her face to give herself time to think. 'I work for Mr Bartlett, really, and if he found out I was lounging around being drawn, when I should be busy in the house…'

Alessandro threw off her objection. 'You're working for me at the moment. Not Terence.'

Michelle paused. There was nothing she could say except, 'If you put it like that, I can't refuse.'

He smiled. 'Yes…' he said thoughtfully. 'The more I see of you, Michelle, the more I realise you're wasted here. You ought to be immortalised somehow. And I'm exactly the man to do it. Wait here. I'll go and fetch my things.'

She had no choice. He vaulted out of the pool and picked up a robe from one of the poolside chairs. He pulled it on and walked quickly into the villa.

Michelle knew she should be feeling cold. She wasn't. The sight of his muscles sleek with water had brought a slow-burning fire to life deep within her body. Alessandro Castiglione had a lot to answer for. From the moment he'd landed he had invaded every part of her life. First he'd stopped her sleeping. Then he'd aroused her by touch, outside the studio house. Now he had persuaded her to wait for him, wet through and waist-deep in water.

As he disappeared from sight, a chill wind rippled across the pool. Michelle's skin contracted with the cold. Sinking beneath the wavelets, she let the water waft her feet off the floor of the pool. She knew she ought to thrash through a few lengths to warm herself up. Her heart wasn't in it. Exercise no longer had the power to distract her. All she could think of was Alessandro. Big, strong Alessandro Castiglione. He acted the part of blasé tycoon to perfection, but his bitter-chocolate eyes told a different story. When Michelle shivered now, it was at the thought of his deep brown gaze. If only she could decode its meaning.

Twisting in the water, she saw Alessandro walking back towards the pool. He was dressed now in jeans and a tight white tee shirt. His muscles were still on display, and Michelle felt them through her fantasies. Those jeans were so well cut they were obviously made for him. 'Casual' still meant 'designer chic' in his circles. The sketchbook under his arm was bound in leather, and he was carrying a long metal container. He put this down beside one of the poolside chairs.

'If you could swim a few lengths for me, Michelle, I'll try out a few ideas…I need something to make my working days worthwhile. Art is my therapy.'

'And mine. I always wanted to go to art college, but it wasn't possible for me to finish the course,' Michelle said shyly.

He was already rifling through the contents of his art box. Selecting a piece of willow charcoal, he made a few swift, sweeping strokes across his sketchbook.

'A little taster for you.' He showed her the pad. She was amazed. In a few strokes he had laid her down on his plain white sheet with nothing more than a sliver of burnt wood.

'You swim slowly, up and down.'

As he sketched, he asked her all sorts of questions about her own work. His conversation was light and insubstantial—until he asked her something that really burst her bubble.

'What made you give up your art course?'

She didn't answer for a while. Then she rolled onto her back to watch him.

'The answer to that is the same as it is to most of your other questions—my mother,' she said at last. 'Mum didn't consider art to be a proper job. There was no room for anything in my life unless she thought it had value. As a child, I was a disappointment to her. If I couldn't be beautiful, then I had to be useful.'

Alessandro frowned. Michelle was struggling to keep her mind on their conversation, but his disapproving expression helped keep her on track.

'"Art isn't a job, it's almost as much a waste of time as reading."' She quoted one of her mother's favourite sayings.

Alessandro's mood darkened further. 'I thought you said in the studio house that you had some books?'

'I do—and that was the problem. They're art books, and Mum hated them most of all. If I wasn't painting or drawing then I was reading about it. She thought I was doing it to spite her.'

This softened his expression, but only a fraction. 'It might be for the best. I'm in the trade, and art colleges turn out far too many indifferent graduates, in my opinion.'

Alessandro worked quickly, changing medium and trying out several grades of paper. He was enjoying this. Any man could take a woman—Alessandro did, frequently—but this was something altogether different. The more he worked on his sketches of her, the more relaxed he became and his stress fell away. It was a circle of satisfaction.

Eventually he put down his work and stretched, long and luxuriously. The sun felt good.

'Shall I stop swimming?' Michelle called as he stood watching her, hands on his hips.

'Yes. Come and lie on one of these loungers for a while.'

The water accepted her once again, showering her with a thousand droplets at she swam towards the steps. Alessandro watched them tumbling over her smooth wet skin. Each time she raised her arm he marvelled at the perfect curve, the sleek, easy beauty of her.

Stepping out onto the hot white tiles, she slicked her wet hair back from her face. He felt his body rise in anticipation.

Grabbing a towel, he enveloped her in its folds. Michelle immediately pulled up a corner and made to rub at her hair.

'Wait—leave that. I want you to look as though you've just left the water. Relaxed, and soaking up the sun.' He took her hand to lead her over to the seats.

In a flash Michelle was swept right back to his goodnight kiss. Alessandro took away her towel and, dropping it in a heap, told her to sit down on the sun lounger.

'Do you want me to do anything special?'

'You look just fine as you are.' His gaze grazed her body appreciatively. 'All you need to do is lie back and close your eyes.'

It took Michelle a little while to get comfortable, and longer to relax.

'I feel a bit self-conscious,' she said apprehensively. She often wore a bikini, but this was the first time she had been within touching distance of a man as gorgeous as Alessandro.

'Don't worry. I've drawn dozens of women—most of them wearing less than you are now.'

Michelle giggled. That made her feel so much more comfortable in his company. But still, when his hand reached out to arrange her wet hair, she flinched.

'Did I hurt you, Michelle?'

'No—not at all. I just have this thing about being touched, that's all. I *know* I'm never going to be struck again, but my body isn't so sure.'

She tried to laugh it off, but Alessandro was shocked. He withdrew a fraction, until her smile reassured him.

'Then I shall be very careful how I position you,' he smiled.

He was more than careful. Each time he reached out to touch her, he hesitated before making contact. She had the double pleasure of anticipation and effect. His touch when it came was so light it was evocative of their evening in the starlight. She could hardly bear it. She knew exactly how each touch would feel, because she had already imagined the grain of his fingertips drifting across her skin. When she reacted with goose pimples, it wasn't from any chill.

Alert as ever, Alessandro fastened his attention on a droplet of water coursing over the downy skin of her forearm.

'Tell me if you get too cold,' he murmured, reaching for the towel. With one long, slow movement, he stroked down the entire length of her arm.

As his touch trailed away, she sighed. It was a sound of total contentment. She leaned back against a cushion and closed her eyes.

'Before you settle down, I think I'll have your hair over *this* shoulder...' He swept her wet hair around and settled it, lock by lock.

Feeling his fingers stroking each strand into place sent shimmers of energy through Michelle's body. Alessandro had started wiping droplets from her skin and she shivered. As a trickle of water meandered over the generous curve of her breast his fingertips reached out to trace it...

CHAPTER FOUR

A LITTLE cry of anticipation escaped from her lips.

He stopped. His hand was hovering so close to her skin she could feel its warmth. It raised her temperature faster than the sun.

'I can see you're getting cold.' He leaned back, letting his hand fall onto his thigh with a slap. 'Come on, let's get inside—I've made you suffer long enough.' His rich accent rolled over one fantasy, but with smooth assurance he replaced it with another. 'I've arranged a little treat to thank you for your patience.'

'Oh, but you shouldn't have,' Michelle stammered, secretly feeling very glad that he had.

Waving aside her pleasantries, Alessandro picked up two more big towels from the neatly folded pile on the poolside chair next to his. Swirling one around her shoulders, he draped a second over her wet hair. Michelle revelled in their soft, sun-warmed folds. That was luxurious enough. Then she felt his hands moving over them, blotting moisture from her shoulders and hair. She leaned into his touch, enjoying more intimacy than she had ever imagined.

'This is more than a treat, it's heavenly!' she murmured.

'*Dio*—this isn't it.' He chuckled. 'There will be warm croissants and hot chocolate for your breakfast. That's the surprise. I'm guessing you won't have eaten yet?'

Michelle shook her head. She hoped nerves wouldn't stop her eating now! To be served by a guest would be a real turnaround.

He was already heading for the villa. She followed him at a respectful distance, but the gulf between them couldn't stop her dreaming. The villa Jolie Fleur was her workplace. This morning she was almost entering it as a guest. Her normally quick footsteps slowed, and she paused on the threshold. It was a beautiful house, ten times the size of the poky flat she had left behind in England. Pastel paint and mirrors were everywhere. She tried to concentrate on the flower arrangements. This was a great opportunity to see the place through the eyes of a visitor, and she was glad to discover it looked really good.

Alessandro had complimented her on her housekeeping, and that meant a lot. Now he had arranged breakfast. She had never been given a meal by anyone she worked for. It was unlikely to happen again, and definitely not with anyone as gorgeous as Alessandro Castiglione! Michelle was determined to enjoy every second, and make the experience last as long as possible.

'What are you waiting for?' he called back at her over his shoulder. Then he walked on. The crooked smile he flashed so rarely had hidden depths. It made her yearn for his full attention, but it wasn't to be.

'Fancy me having my breakfast served by the world's most eligible bachelor!' she breathed as he led her into the enormous kitchen.

'That's just a title from the tabloids. The woman

hasn't been born who can tie me down.' He smiled wolfishly as he directed her out onto the sun-drenched terrace. 'This is to thank you for acting as my model.'

The terrace's stunning sea view was framed by pink bougainvillaea. It made the perfect setting for breakfast. When Michelle had thawed out over a mug of hot chocolate they ate warm buttery croissants, brioches and apricot conserve. She was so nervous she spent more time pretending to admire the view than she did eating. That way she could watch Alessandro.

He ate well, and didn't have much patience with her excuses of not being hungry. With his encouragement, she eventually ate almost as much as he did. Later, over a cup of creamy cappuccino, she relaxed back in her chair and tried to decide whether the sea or the sky was the lovelier shade of blue.

'I could stay here all day,' she said eventually.

'*Perché no*? Why don't you?'

'Because I have to work, of course.'

Alessandro looked around the spotless terrace, and beyond it into the gleaming kitchen. Finally his gaze turned on her.

'This place looks tidy enough to me.'

Reaching out, he brushed a pastry crumb from the sleeve of her robe. It was such an intimate gesture Michelle tensed, wondering how he would follow it up. All he did was look at her, long and intently. It was the same expression he'd used when trying to capture her in his sketchbook.

'It won't take me long to settle into the studio house. Then I shall be able to start planning my next painting properly. I hope you're prepared for me to haunt you day and night, until I get all your features exactly right?'

If only you knew how you haunt me already, Michelle thought. *You are the cause of my sleepless nights.* A delicious tension increased inside her each time she looked into those melting brown eyes.

He checked his watch, and the moment evaporated. 'What time does the caretaker arrive?'

Instantly Michelle knew he had moved on. It signalled the end of her fantasy. He was dismissing her. Much as she wanted to stay, Michelle knew it was for the best. If the caretaker arrived to see her leaving the villa in her dressing gown, she would never hear the end of it.

With a sigh, she realised she couldn't spin out her time languishing in the villa any longer. This was his holiday. But it wasn't hers. She took as long as possible packing up the breakfast things and loading the dishwasher, just to be near him. But however long she lingered, the evil moment couldn't be put off for ever. Eventually she had to say it.

'Thank you so much for breakfast, Alessandro. Now I really must go.'

'Goodbye, Michelle.'

She left the house feeling flat and disappointed. He had changed in an instant, almost as though he'd sensed she might be getting ideas about him. His manner at the pool had been so relaxed and charming. It had put all sorts of crazy ideas in her head. Now he seemed to be doing his best to put up a barrier of indifference. She couldn't help wondering why—and dreaming about what she might do about it.

Alessandro was restless for the entire day. He couldn't settle to anything. The morning newspaper didn't tell him anything he hadn't already heard from his business associates. Opening the book Michelle had lent him released a drift of her perfume. His eyes tracked across the page, but somehow the words didn't sink in. Instead of Renaissance art he kept being distracted by modern beauty.

Michelle moved around the villa almost silently, freshening flower arrangements, topping up drinks trays, plumping cushions. She never made the first move, but whenever he spoke to her she would pause and talk shyly with him—whether it was about Raphael, the day's menus or something as mundane as the weather.

He took lunch in the garden that day, but that didn't help either. Michelle had moved outside too, gathering lavender from the herb garden. He couldn't see her from his seat on the terrace, but the sound of snipping scissors and the fragrance of crushed flowers told him exactly what she was doing. It reminded him of their evening talk, with all those warm, intimate scents and sounds. He could visualise it so perfectly he began sketching her from memory.

The women in his circle rarely showed the natural beauty and honesty of Michelle. She was unique. His own mother had been a shop girl, until Old Sandro Castiglione had tried hauling her up the social ladder. She had loved the lifestyle but hated the life. All the Castiglione men had lived to regret being related to her. Alessandro grimaced at the memory. Now his world was full of women who rattled on about clothes and make-up as though it should mean something. They were a complete mystery to him.

Early on in his adult life, he discovered that the more money you gave women, the noisier their demands became. There had been one woman who had taken all he had to offer, and more. Then, when he'd least expected it, she had delivered a blow that had almost destroyed him. She had used him as a pawn to make her husband jealous. Experience was a harsh teacher. These days Alessandro took care to keep moving. He took control. It was the only way to enjoy life.

He spent the rest of that day working on the sketches he had made of Michelle. That made his sense of dissatisfaction worse. She claimed she didn't mind him distracting her, to check the exact line of her shoulders or the precise size of her eyes. Each time he promised it would be the last. He admired the way she pretended to be disappointed, with an almost professional skill.

As the day dwindled away he shut himself in the studio house, determined to get down to work. After all, the place was perfect. The light was good; there were no distractions; he could lay all his artist's materials out. The only thing it lacked was a live model. He wondered about going to check on the original for a fifth and final time, but he could hardly disturb her again. There were limits—even for him.

He roamed over to the French doors, which were standing open. Shadows were lengthening out in the garden. A walk through that oasis of calm might help him to cool down. Throwing his sketchbook aside for the final time, he strode out into the evening.

He spotted Michelle almost at once, and stopped before she saw him. She was standing on the grass, only a hundred yards from the studio house, gazing along the flower-filled border. A playful breeze pressed the thin cotton of her uniform against her body. The gentle curve of her breasts contrasted beautifully with her small, well-defined waist. He noticed all this with an artist's eye, but testosterone filled in plenty more details.

Beneath that dress her spine curved into the flare of her bottom—which would be soft and peach-like, he knew. And he had already seen those long, slender legs in the pool that morning.

Arousal drew him on. When she turned and saw him, her lips parted as though she was about to speak.

No words were needed. His hands reached out for her as he approached, and he drew her into his arms.

Shock was almost as powerful a feeling as lust, Michelle realised. She tried to speak, but once she felt the insistence of his flesh against hers she was lost. Her body trembled, and she gasped at the power of its response. Then Alessandro eclipsed the setting sun as he kissed her with a passion so primitive all her inhibitions were swept away. She returned his kiss, her heart beating erratically as she revelled in the experience. She was being tasted by the man who filled her days and dreams.

Clutching at him as though she would never let him go, she raked his back with her fingers. He responded by moulding her body beneath his hands. She was his. Dizzy with a tumble of emotions, Michelle knew she was unleashing feelings she could never control. Her body pounded with an urgent burning desire, flooding through her veins in a tidal surge.

She had never felt like this before. Her body reacted purely on instinct, alive to all the sensations he was igniting in her. His kisses released her mouth and she threw back her head with a moan. Alessandro's mouth skimmed over the sensitised skin of her throat. Time lost all meaning as her torment increased. Her body sang with an almost unbearable torment. A heavy drawing feeling deep within her made Michelle press herself against his unyielding body. She leaned into his touch, feeling the most feminine parts of her opening, waiting for his touch.

Alessandro was more than ready for the experience. He pulled her close, the ridge of his erection rubbing against her. With a gurgle of pleasure she let her hands swim from his shoulders to his waist, then on. Light-headed with longing, she caressed the taut curve of his buttocks—but her fingers craved more. Soon they were dancing over his groin, desperate to discover its mystery.

'Oh, Alessandro…' she breathed.

If he didn't want her heart, then she was ready to give him the only thing she knew he would accept. As his hands caressed the heavy fullness of her breasts, she struggled to release his zip. His kisses closed over her mouth again as she shut her eyes and pushed her hand inside his jeans. With a lurch of excitement she discovered he was naked inside them. In mounting wonder she ran her fingers over the rigid length of him.

'*No*—not yet.'

She reacted with pained surprise at the note of command in his voice. He moved back a fraction—far enough to unfasten her uniform. He removed it from her body in one practised movement. She gasped, but he wasn't finished yet. Pulling down her bra straps, he peeled back the lace and put his mouth to her naked breast. While his hands cradled and caressed their fullness, his teeth teased first one nipple and then the other into hard beads.

Michelle was faint with pleasure. Her breath came in ragged gasps as she called his name into the lonely dusk. She clutched at him, and their bodies became one.

Revelling in sensations they both needed to satisfy, Alessandro laid her down gently on the camomile lawn.

It was warm and fragrant, reflecting the primitive heat of their passion. With a pang Alessandro wondered if his need for her was simply a symptom of his shallow lifestyle. If crossing the divide between his world and hers just introduced a little danger into the relentless routine of his life. A million thoughts formed and vanished in his mind as Michelle moved beneath his body. She had a supple delight he needed to experience.

Rolling over the sweet herbs, he took possession of her. All his consciousness was centred on filling the void inside himself. He thrust into her, feeling resistance and hearing her little cry as her muscles tensed and then closed around him. She made a sound of the deepest, darkest female pleasure, arching her back to meet him until they melded into one being. He leaned forward, entering her as deeply as he had done in his dreams. His pleasure was so intense he wondered how he had managed to resist her for so long.

Michelle clung to him, riding the waves of new sensation and wishing it would never come to an end. She wanted to absorb all his body, to give herself to him as completely as he was possessing her.

This was her life, and she was giving it to him. Nothing would ever compare to this moment, here with Alessandro, beneath the darkening Mediterranean sky.

'Oh, Alessandro,' she whispered, as soon as the breath seeped back into her lungs. 'I never dreamed making love could be as wonderful as that. I wanted my first time to be the best…'

Her lids were heavy with emotion and her words full of sincerity, but they froze Alessandro to the bone.

What the hell have I done? he thought, knowing full well it was the worst possible thing. Gently, but as quickly as he could without hurting her, he withdrew. The little gasp she gave told him more than he wanted to know.

'*Dio*, Michelle. I'm sorry…'

'Don't be. It was fantastic.' She reached up, cupping his face with her hand. Her eyes were liquid with sincerity.

Alessandro was appalled. How could he have been so stupid? He had heard that tone, seen that expression and felt that touch in his dim and distant past. It had spelled disaster then, and would do again.

'It was a mistake,' he said firmly, hardening his heart and looking away in case she winced. 'It should never have happened.'

'I know. I *know*,' she said quickly, in a small voice that seemed to come from far away.

He felt her moving beside him. Unable to look her in the face, he rolled towards her again, pulling her head into his shoulder and holding her close. Everything had changed between them. He had expected tears and accusations. Instead he'd got silence. That was worse. He had hurt her, and not only physically. The knowledge pierced him like a blade. It was the first time someone else's pain had rebounded on him, and it was a shock. Facts and figures were so much easier to control than feelings—especially when they belonged to other people.

It made him think. This would be another sleepless night for him, he vowed, but it would be one with a purpose.

He had work to do.

CHAPTER FIVE

Four months later

ALESSANDRO sat alone in the boardroom of the House of Castiglione. He looked over the accounts he had been handed a second and then a third time. The figures refused to make sense.

His people kept telling him what a success Michelle was making of her new life back in England, but he couldn't see it. When he looked at the dust-dry columns of figures all he saw was her luscious body, so soft and willing beneath his hands.

His initial anger over his own irresponsibility had taken a while to subside. When he had arranged for his charitable trust to set her up in business, he'd assumed that would be an end to it. His growing hunger to experience her again disturbed him. The mere sight of her name on this file inflamed his need. Something had to be done to get her out of his head—once and for all. He wanted to possess her again, to take her with the same fierce passion that had overwhelmed her on that sultry Mediterranean night. Nothing less would satisfy him.

Throwing the papers aside, he gave orders that he was leaving for England—right away.

Melting with anticipation, Michelle held her breath. Alessandro's smiling eyes looked into hers as though she was the only woman in the world—now and for ever. They were lying on soft, sweet, herb-scented grass in a pool of shade. Above them, leaves rustled in a hot, dry breeze. His hand traced the flickering pattern of shadows over her nakedness. As his fingers trailed from her shoulder, around the curve of her spine to the plump softness of her hips, she moaned and drew closer to the security of his body. He was about to place a tender kiss on her lips—

The alarm clock catapulted Michelle out of her dreams, straight back into real life.

For a long time she refused to open her eyes. She knew millions of people would kill for the chance of the life she had now. That didn't make waking up any easier. Alessandro had written himself out of her life. Oh, he had been madly generous, arranging for his people to set her up with her own art gallery and the Cotswold cottage she had always dreamed of owning. But his guilt had come at a terrible price.

Michelle was still only gradually coming to accept that she would never see him again. The only time memories could bring her pleasure was while she slept. Her dreams always focussed on the irresistible, adorable Alessandro, not on his heartless reality. Once she woke, the pain of their parting was too much to bear.

Waking destroyed the only pleasure she had left in life. This wasn't the sun-soaked South of France. It was England at the dreariest time of year. The only fragrance in her life now came from the lavender bags she had brought back with her. She groaned. It couldn't be morning already, could it? Squinting at her alarm clock, she tried to make out its digital display. Before she could manage it, the realisation of what mornings had come to mean hit her like a lead weight.

She rolled over, pulling the duvet over her head. *Please, please let me have just five more minutes' calm before the heaving storm begins—*

It was no good. Her stomach was already turning somersaults. *How can one tiny baby wreak such havoc?* she thought, staggering into the bathroom to lean her forehead against the cold china of the washbasin. She shut her eyes.

If only events could be blacked out so easily. She had given her heart to a man with a terrible reputation, who had dropped plenty of hints about his hatred of commitment. The one time she had tried to contact him directly his firewall of personal staff had closed ranks around him. She had been abandoned, and it was no more than she should have expected from a man like Alessandro Castiglione. What hope was there for someone as stupid as she was?

When she began to feel better, she opened her eyes. There was no point in raking over past mistakes, but she couldn't help it. Gently she stroked the front of her nightdress. Her life must centre on what was best for her baby now. Memories of its father were all she had left—and one single letter.

A chill ran over her body. Suddenly she was back in the villa Jolie Fleur, the morning after their lovemaking. How she had tortured herself as she'd got ready for her working day, wondering how she could ever look Alessandro in the eyes again. And then she had opened the door of his suite and found her book on Raphael, returned with a note to say that business had called him away but that his staff would be in touch with her.

Only the abandoned house had heard her tears. Right from the start she had known he was lying. How could work have contacted him when she knew his phone wasn't working? Running straight to the studio house, she had found it empty and abandoned. Alessandro had taken all his art equipment and was gone.

When two smartly dressed representatives of the Castiglione Foundation had arrived later in the week to present her with the keys to a house and a business in the most exclusive part of the English countryside, Michelle's impulse had been to throw it straight back in their faces. But although she was proud, she wasn't stupid. She had listened to their assurances that Signor Castiglione often used his wealth to set hard-working, deserving people up in business. They'd known all about her temporary contract coming to an end, and that she would soon need a new job. It had seemed like the ideal solution to all her problems. Like winning Alessandro's heart, security had been an impossible dream for Michelle. Accepting his offer would satisfy them both.

After completing her contract at the villa, she had returned to a new life in her old country with everything she had ever dreamed about—and more. Within weeks she had discovered she was pregnant. It was both the best and the worst thing that could have happened. With another life to protect, Michelle couldn't afford to grieve for what she had lost. Instead she had a whole new set of worries.

How could she give her baby a better childhood than her own if it was going to grow up without a father?

* * *

Michelle always arrived at the gallery very early to make sure everything was spotless. This village was a tourist honeypot in the Cotswolds, famous for its royal connections. Her clients loved Michelle's efficiency, and she never disappointed them.

She went in through the front door, half noticing a sleek, pale blue car prowling around the market square. Checking her mobile, she disappeared into the office. The phone had been bought during her very first days of freedom, straight after her mother's death. It had been an important milestone on Michelle's road to a whole new life.

I've certainly accelerated along it since then, she reflected as the bell on the shop door announced she had forgotten to lock the door behind her.

'I'm afraid we aren't open yet, but please look around!' she called out, in her best gallery-owner's voice.

Concentrating on her phone, she pressed the button to retrieve her messages. As usual, the only messages were from friends and customers. Another twenty-four hours had passed without any word from Alessandro. That made two thousand, nine hundred and twenty-eight hours in total so far. Not that she was counting, of course. There was no point. He'd always stressed he wasn't interested in commitment. And since returning to England, she had found out exactly how true that was.

She addressed every bit of correspondence about her business direct to him, but the Castiglione Foundation's faceless finance department always dealt with it. Not once had Alessandro ever got in touch himself. Every single magazine she'd ever read warned that holiday romances like hers always led to disaster. *So why didn't*

I believe them? she thought bitterly. *It would have saved me an ocean of tears.*

'Michelle?'

His voice swept in from the gallery, rich with all the bitter darkness of continental chocolate. It was unmistakeable. She froze, struggling to believe what she had heard.

'Alessandro?' she whispered. Then common sense stopped her rushing out into the gallery. She wasn't going to make a fool of herself a second time. She had shrugged on a shroud of cynicism the day Alessandro had abandoned her at the villa. It was time to see how well it fitted. She needed answers, and she turned to confront him.

Time stood still. All her rage and disappointment went into suspended animation. She stared up at him, transfixed. His tall, imposing figure instantly filled her mind and her senses with a heady mix of memories. Every important detail, from his luxuriant dark hair and piercing graphite eyes to the tang of his individual aftershave and all that essential maleness, was exactly as she remembered. Today he wore a classically tailored suit. A tie in midnight-blue silk and solid gold cufflinks graced his formal white shirt. The effect was understated, and obviously expensive. He was standing before her in the totally desirable flesh, and it made quite a contrast to the naked splendour Michelle was trying her hardest not to remember. She knew the only thing that should matter to her was why he had walked out on her, all those lonely weeks ago.

But as she met his gaze Michelle forgot everything but the torrid passion he fired in her. It sizzled through her veins, drawing her close enough to inhale the distinctive warm scent of his aftershave. It made her want him. She had been forced to put on armour when he abandoned her, just to get through every day. Now he was here she wanted him to remove it, piece by piece— but her body had other ideas.

A second, different sort of surge made her step back, both hands reaching for her throat in a mixture of panic and embarrassment.

'Oh… Oh, dear… I feel sick…'

'I don't normally have this effect, *tesoro*—' Alessandro began, but his smile vanished as she shook her head.

'No, I mean *really* sick—'

He sidestepped smartly as she rushed past him and into the tiny bathroom beyond the office. She reached it just in time. Almost immediately she felt Alessandro at her side. When she'd finally stopped throwing up, he pushed a wet cloth into her hands. Michelle had never felt so grateful for anything in her life. She pressed it against her face, glad to hide her burning cheeks.

'Is there anything I can do?' he asked, his beautiful accent thick with concern. It broke her heart all over again.

'You've done enough already, don't you think?' she croaked.

Taking the flannel from her hot, clammy hands, he replaced it with a glass of ice-cold water. When she had finished drinking, he took it back. Then he helped her to her feet. Feeling as weak as a kitten, Michelle clung to him. For a few seconds she deluded herself she was back in heaven. Then she discovered she wasn't the only one who had changed. Alessandro was not melting against her as he had done on their glorious first and last coupling. His body was tense and unyielding. He reached for her hands, held them for a moment, and then released himself.

The ice in his voice matched his wintry expression. 'I've set you up with a home and a job for life. You didn't have either when we met.'

There was a dangerous look in his eyes that made her wonder what more could go wrong with her life. When she challenged him, she soon found out. Her dreams met reality and came off worse.

'You want me to be grateful? For the fact you've been keeping me safely at a distance? Is it because you want to feel you've done your duty? Or so I can't embarrass you in front of your friends, like Terence Bartlett?' She put all her pain into the words. Her heart had taken a thousand knocks over the past few months, but she had never felt as bad as she did right now. 'You've left me quite literally holding the baby, and you expect me to be *grateful*?'

'No, but if you can't be thankful you could at least—' He stopped and stared. His eyes had been riveted on hers. Now their penetrating gaze dropped slowly, inch by inch, down her face to her body.

Michelle watched the broad expanse of his shoulders rising and falling rapidly. Their irregular rhythm betrayed a seething tumult within him. When he could bring himself to speak, Alessandro had to make an obvious attempt to remain civil.

'You are pregnant? Now, why doesn't that surprise me?' he hissed through the mockery of a grin. 'Children are such good bargaining tools. I hardly need ask if you're going to keep it.'

The image he projected was pure Vesuvius. All those terrible rumours about him came back to taunt her.

'I've been left completely alone in the world. I know what it's like to be unwanted.' Michelle edged her bitter words into the simmering silence between them. 'I have to make amends. What else can I do?'

'I think we've both done far too much already.'

For long moments she watched him in terrified silence. At first his head was bowed. Then gradually he raised it, until his words were being spoken to the top left hand corner of the room.

'From now on it's a matter of damage limitation. It can start with the fiction of a happy reunion between us.'

Michelle stared at him. Back in France this man had taken everything she had to give. When he had vanished from her life it had created a void so vast she knew it could never be filled by anyone else. Now he was standing right here in front of her. She had so many questions they tangled in her throat, silencing her. She wanted to reach out and touch him, to recall that painfully short time they'd spent entwined, but his expression reflected her experience. His eyes blazed.

'How have you got the nerve to stand there so calmly, Michelle?'

The bitter reproach in his voice ignited all her protective instincts.

'I'm making the best of the situation. That's all I can do,' she said staunchly, but colour flared into her cheeks.

Her reaction seemed to draw the sting of his anger. His shoulders relaxed a little.

'Yes. Of course.'

Her anguish increased as the fire in his eyes died and was replaced with distaste, as though he was waiting for her to justify herself. Once he had been closer to her than she had been to herself. That sliver of time they had spent together had been the stuff of fairy tales—*and he still is*, she realised. His soft, dark curls might be shorter now, but they were equally impossible to tame. And the cool aristocracy of his cheekbones remained, though he was thinner. Was he working too hard? She ached to know.

Her news was a hammer-blow to him. She could see that. Despite everything he had put her through, she was desperate to stretch out and comfort him. The familiar rasp of his chin against her palm would feel so very good… With an involuntary shake of her head, she gave up on the idea. Alessandro was clean-shaven now. Even that had changed. Everything was different between them—especially the expectation in his eyes. It had become as hard as mahogany.

'Well? Don't you have anything to say for yourself, Michelle?'

She squared up to him. It had taken the two of them to reach this point. However frightening his reputation, he ought to be told a few home truths.

'Like what, exactly?' She tilted her chin, mirroring his determination. Hurting badly, she struck back in the only way she could. 'You betrayed my trust, Alessandro. What happened to us? Where did you go? From the moment you left me in France, all I've done is work, eat, sleep—and try to forget you.'

'Well, now you and I are going to give the world the happy-ever-after it wants.' His voice crackled, and she saw defiance in his eyes. 'No bad publicity must ever be allowed to harm my company. The headline "*Billionaire left me pregnant, sobs virgin*" will sell a million newspapers. I'm not in the business of giving journalists an easy life. Last year I sued a tabloid to within an inch of bankruptcy for claiming I had an affair with the wife of a business rival. Now they're waiting to catch me out for real. But it isn't going to happen.'

There was no question about it—whatever 'it' might be. Michelle saw cold determination in his eyes. For the first time since meeting him all those weary months ago she felt fear.

Reaching into his jacket, he pulled out his phone. One long, irritable call later, he shut it and confronted her again.

'My people will tip off the media that I am meeting you here today. There will be a photo opportunity, and a press release drafted to go with the pictures,' he told her. 'That will keep the papers happy for a while.'

'Will the handout explain why you haven't been in touch with me since—?'

A raised brow from Alessandro snapped off her question, as though his being reminded of their last moments together was nothing more than an irritation to him. Outwardly calm for a moment, he adjusted his tie. Its sleek blue silk was an ideal complement to his dark handmade suit and brilliant white shirt.

'As I always told you in France, I was looking for relaxation, not commitment.'

His voice was stiff with self-justification. He continued smoothing down his sleeves and checking his cufflinks, but as far as Michelle could see nothing about him needed altering. As always, he looked perfect. But to her, right now, he seemed an empty shell. The man who had beguiled her at the villa Jolie Fleur had vanished. She searched his expression, but the more she saw the less she understood.

'If rescuing you today silences the scandalmongers, Michelle, then this is for the best, too.'

As he spoke, the look in his eyes softened slightly. She took another step towards him.

'Why didn't you ever ring me?' she whispered.

Suddenly every second of the good times came back to her in sparkling detail, and it hurt. There could be no hiding the resentment in her voice as she added, 'You abandoned me, Alessandro!'

His lids lowered, giving those beautiful dark eyes an added mystery. 'You have hardly played fair with *me*.'

'I couldn't help it!' she wailed, but Alessandro wasn't listening.

'But I can. And I'm going to.'

He spoke with grim determination, but for a second it was tempered by his expression. He lowered his chin and arched his brows, and in that moment a spark of recognition flared within Michelle. Somewhere beneath this flinty new exterior was the Alessandro of midnight conversation and dawn swimming. Passion had sizzled through Michelle's veins then. It was rekindled now, as she drew close enough to inhale the distinctive warm scent of his aftershave. Her body urgently wanted to make physical contact with his. It might hold the key to her prison of regret. Warmth rushed over her skin as she willed her hand to rise and stroke his cheek, but her body had other ideas.

A second, different sort of surge made her step back, both hands reaching for her throat in a mixture of panic and embarrassment.

'Oh… Oh, dear… I feel sick again…'

'It will be better to get it over with now, before we leave,' he said with resignation. 'We will be safely in Italy by lunchtime.'

Michelle didn't have time to ask what he meant. The word-association between 'lunch' and 'food' sent her stomach over the edge again.

His jaw was resolute as he knelt down beside her a

second time. His efficiency with wet cloths and cold drinks in the face of the turmoil going on inside her body made Michelle feel completely hopeless. She groaned, and then groaned a second time as she thought back to his mention of journalists, travel to Italy, and all the on-lookers it was bound to involve.

'Oh, no—what will everyone think?' she moaned.

Alessandro flung his hands high with a ferocious ex-clamation in Italian. 'At a time like this she worries about *modi*—good manners!' he marvelled, incensed. 'Right now there's only one thing you should be con-cerned with, *tesoro*—and it isn't other people!'

CHAPTER SIX

IT TOOK her some time to recover. Alessandro made tea, and a lot of calls on his mobile in terse Italian. By the time Michelle felt stable enough to leave the back office and walk into the gallery there were half a dozen photographers gathered outside.

'They're never far away. The Cotswolds are full of royal residences and megastar hideaways to be staked out,' he explained with scorn for the subject.

'And they'd abandon all that for a shot of you?' she said cautiously.

'I can't help that. I never asked to be catapulted into the public eye, but it's something I have to live with. Like you, I must do the best I can. It's really only the House of Castiglione that is important to me.'

She gave a wry smile, unable to deny it. His work *was* seemingly the only thing he cared about. Alessandro had stressed there would be no future for them. But at the time it hadn't stopped her fantasising about living the simple life of an artist's wife. Now her dreams past and present burned to ashes under the searing gaze of the world's press.

I knew my holiday romance was too good to be true, she thought sadly to herself.

'Well, I suppose I should be grateful for your help. I could have done without your army of fans, though.' She almost managed to smile, but when Alessandro tried to do the same it ended with a shake of his head.

'As I said, I have a rescue plan, Michelle. I'm offering you an escape, should you wish to take it.'

He bit through his words like silver foil. Whatever he was offering, Michelle could see it involved him in great sacrifice. She thought back to what she had given him that glorious Mediterranean evening.

When she spoke, her voice was dangerously quiet. 'You abandoned me, Alessandro.'

'Now you know why.' He gestured towards the long lenses trained on her, ready to snap the moment they stepped out of the gallery door. The firm line of his jaw still had the power to make her feel weak at the knees, but now it was clenched with barely concealed anger.

All the hours of waiting, the worry and the fear rose up and forced her to challenge his shark-sleek fury.

No, I don't! I don't know anything, Alessandro! she thought. *I don't know why you left the villa so fast, I don't know why my business is being besieged by paparazzi at eight o'clock in the morning, and worst of all—* She tried to fight back tears of confusion. He had been a wonderful man of mystery during his time at the villa Jolie Fleur, but that same blank canvas was now a frightening, frustrating shield raised against her.

Looking up at him, she whispered, 'What happened to the funny, romantic artist I met in France?'

'Life. That's what happened to him,' he said briskly. 'It's what goes on behind the scenes when you're busy having a good time. Now, give me the key to your house. Your things will need to be packed.'

Dizzy with exhaustion, and hardly able to think straight, Michelle nearly laughed out loud. 'Wait! Wind back a bit—you're going too fast! How am I supposed to get back to Rose Cottage through all those photographers? Will they let me past?' More were arriving by the minute. 'I can't face them feeling like this…'

He drew in a long, deep breath. Michelle studied his face, desperate for clues. It was hopeless. His raven eyes were more full of mystery than ever.

'You won't need to. My people will do it all for you. That's how things will be from now on.' He spoke slowly and deliberately, as though she were a child and he was a parent hardly able to keep a lid on his anger.

'Here? Or in Italy?' she said, piecing together the fragments of his earlier announcement.

'At my home, of course. You can't possibly stay here after all this.' He cocked his head in the direction of the crowds outside. 'I don't intend to leave you and my child here a moment longer. Left here alone, you're a danger to yourself. And to my business,' he finished bitterly.

'Is it true that you sacked your own relatives from the House of Castiglione?' She couldn't stop herself asking the awful question.

'I really didn't expect that *you* would listen to gossip.' His voice was a diamond tip, etching the remains of her heart. 'I thought you were above that sort of thing, Michelle. But at least it shatters the last illusion either of us might have. We know nothing about each other, so we can start our new life together from scratch.'

'Our new life?' She stared at him, bemused.

'That's what I said. Now, let's go. The paparazzi will sit around outside for days, waiting for what they want.

They have endless patience. I don't.' He looked her over
with a critical eye. 'Do you have your keys?'

'Yes.'

'Show me.'

Distracted by the arrival of a huge man in shades and
a sharp suit outside the front door of the gallery,
Michelle rummaged in her handbag. She found nothing.
As Alessandro fidgeted, she went through each of her
pockets in turn. With relief she put her hand on them in
the last possible place they could have been hiding, and
pulled them out with a flourish.

'At last. Now, we go.' He nodded, ushering her
towards the door. 'Leave me to field any questions.' His
accent was thickened with tension.

The giant was obviously employed by Alessandro.
He opened the gallery door to let them out. Without a
word, Alessandro handed him the key to Rose Cottage.
Michelle quailed, until Alessandro's hand fell heavily
on her shoulder. 'That's Max. He'll see to your packing.
I have a car waiting for us—stay close to me and say
nothing.'

She nodded dumbly, and then noticed the beautiful
pale blue car she had seen earlier. It was drawn up in the
nearest possible parking space, only a few yards away.

'Is that our transport to the airport?'

Alessandro nodded.

'When does our plane leave?'

'It's my own jet, so departure time is the moment we
get there. And now—*silencio, per favore*.' He took her
arm with cold determination. 'We must smile for the
cameras, Michelle.'

She did as she was told.

The crowd surged forward with a sparkle of flash-guns. Far from bundling her through them, as she'd expected, Alessandro stopped and raised his hand.

'Please, ladies and gentlemen! Remember our agreement. Michelle and I will give you the one shot I promised you could have. Then you leave us in peace, OK?'

Michelle wasn't aware what the crowd made of this, because in the same instant Alessandro hijacked all her senses at once. Pulling her into his arms, he kissed her with such verve the universe exploded around them. His mouth pressed hard against hers until all she could think of was the one burst of totally priceless passion they had shared.

Her hands reached up, desperate for the reassurance of his powerful bulk. The fragrance of him, the hard, perfectly defined muscles beneath the designer clothes, brought all her feelings for him powering back. Only one thing was missing. That moment in the garden, when he had reached out to her, his eyes had been alive. Right now they were magnetite, cold and hard, despite the hot fluidity of his body against hers. His fingers dug into her shoulders, but it was a grip of possession, not warmth.

Seething against this conflict of emotions, she held on to him, desperate for encouragement. Instead he drew back, just far enough for his whisper to be heard by Michelle alone.

'There. That's it.' His words to her were deadly as diamonds, but all threat vanished as he turned another winning smile on for the cameras. 'If the photographers among you weren't quick enough to catch it, *peggio per te*! There'll never be another one.'

'You sound awfully sure of that, Alessandro!' Michelle quipped, but his reaction seared her into silence. He shot such a poisonous glare at her that she jumped. It happened so fast no one but Michelle saw it, but it was a look she would never forget.

With an eloquent shrug for the rest of his audience, Alessandro changed his hold on Michelle and started propelling her towards his car. While he might be smiling with those perfect white teeth, all she could focus on was the rigid line of his jaw.

Her shock at his expression turned to horror as questions began firing from every part of the crowd. Alessandro's people had made a good job of alerting the press. More vans were pulling up along Market Street all the time. The forest of satellite aerials grew. This was a worldwide sensation.

Desperate for guidance, she called out to Alessandro. It was a mistake. In the privacy of her office he had been rigid with fury, but the total lack of emotion he turned on her now was far worse. With a smile that did absolutely nothing to soften his features, he turned his cool professionalism on the questioners. They were crowding in on every side. Despite her fear of this new, unrecognisable Alessandro, Michelle found herself shrinking towards his protection. He had a vice-like hold on her hand, and his complexion was pale, but he used every ounce of his easy charm as he spoke to their tormentors.

'Please don't hassle my fiancée, gentlemen.'

As they reached the car, its uniformed chauffeur opened the rear door for her. Michelle was stunned, and stopped. Alessandro let go of her, but his attention never faltered. Sliding his fingers across to the small of her back, he directed her towards the yawning cavern that was the interior. His towering presence blocked her retreat, so there was no chance of bolting back into the familiar sanctuary of her gallery. The driver and the open car door blocked any hope of escape on one side. She cast a hopeless glance in the other direction. Swollen by the arrival of practically all the villagers, the crowd surged forward. If she ran, where could she go?

A ripple of excitement passed through the crowd. Pens clicked, notebooks were flicked.

'Fiancée? But you've never told us about any engagement, Sandro?'

There was a hint of accusation in the anonymous question. The rest of the crowd was quick to echo it. Alessandro laughed it all off.

'For the first time I've surprised you, gentlemen.' He grinned affably, but Michelle saw his mask slip ever so slightly as he added, 'And, please, Sandro was my father's name. I am Alessandro—apart from genetics, my late father and I have absolutely *nothing* in common. OK?'

'Nothing? How about your treatment of pretty girls?' a voice called out.

Alessandro smiled again, but only Michelle was close enough to see that his sudden flush had more to do with rage than flirtation.

'No one who knows me would suggest any such thing,' Alessandro replied lightly, but his eyes were boring holes through Michelle as he did so.

'History looks to be repeating itself, though, doesn't it? A sudden engagement to an unknown shop girl? Have you got something to hide?' another voice chipped in.

The crowd tasted blood. Excitement bubbled through the whole gathering.

'What do the other members of the House of Castiglione think of all this?' a third interrogator yelled from the back of the gathering.

'No comment,' Alessandro snapped as he guided Michelle forward, her legs almost giving way as she entered the false security of the car's interior.

Even as the door slammed shut behind her the press engulfed the vehicle like a tide. Alessandro dived in from the other side and flicked a switch on the console beside Michelle. Instantly, the car windows became opaque. All the grinning faces outside were reduced to dancing silhouettes as the chauffeur settled himself in the driving seat. Alessandro issued some clipped instructions in Italian. Then he raised an electric partition, effectively sealing the passenger compartment of his car off from the rest of the world.

Michelle fought to control her panic. She had no idea what had been in Alessandro's mind when he'd arrived at her gallery out of the blue, but she knew what the trouble was now. Her news was the cause of all this commotion. Her life had been spinning out of control for weeks. Now Alessandro was throwing it right out of kilter. Things were going from bad to absolutely terrible.

Alessandro secured his seat belt with short, sharp movements. 'Let's get going.'

She needed to scrape together a lot of courage to keep her voice steady in the face of her shattered dreams and his coldly formal fury.

'W-why did you call me your fiancée just then?'

'Because that is what you must be.'

He turned his coal-black eyes on her. They were so lacking in the gentle romance she had once experienced she felt a sudden chill of fear. The words she had once longed to hear were distorted by threat.

'Don't I have any say in the matter, Alessandro?'

He gave a derisory snort. 'You could have been

honest with me and said no all those weeks ago. Then none of this would have happened.'

How could he discount the most important moment of her life like that? 'I'm sorry,' she whispered.

'I'm sure you are.' The fingers of his left hand drummed relentlessly on his knee, and he stared out of the window. 'But are you sorry because you wish it had never happened? Or because I've arrived to take control of the situation when you thought you'd be getting everything your own way?'

Michelle couldn't answer. She stared down at her hands, which fractured and blurred as tears filled her eyes. She prayed he wasn't thinking about a termination. It had crossed her mind for a split second, but she knew she could never have taken that route. How could Alessandro, a man who was driven around in a car the size of a super-tanker, ever understand how despair felt?

She shut her eyes and sank back in her seat. She had woken that morning thinking nothing could be worse than a future of loneliness and hard work. Now she knew differently.

Their journey to the airport was tense with silence. Alessandro only spoke to her again when his people had whisked them through the formalities and settled them on his private jet. Alert to his mood, the staff disappeared as fast as they could.

'I assume from that second little exhibition you really *are* carrying my child?'

His voice ran like a switchblade across her nerves. Michelle raised her head, and saw that he must have been winding himself up for a long time to pose the one question that was really preying on his mind. His breathing was irregular, and he nipped his lower lip as he waited for her reply.

'Of course I am. I wouldn't lie to you, Alessandro.'

'In my experience there's no "of course" about it—not where women are concerned.'

His bitterness towards her was one thing. This second-guessing when he hadn't shown any appreciation of her feelings in the past was too much. She was suddenly as cold as he looked.

'How dare you suspect me of lying to you without any proof, Alessandro? Maybe it's the company you keep. I'm sure confidences can be broken and twisted when there's big money on offer. So perhaps I should try and understand how you feel—'

'You never could.' Her appeal was cut off bluntly.

She was aghast. 'Then how can you possibly expect me to marry you if you think that? Surely marriage must be based on understanding?'

He shook his head. 'I *must* marry you. There's no alternative. I won't have a child of mine born illegitimate. Anything less than marriage will give the press exactly the opening they have been waiting for. I've been trying to live down my family's terrible reputation, but the media prefers monsters.

'Last year the papers accused me of having an affair on the basis of nothing more than a few perfectly ordinary photographs taken in a restaurant. I was photographed dining with the wife of a business rival. Knowing my situation, and how much her husband coveted the House of Castiglione, she wanted to buy it for him. We discussed it a few times in secret meetings. I was very tempted, but in the end I decided not to sell. We were photographed during one of our discussions, and the paper made it out as much more. The scandal almost killed her—and their marriage. I sued the rag, and got a retraction of the lies it printed, but the media never forgets something like that. An abandoned woman and a bastard child would give them real ammunition to use against me.'

He looked at her directly, his eyes burning coals of accusation.

'So? Tell me the truth, Michelle. If I hadn't come to fetch you, would you have bothered to tell me about this baby, before you told *them*?'

For one mad moment Michelle had been tempted to keep the whole thing to herself. When she'd got the results of the pregnancy test her impulse had been to run away and hide. And after failed attempts to get in contact with Alessandro she had reconciled herself to being alone with her baby—and her memories. It was the price she would pay for the few days of fantasy life she'd led in France. She had her cottage and her business, but it wouldn't make up for spending the rest of her existence without him and coping alone.

But life didn't get any more real than it was right now. She was pressed into her seat on Alessandro's executive jet like a frightened witness faced with a seasoned prosecuting counsel. Nodding in answer to his question didn't get the reaction she expected. Alessandro exhaled with a noise of disgust.

'So why didn't you tell me straight away?'

Michelle stared out of the window. As the jet gained height her spirits tumbled.

'How could I?' she whispered at last, watching her tears reflected in the glass. They were crossing the coast, and she could have cried an ocean. 'You disappeared,

Alessandro! I went straight to the studio house, but it was all locked and shuttered. I waited and waited for you to come back, but you never did. What was I supposed to think when I discovered I was pregnant? That a man who disappeared so fast after the wonderful time we'd shared would be a good father to my baby? I don't think so!'

She turned anguished eyes on her accuser. But he had looked away, his lips set in a determined line. Michelle's frustration erupted in a strangled cry. With only her baby to protect, she had nothing left to lose. However furious Alessandro might be at what she had to say, she no longer cared. He might think he was riding to her rescue, but this wasn't the fairy tale she had dreamed about. She steeled herself to face his rage, but a strange change was working over his features. The muscles in his face relaxed slightly and he moved his head from side to side. Without even really realising it, he'd picked up a coaster and was sketching on it—keeping his hands busy as he thought.

'*Sì...capisco.* But I'm here now.' Instead of shouting her down, his voice was a slow river. It rose around her as he asked, 'Did you ever think about termination?'

She nodded, fighting against the swell of tears that stung her throat and made it so difficult to speak.

'I couldn't bring myself to do it.'

'But you did consider it?'

'It crossed my mind for a second, yes.' Her voice was thin and indistinct.

Scoring a vicious line across his sketch, he turned away, hissing a torrent of Italian at the window beside him. Leaning his elbow against its sill, he pressed the side of his thumb against his mouth.

Please don't say something we'll both regret, she thought hopelessly. Sunlight flooding into the jet's interior cast a halo around him. When he eventually decided how to put his feelings into words, his silhouette became an avenging angel.

'Why didn't you call the number I gave you?'

Michelle burned with rage. There was no point in remembering the gentle charmer she had met in that sun-drenched French villa. He no longer existed—if he ever had. All the time Alessandro had acted the part of an ordinary man he had been deceiving her. The formidable character sitting opposite her bore no relation to the silver-tongued charmer who had led her astray so easily.

'If I hadn't decided to visit you while I was in the area, I suppose the first I would have heard about this business would have been when you arrived with the child on my doorstep, ready to thrash out the details of a pay-off?'

Aghast, Michelle was stung into a reply. 'No! That was the last thing on my mind!' Calling her pregnancy 'this business' showed only too exactly how he felt. She couldn't stand it, and barely managed to form enough words to explain. 'From the moment I found out I was pregnant I knew I'd have to tell you, Alessandro. And I tried. But you didn't exactly make it easy, did you?'

This was coming out all wrong. Michelle pressed her hands to her face in despair. The loneliness, sickness, uncertainty and downright terror she had suffered over the last few months finally bubbled to the surface. Despite all her best intentions she dissolved, right there in front of him.

With a sigh, Alessandro pulled a brand-new handkerchief from the breast pocket of his suit and handed it to her across the aisle of the jet. Staring resolutely out of the window while she collected herself, he shook his head when she offered it back to him.

'I'm so sorry about it all, Alessandro.'

'I'm sure you are. But not as sorry as our child will be, growing up with coverage of our suspiciously well-timed wedding dragged out of the archives at every opportunity.'

Michelle had been too drenched in her own problems to look that far ahead. When he put it like that, she flared into new life. 'No! I'll do anything to save my baby from being hurt!'

'I'm sure you will.'

In contrast with her dry sobs, Alessandro's voice was unnervingly calm. Unclipping his seat belt, he crossed the distance between them with heavy, measured steps. Michelle willed herself not to shrink away from him as he took the seat beside her. An artist with silken hands had swept her off her feet. Now a tycoon towered over her, the complete master of all the trinkets his lifestyle provided—the executive jet, the gold Rolex, the finest handmade clothes.

As he adjusted his immaculate appearance, one of Alessandro's stewards arrived, carrying a silver tray. Balanced on it was a single glass of chilled champagne and some mineral water.

'You must be thirsty.' Alessandro sat back to let the waiter put down his tray. Michelle gave the man a wan smile. The drinks only served to highlight how far she had been cast adrift from her holiday romance. Alessandro had made breakfast for her at the villa himself, squeezing thick, rich juice from fresh oranges over ice for her to drink. Now a uniformed waiter was opening a sterile bottle and pouring out clear, tasteless liquid.

So much had happened in the past months. When Alessandro left her, back in France, she had felt totally betrayed. He had abandoned her after they shared nothing but tenderness. Today he had plunged back into her life full of accusations, and the press were hounding them both. How could she trust him while things were so bad when he had left her when times were so good?

CHAPTER SEVEN

THE idea that the head of the House of Castiglione might ever let his heart rule his head was one Alessandro wanted to kill straight away. He was still stinging about being compared with his father. He loathed being linked so closely to Sandro Castiglione. In only a few years he had transformed his father's failing business from an old-fashioned art dealership into an international concern.

Alessandro's fortune diverted a constant stream of spoiled beauties through his life. He always made a point of treating women well—until they threatened to get between him and his work. It was a reaction against the way his father had always behaved. In common with most of Alessandro's other relatives, Old Sandro had possessed the morals of a *bracco Italiano* and the loyalty of a cat. He'd treated work as a distraction from his real career of infidelity. Old Sandro had used women as possessions, abandoning them as easily as he had thrown away money.

Alessandro was no prude, but he conducted his own affairs with care and discretion. With one spectacular exception he had always chosen carefully—women who understood his lifestyle. They knew the score. Castiglione men might sample a thousand flowers, but their wives would be chosen from among a tiny caste of the most influential and ancient Tuscan families.

Then this little foreigner had edged her way into his life. With hair the colour of *caramello* and a laugh that acted like balm to his soul, she had made him forget a thousand years of history. From the instant he'd seen her, nothing but the moment had existed for him. They had been two strangers, enjoying a break from real life with no pressure, no commitments and no comeback. Alessandro hadn't given the House of Castiglione a single thought for the whole of his stay at the villa. It had been the perfect summer indulgence—nothing more.

Or so he had thought.

Months later, here they were—together again. Circumstances could not have been more different. He watched Michelle covertly as she sipped her drink. The more he saw of her, the less he liked himself. *It's all my doing,* he thought ruefully. *I took that glorious, sun-kissed creature and turned her into this scared, world-weary woman.*

Trust was a delicate thing. Alessandro knew that only too well. It was why he never offered anyone any more than he could afford to lose. Until now he had always let women come to him and leave when they liked. This girl was unique in that she was the only one he had approached. She was also the only one he had walked away from. The thought of that made him restless.

Something had been working away inside him, like grit in an oyster. It had been nothing more than a minor irritation to begin with, but the feeling had grown day by day. He could pinpoint the exact second it had started.

He shut his eyes and pictured the scene exactly.

Swifts had screamed past the helicopter taking him from the yacht to the villa Jolie Fleur. The sky had been Madonna-blue, and the sun so intense it had been no surprise to see her lingering in the shadows. And then it had happened. Alessandro had realised she was trapped, and completely at his mercy. No Italian man with a pulse could have resisted such a delicious opportunity. From that moment on he'd forgotten all about work, and had gone to offer his assistance. When she had turned that wide-eyed loveliness directly on him he'd been lost.

After that, things had gone from bad to disastrous. With a smile and a giggle, Miss Michelle Spicer had slipped under his defences and made him forget every rule. Alessandro's only excuse was that her uncomplicated, easy charm had been so different from any woman he had seduced before. It had made him blind to the dangers. It was exactly those qualities of innocence and gentleness that had made him reach out to her in the garden. And that had been when it had all gone wrong. By not telling him she was a virgin she had deceived him. Her silence had turned his fling into something dishonourable, and confirmed Alessandro's low opinion of women. He had done wrong, but her silence had been worse.

He opened his eyes. What else could he expect? All women were the same. Show them a rich man and they became leeches, out for everything they could get. But Alessandro knew what could happen when neither parent took responsibility for their actions, and he was going to make damned sure it never happened to any child of his. This whole problem was something far more important than either his feelings or Michelle's.

'I am not one of these men who take pride in leaving a trail of bastards wherever I go, Michelle.' His accent thickened as he got ready to confront the subject that was crouching on his shoulder.

Her head whipped around and she stared at him.

He carried on. 'I am interested only in the baby. That innocent child needs a parent with morals and values.'

With a moan of horror, Michelle put her head in her hands. How could he speak to her like this? What had happened to the softly spoken man who had taken her to paradise? He had changed, turning from a lover into a mean-minded monster. This was no longer a rescue but an entrapment. She needed to escape—sooner rather than later.

'I can't take any more of this.' She flapped her hands, desperately searching for the handkerchief he'd given her earlier. Finding it, she scrubbed her face dry and confronted him. 'The moment we land, I want you to put me on a plane going straight back to England!'

Alessandro picked up the fine lead-crystal glass before him. Turning it slightly, he inspected his champagne's filigree of tiny bubbles.

'No. You're coming with me to my villa. As I said, if you are claiming the right to be the mother of my child, you must take the responsibility of becoming my wife. A guest wing is being made ready for you right now. It will be perfect by the time we arrive.' He took a sip, and smiled appreciatively at the taste of his favourite vintage.

Michelle blinked at him. 'Then you were serious when you called me your fiancée?' she said in a whisper.

'I would never joke about something like that.'

'But what if I refuse?'

Alessandro drained his glass and called for a refill.

'You won't, if you're a clever girl and listen to reason. I need an heir. You have my child. Marry me and I will support you and care for you and the baby from now on, no questions asked. Refuse, and I will have that child the moment it is born. I would rather avoid scandal, Michelle, but not at the expense on my child. My legal team will ensure you never see it again, or one penny of compensation.'

His eyes were blazing. Michelle was terrified, but she could not go down without a fight.

'Mothers have rights, too,' she said staunchly, her hand moving nervously over her stomach.

'If it wasn't for the generosity of my charitable foundation you wouldn't have a job or a home. A condition of your tenancy at Rose Cottage and the gallery is honesty. You withheld from me the fact that I was to become a father. That means you'll lose both, in case the press decide you got the job and the house by blackmailing me. No court in the world would leave a child to grow up homeless with an unemployed mother. Not when the alternative is better in every single way,' he finished acidly.

Michelle didn't need to dwell on her own miserable childhood to recognise that truth. Her only hope was to appeal against the scorn in his eyes.

'Alessandro, how can I stay in your home, let alone marry you, when all you face me with is accusations? What basis for a relationship is that? If you're deaf to the truth then there's no point spending any more time together than we must.'

'I told you back in the summer—I'm not interested in a relationship with you. But there is every point in the two of us presenting a united front, Michelle.

Remember the international press filling your little street in England? That was a picnic compared with what you will face in *Italia*. There, the paparazzi are on home ground. My estate in Tuscany is secure. They don't bother me. It is my own private haven from them. But for a woman who refuses my protection—well, I couldn't guarantee anything.'

His words were almost a threat. Michelle looked at him, but his expression was impassive.

'All those people back in Market Street will have gone by now. They'll have forgotten about me,' she said with an attempt at defiance. 'They'll have found a new scoop.'

'No.' Alessandro shook his head, and all his authority escaped in that single word.

As he put his glass down on the table in front of them the champagne inside it shivered. So did Michelle.

'That's not the way the international press works when a member of the Castiglione family is at the heart of the drama. For the past two years *I* have been the House of Castiglione. Me! I have turned it from a laughing stock into a respectable institution. Because of that, everything I do is news in my own country—which is good for my family's company as long as the publicity is of the right sort. I don't intend to jeopardise the lives and careers of all the people who work for me because the press turns your little drama into a full-blown scandal. You have a choice.'

His kept his voice level, but it was crackling with reproach.

'If you add to the media frenzy by making a scene when we land, or refuse the protection I can give you at the Villa Castiglione, it will guarantee they follow your every movement from now on.'

All the arguments Michelle had been itching to voice died on her lips. The thought of exciting any more attention was truly chilling. All she wanted to do was disappear and keep her baby safe. There was no way she would willingly throw herself into the jaws of the press.

When they reached the airport, Alessandro's party was fast-tracked through the formalities.

'Where's my luggage?' Michelle looked round in panic, remembering the queues and confusion of her one other trip abroad.

'I'm surprised you ask,' Alessandro said with grim humour. 'You'll never need to worry about anything like that again. It's all being dealt with. You aren't the housekeeper any longer, Michelle.' He took a firm grip on her elbow and guided her towards a private exit. 'Forget it. Just concentrate on smiling, in case a stray cameraman spots us.'

Tuscan sunshine gleamed on the glassy surface of a sleek black sports car waiting for them outside. Alessandro, always preferring to drive himself, had made sure it was dropped off earlier by a member of his staff. Opening the door, Alessandro waited until Michelle was settled before going round to the driver's seat.

'Here comes a photographer. And where there's one, there will be others,' he explained with a heavy sigh, and he was right.

He had to slalom the car around the figures leaping off the pavement, trying to make them slow down. Everyone was desperate for a taste of Alessandro's action.

'They're like ants.' He hit the switch that darkened the car's windows.

Michelle was glad no one could see in, but as the car

threw off its pursuers and moved out onto a main road she wished she could see out. Pressing one of the buttons on her armrest, she lowered the window beside her.

'Why not use the air-conditioning?' Alessandro said as the glass slid down silently to let hot, dry air whip around the car's interior.

'I wanted to see out,' she said. 'This is lovely,' she breathed as the amber and gold countryside of Italy sped past outside.

'It's hard not to love it here,' Alessandro said in a voice heavy with irony.

He drove smoothly and powerfully, and Michelle found his silent efficiency amazing and strangely appealing. She had only known him as an artist, with talent in his fingertips. Now he mastered the car with effortless ease. It was difficult to keep her eyes off him. Although the timeless landscape outside tugged at her attention, she could not look away from the man who had come back into her life so suddenly. His personality filled the car, and she could feel her body respond to his closeness. Alessandro was impossible to ignore.

Eventually he turned off the main carriageway and continued along a series of winding lanes. Rolling hectares of farmland on either side of the road became hemmed with small fields and stone walls. The road began to climb, and Michelle saw a small village clinging to the hillside ahead.

'That's where we're heading. The other side of the valley is prettier.'

His words were prophetic. The small stone walls on either side of the lane suddenly grew taller, until the car was running through shadowy canyons. Ancient multistoreyed houses reared up, shutting out the sun.

Geraniums spilled down from every ledge, doing their best to cheer the roadside homes, but it was an uphill struggle. Finally he pulled in and stopped.

'We're here,' Alessandro said simply.

Michelle sat up straight in her seat. They were parked in front of a large pair of metal gates. As Alessandro keyed a security code into an intercom, she tried to take everything in. This part of the road was in deep shade, made all the more sinister by towering evergreens leering over the top of the wall. It looked like the entrance to a cemetery. Michelle's spirits had never been very high. Now they sank with her, back into her seat. Only when the automatic gates swung open could she dare to hope again.

Her first glimpse of Alessandro's world was stunning. A broad, mile-long drive was hemmed on either side by an avenue of shady lime trees. Between their trunks Michelle glimpsed parallel lines of vines hugging the rolling contours of Alessandro's estate. The end of each row billowed with roses, their lissom banners of pink and white flowers making a vivid contrast with the rigidly trained grapes.

'It's beautiful. Absolutely beautiful,' she whispered. 'Look how the vine leaves are turning red already!'

'Yes…' Alessandro mused, as though noticing for the first time how autumn was searing the foliage. 'The cold nights and low sun make it happen every year at about this time.'

Michelle shot a quick glance at him across the car's interior. He scanned his surroundings, and then returned his focus to the road ahead. Disappointed, she tried to recapture her first flare of excitement at the scene outside. It didn't take long. Ancient chestnut woodland softened much of the Castiglione estate, but there were enough pines and cypresses standing guard on the horizon to remind her that this was the real Tuscany. He was driving towards a large, rambling villa perched on an outcrop of rock. Golden stone and terracotta tiles gave it an apricot glow in the soft afternoon light. As the car growled up the dusty carriageway it became obvious that they really were heading straight for the palace on the rock.

Michelle gasped. 'Good grief—is that your home?'

'It's where I live—for some of the time, at least. You're impressed?' Alessandro sounded surprised.

'Of course I am. I've never seen anything like this before. The South of France was my one and only trip out of England.' She was craning her neck, twisting in her seat to see as much of the vast estate as possible. 'Did you ever build the artist's studio you wanted?'

He shook his head. 'Not yet. It will be a wrench to change from the building I've used for so long. You can't see that from here. It's at the far side of the estate, to make sure I can control who goes there.'

His terse reply brought Michelle up short. It was as though this new, unfamiliar Alessandro was trying to shut her out of the best part of his world. Resentment led her to make an equally acid retort.

'I suppose that means you only use it to entertain people who aren't as grand as you?'

'No. I go there to be alone.' His reply ricocheted back to her. 'My working days are crammed full of people and problems. My studio isn't. Unless I invite them.'

Their car was approaching the villa's entrance. There couldn't have been a greater contrast between the little studio house in France and this gracious collection of buildings. The original, ancient villa had been extended over centuries. It was now a rambling wonderland of tiles, towers and balconies. The car came to a halt in a big cobbled yard, overlooked on every side by dozens of windows. Each one spilled waves of glowing scarlet geraniums over the ancient stonework. It was a startling farewell to summer, but Michelle was in no mood to appreciate her surroundings any more.

'If you feel like that, Alessandro, then I'm amazed you let *me* into your secret world.'

'At the time I thought more of you than I do now.'

Before Michelle had time to think of a reply, Alessandro got out of the car and walked around to open the door for her. As he did so she looked up, first into the closed mystery of his face and then at the towering glory of his ancestral home. Both made her very aware of her insignificance. When staff surrounded the car and began unloading the luggage from its boot it was final proof that Alessandro's lifestyle was as far removed from hers as it was possible to get. It was an awful lot to take in.

One foot poised over the cobblestones, she hesitated. 'This place is enormous!'

Alessandro was in no mood to linger. He caught hold of her hand and drew her out of the car. The smooth, firm touch of his skin was at first reassuring, but his unsettling gaze was too much for her. To her alarm, a tingle of something she had almost forgotten shot straight through her body. With growing warmth she recognised it as physical arousal. She tried to draw back, but Alessandro refused to let her.

'I'm sure a clever girl like you will soon get used to it. Now we must eat. I'll take you to your rooms while my staff take care of everything else. There will be time for a guided tour later on—but only if you're not too tired.'

The mention of food did something strange to Michelle's stomach. It began to whirl as fast as her brain. Things had been moving far too fast. Alessandro might think he'd been gracious in giving her a choice of struggling on alone in England or being overwhelmed in Italy. In reality, his alternatives gave her no choice at all. The height of the surrounding walls, the size of his house and estate were incredible, and those great gates were a comfort. All the same, they made her feel like a bird in a gilded cage. The thought made her light-headed, but before she could decide if her situation was good or bad a more unwelcome feeling arrived to overwhelm her.

'Michelle? What is it? Are you all right?' Alessandro's voice was dark with concern as he stopped and turned to face her.

She tried breathing slowly and deeply. Sometimes it could delay the inevitable. This time it didn't work.

'Do you have a bathroom?' Swallowing hard, she got the words out somehow.

Lifting her into his arms, Alessandro carried her into the villa. Half a dozen of his long strides got them to a door at the side of the entrance hall. He carried her through into a smartly spartan office, and throwing open the door of an executive washroom, placed her down carefully.

'This must be one of the benefits of working from home,' he muttered as she made a dash for the lavatory.

That it should come to this, she thought. *I'm crumpled on a strange floor in a foreign country.* Her shame surely couldn't get any worse. For a sophisticated man like Alessandro, this must be the worst possible lapse in behaviour.

When it was over, she struggled slowly back to life. Behind her, someone was running a tap. As her vision cleared she could see exactly how luxurious this bathroom was. The walls and floor were covered in sea-green marble. It provided the perfect background for all the gold fitments, and the cold, white porcelain she had been so glad to lean against. It was then that her focus steadied on the highly polished black shoes inches from her. She followed the impeccable knife-edged creases of Alessandro's smart suit and realised he had come to her rescue with another welcome glass of water.

'I—I'm sorry, Alessandro…' Too weak and wretched to stand, she drained the glass while still sitting on the floor of his executive bathroom.

'I thought it was supposed to be morning sickness,' he said calmly.

'So did I.' Her reply was heartfelt. 'The past few weeks have shown me otherwise. It can happen at any time during the day or night.'

'I'll get my doctor to give you something.'

'No…I'd rather not.' She shook her head, wincing at the rawness of her throat. 'I haven't taken so much as a paracetamol since I found out about the baby. I don't want to start now.'

'Are you sure?' Alessandro searched her face.

Despite the feeling she had been turned inside out both physically and mentally, she nodded.

'That's good.' He nodded appreciatively and took the glass from her hands. 'You look exhausted. You should rest while you can. I'll take you straight up to your room. My doctor will be sent for—' He was already keying a number into his mobile, but Michelle held up her hand.

'There's no need, really. I'm feeling better already. It was probably all the travelling, and the fact I haven't eaten since breakfast.'

He muttered something in Italian, and then patted her shoulder absently. 'My mistake—I should have insisted you ate more. And you'll be too tired for visitors today, by the time you've settled in. I'll tell the doctor to call first thing in the morning. Merely as a formality, you understand, as I agree with you. You shouldn't take anything beyond the best food and drink—only the best *Italian* sort, of course—while you are carrying the Castiglione heir.'

Somehow his words managed to make Michelle feel better and worse at the same time. Everything was being taken out of her hands. She had no say in anything any more. While the baby played havoc with her body, Alessandro was putting himself in charge of every other detail. She knew she should have been glad of the help. Instead, the last few troubled hours all crowded in on her at once. The long, stressful day, the travelling and her unruly hormones dragged her down into the depths of despair. Pushing her sweat-damp hair back from her face, she couldn't hold back her feelings any longer.

'I never wanted this to happen,' she said softly.

Alessandro sighed. 'It happens.'

Slipping his hands around her waist, he lifted her carefully to her feet. Michelle felt so weak and wobbly she couldn't avoid leaning against him. She expected him to recoil at such a pathetic show. After all, he had been in a towering rage from the moment he strode back into her life that morning. But instead of pushing her off he stood firm. Tension kept his body rigid, and his arm dropped onto her shoulder rather than enfolding her, but at least he made the gesture. Michelle guessed it was the only support she could expect, and she was grateful for it. She closed her eyes and tried to forget everything else but her baby.

'After everything that's happened, how can I put things right, Alessandro? You say you want to improve your family's reputation, but when the baby comes early everyone will know we *had* to get married!'

'I will deal with it.'

'How?' She gazed up at him as he helped her through his office and out into the entrance hall again. His jaw was a resolute line.

'I employ the top PR team in the country. Press exclusives come and go, but the House of Castiglione must go on for ever.'

There was such an unusual edge to his voice that Michelle couldn't bear to ask what he meant. As though reading her mind, he closed his hand over hers. It had all the warmth and gentleness that was missing from his expression and voice, but the feeling lasted only seconds. After a fleeting squeeze he let go, and guided her in the direction of a grand marble staircase.

'I'll deal with it,' he repeated firmly.

CHAPTER EIGHT

MICHELLE wished she could feel relieved at Alessandro's words. Instead, she became more confused than ever. This whole disaster had come about because she had put all her faith in him once before. Knowing what she knew now, it would be a leap of faith to trust him to sort anything out. And as for marrying him...!

She was shattered—physically, mentally and emotionally—and no longer knew what to think. There had been one new experience after another, and now she hardly had the strength or will to put one foot in front the other. When a maid hurried up with a smile and an unintelligible question, it was the last straw. She burst into tears.

Alessandro dismissed the girl with a nod of his head. He waited until they were alone again before speaking.

'What is the matter, Michelle?' His questioning was cool and offhand.

'I c-couldn't understand what she said...she wasn't speaking English...' she blurted out between sobs.

'Why should she?' Alessandro lifted a quizzical eyebrow. 'You're in Italy now. You'll need to learn our language. But don't worry. I'll get someone to teach you.' He batted her problem away with a casual gesture.

The last thing Michelle wanted right now was lessons. She found it hard enough speaking to this new, dynamic Alessandro. The idea of having to work with a tutor in a foreign language brought back all her worst memories of math lessons at school. Her tears kept coming. With a long-suffering sigh, Alessandro found the handkerchief he had given her once before and put it into her hands.

'Couldn't you teach me?' She sniffed into its folds.

He shrugged off her suggestion. 'I don't spend enough time here. As I told you, the Villa Castiglione is my retreat from business life. I'm often away for long periods.'

'So I'm going to be left here on my own?'

'There are worse places,' he reminded her with a glance that took in the sunlit hallway. It was lined with antique furniture and priceless works of art—a silent oasis of calm. 'Market Street filled with paparazzi, *per esempio.*'

Michelle didn't need to speak Italian to understand the veiled threat behind his words. *If you don't like it here, you can go back to all that.* She tried to challenge him with a stare, but it was impossible. Her eyes were too red and raw. The golden light flooding in from the windows overlooking an inner courtyard made him seem more aloof and aristocratic than ever. It cast his eyes in mystery, and emphasised the feeling that he could bring emotional shutters clanging down against her at any time he liked. Appealing against any decision he made would be like banging her fists against a brick wall.

She could do nothing but follow in silence as he led her upstairs towards one of the villa's guest wings.

Alessandro's childhood had taught him emotions were a weakness. As far as he could see, strong men could not afford them. That had become his reality. His true feelings were so deeply buried that he barely knew they existed. But Michelle had nearly achieved the impossible. Several times he had almost told her exactly what he thought about gold-diggers who manipulated circumstances to suit themselves. Then she'd turned those big, limpid brown eyes on him. Every time the words had died on his lips. God, the girl could act. He had been completely taken in by her soft words and seduction in the summer, but it wouldn't happen again.

As he led Michelle past statues and priceless paintings on the way to her suite, he tried to concentrate on his surroundings. When she pointed out exactly how lovely the old place was he made a mental note not to take anything for granted any more. He realised how rarely he took the time to really look around him nowadays.

The Villa Castiglione was the nearest thing Alessandro had to a home—although, in view of his tempestuous past, 'home' was too cosy a word for it. Visitors to the place made him uneasy. It was like exposing a raw nerve. Bringing Michelle here was difficult, but he felt it was the least he could do. No parent should be expected to raise a child alone.

He told himself he should be glad she'd accepted so meekly. He wasn't a bully by nature, and disliked having to force her in any way. The memory of those few delicious summer days they'd shared was still so sweet and fresh in his mind and he wanted to keep it there. Michelle had been so unspoiled, so willing. Everything about her was so inviting—especially, he thought with a lurch of lust, her body.

He cast a sidelong glance at her as they walked along the villa's upper gallery.

'You are looking better,' he observed.

'It comes and goes.'

Like a woman's loyalty, he thought to himself, managing not to let memory taint his expression. Today Michelle looked even more impressive than he remembered, with her breasts cupped invitingly by a close-fitting top. It clung to her perfectly. He could see where her natural softness spilled over the firm outline of her bra. The thought of cradling that pale tenderness in his hands again unleashed a tidal wave of desire in him. But even as Alessandro managed to restrain himself he knew it was going to be tricky.

Each time they passed one of the indoor staff heads were inclined towards Michelle, as though she was royalty. Despite the long, infuriating day, Alessandro found himself smiling at her reaction. She was delighted every time. He liked that, despite the current circumstances. After all, pleasing women was one of his favourite pastimes.

Alessandro's expression clouded only once as he guided her along the gallery towards her rooms. It was when he felt the thrum of the PDA in his pocket. He killed the call without answering it.

Recently voted the world's most outstanding entrepreneur, Alessandro had succeeded by being ruthless. The tribe of Castiglione hadn't believed any Italian man worth the name would sack his own relatives, but he had done it. The least he could do for the family after that was marry a good Tuscan girl, they'd argued—and by that they meant one of his cousins. He was supposed to raise *bambini*, secure the future of the House of Castiglione, and keep them all in jobs for life.

Alessandro's finely sculpted nostrils flared at the

mere thought of it. He'd never taken orders from anyone in his life, and he wasn't about to start now. He owed his extended family nothing. And when he remembered the way his father had always treated him—

'Alessandro? Are you all right?'

'What?' Emerging from his waking nightmare, Alessandro looked down at Michelle. Focussing on her sweet, apprehensive smile reminded him of why she was here in his sanctuary.

The Castigliones want an heir to the family firm. Well, here it is, he thought bitterly.

He shrugged. '*Certo*, Michelle. I was thinking about work, that's all.'

'Oh, I know exactly what you mean,' Michelle said with a rush of feeling.

Her response was so heartfelt Alessandro laughed. He couldn't stop himself. It was the first time in weeks he had done anything like that. They glanced at each other, exchanging a look of shared suffering. For one single second the magic of understanding united them. Michelle's eyes widened, but her own laughter died before she could make a sound. Her lips parted in a way that told Alessandro work was suddenly the very last thing on her mind.

His desire for her rose up again, threatening to rip off his mask of civilisation. He needed to kiss her senseless right there in the gallery, to run his hands over her warm soft skin, to carry her to his bed and make love to her all night long—

That won't solve anything! he told himself sharply. Using sex to block out painful memories had never helped him in the past. But even as he felt the need to try the easy route to oblivion, Alessandro became aware of a new and shocking truth. For the first time in his life he admitted to himself that sex on its own would never be enough to dull his pain.

He wanted someone to take away the terrible hollow feeling that echoed right through him.

Trapped by the look in his eyes, Michelle could not move. His gaze ran over her like quicksilver. He used it, and her reaction, with practised skill. The touch of his fingers could not have affected her more. His expression played her as though she were a priceless violin. It made her want him. But all the time she knew from experience that once this man started something there could be no going back...

At that moment a strand of Michelle's hair fell free from the ponytail she was wearing to keep it away from her face. With a slow, calculated movement, Alessandro reached out and brushed it back behind her ear.

'It still feels like silk,' he murmured, leaning in close so she could catch the longing behind his words. When he spoke again, his voice was as sweet and low as a stream in summer. 'I was curious—I thought pregnancy might force all sorts of changes on your body.'

His gaze was as intense as ever. Michelle could feel it as surely as the whisper of his breath against her skin. In an instant she realised he was going to kiss her. Anticipation crackled through the air like an electric charge. Irresistibly drawn towards him, she closed her eyes, waiting for his touch. Fatigue, resentment, loneliness... She forgot everything. This was going to be heavenly. The sound of her heart pounded insistently in her ears, making her dizzy.

Then she felt Alessandro hesitate, as something outside

their little bubble of solitude caught his eye. In that second a formal greeting echoed through the gallery. It was a maid, rustling up with a message for him. In response he laughed, and the spell was broken. Michelle had to stand by and watch Alessandro and his staff member smile and chat away easily in their own language. It meant nothing to her. She felt painfully isolated.

Her job done, the maid walked away without turning a hair. All the staff acted as though Alessandro escorted young women through his villa all the time—which, Michelle reminded herself sharply, he probably did.

'Your rooms are ready.' Alessandro's tone was back to business—they were strangers again.

As they reached the end of the corridor Alessandro opened a great oak door.

'Welcome to your suite, Michelle. I'm sure you'll be happy here.'

She had a sudden vision of being just another girl in Alessandro's regular parade of female guests. Her face twisted with cynicism—but only until she saw inside the door he was holding open for her. All her doubts vanished the moment he stepped aside for her to go in.

She had expected nothing more than a simple bedroom, with possibly an *en suite* bathroom. What she found was a large, sunlit room with comfortable seats and a table—and this was only the reception area. On the far side a glazed door gave a glimpse of a wide colonnaded walkway beyond. That led to one of the villa's towers a few metres away. Alessandro led her over to the door and opened it for her. Michelle crossed the threshold, but only took a couple of steps before stopping.

'Go ahead. What are you waiting for?' he prompted.

Michelle was too busy gazing at the scenery to

answer straight away. The loggia overlooked slopes spread out below the villa, and it felt like being on top of the world. 'The view...it's breathtaking!' she gasped.

'Careful—it's a long way down.' Alessandro shadowed her as she went to lean on the loggia's wide stone sill.

He was right. The villa's hilltop position meant the ground fell away alarmingly. Michelle was careful not to look straight down—that would have been too much for her delicate stomach. Instead, she gazed across the valley's chestnut woods. Autumn was already spinning gold through the leaves.

'Are you cold?'

'No, I'm fine.'

It was Michelle's turn to frown. She had been so careful not to let him see her shiver. How had he known? Then with alarm she realised what had tipped him off.

Letting go of the balcony, she raised her hands to clasp them in front of her, trying to hide the buds of her nipples. She had been enjoying the tingle of their arousal pressing against the lace of her bra, but his gaze was too appreciative. Her body simmered with an illicit longing to feel his touch again, but he already thought the worst of her. She wasn't about to confirm his suspicions. A flare of colour ran straight to her cheeks. Alessandro gave her a knowing smile, then moved away along the walkway.

'Let's carry on into the tower. It sounds like dinner is ready.'

His hearing must be as acute as his eyesight, Michelle thought as he gestured towards the far end of the loggia.

She had been given the whole of one of the villa's fairy-tale towers as her temporary home. A sunny sitting room led out onto a terrace with more breathtaking views of the beautiful countryside. That wasn't the only surprise. A uniformed maid was setting out a meal for two inside a conservatory banked with flowers. It had been designed as an intimate dining area for when chill breezes ran up the valley. Here, the fragrance of citrus bushes and peppery cyclamen mingled with the oriental spices of their meal. On a table just large enough for two, silver salvers had been covered with a wonderful display of salads and titbits that would have tempted the most reluctant diner.

'Today has been a bad experience for us both, Michelle. Let's sit down, enjoy a good meal and take stock.'

He pulled out one of the delicate wrought-iron chairs for her to take a seat. Michelle's appetite did one of its now familiar U-turns. Looking at the food revived her. She couldn't help giggling nervously as she took her place. Twenty-four hours ago she had been eating egg and chips from a tray in front of a portable television set. Now Alessandro Castiglione, billionaire business-man, was entertaining her at a table filled with exotic hand-made treats. He looked good enough to eat, and so did her stunning surroundings.

This is the perfect setting for seduction, she thought with a painful pang. That set all sorts of alarm bells ringing. Michelle knew she ought to be on her guard. She had already given Alessandro everything. He had responded by abandoning her. Yet the knowledge that his thigh was only inches away from hers beneath the table was pushing that episode right out of her mind...

'This is just a taste of what my chefs can do. Let me know what you like, and I'll make sure it's on the menu,' Alessandro said as he picked up one of the silver dishes and handed it to her. Their fingers touched as she took it, and he smiled.

It was the simplest of gestures, but the expressive look in his eyes told Michelle more than words ever could. He was weighing up the difficult situation, too.

'I don't eat much these days,' Michelle said, scooping a tiny portion of tabbouleh onto her plate. She was starving, but wasn't sure nerves would let her eat. And it would be unthinkable to leave anything on her plate at a time like this.

Alessandro regarded her sharply as he offered some fresh orange salad.

'You must. Everything that goes into your mouth should do the baby good. You're lucky to be in such a position of influence over its health and welfare.'

Michelle cringed. His mention of their child was nothing more than a device to make her do the right thing. She accepted the salad, but knew she had to divert him onto some other subject. False interest in her well-being was the last thing she needed.

'And *you're* lucky to live in a place like this!' she said brightly. 'It must have been so lovely for you to grow up here. Lots of servants to do all the chores, and no need to worry about getting good grades in school.'

She looked at the metalwork forming the conservatory's glazed roof. It was as light as lace. The architecture here was as stunning as the food and flowers.

'Luck has nothing to do with it. It was my misfortune to be born here, but I made the best of the hand life dealt me.'

Michelle's mouth dropped open. It was an outrageous view of his privileged life, but Alessandro was too busy creating his meal to notice the effect his words were having on her. He carried on talking.

'The only reason I am rich is because I work hard. This place has nothing to do with the House of Castiglione. Rather, it is my sanctuary from it.'

His arm brushed lightly against hers as they both reached for the same dish. She immediately retreated.

'After you.' Alessandro nodded.

The gesture was as straightforward as his words, and Michelle realised that when Alessandro was on form, what you saw was what you got. He might have faults, but false modesty wasn't one of them. Her heart began to accelerate at the thought of his other vices. *How many other women have been entertained right here, like this?* she wondered. *And what happened to them afterwards?* Watching Alessandro in his natural habitat made her temperature rise. She put down her cutlery. How could anyone think of eating at a time like this?

He took her hesitancy as a hint, and dropped a couple of tiny filo parcels onto her plate.

'If we're to marry, Alessandro,' she said slowly, 'I ought to learn something about you.'

'You could have done that a lot sooner by phoning the contact number I left in my note,' he said coolly.

Indignation flared in Michelle's cheeks. 'I tried— believe me! When I rang, your secretary refused to put me through to you. I overheard her say "It's another one!" to someone else in the office. I took that to mean you give all your women the same number, knowing they'll never get past your firewall of lackeys!' she finished in a rush.

There was a long and threatening silence. When Alessandro eventually replied, it was with such cold venom that Michelle actually shrank in her seat.

'So you think I'm the kind of man who lies to women, do you?' He held her eyes with his as he took a fork and stabbed at his meal. 'Let me tell you, Michelle, I consider that the worst form of deceit.'

She looked away, trying to hide the pain as she recalled the happier times they had spent together. Honesty clearly had a different meaning for Alessandro.

'You were so unlike all the other people I'd worked for—so *ordinary* when we first met! Now I discover you've got a million staff, a private plane, different cars in every country and apartments all over the world—' She brought herself up sharply. She didn't want him to think she was obsessed with the perks of his jet-set life-style. Alessandro already imagined she might try and take advantage of him. If he thought she'd been reading up on him in the glossy magazines, he might think she was out to make something from her situation. 'I mean, you've told me you have to travel a lot for your work, of course...' she finished lamely.

'The House of Castiglione is a good enough reason to keep me on the move,' he agreed, flashing the briefest of smiles. 'But there's more to it than that. As I've told you before, I don't like to be tied down—either by people or places.'

The atmosphere eased, but despite that twitch of his lips there was no amusement left in Alessandro's expression. His words were clearly meant as a warning, but the nearness of him was a reminder of the pleasure they'd shared. It was as if he sensed the depth of her attraction for him but refused to give her any encouragement—quite the opposite, in fact.

Michelle struggled to concentrate on her food. Her mind was befuddled. She felt as though Alessandro was a master hypnotist. He could convince her of one thing, and then wake her suddenly from a dream to tell her something else.

He continued with all the smooth assurance of a professional host. 'Before I inherited my father's business concerns I made myself successful on my own account. I left school as soon as I could, got a job at a burger place and worked my way up to become managing director.'

'You worked in fast food?' Michelle gasped, her own situation temporarily forgotten. She could hardly believe it.

He shrugged off her amazement with a hollow laugh. 'I wanted to prove myself in a field where no one could say I'd traded on my family's name. So that's exactly what I did. While I was in charge the place went from an also-ran to the market leader, and won any number of nutritional awards.'

That was some achievement. Michelle was ultra-cautious when it came to food. The chain produced the only type of burgers she would eat. It was amazing that Alessandro could take something so commonplace and mould it into such a success.

She thought back to her own unhappy childhood. 'Your parents must be very proud of you.'

'Ha—*neanche per sogno*!' He snorted, but almost as soon as he had done so a strange expression came over his face. 'Anyway, they're both dead now. But if you read the gossip columns you would surely know that? They would also have taught you my father was the most generous of men…but only with money. When it came to love and loyalty—'

He stopped abruptly. Picking up his knife and fork, he carried on with his meal. His movements were in such contrast with his usual one-handed Italian ease that Michelle knew she was looking into an open wound. She needed to know more, but sensed it was safer to change the subject.

'You had your mother to give you that security, I suppose.' Michelle sighed. Other people always did. It was a pain she suffered every time conversation got around to family life.

'I never had a real mother.'

There was a strange lack of feeling in his words. Michelle picked up on it straight away and looked at him sharply.

'Oh, Alessandro, I'm so sorry.'

He raised his head to look at her. Once again she saw the guards in place in his expression. *He's slammed down those shutters against me again*, she thought, but he waved away her concern.

'It trained me to succeed. When I was catapulted into the top job at the House of Castiglione nothing changed. And everything.'

Alessandro wasn't the only one who could change the subject to good effect. Michelle grabbed the chance to steer their conversation away from parental pain. She had suffered enough of that herself. It was good to realise she wasn't unique, but this wasn't the place for post-mortems.

'You went straight from fast food to fine art? That's quite a contrast!' she said, awestruck. 'How did you manage the switch?'

'It wasn't a problem.' Alessandro dismissed her question with a casual shrug of one shoulder. 'I had spent my whole time fighting to improve international fast food. To me, quality is everything. Pace is nothing.

Going to work for the House of Castiglione was like leaving a busy *piazza* and walking into an ancient cathedral. It's possible to appreciate both, at the right time and in the right circumstances.'

'And you struck lucky?'

Alessandro put down his knife and picked up a decanter of wine. It glistened like blood as he poured himself a glass before replying. 'I don't believe in luck. All my life I've forged my own success, without the help of anyone or anything. Don't you say in English, *he travels fastest who travels alone*?'

Michelle could hardly believe what she was hearing. All her life she'd thought she was the only person who'd had to spend every second of every day proving themselves. Now she knew differently. She had always been so desperate for approval there had been no room for anything in her life beyond working for her mother. It sounded as though Alessandro had similar demons. She stared at him in disbelief.

'People who say things like that are usually lonely. But you're so confident, so successful! You can't be lonely—' She looked him directly in the face, trying to see if they had something else in common. 'Can you, Alessandro?'

He took a sip of his drink, taking his time to replace the glass carefully in front of his plate. Resting his elbows on the table, he netted his fingers and rested his chin against them as he considered his answer.

'That's a very personal question. Did I ever ask *you* why you felt able to leave England so soon after your mother's death?' he asked.

Until that moment Michelle had been gazing at him in wonder. Now she looked back to her meal.

'I don't think we'd better go there. My mother would have died of shame to think I'd become the sort of girl who got pregnant on holiday.' She stopped, conscious of straying into an area that should be out of bounds to them both—at least for a while longer.

Alessandro took the initiative. 'Your mother can't possibly have any influence over you any more, Michelle.' He sat back in his seat, surveying her. 'She's gone, and you're a big girl now.'

His eyes roved over her face. Beneath the table she felt his leg briefly make contact with hers. The touch of his expensively tailored trousers against her sent a shock wave straight through her body. Was it an accident? The seductive glimmer in those graphite eyes of his reminded her that Alessandro Castiglione was a man who never made an unconsidered move.

'Maybe,' she answered, uncertain on several counts.

His next move convinced her. As he leaned forward, his wintry expression melted into something close to a smile. 'You have proved yourself woman enough to carry my heir, Michelle. And right now that's the only thing that matters to me. The only thing.'

His movements began speaking directly to her. The long, artistic fingers of his left hand were stroking the damask tablecloth. The relish he took over the action was unmistakable. When he regarded her with those devastating dark eyes, it was with an intimacy she didn't need to question.

'You'd be surprised if you knew what I was really like,' she muttered, breaking eye contact to pour herself a glass of iced water from the carafe standing between them.

She needed it. Alessandro was sending her temperature right off the scale. Was that faint hissing she could hear the air-conditioning, or the surge of her unruly hormones? It was hard to tell. Her mind was reeling with the possibility that any moment now he might reach forward—and she would be there for him. There could be no question about it—

Her self-control was a hair's breadth from shattering completely. She *had* to stop herself anticipating his touch! She *had* to shift the subject onto something unsexy, before all those memories of the first kisses they had shared came back to haunt her again.

'I—I suppose you bring all your sophisticated friends here to the villa?' she began, and then gave herself a mental kick. *Idiot! Now he'll automatically compare me with them!*

'Only the ones who interest me get as far as visiting this place. And they're as rare as intelligence in the circles I move in. None have been invited to stay in any of the guest suites until now.'

Alessandro poured himself a glass of water and took a sip, moving with an easy assurance that took her breath away. She couldn't escape from his mesmerising eyes. The cast of his features always made her want to reach out and touch him. Her body was reacting to him as surely as if his gaze had been the playful caress of his lips or fingertips. Warmth stole up from her belly, keeping her nipples proud with excitement. She could feel the blood dancing through her veins like champagne. The welcome warmth of arousal made her shift slightly in her seat.

Alessandro lazily impaled some *amori* salad on his fork, but paused before lifting it off the plate. 'Beautiful women, paintings, sculpture…I take an interest in them all, but fine art has always been my first love.'

'You must really enjoy working for an international art dealership like the House of Castiglione,' Michelle said, wondering if she was on solid ground again. Somehow she doubted it. Being so close to him, and knowing not many other people had made it this far, would make it hard to come down to earth ever again.

'I enjoy my work, yes. But the people I work with? That's another matter.' He ate the pasta, then stabbed a roasted cherry tomato. When he had finished that morsel, he tapped his fork on his plate, making the fine china ring. 'Wherever there is money, envy and pain are always close behind.'

'You don't need to tell me that.' Michelle shook her head sorrowfully. She thought of the car she had saved up for so long to buy the previous year. Until she'd got it home she had imagined the worst part of living in a house with no garage would be increased insurance premiums. To find the waterproof cover of her pride and joy slashed on the first night, its paintwork keyed and the wheels stolen was something she still hadn't come to terms with.

'Everyone wants to know me now I've become head of the House of Castiglione. Unfortunately, it is for all the wrong reasons.' Alessandro grimaced.

'I'm sure that isn't true.'

He guffawed. 'That could only be said by a woman who doesn't feel the need to impress anyone.'

Alessandro threw his answer at her in a way that made sure he didn't have to open up any further. This stonewalling only made Michelle want to reach out to him again. She could identify with so many of the things he said. Now she was convinced this beautiful, strangely guarded man would haunt her until the end of time. She also knew she didn't need to tell him that. A sea of admiration must surround him wherever he went. She was only one little fish, outclassed in a shoal of celebrities.

Alessandro held all the cards in life—breeding, money and confidence—while she had none. The sad thing was, he hardly seemed to enjoy any of them.

CHAPTER NINE

MICHELLE regarded him as she took a sip of her drink. 'You really know how to live, Alessandro,' she said, placing the glass down carefully beside her plate.

His eyes were veiled, and he didn't reply. She had so many questions to ask him. Feeling rested and fortified by the wonderful food, she could not resist working her way towards the one that burned most insistently in her mind.

'All this beauty encased by such a hi-tech security system.' She gazed at the banks of pastel-pink cyclamen and trailing ferns ranged around them. Jasmine twining in and out of citrus and mimosa bushes added to the feeling of sitting in a beautiful garden. 'How many people have made it through your defences?' she whispered.

'None so far.' His voice was a low growl, snatching back her attention.

It was the opening she needed. 'Then it's all the more amazing that you called me your fiancée in front of that press pack.'

'I've told you. It's the easiest solution. We'll get married as soon as possible to legitimise the baby. That way I satisfy my conscience, the House of Castiglione gets the heir it needs, and I don't have to worry about adverse publicity any more. Things will improve still further when the baby arrives. We'll project the perfect image of family life.'

He outlined his plans with ease. Michelle could hardly believe what she was hearing. 'You're going to use our baby as a photo opportunity?'

He gave a leonine smile. 'No. In a refreshing break with recent Castiglione tradition, I'm going to be fiercely protective of my child. No offspring of mine will ever be used to get cheap publicity. Neither will it be used as a pawn, currency or its mother's latest fashion accessory.'

Momentarily thrown off balance, Michelle reacted by trying to laugh. 'You sound like a press release, Alessandro!'

He inclined his head gravely. 'I'm a realist. That's why I warned you not to be tempted to fall in love with me.'

Michelle had felt a million things for him over the past few months, although love wasn't quite the right word for any of them. Lust and longing, certainly, but love? She wasn't actually sure what that was. With no experience of how it felt to love and be loved in return, how could she possibly know?

Looking at this charismatic and awe-inspiring man, she felt a new ambition begin to steal over her. She knew what it was like to live within an isolation tank of work and duty. Breaking down the barriers that surrounded Alessandro would be a real achievement. It was something that would do them *both* good. And, she reminded herself, there were worse things in life than moving into the guest wing of a Tuscan villa. Unemployed single parenthood back in England, for one.

Smiling up at him mischeviously from beneath her lashes, she tried to find some chink in his armour. 'Didn't it ever occur to you that I'd taken you at your word, Alessandro? That I might have grown to hate you for abandoning me, and that I might refuse your offer to move in here?'

Her words only proved to Alessandro how inexperienced she really was.

'No, it didn't—not for a second. I saw you needed help. I'm the one to give it, however it might make me feel. There was no way you could turn me down.' He shook his head. 'Are you ready for dessert?'

He looked pointedly at her meal. Michelle had been so wrapped up in her thoughts about him that she had abandoned it. Not wanting to keep him waiting, she nodded. To speak might have broken the spell she was beginning to weave for herself. In her mind she had already started to chip away at his icy reserve.

A maid appeared from nowhere and placed a magnificent gateau in the centre of the table.

'The French call this *nid d'abeilles*.' Alessandro picked up a silver cake slice. 'Would you like some?'

The cake was a cloud of featherlight brioche, filled with *crème anglaise*. Michelle admired the glistening confection with its topping of toasted almonds.

'I can't say no to something so tempting.' Michelle looked up, and when she saw the glimmer in his eyes her cheeks pinkened and she looked away, embarrassed.

But a teasing smile haunted his lips as he watched her reaction, and slowly it fuelled Michelle's budding arousal until she ached for him in a way she had never experienced before. She knew it was wicked, but now she had seen him smile she needed more. She wanted his touch.

Alessandro cut her a portion of gateau. Lifting it onto a delicate bone china plate, he passed it to her. She wished there could be another excuse for their hands to touch as it passed between them, but it wasn't to be. The half-smile in Alessandro's eyes almost made up for it—but not quite. Even so, for a moment she persuaded herself those blinds obscuring his true feelings had allowed a sliver of encouragement to escape. Colouring, she looked down and reached for her cutlery.

'Wait—don't start yet. There's an important finishing touch.'

The maid materialised at his elbow with a cut-glass jar of honey.

'Won't that make this cake too sweet?' Michelle frowned as Alessandro offered it to her.

'My chef uses less sugar in the recipe. Honey is the ideal accompaniment. It's produced on the Villa Castiglione estate.'

With his encouragement, Michelle leaned forward to breathe in the honey's distinctive fragrance. It was heavy with the perfume of flowers.

'Try it.'

She was hesitant, having tried supermarket honey once without liking it. Only Alessandro's persuasive powers made her pick up the intricately cast silver honey server. She twirled it in the jar of bottled sunshine. Trailing glossy liquid over her dessert, she smiled.

'This isn't a bit like the stuff I've had in the past.'

'Would you like more?' His accent turned the words into a purr.

'Oh, yes…' Michelle breathed, in a way that had nothing whatever to do with honey.

There was a pause as he looked at her plate and raised his dark brows.

'But you haven't tried it yet.' Putting the honey jar back on its silver salver, he positioned it between them on the table. 'Later, perhaps?'

Beneath the table, his knee brushed against hers. Light-headed with longing, Michelle hoped it wasn't an accident. She gripped her spoon and fork tightly, concentrating on carving out a little taste of the gateau.

Any worries she had about not liking the *nid d'abeilles* dissolved instantly. Its combination of tastes and textures was a divine marriage. She closed her eyes and enjoyed.

'Quite an experience, isn't it?' Alessandro's voice strolled through her soul.

'It's wonderful.'

She finished the whole slice, right down to the last smudge of honey on her plate. Then she sat back with a sigh.

'Every bit of that was absolutely delicious.'

'I'm glad you enjoyed it.' He had already finished his own dessert, and was watching her over steepled fingers. 'Would you like coffee?'

'I'd better not,' Michelle said with real regret. She would have jumped at any excuse to carry on sitting so close to Alessandro—except that one. 'I haven't been able to stand the smell of it since—'

'I can imagine.' Alessandro cut across her words before she could mention her pregnancy. 'They say it affects every part of your life.'

She nodded, conscious that he must want to skirt around the issue. Powerful feelings were torturing her. They had nothing to do with pregnancy but everything to do with Alessandro.

'And mine…' He stood up, the delicate legs of his chair rattling against the stone tiles of the conservatory floor. 'Would you like a tour of your new home? If you're not too tired,' he added as an afterthought.

The thought of being squired around a Tuscan villa at dusk was wonderful. The fact her guide would be none other than Alessandro took a little getting used to. After an uncertain start, today had been a dream spun from fantasies. She had been whisked into a completely different world. There was so much to take in, and despite Alessandro's simmering resentment, Michelle couldn't resist the chance to spend more time with him. Perhaps she would wake up and find it had all been some kind of feverish delusion. Everything might disappear in a puff of reality. It could happen. After all, Alessandro had vanished from her life once already, taking her happiness with him. What was to stop him doing the same thing again?

She set off on his guided tour determined not to be over-awed. It was impossible. There was so much to take in. The moment he led her down to the custom built spa, her mouth dropped open. The best she could hope for after that was to try and hide her wonderment. It was difficult. The changing rooms alone were larger than her cottage back in England. When Alessandro led her through to the pool and bar, she walked into heaven.

'You should take plenty of exercise. I've checked, and swimming is something you can enjoy right up to the time the baby is born,' he said with satisfaction.

Michelle gazed at the tasteful mosaics of fruit and flowers on the tiled floor and walls of the pool. They glowed with colour from underwater lighting.

'All the steamer chairs are inside today. Normally

they are outside on the terrace, taking advantage of the view.' He pointed across the huge room to the far wall, which was completely glazed.

'It's like a tropical garden!' Michelle looked around at the huge terracotta planters standing in every corner and around the bar. They billowed with all sorts of exotic foliage. Palms, bananas and marantas revelled in the warm, humid atmosphere. She went over to admire a fountain of orchid blossoms, and was amazed to see a pretty little tree frog blinking at her from among the leaves.

'The original pair arrived hidden among some imported plants. They love it here, and have bred happily ever since,' Alessandro said softly from some-where just behind her.

Michelle hadn't realised he had followed her so closely. She spun round on her heel, and saw his expres-sion slip from amusement to gravity.

'I'm happy to let them stay—as long as they behave themselves.'

She raised her eyebrows, wondering if the same rules applied to her. If Alessandro monitored the behaviour of wild creatures so carefully, he might intend doing the same to her.

Alessandro inspired such conflicting feelings. From the moment she'd set eyes on him she'd known no other man would ever exist for her. His unexplained disap-pearance from the villa Jolie Fleur had almost destroyed her. Her self-esteem had been totally wrecked. When she'd discovered she was carrying his child, it might have been a disaster too far. Instead, it had proved to be an unlikely lifeline. Preparing to try and give her child the sort of life she'd been denied had kept Michelle going through those dark, early days of depression. That was why she had to fall in with Alessandro's plans now. However bizarre his actions in bringing her here and arranging a loveless marriage, it would at least give her baby the chance of a perfect childhood.

And it might eventually give me some hope of happiness for myself, she thought, daring to slide a sideways glance at Alessandro as he led her through his vast ancestral home. Until they'd met she had spent every one of her twenty-three years worrying what other people thought of her. Then, for a few glorious summer days, Alessandro had blown all her fears away. He filled her mind and senses until nothing else had mattered. However much she tried to recall the angry side of him, she was fighting a swelling tide of much happier memories. She feasted her eyes on him whenever she thought it was safe to do so. Alessandro's cool, aristocratic presence set her senses dancing. And, to judge by his expression, he was fighting to restrain his own impulses, too.

It wasn't long before Michelle discovered what they were. As dusk crept up from the shadows of the ancient building, their leisurely ramble around the Villa Castiglione reached the great entrance hall on the ground floor.

'This is where I arrived earlier. It must mean the end of my tour,' she said with real regret. She was trying to avoid looking towards his office. That was a place of painful embarrassment for her. She went all hot and cold at the thought of throwing up not once, but twice in front of him.

Alessandro had no such qualms. He was heading over to the white painted door, and when he reached it, looked back at her expectantly. 'You still have the master suite to see.'

He pushed open the door and leaned back against it. There was no escape. Michelle had to walk past him, into the heart of his house.

Alessandro's office was full of the warm, stuffy smell of top-quality paper and brand-new fittings. Without the demon sickness pulling her towards his executive bathroom, Michelle had time to appreciate the pot plants spilling flowers and foliage from every nook. He led her out to the executive lift that would take them right to the top of the building again. When its mirrored doors slid open they were in a world where sound was softened by thick cream carpet and the exotic foliage of planted arrangements. Like the villa's spa area, palm fronds and sprays of orchids were everywhere. They swayed seductively in warm, filtered air. But when they reached Alessandro's suite of rooms, she heard the sound of birdsong.

'Oh, an aviary!' she gasped, seeing tropical birds flitting among the leaves in one protected corner. 'I've always wanted one of those!'

He made a wry face and followed her over to the gilded wire of an enormous enclosure filling one end of the lobby. The birds initially took fright at the sight of Michelle, but when they recognised Alessandro they hopped out into view again.

'Really? *Dio*, it's the last thing I'd wish for.' He marvelled at her. 'It's always been here. My father never believed in leaving anything to chance. Anything he might want to do or see, like birds, had to be on the spot. I don't approve of caging anything, but these little creatures get the very best care around the clock. I wouldn't feel happy entrusting them to anyone else, so they'll have a home here for the rest of their natural lives. But when they die I'll never replace them. Poor things.'

He gave them a smile that touched Michelle's heart.

'But come on—it's getting late. You can visit them again after you've seen the rest of my suite.'

Michelle looked dubiously towards a pair of cream doors leading from the lobby. The clean smell of fresh paint sharpened her senses. Although she wanted to break down Alessandro's distrust of her, this felt like an intrusion too far.

'I'm not sure…we hardly know each other…'

'You are the mother of my child, and I've introduced you everywhere today as my fiancée. There can't be anyone better qualified to judge the redecorations that have been done for me.'

He ushered her through the doors into a large drawing room beyond the lobby. Cool and sophisticated, in pale green and cream, it was made still more beautiful by the accent of dark rugs and tasteful arrangements of antiques and artwork. Alcoves around the walls displayed discreetly lit expensive crystal. Michelle could not stop staring. Lovely things kept catching her eye, but Alessandro didn't give his surroundings a second glance. He led her straight through a pair of tall French doors and onto a balcony.

A delicate tracery of railings was the only thing that stood between them and the Castiglione estate. Although darkness was falling fast, Michelle had a sense of great space, contained only by the bulk of hills that rose up all around Alessandro's ancestral lands. A distant twinkle of lights showed where the road threaded its way along the Tiebolino valley. Now and then the shape of an owl broke away from the shelter of the chestnut trees. The sound of its call echoed like mournful music through the countryside.

'I can waste minutes on end out here,' Alessandro said in a confiding tone she hadn't heard for weeks. 'The whole place is usually deserted by the time I'm free to go on the prowl. But occasionally someone's life comes into my field of vision for a few moments—a member of my indoor staff, or one of the estate workers. I might overhear a few words, or witness a scene—then they're gone. What happens after that is none of my business, only theirs—unless it requires money, of course.' His expression hardened, and she saw his hands clench on the balcony rail. 'Then I'm the first port of call for everyone.'

Despite the jaded tone he used to talk about cash, there was a certain satisfaction in his voice. Michelle was intrigued. She had never known anyone who enjoyed observing others from a distance in the same way she did. Until he'd said that she had assumed his life as an international tycoon was filled with other people's lives.

'It's perfect, isn't it?' She smiled, relaxing a little. 'For a while you can enjoy a kind of intimacy with others, but they can't expect anything from you. They don't know you exist. Watching from up here must give you the perfect camouflage. I wish I'd had somewhere like this back home in England.'

'Why would you need to hide?' he asked unexpectedly.

'Oh, I've always been much happier to melt into the background.'

It was a few seconds before Alessandro replied. His answer was filled with the bitter tang of experience. 'At least you've had a choice.'

Michelle laughed out loud at that.

'You must be joking! My mother entered me for the Miss Bubbles competition every year from the age of one.'

'Miss Bubbles?' Alessandro's beautiful dark eyes were puzzled.

'It's a nationwide beauty pageant sponsored by a British soap manufacturer,' Michelle explained. 'The winner gets her picture on the pack for a year, and their own weight in each one of the company's dozens of products.'

Alessandro tried to look impressed. It was no good. For once Michelle could see right through him. She knew he was laughing at her secretly. Everyone always had—especially the judges.

'Did you win?'

'Not once—in five attempts. My mum spent a fortune on hairspray and elocution lessons for me, but it was no good. She was always disappointed. Right from the moment I was born. She wanted a doll to dress up, but instead she got—me.' Michelle spread her hands wide in a hopeless gesture.

Alessandro gave a hollow laugh. 'I think that is called in English fishing for compliments?'

The look on Michelle's face when he said that brought out the cynic in him.

'Oh, come on! You're breaking my heart, Michelle. Surely it wasn't so bad, being pampered and groomed all the time?'

Instead, she shook her head. 'Exhibiting me was Mum's hobby,' she said simply. 'Much later, when Dad died and Mum was left with no money coming into the house, she realised what my teachers had been saying all along. I'm just not size-zero material and I never have been. We had to find work, and beyond art I wasn't qualified to do anything beyond cleaning.'

'So you had to give up the spotlight?'

'It was a relief! I spent all my time trying to back out of its glare,' Michelle said ruefully. 'And "the older they get, the cuter they ain't," as my dear old mum used to say!'

She laughed, but Alessandro's smile quickly faded into something far more serious.

'Not so. You look cute enough to me.' Slowly, his hand slid along the wrought-iron balustrade. He needed to say something to bridge the gap between them, but English was too revealing. '*Li ho mancati*, Michelle.'

To soften his gruff confession he reached out to touch her arm. As she turned towards him it fell away, like gossamer evaporating in sunlight.

'I don't speak Italian,' Michelle reminded him. 'You said you were going to find me a tutor.'

Laughter came, thick in his throat. 'Of course—how could I forget?'

'So? What were you saying?'

He shrugged. 'I'm not in the habit of repeating myself. The faster you learn my language the better. When I'm at the villa I don't have enough time to waste in translation. I've got better things to do, and other people to speak with.'

Michelle felt his words like a blow. For the first time the reality of a marriage of convenience with Alessandro struck home. He would be calling the shots. Her future would consist of long periods abandoned here at the villa, Alessandro's secrets, and probably more lies.

It did not seem to occur to him that this was more honesty than Michelle wanted. His eyes were as dark as memory, but despite that laughter still danced in them. Michelle was hurting, but she had to hide her pain. She tried to laugh, but it was impossible. All she managed was a smile. His hand returned to her arm and he guided her back into his suite. His movements had a fluidity that distracted her from further questions.

'Come—you only have one room left to see. The place closest to every Italian man's heart—his kitchen.'

The kitchen of Alessandro's suite was as glossy and well equipped as the rest of his home. Michelle took a moment to marvel before noticing something. More than any other room in his beautiful home, this one was totally unnatural. The showroom condition of the glossy cherrywood cabinets was just *too* perfect. Every surface was spotless. The place was totally devoid of any human touch. There were no pot plants, biscuit tins, fridge magnets or noticeboards.

It was chilling. She had been shown the villa's enormous kitchens downstairs, and Alessandro had live-in staff to keep the place clean. That would explain why this part of his suite looked unused, but she suspected it hid a deeper truth. The thing Michelle found scary was that, in common with the rest of his villa, Alessandro's kitchen had no heart.

The last rays of sun vanished as they completed the grand tour. Wearily, Michelle followed Alessandro back into his reception room. Reaching some switches on the wall, he pressed them. Discreet lamps instantly shed soft light around the newly decorated room, but the contrast of light and shade made her feel momentarily dizzy.

Sensing something wasn't quite right, Alessandro went straight back to where she was standing. She had one hand pressed to her brow. Looking into her face, he frowned. 'You're exhausted,' he said softly.

'I'm fine. It's nothing but a dizzy spell. They pass.'

'But what about the baby?'

There was a tinge of reproof in his voice. Michelle bit her lip. She had got so used to pushing herself through all the weary, lonely days of her pregnancy so far. It must be difficult for an outsider, especially a privileged one like Alessandro, to understand how 'the show must go on'.

'It isn't an illness, Alessandro. The doctor says I should carry on as normal.'

He was unimpressed. 'That's *your* doctor's opinion, maybe, but you must be guided by *my* doctor from now on. He's calling first thing tomorrow to check you over.' He clicked his tongue and frowned. 'Are you sure you're OK? Your guest suite is right on the farthest side of the villa. It's quite a walk back.'

'I'll be fine. All I need is a few minutes' rest and a drink, if you have one.'

'Of course.'

He guided her across the room to one of several soft easy chairs drawn up around a big old fireplace. Settling her there with a look of grave concern, he turned his attention to the grate. A neat arrangement of sticks and crumpled newspaper lay in it, ready for use.

'If you can't drink coffee, what can you tolerate?' he asked, kneeling down to light the fire. Any time Michelle tried to do such a thing it inevitably led to messy hands and failure. When Alessandro struck a match, flames leapt into life instantly beneath his fingers, as she had known they would.

'Another glass of still mineral water would be fine.'

Alessandro sat back on his heels and snorted dismissively. 'Do you not want something warm when there's such a chill in the air?'

Michelle had the perfect answer to that. 'I could never find decent tea when I was in France during the summer.'

'Ah, but now you're at the Villa Castiglione.'

Brushing off his hands, Alessandro stood up to admire the blaze he had kindled. 'I got a taste for tea when I was sent away to boarding school in England. I had to—it was either that or stay thirsty. The kitchens here always have a good supply of anything my guests might want. What blend do you drink?'

Michelle was tired and overwrought, but couldn't help laughing at his concern. 'Does your kitchen stock supermarket special?'

'Now, that's something I *can't* offer you.' His face softened with a smile, thawed by the fire and the warming atmosphere. 'Your choices begin with Indian or China, and get more exotic and complicated from then on. So—what do you fancy?'

'I have absolutely no idea.' Michelle began to feel better. She giggled, spreading her hands wide and letting them fall on the arms of her chair.

After that soft sound there was an instant of perfect silence. It was broken only by the crackle of logs on the fire. In that moment she realised exactly what she wanted. And, to judge by the fleeting look in his eyes, so did Alessandro.

'When it comes to tea, I'll let you decide for me,' she said quietly.

He nodded. There was a moment's hesitation—and then he walked over to a telephone hidden away on the window seat.

Only minutes after his whispered conversation with the kitchens, a tray of drinks and more food was delivered.

'Your people feed you so much!' Michelle observed as soon as they were alone again.

'They try, but I prefer quality to quantity,' he said, pouring a cup of tea and handing it to her.

It's little considerations like this that set him apart, Michelle thought as she accepted it. The Royal Worcester cup chimed prettily as she stirred in some milk with a solid silver teaspoon. As she looked at the small display of *petit fours* and miniature *biscotti* laid out for them, the delicious meal she had eaten seemed long ago and far away.

'Go ahead.' He smiled, fixing himself a drink from the tray. 'Don't be shy.'

She chose a perfect triangle of lemon sponge, hardly bigger than her thumbnail, and then a tiny almond *tuile*.

'Have some more,' he coaxed. 'It's all there to be eaten.'

'Oh, but it's such a wicked selection…' she said with real longing, looking at a miniature meringue that was hardly big enough to contain the wild strawberry nestling within its curls.

'I insist that all the ingredients come from my estates,' Alessandro said with satisfaction. 'That way, every mouthful is guaranteed to do you good.'

'I'm sure it will,' Michelle said with relish, and didn't need a second invitation to treat herself.

Five minutes later they had finished everything, and Michelle's eyelids were drooping in the warm, dusky comfort of her armchair.

'You're looking better already,' Alessandro said with quiet satisfaction.

His words jerked her awake. She sat up quickly. He was standing beside her, and raised a hand in warning.

'Take it easy—there's no rush. Would you like another cup of tea?'

'Yes—yes, please.' Michelle automatically reached for the teapot at exactly the same time Alessandro did.

In the soft light of evening his fingers closed over hers—at first by accident, then with a definite pressure. It could mean only one thing, but Michelle was afraid her slightest movement might fracture the fantasy. They were both trying to do the same thing at the same time, so it might have been an accident. But then he bent forward to rest his head lightly against hers…

The impulses Michelle had been suppressing all day pushed her gently into the warm solidity of him. In one movement he drew her hand back from the tea tray and enfolded her in his arms. When he touched her cheek, it freed all her pent-up passion at last. Twisting in his grasp to face him, she accepted his kisses with a hunger beyond caring.

CHAPTER TEN

PLEASURE had been the only thing on Alessandro's mind that morning. The news of Michelle's pregnancy had crushed that, consuming his brain with the need to legitimise his child. That was his duty. So where was the pleasure in that?

The answer was Michelle. The curve of her cheek, the gentle flow of her hair—everything about her was crying out for his touch. When she had crumpled into this chair, so vulnerable and pale, Alessandro had known the time for self-control had come to an end. Gathering her up like this and inspiring her with new life was the most natural thing in the world.

He tried to make his kisses slow and leisurely, but his desire for her had been caged for months. It could barely be contained. Her body was trembling beneath his touch. It had been so long—far too long. He felt her desire burning within the thin cotton of her top. It was wonderful. He covered her face in kisses, teasing moans of pleasure from her as she closed her eyes, full of the aching delight of it all. As her fingers kneaded his shoulders he found her mouth again and kissed her quivering lips.

The soaring power of her response acted on

Alessandro like the most powerful aphrodisiac, but it couldn't stop his mind working. That was the trouble with being a 'face' on the international stage. It made you unnaturally wary. Each time someone smiled or tried to be friendly Alessandro got suspicious. He had the example of his parents to blame for that. Too often in the past people had approached him only in the hope of getting their picture in the paper, or worse. So far Alessandro had outmanoeuvred every plan. He had managed to repair the damage done to the House of Castiglione's image by his mother, father and his warring relatives. Michelle was not going to be allowed to jeopardise his peace of mind. He wasn't going to let her get inside his mind.

He'd have her—but on his own terms. Marrying her would secure his heir. It would also give him every legal opportunity to indulge in sex with her without any emotional entanglement. Romance was for single people. Sex was for grown-ups, like them.

He smiled as his kisses and caresses drew her smoothly towards an absolutely stellar experience. Whispering encouragement, sometimes in the music of his own language, sometimes with the sweetest words she had ever heard, he placed kisses all over her cheeks, lips and forehead. As the tip of his tongue danced around her ear, he murmured, 'Have I ever told you my eyes couldn't get enough of you, from the first moment I stepped off that helicopter?'

'Never. Tell me now…' It was the voice of a husky stranger. Michelle could hardly believe the words had come from her own lips, and giggled.

Alessandro felt his body rise in anticipation. Her voice was a low, throaty chuckle, and it was all woman.

She was his. There could be no doubt about it. For a few glorious moments he allowed himself to focus totally on the sensations rippling through his muscular body. Nothing else mattered for him. Their past and future were irrelevant. Only the present consumed him.

The thought of it ran kisses of fire over his skin as he caressed the inviting curves of her body. Michelle warmed beneath his hands, flowing like honey and equally sweet to the taste. The closer he got to her, the more difficult it was to focus on one single charm. Even the nervous tension that tortured her every moment had a strange fascination for him. He could feel it now, expressed in the taut line of her throat. Pausing, he reassured her softly.

She could hear him whispering, but barely registered what he was saying. It was impossible not to return his kisses, but her muscles were beginning to bunch for flight. Breaking free from his mouth, she managed to gasp, 'You're nothing like the Alessandro I used to know.'

'Aren't I?' He chuckled, deep into the side of her neck. 'But you're *exactly* as I remember you!'

It's not true, he thought. *Back in the summer she was as willing as water. Today—today I cannot tell which woman she is. One always looking out for the next opportunity to fleece a man, or the innocent I had in my bed?*

He knew how Michelle worked, and she'd never be able to wrong-foot him again. Tonight he planned to take what she offered, but it wouldn't make any difference to her future. He'd marry her, ensuring his child could be kept safe at the villa, but otherwise she wouldn't be allowed to affect his life in any way. Like all women, she would soon tire of his work ethic and find other ways to amuse herself. He intended to be the perfect father, providing everything his child could ever need or want. What Michelle chose to do would be absolutely no concern of his—as long as she behaved like the perfect mother in public.

His own mother had strayed in public, but unlike his father, Alessandro was determined not to react by conducting his own affairs across the pages of glossy magazines. He was going to control everything the world learned about his family, no matter how much it cost and whatever the private sacrifice. The future was about this baby, not his feelings. Alessandro's priorities were to give his child a proper upbringing right from the start, and make it a legitimate heir for the family firm. Nothing else mattered.

But at times, in Michelle's looks, her sighs, her words, he thought he saw more in her—the woman he'd once thought she was. But it was dangerous to give that thought free rein.

Michelle's perfume drifted around him on the warm air, bringing him back to the present.

'Alessandro,' she murmured.

Something was definitely happening to him. He could feel it in the way his shoulders were loosening up. And he found he was appreciating all those little details that set Michelle apart from his usual quarry. Her soft, curvaceous beauty felt wonderful beneath his fingers. The feel of her, and those deliciously shy smiles she gave him, stood out in stark contrast to the bony triumph and niggling demands of the women who usually came looking for his attention.

'I don't do fidelity,' he reminded himself aloud, just so she could be under no illusion. 'I told you as much in the summer.'

He had to say it, to stop her getting too close. Alessandro had his suspicions that she was cast in the same mould as his parents. She had hidden the truth from him once before, during those lazy days in the South of France. All the time her apparent expertise and smiles had told him one thing, when the reality had been quite different…

For a split second the memory of taking her virginity acted on Alessandro like a slap in the face. He hesitated, but quickly hardened his heart. Yes, he'd left her while she slept, but he had only done it to secure her future. He'd only wanted a fling, and staying any longer would only have meant putting off the moment when he broke her heart. He had thought his way would be kinder, and he had done his best to make amends.

Knowing her dream of an idyllic cottage and a chance to work with the art she loved, he had arranged it all through his charitable foundation. When she had never bothered to contact him on the number he had put in his letter of goodbye, he had assumed she wanted to forget the whole affair.

In his eyes, there was nothing to be guilty about now. Marrying her would seal the deal. It would stop her trying to cash in on his child by using the poor little mite as a bargaining tool. And marriage would give Michelle the satisfaction of a regular income for life—as long as she played by his rules. In Alessandro's experience, money was the worm at the core of every apple. This way, he got to control exactly where it went…

He sampled Michelle's full, rose-pink lips again. Her deliciousness soon pushed every reproach from his mind. All day her subtle beauty had tempted him with glimpses of what the future held. Now he was going to rediscover the charms of her body as though it was the first time.

'You want me. You've always wanted me. Let me take you now,' he growled.

It was a bold statement, but despite his powerful urge to ravish her right there in the firelight, Alessandro wanted this decision to be hers. He had been too impetuous the first time. When she tensed beneath his fingers he guessed what it meant. He stiffened, silently compelling her to change her mind.

'We both know how good it is between us.' His voice was husky and full of longing.

In contrast, Michelle's reply was clipped and desperate. She peeled herself away from him and looked up into his face. Her expression was searching. 'I can't. We mustn't. I was too carried away to call a halt that evening in the villa, but I have to make a stand tonight, Alessandro. You have to realise I'm not the woman you thought I was. That's why I can't give in to you again before our wedding. It's not in my nature.' Her eyes became hooded in a way that unsettled him. 'If you *really* intend marrying me, you won't mind.'

Alessandro pulled back sharply. With a gasp of disbelief he let her go, and ran a hand irritably through his hair.

'I've spent a long time living down my father's bad reputation. I'd *never* have brought you here for anything less than marriage. Of course I'm going to marry you. What do you think I am?' His voice was dark.

Her reply was instant. 'The sort of man who took my virginity and left me to wake up alone?'

'I did what I thought was the best thing at the time. Was it my fault if you gave up at the first attempt at getting through on my private line?'

'I was ashamed and embarrassed for being so weak-willed and sleeping with you, Alessandro. Ashamed because I'd always intended to be a virgin on my wedding day—and embarrassed because…' She looked down at the floor quickly, blushing as all those conflicting feelings came rushing back. 'Because I enjoyed it. If I *had* found you again the next day, I'm not sure I could have looked you in the eyes…'

Slowly, gradually, his expression warmed, until the hint of a smile parted his lips. 'You've been managing quite well today.'

She looked up, and they exchanged the flash of a quick smile.

'We're in an unusual situation, aren't we? Perhaps… well, perhaps there were faults on both sides,' he continued with difficulty, adding quickly, 'Don't be too hard on yourself, *carina*.'

Closing the gap between them again, he placed a delicate kiss on the tip of her nose. Cupping her head in one of his warm brown hands, he burnished the gleam of her hair. 'We've both been having a rough time, but that's all behind us now. I told you back in the summer—it's OK to enjoy life, Michelle. Relax, and give yourself the chance to live.'

Tentatively, she returned his smile. When she leaned against his touch this time, Alessandro bent his head and dropped a tingle of exquisite kisses over the thin skin of her throat. It silenced Michelle, but couldn't calm her mind. She had always thought she was less than human, because for her, enjoying life seemed impossible. Guilt was everywhere, and never more painful than today. She was pregnant, and desperate enough to believe the promises of a man who'd already abandoned her once.

What would Mum have said? The thought tortured her. It tried to push her out of Alessandro's arms. But she could hardly tell him that.

Suddenly she realised she couldn't tell him anything at all. He was filling her senses to the exclusion of everything else. All her worries evaporated as he nuzzled her breast through the thin cotton of her top. With a gasp her head fell back, and she revelled in the deliciously sensual feeling of his lips pressing the fabric against her aroused nipples. Unless she stopped him right now, she would be lost all over again.

'Michelle…' His warm breath whispered through to her skin. 'There's no need for you to deny yourself any more… Unless you really, honestly want to…'

It was the chance of a lifetime. Michelle thought back to their days beneath the summer sun. The experience was still so sweet in her memory. What was to stop her enjoying it all over again? And this time would be even better. She would be Alessandro's wife, living right here at the hub of everything that meant anything to him. If she was accepted into his home she could try to work her way into his life. She could start by trying to grab back the brief happiness they had shared in summer with both hands—

Cold, hard reality trampled that fantasy underfoot. Alessandro was offering her an all-expenses-paid life in return for a share in their child. That was all—no promises of love or romance. She would be reduced to living off him. Life alone in England had been hard, but Michelle had been discovering her independence and making it work. Now Alessandro had taken complete charge of where she would be living and what she would eat. She began to panic. She would lose everything, and be absorbed by him. She would be totally dependent on him for everything.

Alessandro was caressing her in a way he knew she couldn't resist. In desperation, Michelle knew she had to stop him before her body bypassed her mind and started giving the orders.

'No—stop, Alessandro. I can't.'

Digging her fingers into the curve of his back, she pushed him away. It was a rougher action than she'd intended, but she had to be harsh. Betraying her feelings would give him too much leverage over her emotions.

'I can't marry without love, Alessandro.'

'Why not?'

He stopped and gazed at her, nonplussed.

'Because it wouldn't be right!' she said, amazed he could be so cavalier about something so important.

'Rubbish! It is the only option. It will legitimise our baby, secure the future of the company and make sure this lovely old house carries my family's name into the next generation.'

Michelle looked at him with new eyes. Despite her past experience of him, there was no doubting his sincerity about this. Tradition was so important to him, and she knew his pride would be her downfall. If she refused to marry him he would sever all connection with her for ever.

She thought of her poor, innocent little baby, cast adrift because of her scruples, and came to a decision.

'I suppose the Castigliones have been doing this sort of thing for centuries?' she said slowly. 'Choosing a wife for hard-headed, practical reasons rather than love?'

Alessandro nodded with satisfaction. '*Certo.* Can you think of a more logical thing to do? You'll live here as my wife, and supervise the upbringing of my children. Everyone will be happy.'

Something about his bold assertion made her wonder.

'So...you're planning on having more children?' She stroked her tummy thoughtfully. 'I'm still coming to terms with carrying this one.'

'Don't worry—you won't necessarily have to *do* anything. That's what staff are for,' Alessandro murmured. 'It's your presence in the Villa Castiglione that is important. You'll be the heart of my home. I want you on call twenty-four hours a day, every day.'

'And what will you be doing while I'm being Queen Bee of the nursery?'

He stared down at her as though it might be a trick question.

'I'll be at work, of course. I've already told you I don't spend much time here.'

'And you'll be in the Florence office?' she ventured hopefully.

He looked puzzled. 'Possibly...sometimes. I travel all over the world. Wherever the House of Castiglione wants me, that's where I'm based.'

'But...not always here at home?'

He frowned at her continual probing.

'Hardly ever.' He shrugged. 'That's the way these relationships work. Distance can often make them stronger.'

'Can it? Who told you that?'

His eyes evaded hers. 'Oh, I must have picked the saying up from somewhere.'

'A child needs two parents.' Michelle sent his own words spinning back to him.

'Yes—one to work, and one to care.'

'I'd rather we both cared for our child—together.'

'Neither of you will ever want for anything.' His intensity was completely convincing. Michelle would have nodded, but she still needed to make a point.

'I'm not interested in money or things. You can keep it all, Alessandro, as long as I can keep my baby,' she said simply.

He dipped his head. 'Thank you for being so reasonable.'

That brought a smile to her lips. 'I don't feel reasonable. I feel ungainly and uncomfortable.' She looked down at her damp pink palms and sighed. Making a move to rub them over her jeans, she remembered where she was just in time and stopped. The corner of an immaculately pressed handkerchief flipped into her field of view. With a sigh she took it, glancing up at Alessandro as she did so. There was a fragile smile on his lips.

'As far as I'm concerned you look radiant,' he said softly.

'I must look hot, bothered, and the worst possible advertisement for pregnancy,' she persisted.

But Alessandro had no time for her self-pity. His body swayed closer, touching hers. One hand cupped her shoulder. The other pressed an index finger gently against her lips.

'You're talking like a risk-assessor, *carissima*. Stop it—and fly.'

She closed her eyes, remembering their first and last carefree coupling. But there was a direct route from that indescribable happiness to Alessandro's coldly efficient marriage proposal. She had given her all to this vibrant, sexy man, and seen him reduce her dreams to a cost-benefit analysis. Now he was turning the charm on again. It was so *very* tempting…

'Oh, how I wish I thought I could trust you, Alessandro.'

'A Castiglione never breaks his word,' he said quietly. 'I will care for you for as long as you are the mother of my child.'

The thought of what he had been to her in the past pressed Michelle on. She wanted to experience that special fulfilment only Alessandro could bring her. Surely the life sentence of being his wife in nothing but name was worth it for the chance to soar with him once again?

Or twice…? Or maybe more times…?

He had suggested there would be more children…

Michelle came to a decision. If that was what it took to stay within Alessandro's orbit, then she would do it. If she went back to England she might never see him again. At least he said he visited the Villa Castiglione from time to time. That was something.

'Then, yes…I'll marry you, Alessandro.' She ducked her head, anticipating a guffaw of relief, laughter—in fact, anything rather than what actually happened, which was silence. After a pause, she heard him draw in a staccato breath.

'I'll make sure you never regret it, Michelle,' he murmured in one single exhalation. 'Let me show you…'

His arms fastened more tightly around her. *We fit so exactly. It's as if our bodies were made for each other*, she thought. *We're in one mind about the baby too, but beyond that, what have we got?* She drew back a minute distance, wondering if she had the strength of will to resist him. *Can my physical need for him make up for the bad times?* she thought. *When I don't know where he is, but I can guess what he's doing?*

The answer came back: *I don't know.*

'I may not offer you love, Michelle, but at least I'm being honest about it,' he murmured into her ear. 'We're both adults. I need you, you need me. And the baby comes before us both. This will be a perfect arrangement. We'll all get everything we could possibly desire. You'll live a life of luxury here, and the baby will always have first call on my time. Any time, anywhere, my heir takes precedence. I'll be here,' he finished, so emphatically that she believed him.

It was a turning point. Until then Alessandro had only seduced her through her dreams. Now it was happening for real. He was kissing her and caressing her and driving her out of her mind with longing. Despite and because of everything that had happened between them, Michelle could not resist. All sorts of alarms rang in her head, but they were muffled. She could think of nothing more than the pleasure of being in his arms and under his spell.

She gazed up at him, knowing that a man like this could never confine himself within the arms of one woman. She knew she was setting herself up for heartbreak all over again. *But then*, she reminded herself, *I'm used to that.* At least she could grab these minutes, maybe even a few hours of pleasure, before grim reality kicked in again. For now, for once, it was enough to relish every second she could, enjoying Alessandro while her feelings for him were still free of any regrets.

When he asked her again, there was only one possible answer she could give him. With a sad, sweet smile she told him breathlessly, 'Yes…take me again, Alessandro. Please…like the first time.'

CHAPTER ELEVEN

HER words brought Alessandro's body to boiling point again. He caught her hand, ready to lead her towards his bedroom, but lust overcame him. He stopped and took her face between his hands. Then he kissed her, long and hard. As his hands slipped down to roam over her body, his tongue probed the intimacy of her mouth with a precision that took her breath away.

Between kisses he murmured, 'I'm all yours. Undress for me.'

Unconsciously, Michelle drew back. Alessandro frowned. He tried to question her eyes, but her lashes flickered down, hiding them from him.

'I'm not sure…' she muttered, blushing self-consciously. It was hard to believe she had found enough courage to get the words out.

'You know you don't have to be shy with me any more. The time for that is gone.'

Slowly, nervously, she peeled off her top and jeans. Alessandro watched, absorbed by her body. Grasping her hands, he tugged her down onto the warm, soft rug before the fire. His practised fingers removed her lacy, insubstantial underwear. Pulling her into his arms again, he compressed the fullness of her breasts against the rough warmth of his clothed chest.

'I'm going to make this incredible for you.' Arousal turned his quiet laughter into a throb of anticipation.

Shocked by the power of her body's response, Michelle was excited, too, as fiery sensations overwhelmed her. His kisses plundered still more passion from her mouth while his hands moulded her naked breasts. Teasing her nipples into peaks between his thumb and forefinger, he sent a fizz of arousal straight to the most feminine parts of her body. Cat-like, she arched to meet him. Her teeth grazed his shoulder as she tried to stop herself moaning with pleasure. Her reaction enticed him to increase her torment until she felt dizzy with desire. The way he played her nipples set her alight with passion.

When she realised she was biting him in her desperate need to stay silent, she forced her mouth open with an agonised cry. Desperately, her fingers clenched in the yielding luxuriance of the rug beneath their writhing bodies.

Driven half out of his mind by the passion of her response, Alessandro discarded as much of his clothing as he could without releasing her. He couldn't bear to let her go. He could not get enough of her: her perfume, her taste, the feel of her beneath his fingers...

Naked at last, he switched his attention back to the swell of her breasts and their pouting peaks. His lips enclosed one nipple, drawing it into his mouth, where his tongue encircled it. The same raw masculinity sent his hand swooping down her body to part her legs and find the warm heart of her female need.

Michelle's whole body rippled with unexpected

feelings of wanton heat. Her fingers slid through Alessandro's hair, keeping his mouth close to her breast as she rode the waves of delight he stirred within her. She could feel the moist excitement of her sex opening like a flower as it responded to his touch.

'Alessandro… Oh, Alessandro…' A voice was calling his name, and it was hers. Michelle was hardly aware her lips were forming the words.

Alessandro paused. He sensed she was on the edge of orgasm, and he wanted his own fulfilment to be part of her soaring enjoyment.

He moved over her easily, his hands gliding over her body to pull her still closer to him. As he thrust, his kisses increased. Michelle rose to meet him, her body searching for something her mind knew little about, but which felt good. So very, very good. Her body stretched, drawing him in with a desperate urgency to hold him as close as possible. Though he fought to control his body, it would not be denied.

The explosion of his orgasm swept Michelle up to heights she had never dreamed existed. Then, as she felt Alessandro pulsing into her with his own release, great swooping waves of pleasure ran through her body as she reached fulfilment in the shelter of his arms.

As she drifted back to earth, his enfolding warmth made her whole being sing with happiness. She was so totally content, even when Alessandro withdrew from her body. She knew now that although she might never keep him, her mind would store the few precious moments when he was totally hers. The memory of him would be hers for ever. The afterglow of their love-making brought Michelle the kind of warm satisfaction that had been missing from her life for too long. She revelled in it, watching Alessandro from beneath drooping lashes.

Struggling to keep awake was almost impossible—until she managed to focus sleepily on his expression. He was watching her drifting between wakefulness and sleep. But she could see his eyes were totally lacking in emotion. Once again, Michelle was knocked back. A single tear escaped and ran over the curve of her cheek. Alessandro saw it. He took her in his arms and kissed it away, whispering to her in his own language.

She could not understand what he was saying, but she knew only too well what was making him sound so grim. Marriage vows would bind her and his child to him for ever. He must be warning her what to expect. Total loyalty on her part could expect only occasional fidelity from him.

He might kiss away her tears now—but only for as long as *he* chose…

Alessandro woke with a smile on his face. In seconds it became dread. What on earth had he done? What had possessed him to take her again and again when she had said she wanted to wait? Something wild had overcome his natural gallantry. That was as unforgivable as taking her virginity in the first place. What was it about this woman that made him forget everything except his delight in her body?

He moved his head slightly, and confirmed what the warm, solid presence at his back was telling him. Michelle lay beside him. She was still fast asleep.

'You are a minx and a schemer. I was intending to wait for our marriage also—what happened to all my good intentions?' he muttered into the cool morning air.

Carefully, so as not to waken her, he managed to look at his watch. It was nearly 7:00 a.m. At some point during the night they had made it as far as his huge double bed. Eventually sated, they had fallen asleep in each other's arms.

Alessandro knew he should get up, forget the night, and turn his attention to the working day. Instead he lingered, gazing down at Michelle. He could hardly bear to abandon her a second time—not after what had happened to trigger all this in the first place. It would have to be done…although not for a few minutes. He wanted time to savour what he was looking at.

The fullness of her breasts was accentuated by the gentle rise and fall of her breathing. She was dead to the world, and it transformed her face. For now she looked totally at peace. Alessandro knew she would be worrying away at something from the moment her eyes opened, so he let her sleep on. The sight pleased him almost as much as his own body's total satisfaction with their lovemaking.

Then she moved slightly.

'Alessandro?'

He leaned forward, trying to catch her first words. Almost in the same instant he realised she was still asleep.

He needed to go, but something kept him at her side. He told himself it was because he could not possibly leave her to wake up alone a second time. Just as he was convincing himself that was the only reason keeping him there, Michelle moved again slightly. The sheet slipped away, leaving the whole of her naked body on show. Now he needed no excuse to linger. He was spellbound—especially when he caught sight of the scene reflected in one of the vast gilt mirrors lining his bedroom.

Tousled and unshaven, he looked like what he was—but Michelle looked like an angel. Totally untroubled in sleep, there was a wild sensuality about her that wouldn't have been out of place in one of the finest Old Masters. It almost stopped his heart. She was totally irresistible. Lifting his hand, he was about to stroke her awake, but hesitated. He knew he mustn't encourage her. It would be unfair to pretend he could be faithful. His father and all his uncles had been serial adulterers. And his mother... Alessandro's face contorted at her shimmering, faithless memory. His heart sank. He had inherited trouble from both sides of his family.

Lying back, he wondered what had happened to his once legendary self-control. This should never have happened. Michelle had wanted to delay sex until their deal was sealed by the marriage ceremony. If she woke to find herself in his bed, she might blame herself for caving in. Despite her willingness...

Silently, he got up and lifted her gently. She only stirred to snuggle more securely in his arms. After carrying her quietly through the villa, he placed her in her own bed. Her whole bedroom was flooded with light, shadowing the gentle curves and hollows of her body. Alessandro watched her, transfixed. In sleep, all her cares had fallen away. She looked so fragile, so utterly desirable. He feasted his eyes on the place where his child was growing, safe and sound. No harm would come to it now, or in the future. *I've got everything completely under control*, he thought with a smile.

Kneeling on the edge of the bed, he kissed the taut, silken skin of her belly. It was so delicious his lips lingered—and felt the unmistakable flutter of a first kick. He waited, desperate to be sure—and there it was again!

Michelle murmured something, but when Alessandro turned to her in delight he saw she was still asleep.

His smile vanished. She hadn't said anything about feeling their baby move. The thought struck him that perhaps this was the first time it had happened. He wondered whether to wake her up and ask. But what if it was? As the baby's mother, Michelle should be first to experience it. How could he rob her of her body's best-kept secret?

With agonising care, he got off the bed and pulled the duvet gently over her. Then he backed carefully towards the door, praying the baby would dance her awake right now, so they could share the moment.

It didn't happen.

Alessandro closed the door on her and came to a big decision. However much he wanted to share his joy, he had to keep silent. Michelle must think *she* was the first to feel her baby quicken.

When she woke up in her own bed, and alone, Alessandro's message came through loud and clear to Michelle. *I've got my uses, but nothing can keep me in his bed the whole night long*, she realised bitterly. And when she discovered he had already left the villa for his office in the city, her pain was indescribable. He had satisfied himself, so that was an end of it.

She felt sick. This time it wasn't the baby provoking her nausea; it was its father—and her own behaviour. Last night she had been too lost in sensuality to remember all the pain he had brought her in the past. Now, in the bleak chill of the morning after, she realised all too clearly the reality of life with Alessandro.

Oh, what have I done?

She got unsteadily out of bed and looked at her reflection in the cheval glass on the far side of the room. She had agreed to a marriage of convenience where all the convenience was on Alessandro's side. The vows would only be binding on her.

She walked over to the windows, feeling the Tuscan sun stream over her body like warm honey. The sky still had the soft blush of dawn about it. As she looked down on the intricately cut box edging of the parterre garden, Michelle wondered how many generations of aristocratic husbands had parked their wives in this lonely paradise over the centuries. She thought back to the history lessons she had loved so much at school. Mistresses had fun in town. Wives and children were kept at a safe distance in the country. *I'm not alone. I'll be following in a long tradition*, she thought, trying to come to terms with her situation.

Alessandro had suggested she could turn her back on his generosity and walk away. *That only goes to show he doesn't understand me at all*, Michelle thought. She wrapped her arms around her body and gazed down into the sunlit garden. Her life had been hard before she met him. Losing him and going back to England as a single parent would be impossible. She could never find it in her heart to condemn a baby to the sort of childhood she'd had. The poor little mite deserved everything she could give it. If that meant legally binding herself to Alessandro, then that was what she must do.

The artist she had loved had gone. In his place was a flint-hearted businessman. Both were called Alessandro Castiglione, but one was real, and one was a disguise put on according to his whim. Last night had been a more truthful glimpse of his character. From now on he would consider sex with her as his right and duty, not a lasting pleasure.

A wave of embarrassment and shame engulfed her. It was bad enough to have indulged herself like that, but when she next met Alessandro she'd have to face him knowing she meant so little to him he didn't want her sharing his bed all night. Oh, no doubt he'd be tactful and charming about it, but Michelle knew in her heart that Alessandro was one of those men who should have a neon sign saying 'For one night only' over his bedroom door.

She went into her bathroom. It was a mirrored wonderland, but Michelle could not look herself in the face. What had she been thinking of, giving herself to a man like that in the first place? That question was only too easy to answer. All those stars in her eyes had blinded her to his real character. Alessandro would never be interested in turning their original passion into a lasting love, or for that matter any sort of love at all. Why should he? He must meet wave after wave of classier contacts and more beautiful women every working day.

I might become his wife in name, but I'll never be anything more than a one-night stand for him, she thought bitterly.

When they'd first met he hadn't been looking for anything more than fun. He'd found it in her. For him, that was all it would ever be—but Michelle now knew the cost to her heart would be almost more than she could bear.

Despite Alessandro's determination to treat marriage as nothing more than a convenience, his mind kept wandering back to Michelle. The Castiglione building in Florence was full of reminders of his home. The boardroom, the dining room and the corridors on the executive floor were all hung with his acrylics and watercolours of the villa and its estate. And taking pride of place on the wall opposite the desk in his office was a life-size study of Michelle at the poolside of Jolie Fleur, worked up from the sketches he had done of her.

If Alessandro was honest, it was the best thing he had ever painted, but he could not bring himself to admit that—even to himself. The more he looked at the canvas, the more he found to dislike in what he had done. He'd been too heavy handed. He hadn't planned properly or taken enough care. The whole thing was emotionally charged—a world away from the measured, bloodless way he conducted business. And it was having a bad effect on him, he realised, as a representative from one of the city's museums felt the need to clear his throat twice before he could drag Alessandro's attention away from the painting.

'And you're an engaged man now!' his elderly client teased him. 'What in the world will your fiancée say when she walks in and sees *that* little peach on display?'

Without once taking his eyes off the painting, Alessandro stood up and crossed his office. He stood within touching distance of the voluptuous curves that were now nourishing his child, gazing at them long and hard.

'She will have no interest in coming here. But you're right. This is far too much of a distraction,' he said brusquely, turning the picture round to face the wall. 'The days of pleasures like that are long gone.'

The thrum of helicopter blades sent all the staff of the Villa Castiglione into a panic. Michelle rushed out onto the upper gallery to see what all the fuss was about. She was just in time to see a helicopter with the House of Castiglione logo descend past the windows. By the time she reached the ground floor Alessandro had neatly settled his craft in the inner courtyard. Ducking from beneath its slowing blades, he met Michelle on the threshold.

'Alessandro! I thought you'd be away for ages!'

'I can see that.' Checking his watch, he looked into her face carefully. 'Didn't you get the list of instructions I left behind? You should be resting at this time.'

'I was—until you arrived. When I heard a helicopter rattling the roof tiles I got scared…'

He snapped his fingers irritably. '*Dannazione!* I warned Security as I flew in. They should have told you.'

Michelle shook her head. 'You've also ordered them to keep the house an oasis of calm for the good of the baby, remember? Security might well have told the house, but the staff would *never* have disturbed my nap. They were probably scared of what you'd do if they woke me. And they would have expected *you* to let me sleep, too,' she finished pointedly.

He grimaced. 'Point taken—it won't happen again anyway. I'm going to be staying here full-time from now on. I've decided to take a short sabbatical from work.'

The announcement puzzled Michelle, but she tried to look on the bright side. While he took a break from business, at least she would always know where he was. Her spirits began to lift as she realised there could be another advantage, too. With all the troubles of commuting and the business day taken off his shoulders, Alessandro might be able to relax. The carefree artist who had swept her off her feet might reappear in her life…

'Oh, good—you'll be able to spend some time in your studio, painting!' she said with relief.

He silenced her with a look. 'What makes you think there will be any time for that? I've got far too much to do—organising everything in time for the arrival of my heir. You should go back to bed. Monsieur Marcel will be here in—' he checked his Rolex '—forty-eight minutes' time, and you'll want to be wide awake to discuss designs for your wedding gown, won't you?'

He dropped a kiss on her brow. Michelle suspected this was for the benefit of the servants, who were all watching and smiling.

'But—shouldn't getting ready for our baby be a joint effort?' she said, one eye on the staff. They made her nervous, despite their kindly expressions.

Alessandro patted her arm. 'It is. Your body is doing all the hard work, I'm making sure everything else runs like clockwork.'

With that, he strode off into his office. Michelle was left to trudge back upstairs alone.

She didn't have a chance to go back to sleep. Within minutes cars began arriving and doors started banging. People were already arriving for consultations with Alessandro.

Later, as Monsieur Marcel took her measurements and showed her his portfolio of dresses he had designed for celebrities, a maid brought Michelle a timetable for the following day. It was laid out with meetings: dieticians, nursery staff and lifestyle experts were all going to be consulting with her. Michelle had no idea why. Alessandro was so confident *he* would be making all the decisions.

Tired and disappointed, she was beginning to feel like nothing more than an apple tree nourishing a mistletoe baby—or a convenient brood mare. There would be no room in Alessandro's life for her once the baby arrived. Michelle was certain of it. As a person in her own right she might as well not exist. All she could focus on was the way she would be sidelined. She had been so blind! The more she thought about it, the more she realised she had lost the Alessandro she loved long ago. It had happened the first time he walked out on her in France. She couldn't face married life walking on eggshells, waiting to be cast aside again. And this timetable was the end.

Apologising to the dress designer, she leapt up and marched through the villa on a whirlwind tour to find Alessandro. She had never felt so determined to stand up for herself. *He thinks that taking responsibility for my pregnancy means he owns my days as well as my body!* she thought fiercely. She had to get her argument in first—before he distracted her with those come-to-bed eyes and his easy charm.

Those eyes… She wavered.

Her steps slowed and became more hesitant as an image of him danced through her mind. Then she gritted her teeth and marched on with renewed intent. Without Alessandro her life was empty on so many levels—and she resented it. She wanted independence, but life was nothing without him. The more she thought about being a wife in name only, the more trapped she felt.

Righteous fury sent fear and resentment coursing through her veins. When she discovered Alessandro in the villa's vast library, talking to his architect, she was ready to blow. Hearing her familiar light steps, he turned with a smile that would have stopped lava. It had no effect on Michelle. She confronted him, hands on hips.

'I've been looking everywhere for you!'

Alessandro was taken aback by her outburst. The warmth of his smile vanished behind a cloud of suspicion, as he dismissed the man he had been talking to.

'Well, now you've found me. What has happened? What's the matter?'

'Don't start! You've put me off in the past, Alessandro, but you aren't going to do it again!'

'Now, wait a minute, Michelle!'

'No! Let me speak! I can't go on living like this a minute longer! You storm back into my life and drag me off to live behind ten-foot-high walls. My every movement is monitored, but you still can't commit to me. Well, this might be your own personal kingdom, Signor Castiglione, but that doesn't mean you can dictate every second of my life!'

'Are you trying to tell me that you won't like living here?' As cool and collected as ever, Alessandro went over to the iced water dispenser.

'Water! Is that all anyone can ever think of to give me?'

'Some men might smack your bottom, like the spoiled child you are turning out to be,' Alessandro drawled, looking down at her. 'Myself, I prefer a more dignified approach.'

'Me? Spoiled?' Michelle was aghast. 'How can you have the nerve to stand there and accuse me of that when *you're* the one who wants everything his own way!'

'I'm always willing to negotiate.' Alessandro remained totally unfazed. He peeled an absorbent paper coaster from a pile beside the water cooler. Placing it on the highly polished library table, he put the glass of water down.

'Who *are* you, Alessandro?' Michelle asked, exasperated. 'Not the man I met in France, that's for sure! What happened to the gentle, funny man who seduced me in summer?'

Alessandro gazed at her, long and hard. Then he looked away abruptly.

'He became a father. I take my duties and my responsibilities seriously. That's what I'm doing, and so should you, Michelle. The time for fun and games has gone.'

'Some marriage this is going to be,' she retorted.

Alessandro inhaled, long and slow.

'That, of course, is up to you.'

'Are you saying I have a *choice* in all this?'

'There's always a choice,' he said, his voice as coldly insistent as a mountain stream. 'You could put an end to everything right now. Turn and walk away. If you genuinely believe I don't have my child's very best interests at heart, and that you could do better for him by yourself, then I won't stop you.'

His face was totally impassive. Michelle looked into it and believed. He couldn't care less about her. Her life was in ruins, yet he could stand calmly by and give her the chance to make things still worse for herself. If Alessandro was truly so unfeeling towards her, she had nothing left to lose. It made her stake everything on one last, desperate gesture.

'I can't. You know that as well as I do, Alessandro. In your own selfish, twisted way you want this baby every bit as much as I do. The only way I can keep my child safe is by making sure I'm never more than a heartbeat away from it. As far as I'm concerned, that chains me to you tighter and more permanently than any padlock.'

He wheeled away, grasping at the high marble mantelpiece for support. His fist bounced against the cold white stone and his voice had the accuracy of a mason's blade.

'I knew this would happen the moment I let anyone into my life!' he said fiercely. 'It was exactly the same with my—'

He stopped. Pushing himself away from the fireplace, he confronted her. The light of battle was switched off. He glared at her, his chest rising and falling rapidly as his anger boiled away. His face was contorted in the way of someone who had said too much. He was obviously wounded, but Michelle wasn't going to let him get away with it.

'With *who*, Alessandro? All your other girlfriends? Well, pardon me if my heart doesn't exactly bleed for you! I don't have the luxury of being able to compare. You were the first and only man for me.'

She levelled a look of vivid disappointment at him. When he took a step back she tried to feel victorious. Instead she felt nothing but the ache of loss and longing. It pressed tears against her lids and forced badly considered words from her lips.

'And if this is what life with you is going to be like, then I'm better off out of it!'

She turned and blundered blindly for the door, scrabbling past chairs and furniture in her desperation to get away. The only thing more important than escape was the need to feel Alessandro make a commitment to her. She wanted him to reach out, pull her back into her rightful place in his arms and never let her go. Instead he sent nothing after her.

The flood of tears she refused to let him see choked into an indistinct gurgle of grief. 'I'm sorry to have wrecked your master plan!'

She reached the hall, but did not stop. Staff rushed forward with her coat and gloves, but she pushed past them, desperate for the door. Bursting out of the villa, she gasped as cold fresh air seared her lungs. Every breath burned with the rage and disappointment she had been suppressing for so long. Despite her frustration, she was still determined not to cry in front of him. Rushing away from the house, she plunged out into the estate, not caring where she was going.

CHAPTER TWELVE

MICHELLE ran until her legs wouldn't carry her any farther. Finally, despite the cold, she sank down, exhausted. Her resting place, beneath a gnarled olive tree had been sucked dry by its ancient roots. It was as drained as she was.

Like everything and everyone else on this estate, Signor Alessandro Castiglione owned it. *And that includes me*, she thought. It wasn't fair. Her life had never been her own. First her father had pushed her into winning a scholarship. Then when he was killed, her mother had wrecked that future. Only when her mother had died had Michelle managed to get a life. And then she'd met Alessandro.

She wiped a dusty hand across her faced and looked around. Almost all the vast Castiglione estate was visible from this viewpoint. Autumn sunlight sparkled on the metal ladders of men pruning the olive trees. A tractor crawled slowly over the shoulder of a distant hill as an army of grape-pickers moved backwards and forwards, emptying their bags into its trailer. Estate workers were clearly kept hard at it from first light until dusk, bringing in the harvest.

Michelle began to realise they were as tied to boring routine as she had been once upon a time. Alessandro had changed all that for her. He was a good man. Learning about the baby after so long apart had been a shock for him. It was no wonder he'd acted in the way he did. *He's only making the best of it, bringing me here to make sure his child gets a good life.*

Despite her trampled dreams and the cold, despite everything she had been through and everything that was surely to come, Michelle started to laugh. *Oh, poor me! I flew into a rage and sent away a top dress designer, picked a fight with my irresistible soon-to-be husband and ran out into the freezing cold—all because I'm trapped in paradise with nothing to look forward to but the birth of my totally adorable baby!*

Put like that, self-pity was the last thing she should be feeling. Picking herself up, Michelle tried to brush the silver-grey dust from her clothes. She realised her hands were plastered, and then remembered touching her face. Sure enough, she felt powdery streaks. It wouldn't do for anyone to see her like this—crumpled, tearstained and grubby.

She looked around at the paradise she had been finding so hard to appreciate. As her gaze travelled down the hillside she spotted the studio Alessandro had told her about, set in the boundary wall that snaked around the estate.

A smile spread across her face. She knew there would be a sink inside, where she could freshen up. There would be other things, too. Alessandro might not have put up any resistance to her running away, but it hadn't always been like that. There was another side to him—his art. She wanted to glimpse it again, and relive those few tender moments they had shared.

Alessandro's studio was a one-roomed, low-roofed building. All the windows were on the north side, which faced into the estate. This made it totally private. Getting inside was much less trouble than Michelle had expected. Confident in all his security systems, he hadn't bothered to lock the door. Its handle was stiff with disuse, but Michelle persevered. She needed all her strength to work it. There was nothing wrong with the hinges, which swung open smoothly without a sound.

She paused on the threshold. Alessandro's workshop was not a bit like the studio house in France. This place was dark and sad with abandoned dreams. She shivered—and not only because of the cold. This wasn't a place to linger. Turning to leave, she discovered she was in trouble. The door wouldn't open. She had closed it against the wind that threatened to scatter Alessandro's already tumbled papers and artwork. Now it refused to open.

She groaned. If only she hadn't dashed out without picking up her coat and mobile phone! She blew on her hands, but it did no good. There were so many chinks in the old building, and the wicked wind found every one of them. Luckily, as an artist's studio, it wasn't short of rags. Blocking every draught she could find took Michelle's mind off the fact it would soon be dark. Poking around the small single room, she discovered a little oil lamp. Eventually she found a heater, too. Alessandro had been using it as a table, she noticed disapprovingly.

As she tried to slide the heater out from its hiding

place, piles of books, papers and abandoned projects began to shift. She tried to stop the landslide, but it attacked on too many fronts. Although she managed to catch some, sheaves of work flowed past her open arms and slithered to the ground. Her hands were so cold it would take ages to stack it all up again. She decided to warm herself first, and then set to work.

The heater's burners were black with soot, but eventually she got it going. She had done a good job with the draught-proofing too. Within minutes she was beginning to thaw out. Kneeling down on the floor, she began sorting out the paperwork covering the floor. There was no system to any of it. Books and back copies of craft magazines had been heaped up anyhow. Many of them had old receipts or sketches used as bookmarks. It was quite a contrast from Alessandro's great formal library back in the villa!

As she tidied around, Michelle found a packing case filled to the top with all sorts of interesting things. She didn't mean to look, and mostly she didn't have to. Everything was neatly filed in plastic wallets or cardboard covers, with a line or two of description on the front and some dates. The first file she pulled out was dated only a few weeks earlier.

Remembering the old saying 'eavesdroppers hear no good of themselves', she put it back quickly, afraid it might contain something about her. She imagined she would be on safer ground with the volumes of school reports and photographs, further down. She was wrong. Alessandro had been clever and keen at school, which was more than could be said for either of his parents. She read a dozen variations on the theme of '...*it would be useful to see you both at least once...*'

The Castiglione family might be long on tradition, but they were short on affection. Reading through the paperwork, she discovered that Alessandro had spent virtually all his school holidays marooned in the boarding houses of the best English public schools. That was no life for a child. Michelle burned at the injustices done to him. Curious to see who had inflicted such a sentence, she delved further into the archives.

There were typed letters signed in flowing hands, claiming important business as far afield as Kentucky, Melbourne, London and the South of France. For every apology there was a newspaper clipping dated in Alessandro's writing: photographs of an aristocratic, self-satisfied man at the races, a gaunt supermodel watching Wimbledon from behind enormous designer sunglasses or on the red carpet at Cannes. Michelle scowled. No child of hers was going to suffer absentee parents.

I bet he hated being treated like this, she thought, remembering headlines like *'Poor Little Rich Boy'*, and the press coverage of his abandonment and isolation. *If I go in all guns blazing, accusing him of inflicting the same life on his own child before it's even born, we'll fight and achieve nothing.*

She sat down with her back against the packing case, considering. There had to be another way. When she was a child she'd sat back and taken everything life—or rather her mother—had thrown at her. That had got her nowhere. But arguing with Alessandro was pointless—and painful, too. She had been smothered as a child. Alessandro had been left to fend for himself. With a pang, Michelle realised she had been trying to turn the tables too completely. She wasn't used to independence. It made her heavy handed when it came to getting what she wanted.

As she thought her way around the problem, she began to see a way ahead. Alessandro was a tycoon. Businessmen spent their time negotiating. He was used to that way of working, so she'd learn to do it too. Then she could make sure their baby got a fair share in its father's life. She smiled. A lovely warm glow of satisfaction spread through her. Any minute now she would try to get out again and head back to the villa, ready to apologise and put her new plan into action. But not quite yet…

The studio had warmed up well. *It's almost stuffy*, she thought with a frown. But letting in fresh air would mean cooling the place down. She closed her eyes. It would be a shame to open a window when she'd worked so hard to get the place warm. And taking a nap might stave off the headache that was starting to creep up on her…

Deep in thought, Alessandro rubbed a forefinger back and forth across his upper lip. It was a complete mystery. Michelle had vanished from the face of the earth. The last time he'd seen her she had been storming away from the villa, furious enough to walk all the way to England. Yet no one had seen her leave the estate. He was concerned. Michelle had turned his carefully ordered life on its head, and now she had disappeared.

It wasn't possible. Part of him laughed off the idea of a woman walking out on him. But way down in the deepest corners of his soul another emotion was stirring. It was an overpowering need to know where she was. This was an alien feeling for him. In the past he had secretly felt glad whenever a woman tired of his attitude and flounced away. It had saved him the trouble of ditching her.

Losing Michelle was a completely different prospect.

He hadn't expected her to call his bluff. He'd never dreamed she would actually storm out.

And his reaction to what had happened stunned him most of all.

He wanted her back.

Now he came to think of it, he'd actually wanted her back in his life from the moment he'd left her in France.

He stared deep into the flames flickering in the library hearth, remembering. Her wide-eyed nervousness at their first meeting had been delicious. Their midnight talk on the swing-seat had turned out even better. And as for that morning in the pool…

A smile lightened his lips. Firelight danced in his eyes as he thought back over those few happy days. Where had they gone? He thought about the sketches he had made in France, the painting in his office, and the furious work he had done in his studio when he returned home. The images that had captured the raw intensity between them in France…

No one had seen her leave the estate.

It was the clue he needed. Michelle was so like him— they both craved solitude, yet deep down shared a need for security. She would have gone to the one place inside the estate boundary where Alessandro needed to go himself. Now all he had to do was fetch her back. Michelle might resent having to accept his help, but her independence and stability was exactly what *he* needed to experience right now. Striding out of the house with new determination, he went off to find her.

The evening was brittle with cold. Plunging out of the villa, Alessandro entered a shadowy world of starlight. Owls in the valley sent out mournful wails and quavers.

He barely noticed. Covering the distance between the house and his studio in less than ten minutes, his footsteps crunched on the gritty path.

Breasting the hill, any chill vanished instantly in his warm glow of satisfaction at being proved right. A feeble orange light stood out against the darkness. Alessandro stopped to savour the moment. It was then he wished he'd brought his jacket. Wrapping Michelle up in it to carry her home would have felt so good… The thought made him smile as he set off down the hillside.

His good humour didn't falter until there was no reply to his knock at the studio door. He tried again.

'It's me, Michelle. I've come to say—' The word stuck in his throat.

She had accused him of being a different man. If she still wanted the man who had seduced her in France, then he wanted to change back. But apologising at the top of his voice through solid oak was a challenge too far.

He tried the door. It wouldn't budge. Annoyed, he looked through the window. The light was fading fast, and he could hardly see anything in the growing gloom—except the old heater he'd been using as a temporary table.

The last time he'd lit that, the pounding headache he'd developed had been enough of a warning that it wasn't working properly.

But now it was standing in the centre of the room.

There was no time to think. Alessandro kicked the door down, recoiling at the thick, suffocating atmosphere. The little oil lamp flared in the sudden rush of fresh air. In its ghastly light he saw Michelle, slumped against a packing case. Taking a deep breath he darted into the airless studio and pulled her outside.

The shock of being so roughly handled combined with the cold night air brought her back to life with a groan.

'Oh…my head…'

'*Idiota!*' Alessandro struck his forehead with the heel of his hand.

'Hold on…' Grabbing at the flotsam and jetsam of their last argument, Michelle dog-paddled back to consciousness. 'Don't start calling me names—'

'I was talking to myself. I let you run off, and I thought I'd lost you—' Alessandro began desperately, but words were no longer enough. He pulled her into his arms, hugging her so hard it squeezed nearly all the breath out of her lungs. 'Oh, Michelle…'

She was confused, but she didn't care. Alessandro was here, she was in his arms, and in her mind there was only one thing more important than that.

'The baby…' she wailed.

'No, Michelle—I'm more worried about *you*!'

The intensity of Alessandro's desperate cry brought them both to their senses. They stared at each other, white-faced. It was an impulsive show of emotion neither had expected. Desperate to distract Michelle from his slip, Alessandro started to lower her to the ground. Changing his mind, he took a firmer grip on her, and fastened a manfully flinty gaze on the horizon.

'That is…what I *meant* to say was—you have to be OK, Michelle, if our—*your*—baby—I mean, my *heir*—is going to have any chance of survival.'

No matter how many alterations he made to stiffen his story, Alessandro was determined to the end. Michelle searched his face, trying to spot some glimmer of tenderness behind his stony facade.

Still trying to cover his tracks, Alessandro dragged his feelings onto higher moral ground. 'Didn't you have the sense to know that old lamp and the heater might use up all the oxygen? You could have killed yourself!'

The breath caught in his throat, and his expression changed abruptly. His eyes became dark points of pain. Michelle watched as some other, far worse conclusion contorted his features.

'Or is that what you intended? After the way you stormed out of the library?'

There was no pretence about his voice now. Only pure dread.

For a long time Michelle could not answer. She shut her eyes, unable to bear the horror in his gaze. How could he possibly think such a thing? Tears couldn't wash away the pounding pain from her head, and her throat was raw. Eventually she managed to move her head, first to the left, then the right.

'Never.' The single word whispered into the cold, clean air between them. 'I couldn't bear the thought I might never see you again.'

After she said that, Alessandro was so quiet for so long that she opened her eyes. He was looking down at her, and his face was transformed. Words came out eventually, through a haze of disbelief.

'After all I've done? Taking away your independence and bringing you to a place where you don't even speak the language?'

Her eyes never left his as she took hold of his hands and squeezed them between her own. 'You only did it because you cared for our baby—in a way that no one ever cared for you when you were young.'

His lines of concern for her deepened, then his beautiful dark eyes flicked towards the studio. 'You found the press cuttings?'

She nodded. 'And that isn't all. I read some of the correspondence, too, Alessandro. It was wrong of me, but I couldn't help it. I'm so sorry.'

'Don't apologise. I've read plenty of things I shouldn't have in the past—'

'No—I mean I'm sorry that you went through such torture,' she interrupted him, finding renewed strength at the memory of all those icily formal letters. 'Now I can see why you are so absorbed in our baby.'

'If you picked that up from the personal things,' he said, his eyes guarded, watching her for any clue to her reaction, 'then the newspaper articles about my parents must have told you all you need to know about me.'

She gazed at him, trying to fathom meaning from his pained expression. Slowly she shook her head. 'No...all I saw was a bewildered little boy treated as nothing more than a bargaining chip. The two people in the world you should have been able to trust and rely on to put you first seemed to spend their whole lives trampling over each other in their search for publicity.'

'That's why it is always such a relief to escape from the public eye and come here, to the Villa Castiglione.'

'Then surely that's all the more reason for you to make the effort to stay here more often?' she said quietly.

'You're the last person who should be encouraging me.' He gave a mirthless laugh. 'Why would a treasure like you want to spend time with someone who has adulterous genes on both sides of his family?'

'*Adulterous genes?*' Michelle erupted in laughter, before clapping a hand to her throbbing head. 'What in the world are they?'

'Neither of my parents had it in them to be faithful.'

Michelle narrowed her eyes. 'Why go looking for trouble? You work hard, and all the arrangements you're making for this baby show how selfless and generous you can be. That makes you the complete opposite of your parents, from what I've read about them. I certainly work hard not to take after *my* mother. She was a hypochondriac. That's why I really hated it when you saw me being sick. I like to keep my troubles to myself.' She patted her tummy thoughtfully.

He slipped his arms around her again. Keeping her warm felt *so* good. 'It was no trouble. I'm responsible for the way you are feeling. I want to help.'

His concern was so genuine she couldn't help smiling. 'Thanks, but don't worry. It's my problem! I can't stand anyone seeing me ill. I'm convinced they'll think I'm putting it on, because that's the way Mum always—' Her smile faltered. 'Alessandro…'

He was alert instantly. 'What is it?'

She grabbed his hand and pulled it towards her.

Alarmed, he wrenched it free and started fumbling for his mobile. 'It's OK—I'll ring for an ambulance—'

'There's no need!' With one hand Michelle snatched his phone, while the other pressed his palm hard against her body, low down. He looked deep into her eyes, questioning. She returned his look with one of distant concentration, moving his hand around to find exactly the right spot.

'There! Did you feel that?' She looked up at him earnestly.

Alessandro had wondered if he would be able to act surprised when Michelle first felt their baby move. He needn't have worried. After a struggle to find any words at all, he managed.

'It's…the baby…*our* baby,' he said with dawning wonder. 'Michelle…I don't know what to say. I want to pick you up and carry you home to keep you both safe for ever, but I suppose you won't want me to mollycoddle you.'

'From now on you can do as much mollycoddling as you like,' she smiled. 'You'll get no complaints from me.'

'Do you mean that?'

'I've never meant anything more in my whole life.'

'But…'

Emotions flitted across his face as he tried to take in what she had said.

'After all I've done to you?'

'After all you've done *for* me.' She reached up and touched his face. He closed his eyes as their joined hands made slow, gentle movements over the place where she was keeping his child safe and secure.

'My parents acted as a terrible warning to me, but I've gone too far the other way. They both lived life at a thousand kilometres an hour. Neither was faithful, and both spent their time in the search for celebrity. They prized only things that seemed shallow and short-lived to me. I grew up determined to do things differently in every way I could. But there's one point where both my father and I touch. We both produced an heir for the Castiglione family by accident. The difference is, I'm going to take full responsibility for my child. And for you, *cara mia*. I am going to succeed where my father failed.'

He spoke with such quiet authority Michelle knew he would.

'And that's why my pregnancy is so important to you.'

The warmth of his hold on her fingers reminded her

of the heady times they had shared. She wanted to tell him how happy she was, but now was not the time. Her own pleasure was unimportant beside this chance for him to open his soul.

'I don't want conflict and disappointment in my child's life. I want everything to be perfect.'

Michelle thought back to the way he had made that helicopter land precisely in the right place on the lawn of Jolie Fleur.

'I think parenthood might mean making compromises,' she said diplomatically. 'I want our baby to be happy, not perfect. It will have two parents on call all the time, and plenty of space to run and play. That's a far better start in life than lots of children get. Myself, I would have settled for a chance to be my own person when I was little, and not have to live up to someone else's expectations.'

Alessandro smiled and kissed her. His hold on her changed subtly as he caressed her waist, encircling it with his hands to bind her body to his. Then he pulled her into his arms and held her tight.

'From now on that's exactly what you'll have, Michelle—the chance to be yourself. I am going to spend my life making sure you are never sidelined, or lonely, or left out again. That's a promise.'

The expression in his eyes told her she was safe in his heart, now and for ever. Lifting her gently into his arms for the journey home, he kissed her more tenderly than he had ever done before.

'I believe you.' She smiled.

* * * * *

Special Offers

Every month we put together collections and longer reads written by your favourite authors.

Here are some of next month's highlights— and don't miss our fabulous discount online!

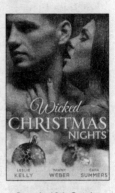

On sale 1st November   On sale 1st November   On sale 18th October

Save 20%
on all Special Releases

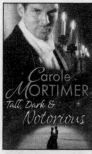
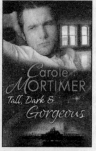
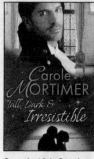
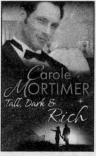
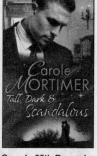

Wrap up warm this winter with Sarah Morgan…

Sleigh Bells in the Snow

Kayla Green loves business and hates Christmas.

So when Jackson O'Neil invites her to Snow Crystal Resort to discuss their business proposal… the last thing she's expecting is to stay for Christmas dinner. As the snowflakes continue to fall, will the woman who doesn't believe in the magic of Christmas finally fall under its spell…?

4th October

www.millsandboon.co.uk/sarahmorgan

1013/MB435

Come home this Christmas to Fiona Harper

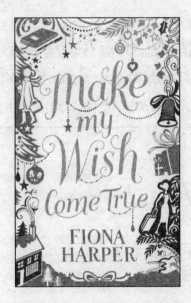

From the author of *Kiss Me Under the Mistletoe* comes a Christmas tale of family and fun. Two sisters are ready to swap their Christmases—the busy super-mum, Juliet, getting the chance to escape it all on an exotic Christmas getaway, whilst her glamorous work-obsessed sister, Gemma, is plunged headfirst into the family Christmas she always thought she'd hate.

www.millsandboon.co.uk

The World of Mills & Boon®

There's a Mills & Boon® series that's perfect for you. We publish ten series and, with new titles every month, you never have to wait long for your favourite to come along.

Blaze®

Scorching hot, sexy reads
4 new stories every month

By Request

Relive the romance with the best of the best
9 new stories every month

Cherish™

Romance to melt the heart every time
12 new stories every month

Desire™

Passionate and dramatic love stories
8 new stories every month